Faith Bleasdale lives in North Devon with her ten-year-old son and her cat. She studied history at the University of Bristol, has enjoyed a wide variety of jobs, but is now lucky enough to write full time. Having lived in Bristol, London and Singapore, she now enjoys the countryside and seaside life in Devon, happily swapping the city for wellington boots, although she dusts the heels off frequently to visit London. She has previously written seven fiction books and one non-fiction.

By the same author:

A Year at Meadowbrook Manor
Secrets at Meadowbrook Manor

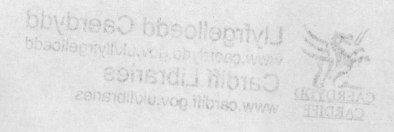

THE TICKET TO HAPPINESS

FAITH BLEASDALE

avon.

Published by AVON
A division of HarperCollins*Publishers* Ltd
1 London Bridge Street
London SE1 9GF

www.harpercollins.co.uk

This paperback edition 2019

First published in Great Britain by HarperCollins*Publishers* 2019

A catalogue copy of this book is available from the British Library.

ISBN: 978-0-00-830698-4

Typeset in Birka by Palimpsest Book Production Limited,
Falkirk, Stirlingshire
Printed and bound in UK by
CPI Group (UK) Ltd, Croydon CR0 4YY

MIX
Paper from
responsible sources
FSC
www.fsc.org   FSC C007454

To Sally, wishing you love and happiness
in your new adventure!

The Singer Family Tree

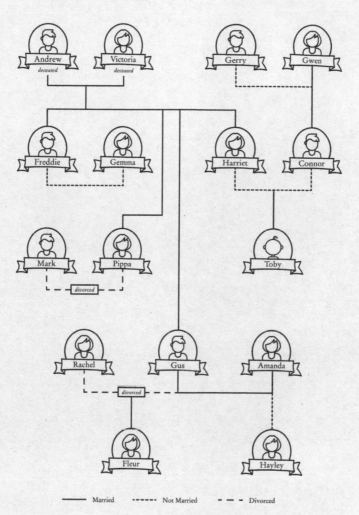

Prologue

The Californian sun streamed through the window, highlighting the house she was looking at on the computer screen. Meadowbrook Manor, a boutique hotel in Somerset, the UK. The house drew her in as she peered at the big windows, the impressive front door, the inviting interior as shown in the photos that had been taken of the inside. She could almost see, almost *feel* herself there.

She noticed a tear sliding down her cheek, which surprised her, as she hadn't realised she'd been crying. She angrily brushed it away. There had been so much, too much that had brought her to this point, and as she stared at the hotel she begged it to give her the answer she needed. Although it felt hopeless, she was desperate to understand. After a while, she felt her heart start to warm. She knew it was crazy, but it really felt as if Meadowbrook was talking to her, calling her.

Before she had time to change her mind she pulled up another website, this time for flights, and with a few clicks she'd booked herself a ticket. She hoped, no she *knew*, in her heart that it was the right thing to do. That ticket was going to take her to just where she needed to be.

Chapter One

Pippa could feel a smile inching its way across her face before she opened her eyes. Today was going to be a good day. She sprang out of bed with childlike enthusiasm, opening the curtains in her small bedroom that overlooked Meadowbrook's magnificent gardens. Meadowbrook Manor, a grand Georgian house, had been home to her and her three siblings for their entire childhood. They'd lived with just their father, Andrew Singer, throughout most of this time, as their mother had passed away when Pippa was only four years old.

And since Andrew's death, Meadowbrook had become much more than just a family home to the Singer siblings. They'd turned it into a boutique five-star hotel.

Pippa looked out at the sweeping gardens. Even in winter, they were perfectly maintained and deserving of the reputation that made them an attraction. They had been her father's pride and joy, so they remained important to Pippa and her three siblings, as did the animal sanctuary that lay just beyond – another great love of their father's before he passed away.

She took a moment to enjoy the view that stretched out over the Mendip countryside. It was a rare interlude, as Pippa was now busier than ever. Opening and running the hotel was pretty much the only job she'd ever had, but she was lucky that she loved doing it. She was a people person, so managing a hotel, charming the guests, making sure their every whim was catered for, played to her strengths. Although her sister and two brothers were involved in the hotel in their own way, it was still largely her baby. The only baby she had.

She brushed this negative thought away. She often thought about how just a few short years ago she'd been married to Mark, a controlling man who'd turned out to be ruthless and uncaring. But she didn't see it until it was almost too late, as one often did in such relationships, and since then she'd been largely single.

Before her divorce, Pippa had always thought she'd have children and become a mum, rather than run a hotel, but she had learnt the hard way that life didn't always work out the way you thought it would. And she was better off now. Surrounded by her siblings and their partners, she did some-times feel a little sad about being single, but she was only thirty-two, after all – it wasn't as if she was an old maid just yet ... although she felt like it at times. Pippa once again pushed those negative thoughts away. Lately, she'd been letting negativity creep into her head, but not today.

She hopped around the room with an energy that seemed on endless supply since the hotel opened. Though the first few months had been anxious ones, Pippa had barely come up for air, but now the hotel had found its rhythm. In fact, Pippa was preparing a party to celebrate its one-year anniversary.

Like with many things at Meadowbrook, the anniversary was slightly unconventional in that they were celebrating over a month early. The official opening of the hotel had been held on Valentine's Day last year, and her brother Gus's wedding to Meadowbrook garden designer, Amanda, had marked that occasion. But as they had bookings this year for those in search of romance, they were holding the party early during the first week of January. Not only was it quiet, but everyone involved with Meadowbrook would also welcome a party to fend off the post-Christmas and New Year blues. No one she knew did dry January, after all. Her brother Freddie said if you were going to pick a month to give up drinking, why pick the coldest, longest and most depressing? She had to admit he had a point.

Although they all had different strengths and often bickered, the Singer siblings all agreed that Pippa should take the lead on the hotel as manager and they supported her in different ways. She often wondered what her father would think of her now. Andrew Singer was driven, complicated, successful and loving, and she missed him every single day.

Harriet Singer was the business brain behind Meadowbrook, the hotel and the animal sanctuary, as well as their father's various investments and complicated estate. Gus, the second oldest, took care of the gardens; Amanda and he ran a gardening company that was hugely in demand. He also painted and ran increasingly popular painting workshops at the hotel. Freddie, her third sibling, was sort of her co-manager but he ran the bar, his particular area of interest, and took care of all the marketing and social media. Somehow, they'd figured out how to do this together, without too much fighting. They'd almost made it to a year with no casualties at the very least, and Meadowbrook was open for business.

After showering, Pippa dried herself and pulled on a pair of jeans and a new cream jumper. Having kept this weekend free of guests for the anniversary party, the hotel felt eerily quiet, and Pippa wasn't used to being here on her own. But this morning, for a little while at least, it was just her. She smiled as she made her way to the kitchen and poured a large mug of coffee. She leant against the counter, thankful for a moment's peace and quiet. Yes, today was going to be a good day ...

Chapter Two

Hilda, Harriet's dog, bounded through the door and jumped up at Pippa, knocking her mug of coffee all over her and getting muddy paw prints on her jumper. What on earth had possessed her to wear cream?

'Thanks, Hilda.' Pippa rolled her eyes but petted the big Old English sheepdog, who was boisterous but adorable. Harriet and her partner, Connor, a vet, had adopted her from the animal sanctuary a couple of years back and she was part of the family.

'Sorry, Pip. I tried to contain her but you know what she's like,' Harriet sighed as she walked in behind Hilda with her new baby, Toby, strapped to her chest.

They were in the Meadowbrook kitchen, the hub of the house. It had been the scene of many a family meal growing up when they'd shunned the formal dining room for the warmth of the kitchen, with its Aga and Gwen, their housekeeper, baking, which kept the kitchen smelling inviting. Now, it was more of a commercial kitchen, but they managed to retain some of its history, not least with the huge, old kitchen table that sat in the room, etched with their childhoods on it.

'Can I have my nephew?' Pippa asked, itching to get her hands on four-month-old Toby.

'If you can figure out how to get into this bloody thing. It almost needed an engineering degree to get it on; you should have heard my language. If Toby's first words are all swear-words then you'll know why.'

Harriet, the oldest at forty, sounded harassed, which was unlike the normally cool-headed woman, but then Pippa guessed being a new mother could do that to you. Harriet was taller than Pippa, with dark hair cut into an efficient bob, and she looked a little like their father, whereas Pippa took after their mother. Harriet was attractive and slim, with trans-lucent skin and brown eyes, while Pippa was more delicate with her blonde hair, pale skin and bright blue eyes. They did share some similar traits, but initially to look at them you wouldn't guess they were sisters.

Pippa managed to unhook Toby and engulfed him in her arms, where he wriggled before nuzzling into her. She sniffed his head, something she couldn't resist doing. He looked like Harry, she thought, but his eyes were similar to his father, Connor. He was the most beautiful baby she'd ever seen. Although she was, of course, biased.

'Right, I need coffee, and loads of it,' Harriet announced as she left Pippa cooing and moved to the coffee machine, Hilda wagging her tail at her heels.

Pippa opened her mouth and then promptly closed it. Harriet appeared to have her jumper on inside out but Pippa wasn't sure she dared point it out.

'Are you all right?' Pippa asked instead.

Harriet was so strong she rarely showed weakness, or rather vulnerability; she didn't believe in it. As sisters, Pippa and Harriet were polar opposites. Harriet took being the oldest seriously and Pippa did the same with being the youngest, even milking it, some might say. They bickered, all four of them did, but they were closer than they ever had been – closer than their father even imagined they'd be, Pippa often thought.

'Yes, I'm absolutely great,' Harriet said, taking a large gulp of coffee. 'Even better now.'

'Good.' Pippa frowned. She knew she worried about her siblings, but Harriet wasn't someone who took kindly to being worried about.

'Anyway, what needs doing for this party?' Harriet asked.

'I think it's all under control. But you're all staying here, aren't you?'

'Yup. I've got a baby monitor for Toby, so I can put him to sleep and enjoy the party,' Harriet grinned.

'You're going to drink actual alcohol?' Pippa asked.

Harriet had barely taken a sip of wine since Toby's birth. Personally, Pippa thought maybe it would do her good.

'Yes, I've pumped milk for his feeds for tomorrow, and then I can pump and dump in the morning,' Harriet explained.

'What?' Pippa grimaced.

'There might be alcohol in the breast milk if I drink, so I have to pump it out and get rid. It's called pump and dump according to the baby book.'

'Yuk. Anyway, can we stop talking about your breasts?'

Just then, Toby gave out a wail.

'Well we can, but I'm going to have to whip them out now as my baby's hungry.'

Harriet reached out and took her son, settling herself down at the kitchen table to feed him.

'Why is my timing so bad?' Freddie said as he walked into the kitchen with a grimace on his face.

'For God's sake, Fred, you can't even see anything,' Harriet snapped.

She had a muslin cloth covering both her and most of Toby. Freddie was the youngest of the male siblings. Only two years older than Pippa, they looked the most alike. Freddie was tall and slim, with the same colouring as Pippa. His messy blond hair crowned his head, but he had the same strong nose as their father and their other brother, Gus.

'You know what he's like. Hello, guys,' Gemma said, appearing from behind him.

Gemma was originally Meadowbrook's hotel consultant and although there was a huge amount of drama before they opened the hotel, she'd done an amazing job. Gemma was thirty and she was shorter than Pippa, with dark blonde, highlighted hair, but was far prettier than she ever thought she was. When she'd worked for the hotel, Gemma and Pippa had become firm friends. But then just as the hotel opened, she and Freddie fell in love – a case of opposites attract, obviously. Freddie was her loud, party-loving brother and Gemma was shy, quiet, anxious and, especially when she first arrived at Meadowbrook, a bundle of nerves. But she was also bright, sensible and with a fun side, and Freddie seemed to have unearthed those qualities in her. In fact, they brought out the best in each other. When the hotel opened, Gemma had resigned. She wanted to do something outside the family now she was dating Freddie. But Meadowbrook Hotel still felt as if it were a part of Gemma; it was important to all of them and of course Gemma was roped in to help when they needed her. She'd gone to college to study business as a mature student, which she loved.

'Right, well, back to this party. What do you need us to do?' Gemma asked.

'I need you guys to stay here and help set up, if that's OK?'

'Sure, but I need to go and get my cocktail bar ready,' Freddie said.

The bar was his domain, which given his predilection for alcohol could have been a bad thing, but Freddie took the bar seriously and hadn't – yet – drunk it dry. He was becoming known for mixing fantastic cocktails and actually, having the responsibility had done him good. That and Gemma, of course.

'Can't wait to try them; although seeing's as I've hardly touched a drink for the best part of a year, you need to go easy on me,' Harriet grinned, the old spark seemingly back in her eyes.

'Harry, have you got your jumper on inside out?' Freddie asked.

Pippa carried two mugs of steaming coffee out through the back door of the kitchen and into the garden. She wasn't surprised to have seen Gus pottering out there earlier. Gus, her eldest brother, loved the gardens and he could often be found out there when he wasn't painting or with his family.

'Hey,' she called, waving at him as he was trimming one of the garden's many bushes.

He stopped, squinted and then beamed.

'Pippa, just what I need,' he said as he bounded over to her.

Gus was thirty-nine and looked like a male version of Harriet, apart from his nose. He was tall, with thinning dark hair and a stocky build. Despite his looks, he was sensitive, quiet and creative. Definitely the most creative of the Singers.

She handed him the mug and they stood side by side in silence, looking at the winter sun glinting in the greenery.

'It looks beautiful,' she said, which was true.

'All the hard work's definitely paid off. Amanda's flat out today, but she's going to finish early so she can come up to the house. I know you probably need me to help with the party, but I just fancied being out here alone for a bit.'

'I understand, Gus.' Pippa gave his arm a squeeze. 'But, yes, when you're ready, it's all hands on deck. Where's Fleur, by the way?'

Amanda, who was in charge of the Meadowbrook gardens and had worked for their father, was Gus's second wife. Fleur, her niece, was his sixteen-year-old daughter from his first marriage.

'She'll be up later with the rest of the family; although I'm sure she'll be wearing something inappropriate and trying to sneak alcohol,' he complained.

Before Toby's arrival, as their only niece, all the Singers doted on Fleur and she was also very close to their late father. Gus and she had a tempestuous relationship, mainly owing to the fact that he was overprotective and not ready for his little girl to grow up.

'I'm sure she won't,' Pippa lied, as that was exactly what Fleur would be doing. 'Anyway, I'd better go and check on the caterers. All OK?'

'Yes, I'll finish up here and be in in a bit to help.' He gave her a hug, handed the empty mug back to her and went back to his pottering.

The peace of earlier in the day was forgotten as Pippa moved around the house. The kitchen was full of catering staff now, who were preparing food for the evening, so Pippa, on discovering everything was under control, ducked out. She stood in the doorway to the bar, watching Freddie and Gemma laughing.

It was heartwarming to see how close her best friend and her brother were, they were so in love. Gemma was passing bottles to Freddie, who was making drinks, but every now and then he'd stop to kiss her. Pippa felt a little like a voyeur, but she didn't want to interrupt their moment, so she carried on.

She ran upstairs and checked the rooms were all ready. It might seem silly but she wanted her siblings and her to sleep in their old rooms for one night. She'd got them all prepared, her room, Harriet's, Gus's and Freddie's. Fleur and Gus's stepdaughter, Hayley, had rooms on the top floor, which used to be the attic rooms for staff back in the day, and Gwen said she may stay over with her partner, Gerry, but she hadn't quite committed. Gwen had never slept in the main house, only in her apartment, and although she was family, she still said it didn't seem right. The rooms weren't the same as when they all lived there, of course, for they were now decorated as hotel rooms, more neutral. Pippa finished her inspection, satisfied that it was all ready as she headed back downstairs.

Flower arrangements were being set up in the reception area as well as the bar and dining room. Pippa had a florist who delivered every week to ensure the hotel always looked its best and in summer they used flowers from the gardens, too. The dining room was ready to receive the buffet food, which would be laid out on the huge dining table. It was all under control and Pippa was almost disappointed to find that she really didn't need to do anything.

She decided to head out for a walk before it was time to get changed. As she passed the drawing room, she glanced in and saw that Toby and Harriet were on the sofa. Toby was on her chest and they were both fast asleep. She smiled at the sight of mother and child and quietly headed out.

She found herself at the sanctuary, where the animals, oblivious to the festivities, carried on as normal. One of the paddocks saw the donkey, Gerald, and the ponies grazing, while another was home to four goats – three adults and a baby. The pigs, who were Gus's favourites, had a space beyond that, next to the field where the two alpacas, Sebastian and Samantha, glared at everyone who passed. In the far field were the cows, or to be precise, the bull, David, the cow, Madonna, and their baby calf, Drake. They weren't the friendliest, either. Fleur got to name most new arrivals, and liked to name them after rappers – hence baby calf Drake and baby goat Kanye.

As Pippa made her way to the sanctuary office, she passed the chicken pen, the cat quarters and the large kennel, which was apparent by the noise coming from it. Although she loved the sanctuary, she wished that the domestic animals had all been re-homed. She wanted them all in loving homes and the fact they weren't made her sad. Although Meadowbrook did have a good re-homing success rate, there were always animals coming in to replace those who left and that wasn't good – or at least not for the animals, as it generally meant they'd suffered.

'Penny for them?' Connor asked, interrupting her thoughts.

Connor, Harriet's partner, was tall, good-looking in a scruffy way, with unruly dark hair and the kindest smile. He had dimples that Toby seemed to have inherited in his cheeks and where Harriet could be scary, Connor was the most laid-back person Pippa had ever met. Yet again, opposites in many ways, but they'd been soulmates from childhood; although they didn't realise it until after Andrew's death and when it was almost too late.

'I'll have you know they're worth more than a penny,' Pippa

replied. 'I was at the house and everything's under control for tonight, so I thought I'd get some fresh air and I found myself here, maybe thinking of Dad a bit today, you know.' Pippa tried not to get emotional but she always did when she thought of her father.

'I know, and look how far you've come. He'd be so proud of you.'

'And you and the sanctuary.'

'Hey, we're like a mutual appreciation society. By the way, I seem to be missing a girlfriend and a baby.'

'At the house, both fast asleep,' Pippa smiled.

Connor ran his hands through his hair.

'Harriet, day-sleeping? Wow. Right, well, I'll finish up here and head up in that case.'

'See you soon.'

Pippa watched him depart and then headed back to the house. She was so happy that all three of her siblings had such wonderful partners – however, she did wonder, just briefly, when it would be her turn.

Chapter Three

Pippa called it the Meadowbrook magic as she happily floated around the group of partygoers. The celebration was going exactly to plan. The family were having fun, as was most of Parker's Hollow – their village, their community. There were a lot of people who were important to Meadowbrook, and there were also many who Meadowbrook was important to, so they all deserved to be part of this: of Meadowbrook's success. Their father had always taught them the value of community and he'd involved as many of the local people as possible in Meadowbrook life. Pippa and the rest of the Singers had carried this on and it was heartwarming for her to see everyone here tonight, people who loved Meadowbrook, people whom she loved.

She took some time out to watch and listen to them all as if she were invisible. Gus was dancing with his wife, Amanda. This was almost their anniversary party, too, in a way – albeit a bit early ahead of their real anniversary on Valentine's Day. Pippa felt warm to see bliss written across both of their faces. They made a great couple – Gus a little serious and a worrier, and Amanda who loved the outdoors and embraced life in a way that was helping Gus to do the same.

Freddie was ordering the bar staff around and trying to

ply Gemma with alcohol so he could also ply himself with it, without getting into trouble. Gemma's cheeks were flushed and she was giggling with happiness and alcohol. Pippa knew her friend well and Freddie's plan seemed to be working.

Fleur was trying to sneak drinks off the tables that were dotted around and she was followed by Hayley, her stepsister. They were being so obvious but luckily, Amanda and Gus hadn't yet noticed. Gwen, Connor's mother, was laughing at something Gerry was saying. Gwen had met Gerry at Meadowbrook and although they both claimed their relationship was really more of a deep friendship, they all noticed how much time Gerry spent with Gwen these days; in fact, he practically lived with her. Pippa impulsively landed a kiss on Gwen's cheek. She was like a second mum to them all and she felt so much love towards her in that moment.

The music that Freddie had selected was loud and vibrant but didn't seem to be a deterrent to the older members of the community, from what she could see. Many of the gardening club ladies, ladies who were retired and who loved gardening so came to Meadowbrook regularly, were dancing with the enthusiastic morris dancers. Even the volunteers and workers from the sanctuary who didn't often let their hair down were giving it a good go. Pippa let John, the vicar, who was also the leader of the morris dancers, spin her around the makeshift dance floor a couple of times before giggling and going to find another drink.

After checking all the guests were having fun, Pippa went over to Harriet and Connor, who were both pale-faced, talking to John – his wife, Hilary, by his side. John and Hilary were pillars of the Meadowbrook community. Not only was he the vicar and head of the morris-dancing troop, but he and his wife were also the people who knew everything that was going on in Parker's Hollow, the village. They also looked scarily alike, both tall, slender or bony, as Harriet said, with glasses that dominated both of their faces. Freddie still found this hard to accept – to him, they looked more like brother and sister than husband and wife.

'You really shouldn't leave it too long to get the lad christened,' Pippa heard John say as she approached.

'Pip,' Harry said, grabbing her.

Harriet was holding a baby monitor, so she could hear if Toby so much as murmured in the room he was sleeping in upstairs.

'Yes?' Pippa smiled.

John, the vicar, was grinning enthusiastically.

'John thinks we need to organise a christening for Toby.'

'You should. We've got the family christening robe and the way he eats he won't fit in it if you don't hurry up,' Pippa laughed, thinking that a christening would be another wonderful Meadowbrook event. She might even get to organise it.

'Thanks for the support,' Harriet hissed in her ear. 'OK, that's great, John, but Connor and I still need to find godparents and then we need to organise a party, I guess,' she said carefully.

'I'll do the catering,' Gwen cut in, as it turned out she'd been listening. 'And I insist on making a very special cake. I'll go and get some brandy from Freddie now while I think of it.'

'Mum, are you all right?' Connor's brows etched in concern.

'Oh, yes, just had one too many sherries,' Gwen replied, swaying slightly.

'Now, if I might interfere, I'd be very happy to put my hat into the ring for a godfather role,' Gerry offered.

Harriet looked so startled she was unable to speak.

'Gwen's Granny and I'm her partner, so it'd be nice for me to have an official title, too,' he said. 'I'm also willing to dress up as any character he might like for any of his birthdays.'

That was Gerry's pitch. No one knew what to say. Gerry did like to dress up, though, at any excuse, which no one liked to think too much about; although it did come in handy for the Meadowbrook events.

'Oh, and I should be godmother,' Edie – one of the gardening club members and a pillar of the Meadowbrook community – said, appearing suddenly as if from nowhere.

Edie was eccentric to say the least. She'd just turned seventy-something but pretended she was sixty. No one dared argue with her.

Pip stifled a giggle. Harriet's face had turned grey and even Connor looked concerned.

'Great, well, you have two godparents right here. You only need one more man if tradition serves or, as I'm a very progressive vicar, you can have more if you like,' John offered magnanimously. 'I know some people these days like to have quite a few.'

'We'll definitely need more,' Connor said, sounding a little shell-shocked.

'Let's think about it and we'll call you soon to lock down a date.'

It wasn't often that Harriet gave in but, Pippa realised, they'd caught her on the rare occasion she'd had a drink since Toby's birth. She'd have agreed to anything, Pippa thought as Harriet downed the wine left in her glass.

'And after the service we'll be happy to do a special morris dance for Toby,' John finished.

'Oh, how lovely. A christening and morris dancing. Of course, I'll make the quiches,' Hilary offered. 'I should go and find Gwen so we can discuss the menu.'

As Pippa watched Connor shrug helplessly and Harriet's eyes fill with panic, she wondered if she should intervene.

'I think I heard Toby crying,' Harriet said. 'John, it all sounds lovely, thank you.' And grabbing Pippa's hand, she thrust the baby monitor into Connor's hands then pulled her sister with her before she was coerced into anything else.

'For God's sake, we'll need to get Toby other godparents – you know, those who might even outlive his parents,' Harriet whispered when they were in her old bedroom.

Toby was in a Moses basket sleeping soundly, silent but for the occasional snuffling noise.

'Think of the pictures!' Pippa laughed. 'Oh, but Gerry's so sweet, though, and so's Edie. It'll mean so much to them, too. They love little Toby.'

'I know that,' Harriet hissed, 'but I'm not sure it's the best thing for Toby. I mean, aren't the parents meant to choose godparents, not the other way round?'

'I wonder what Edie'll wear?' Pippa felt uncontrollable laughter bubbling up. They loved Edie and she certainly lent colour to Meadowbrook.

'I dread to think, Edie in her finest. I adore her but tonight she was definitely channelling Madonna circa 1988.'

'But she was delighted with her ra-ra skirt; she got it when Gemma took her to the charity shops in Bath.'

'At least Toby'll be oblivious to it all, so that's one good thing—'

The door burst open and Connor ran in, brandishing the other baby monitor.

'Oh no!' Harriet cringed.

'What did they hear?' Pippa said, her heart falling.

'Thankfully, as soon as I heard Harriet blaspheme, I ran out of the room. I think John heard you take the Lord's name in vain, but I definitely saved you from the worst.'

'Oh, Con, how can I ever thank you?' Harriet giggled, throwing her arms around him.

'You could always ask Edie if you could borrow her ra-ra skirt,' he winked.

Chapter Four

Pippa was woken by a quiet knock on her bedroom door. She slowly sat up, acknowledging that hungover, sleepy feeling as her memory seeped back. She was in her childhood bedroom, not her normal room. Of course, the bedroom now belonged to the hotel now. It had a four-poster bed and was one of the more romantic rooms, she often felt.

'Come in.' She stretched her arms above her head.

Harriet walked in clutching Toby and a baby's bottle.

'What time is it?' Pippa asked.

'Half six, but your nephew needs feeding and Connor's snoring, which makes me want to stab him. How can he sleep through a baby crying? It's ridiculous!' Harriet hiccupped. 'Pip, I think I might still be drunk and I'm not sure I should be allowed to be in charge of my baby. Gwen offered to have him sleep at hers but I've never spent a night away from him and ...'

'Hand him over.'

Pippa took Toby, cradled him in her arms and planted a kiss on his head. She loved babies. She loved this baby. When Harriet was first pregnant, Pippa didn't like to admit it but she was jealous, or maybe that was envious, because she was so happy for Harriet and Connor at the same time. When she was married to Mark, she'd been so desperate for a child and now she was single, it wasn't looking likely to happen anytime soon. She loved being an aunt, although she needed to persuade Harriet to let her spend more time with Toby. It would do them both good.

She took the bottle and looked into Toby's eyes as he began to suck contentedly, his eyes flickering as he drank. Harriet collapsed in a heap next to them on the bed.

'Why don't you go back to bed and leave Toby with me for a couple of hours? I'm only going to be pottering this morning. The clearing up can wait and I've got help coming in later anyway.'

'I couldn't—' Harriet started.

'Don't be silly, Harry, you're in no fit state and if you have a few more hours' sleep you'll feel much better; you might even be sober. He's safe with me and I'm not leaving the house, so if I need you, I promise I'll come and get you straight away.' Pippa tried to sound stern.

'I love you, Pip. Hey, why don't you join Edie as Toby's other godmother?'

'You asked me a hundred times last night and I'm his aunt. If anything happens to you and Connor I fully expect to get him anyway. But if you really want me to be—'

'I do. Then if anything happens to Connor and me you'll have a better case to argue with Edie. Godmother and aunt, she won't stand a chance. You'll trump her!'

'I know nothing'll happen to you, by the way, Harry, but you know, those alpacas are a bit evil. Not to mention the no-longer-gay bull.'

Pippa was referring to some of the animals at the sanctuary that were part of Meadowbrook. The two alpacas, Samantha and Sebastian, had perfected being rude to everyone they encountered.

'Now I'm never going to sleep again. Except I will right now, actually. I'll put the nappy bag outside your door and if you need me, then you know where I am. If he sounds upset or anything, please let me know.'

'We'll be fine, Harry. Now go.'

As Harriet staggered off, Pippa giggled – Harry was definitely still drunk.

Pippa finished feeding Toby, burped him and then laid him across her as they relaxed in bed. She fancied a coffee but then she wanted to keep cuddling her nephew for a bit longer. He really was the most divine child and he had the Singer look about him with her father's nose, or the beginning of it. He was beginning to look like a perfect mix of both of his parents, actually.

Pippa's phone rang, interrupting her doting, and she looked at the screen. It was Hector. Why was he calling so early?

'Hector, it's practically the middle of the night,' she said, snatching the phone.

Hector Barber was a long-time friend of Meadowbrook, having been introduced by Freddie as a 'celebrity' at their summer fête. In truth he was a reality TV star, having appeared on a show called *Singles Holiday*, though he'd been kicked off for having sex with most of the women on there. From there, he'd gone on to feature on most 'celebrity' reality TV shows going and was a huge national heartthrob. But he'd become firm friends with the Singers and over time, he'd become like part of the extended family. Just before they opened the hotel, he'd announced he was writing a novel and after they'd all managed to get past the shock, he'd been the hotel's first official guest, moving into the hotel to write his first book.

And despite all the cynics, Hector's book had been a huge bestseller and all of a sudden, he was being taken seriously both as a person and a writer. He'd dedicated his first book to the Singers and Meadowbrook.

'I know,' he'd said in response, 'but I'm at the airport in New York and I couldn't remember the time difference. Oh, and Happy New Year. I'm so sorry I missed the party, but having to promote my book here meant I really couldn't get away.'

Hector had spent Christmas in America because of an extensive book tour.

'I know, you told us and it's fine. We missed you but there'll always be another party.'

Pippa thought about how much everyone loved Hector, especially the gardening club ladies. She surprised herself by thinking that even she missed him.

'Right, well, that's why I'm calling. I'm getting on a flight in a minute and I'm on deadline, so I wondered if I could book into the hotel.'

'Hector, you have a perfectly good flat in London and although of course we'd love to see you ...'

Pippa wasn't sure if Hector was lonely. Now he had his success and was in demand, he seemed to want to be around them more than ever. Freddie said it was because he was in love with Pippa, but she brushed that off. He flirted with her terribly, but then he could flirt with a candlestick, he was that kind of guy. Lovely, fun, clever, not to mention gorgeous, but too young and too frivolous for Pippa. He was only twenty-nine and although he claimed his playboy days were behind him, she wasn't convinced.

'But you know I write best at Meadowbrook. I need to get my next book finished. There's so much pressure on me, Pippa, and I was thinking three months would do it.'

'You want to stay here for three months? You do know we've put our prices up?' Pippa teased as Toby wriggled contently in her arms.

When Hector stayed he'd had opening prices, plus a huge discount. Actually, they didn't want to charge him at all, but he'd insisted. The thing was that the publicity that Hector brought the hotel had been amazing. Not least because of the groups of women booked in hoping to meet him. They should have been paying him, in fact.

'Pip, I'm going to talk to Harriet about the rate, because she'll charge me properly.'

'You're family and you can stay with us anytime, but I still don't see why you'd want to be holed up here for three months.'

'And you call yourself a businesswoman? What would Harriet say if I told her you were turning down paying customers?'

'She'd kill me.'

'I'll call you when I'm in London to let you know when to expect me. Oh, bugger, last call for my flight.' He hung up.

'Hector's coming, Toby. You'll like him. He's fun.'

Hector hadn't met Toby yet. He'd been so busy with his book tours that he hadn't managed to come over since his birth. Pippa had to decide where he'd stay. Probably in one of the attic rooms; for some reason, Hector loved being at the top of the house. She had a few bookings coming up, but they had plenty of space for the quiet season. Meadowbrook only had ten bedrooms, all doubles, and she always knew who was staying. One magazine had said Meadowbrook was the very definition of a boutique hotel. And that was exactly their intention when they'd opened it. Pippa loved that it was small and it ensured they knew what their guests liked and didn't like. They made sure they had food that suited their preferences. Catering to their individual needs, as a small, luxury hotel they were more than able to do so. It meant that guests felt they were having an experience suited to them, rather than just a generic five-star hotel stay.

Pippa was actually pleased that Hector was coming. It would be nice to have him around. She grinned – Harriet would be really pleased. One three-month booking to take them through the slow season wouldn't hurt at all, even if they did heavily discount. Although they weren't empty, they weren't full either for the next few months. They had some short mid-week corporate bookings coming up, a couple of groups embarking on Gus's painting workshop and some more on Gwen's baking course, which had proved so popular. And because of the baking show on TV – Hector had even taken part in the celebrity version of that – people clamoured. Baking was the new knitting, apparently. Pippa knew they might have some last-minute bookings, too, but she'd been prepared for it being quieter after Christmas, probably until Easter at least.

Soon after the hotel opened, they realised that the Meadowbrook hotel kitchen wasn't going to be able to accommodate the baking experiences that they were getting requests for. Especially as it was needed to cater for the guests at the same time. However, next to Freddie's house, one of the barns they'd converted, was another barn that they'd been able to turn into a kitchen – a little like the actual *Great British Bake Off* layout; although not a tent, of course. There were a number of ovens and fridges, and Gwen ran her baking courses there. They were so well-known that she'd had to rope others in to help her now she was working less, or at least trying to. Hilary, John, the vicar's wife, helped out regularly, as she was a keen baker, too.

The good news was that the hotel wasn't running at a huge loss. To Harriet's dismay, it hadn't made a profit yet, either, but then as Gemma pointed out, hotels never made money in the first year, which had almost satisfied her. The fact that the hotel was doing OK was enough. For now.

Pippa sat at her desk in the office going through the bookings. Everyone had left, the housekeeping staff were turning the rooms around and Pippa was nursing her persistent hangover with a much-needed cup of tea while making notes to ensure that during the coming week she was on top of things.

Growing up, with her three siblings and their father, not to mention Gwen and Connor, who were there most of the time, Meadowbrook had felt alive. But when one by one her siblings left – first to boarding school, then university, before going off to jobs in various places – it was just Pippa, the baby of the family, her father and Gwen. They'd filled the house with people: her father's friends, the village community and Pippa's school friends, who'd practically lived there when they were teenagers. When Pippa left Meadowbrook to marry Mark, she'd felt a stab of guilt – no, more than a stab of guilt – about leaving the house with just her father and Gwen. But she'd visited often and her dad never complained about being lonely. He kept busy and that was when he'd started the animal sanctuary.

Pippa felt tears surface. She still missed him and she wished he was with them; although she felt his presence in the house every day and that was why she'd always take care of

Meadowbrook. It was the one place she could feel her father and she never wanted to lose that feeling.

Pippa wiped the tears off her face furiously as there was a knock on the office door. Gus appeared with a big smile. Mainly calm – apart from when it came to his teenage daughter – and level-headed, he was the most sensible of the siblings. He was also creative; although he'd been an insurance salesman before he managed to find his true passion: painting and gardening.

'Why the tears, Pip?' he asked, chewing his bottom lip anxiously.

'I was thinking of Daddy. I'm not sure how I got there but with the party, it was emotional. You know, we've kept this place open for almost a year and it's all going well, but I miss him. I wish I knew what he thought of it.'

'I know.' Gus came over to where Pippa was sat and bent down to hug her. 'He'd be so proud of you, you know. All of us, but especially you.'

'Thanks, Gus. Oh! by the way, Hector's coming to stay. He needs to finish his new book.'

'It'll be nice to have him back. Anyway,' he hopped awkwardly from foot to foot, 'I need to get the details for my painting workshop. And Amanda said to complain about the lack of gardening interest.' His lips curled in a slight smile.

'Gus, it's winter. Who wants to garden in the winter?'

'Amanda!' they both said and laughed.

Gus's wife, Amanda, lived for her gardens. She was even out there in the snow, protecting her plants. But although the gardening courses were popular – funnily enough, especially with the younger generation – they weren't in demand in the winter, when bookings had all but dried up.

'I'll sign Hector up,' Pippa joked. 'That'll keep her happy.'

'She's got enough to do, really,' Gus groaned. 'Not only with existing clients, but she's also taken on a new client. A rich family have bought a crumbling old manor house near Bath and they've got acres of grounds that need restoring. The house, too. Amanda hasn't met them yet, but I think they might be Russian billionaires from the sound of it. Probably Mafia or something like that.'

'Tell her to be careful, then. Although it sounds like a great project.'

'She says it's all grand statues and water features at the moment. But I'm worried she's overstretching herself.'

'Let Amanda do what she wants to do, Gus. Don't clip her wings.'

Gus's first marriage broke down because his then wife ran off with one of his friends, but afterwards she'd said that Gus had suffocated her by trying to please her all the time. Gus could be a bit like that. Unfortunately, he was the sensitive member of the family and their hard-to-please father didn't really do sensitive. So Gus had spent most of his childhood trying to please their father, something their father recognised later in life and apologised for, but Gus was still battling with insecurity as a result. Amanda made him happier than he'd ever been, but old habits died hard.

'I know, she's happy, we're happy, and I need to remember that. You know what a nightmare I can be!'

'Exactly. Right, here's your next two painting workshops.'

'Any sign of Freddie?' Gus asked.

'No. Gemma dragged him home a couple of hours ago but that hangover isn't going anywhere soon.'

'Typical Fred.'

Pippa laughed. The Singers had settled into themselves and for four siblings who were so close, they were all so utterly disparate. Harriet the boss, Gus the sensitive one, Freddie the fun one and her ... Pippa was still trying to find herself. She was on her own now for the first time, she was working for the first time and she was getting to know herself for the first time, but she still had a lot to learn. She might be in her thirties, but she felt as if she was only just now discovering who she really was.

Chapter Five

Pippa was absorbed in reading the latest edition of *Hotels*, a trade magazine, in the office, when she heard the front door bang open and raised voices. The noise startled her and she jumped. Glancing at her watch, she saw it was later than she thought. She must have been miles away.

'Are you here?' Freddie boomed, bursting into the office as she stood up.

'Fred,' she greeted.

'Pippa, gorgeous as ever.'

Hector, with his floppy, public schoolboy dark hair, and his favoured look of chinos and a cable-knit sweater, stepped forwards and engulfed her in a hug. He was tall, well-toned – he liked his fitness – with a smile that lit up rooms. His body was often featured in magazines as being a 'hot bod' and his blue-green eyes were the subject of many a crush. Hector, with his boyish good looks, wouldn't have been out of place in a Hollywood film.

As she felt his arms around her, Pippa couldn't help but smile. It was so familiar, hugging Hector; he'd become one of her closest friends over the years. Pippa didn't have many friends. She had her family, the villagers and Gemma. All of her girlfriends had been lost when she was married – Mark didn't approve of her mixing with anyone he hadn't chosen for her – and that made her sad, but now she knew she should count herself lucky.

'Welcome back, Hector. Hope the drive with Freddie wasn't too bad?' Pippa arched an eyebrow.

Freddie had offered to pick Hector up from the train station in Bath. It gave him a chance to drive his Porsche outside the village and also to catch up with Hector, with whom he was firm friends.

'It was great. Honestly. I'm so happy to be here,' Hector gushed. 'Missed the old place. America was nice but crazy busy and you know, just before I was due to leave I didn't think of my flat in London, I thought of here.'

'Right, first things first, welcome drink,' Freddie announced. 'Come on through to the bar.'

'It's only four o'clock,' Pippa pointed out. 'And I've got to organise food for you for tonight.' Pippa knew that she shouldn't be thinking of work but she always did.

'Honestly, Hector's just arrived back after a successful book tour and you can't even toast him?' Freddie tutted.

'Of course I can,' Pippa argued, narrowing her eyes at her brother.

Freddie had a habit of turning anything into a celebration. He'd celebrate a letter arriving, even if it was a bill. And, of course, they'd only just got over the hangover from the party two days ago.

'So, I'm guessing that we'll be eating pizza tonight and probably won't leave the bar?' she conceded.

She knew when to give in; there was no arguing with her brother sometimes. And, of course, Hector's arrival did warrant a celebration.

'That sounds like my perfect welcome-home evening.' Hector's eyes shone. He was so easily pleased.

'Where's Gemma?' Pippa asked.

'She's gone to visit her nan's grave thingy at the crematorium. You know, she goes regularly but she wanted to tell her about the anniversary party and stuff.' Freddie's features softened when he spoke of his girlfriend.

'Why didn't you go with her?' Hector asked.

Pippa had been thinking the same thing.

'I tried, I'll have you know, but she wanted to be alone. She doesn't have family anymore, as you know, so talking to her nan's important to her. I did offer but she said she'd go when I was picking up Hector. Anyway, she'll be back any minute, so I'll get her to join us.' He pulled out his phone and started texting.

'Listen, I've only just recovered from the party hangover, so I'm really not going to drink much,' Pippa said.

'As long as we get the pleasure of your company, I really don't mind,' Hector replied with his familiar grin that made most people swoon.

'So, how were the women in America?' Freddie asked later as they were all sat around a table in the bar.

So much for not drinking. Pippa could already feel herself on the cusp of tipsy. She poured herself a glass of water. Gemma sat next to her. She'd been emotional after visiting her nan's memorial but a couple of glasses of wine and a pizza later, she seemed to have cheered up.

'Not a patch on here,' Hector replied, looking at Pippa from under his long eyelashes. 'But really, I was working so much I barely had the time to know which city I was in. It was bookshop after bookshop – or store as they say – and radio programme after radio programme. It was great, exhausting, but definitely all work and no play.'

'Freddie should take a leaf out of your book,' Gemma teased.

'Oi, I'll have you know I've worked really hard this year,' he retorted.

'You have and you have to admit that you love your job,' Gemma conceded.

'Talking of that, cocktail, anyone? I can make a pretty mean pornstar martini.'

'It's lovely to have you back,' Gemma said.

She was a big fan of Hector. Didn't ever stop reminding Pippa of the fact. And Pippa did adore him, but just as a friend, as she constantly seemed to remind everyone.

'How long are you here for?' Gemma added.

'The book isn't going to write itself. I'm under huge pressure to make it as good as the first one and you know, I'm actually nervous,' he admitted.

Pippa startled. It wasn't often she saw a vulnerable side to Hector, but there it was.

'You'll be fine, you've got Meadowbrook to inspire you,' she reassured.

'And that's exactly what I need,' he finished.

'Harry, what are you doing here?' Pippa walked into the kitchen, to find her sister sitting at the table with a laptop in front of her.

It was only half past six in the morning. Pippa was in her pyjamas and dressing gown. She'd stuck to her guns last night and not drunk too much, and as Hector was the only guest staying, she didn't need to be up so early, but it had become a habit now. Later today, they were welcoming a small accountancy firm on a team-building break. They were staying for three days – painting one day, baking the next, and the third day they were going to take walks and explore the local area. There were only six of them altogether, so it was going to be quite straightforward, but Pippa wanted to check the rooms, the food and the itinerary well ahead of time.

One of the ideas Gemma had introduced was that as it was a small hotel, they get each guest to fill out a questionnaire before arrival. It not only asked for food preferences, but also a bit about themselves, so they could get to know each person before their stay. It worked well. It not only personalised the experience, but it also acted as forewarning. If someone didn't like fish, they'd know not to serve it. If they preferred a certain type of alcohol, they'd make sure they had plenty in. If they wanted entertainment, they'd organise that, too. It was a very individualised stay, which is what Meadowbrook was all about.

'The accounts. I can't get them to add up. And keep your voice down – Toby's asleep by the Aga,' Harriet said eventually.

Pippa looked over to where her nephew was snuffling away in his pram.

'Right,' Pippa said and flicked the kettle on. 'But it's so early.'

'Yes, Pip, I'm aware of that,' Harriet snapped. 'Sorry, sorry, but Toby was up half the night, and Connor and I took turns, but Connor needs to go to the surgery today and I thought if I brought Toby up here then at least he might get a few hours of decent sleep. But these numbers just don't make sense.'

'Fair enough, but what about you, you look exhausted?'

Pippa made tea but then thought that perhaps Harriet needed coffee. She went to turn on the coffee machine and when the machine had warmed up, she made her sister a double shot Americano and handed it over.

'You're a star. And yes, I'm fine. And anyway, after I've done these accounts and then some admin at the sanctuary, I've agreed to let Gwen sit at mine with Toby for a couple of hours so I get to have a nap. Satisfied?' Harriet snapped again. Then she grinned. 'Sorry. How's Hector? I meant to come up and see him yesterday, but somehow this one kept us hostage in our own home. How can something so small wreak so much havoc?'

'He's a baby and he doesn't know what he's supposed to do yet,' Pippa said.

Harriet had bags under her eyes and although Pippa didn't want to point this out, Harry looked exhausted. No wonder the numbers weren't adding up. She leant over Harriet's shoulder and looked at the spreadsheet in front of her. Pippa's strength wasn't in maths, that was for sure, but she could see the mistake clearly.

'Harry, I think those expenses are in the wrong column,' she said softly.

Harriet narrowed her eyes at her sister then squinted at the screen.

''Course, I knew that. Right, great, it's all fine now, then.'

'Anyway, we've got the accountant guests arriving later and I'm just waiting for Vicky to come up so we can go through the menus.'

Pippa knew when to change the subject. Vicky was Gwen's second-in-command, but she'd been trained up to run the hotel kitchen, although she still deferred to Gwen. Gwen was almost as much of a control freak as Harriet when it came to the Meadowbrook kitchen.

'Ha, I should have asked them to do our accounts. Only joking. Gosh, this coffee is good, Pip. Right, I'm going to finish up here, then I'll take Toby down to the sanctuary with me. Leave you to get ready, and don't worry, I won't be popping up with the baby while we've got guests.'

'You know, I could babysit for a bit this morning?' Pippa offered.

'No, it's fine. He'll need feeding soon; I'd better take him with me. But I'll call you later.'

Pippa decided arguing was futile as she took her tea into her apartment.

She'd just blow-dried her hair, when a message pinged on her iPad. The hotel had been set up so that guests could send instant messages from the mini iPad each room was presented with when they checked in. Another of Gemma's ideas. And it made Pippa's life easier, especially when the hotel was full. If they wanted anything – room service, fresh towels – they could send a message. Mixing modern technology with a Georgian manor house, they liked that at Meadowbrook, the old with the new.

She read the message:

Join me for breakfast?

Of course it was from Hector. Who else?

Meet me in the kitchen, she replied.

No guest ever ate in the kitchen. They had a formal dining room or they could eat in their rooms, but Hector was different. And Vicky would probably be there by now, so she could whip up something for them.

'Hector,' Pippa said as he walked into the kitchen a few minutes after her.

'Pippa, morning!' He grinned his boyish grin.

Whenever he did book signings, it was always full of women who wanted to get close to him. He said he felt a bit like a sex object, as he was sure half of them didn't even read the books they brandished for him to sign. It made Pippa laugh. After all, he'd become famous for wearing swimming shorts and little else, and chatting up women, so he had little grounds for complaint.

'Hi, Hector,' Vicky said, turning a nice shade of red.

All the Meadowbrook staff, both male and female, had crushes on Hector. When he'd stayed here to write his first book, they'd all fallen in love or lust with him.

'Vicky, you look lovely as always. Can I have my usual?' Hector asked charmingly.

'Yes, full English and cappuccino coming up. Pippa?'

'I'll just grab some yoghurt and fruit. Tomorrow, we need the dining room set up for six, unless you want to join the accountants for breakfast, Hector?' Pippa asked.

'No, I really don't want to do that. Can I have breakfast in here?' he asked.

'I'm not sure that's a good idea when we have other guests,' Pippa said.

'Of course,' Vicky said at the same time. 'It'll be fine. I'll take care of you myself.'

Pippa rolled her eyes.

40

'Great. You know, sitting at this wonderful kitchen table eating breakfast in here inspires my writing,' Hector declared. 'As does your very wonderful cooking, Vicky.'

'Oh, that's so lovely to hear,' Vicky said, flushed with pleasure.

No wonder everyone fell at his feet. Apart from herself, of course.

Freddie was doing a stocktake in the bar and Gemma was helping him when Pippa returned from checking the rooms.

'God, the village can drink,' Freddie observed as he started to type into his iPad what he needed to order after the party had depleted a fair bit of stock.

'They learnt from the best,' Gemma teased, giving him an affectionate squeeze.

'Gem, do you fancy coming for a walk down to the sanctuary with me? I never see you these days,' Pippa complained.

She was so happy her best friend and her brother were together, but she missed the times when she and Gemma were setting up the hotel together, both living at Meadowbrook. They'd have late-night chats and early morning chats ... She was lonely, Pippa knew. Not anything bad, but she did miss the companionship of having her friend around. They got on so well and Pippa was still getting used to spending more time on her own. Even when the hotel was full, Pippa would be working and then she'd go to her apartment alone to sleep. There was definitely a feeling of isolation at times, but she knew she was probably being self-indulgent. She wanted the hotel and she'd got it. She should be counting her blessings, not worrying about what she didn't have.

'I see you nearly every day,' Gemma pointed out. 'But sure, I'll come with you; we might get to see Drake.'

'He's very sweet,' Pippa said of the new arrival, the calf that Fleur had named. 'But of course Madonna won't let you go near him.'

'Nor will David. They're a tight little family,' Freddie said. 'I thought parenthood might soften them, but it's actually made them more aggressive. A bit like Harry, actually ...'

Pippa swiped at him.

'I might get to see Toby as well,' Gemma added, pointedly ignoring Freddie.

'As I said, Harriet's about as protective of him as Madonna is of Drake. You're lucky she hasn't tried to charge you when you get too close,' Freddie said.

They both left him to it, shaking their heads. It was almost true. Harriet hadn't wanted anyone to hold Toby for about a week after he was born. Even the midwife had to prise him out of her arms, but she was getting better. She was no way as bad as Madonna was, thankfully.

Meadowbrook Sanctuary was an integral part of the estate, although largely they kept it separate from the hotel. While some guests showed interest in the animals, many didn't, so it was kept at a discreet distance, figuratively speaking. The reality was that you drove past it to get to the hotel, but they'd found a balance, as some of the fields had been concealed with large trees, and it worked. As Gemma pointed out, not everyone who came to a five-star hotel wanted to watch pigs rolling around in mud. Although Connor couldn't think why not, Pippa and Harriet had agreed.

The sanctuary had expanded over the past year. With Harriet at its helm, it was growing year on year and the donations were up. Of course, the result of the sanctuary being so well known meant that animals being brought to them were also on the increase, so they'd had no choice but to expand. Connor would never turn an animal away and nor would he put a healthy one down, so they all had to ensure that they could cope with the demand.

Each of the siblings had their own roles to play. Gus looked after the pigs, Freddie the chickens, while Harriet was more of a general manager and finance person, and Pippa floated between all the animals wherever she was needed. They had more staff than ever now, both paid and volunteers.

She found Harriet with Toby by the paddock looking at the tiny ponies, Cookie, Clover and Brian, along with their latest editions, Star and Bea, a couple of Shetland ponies who'd been mistreated. Many of the stories behind how some of the animals who came to the sanctuary had been treated had them all in tears. No one was immune and Pippa found it hard to believe they could live in a world where people were so cruel. Gerald, the donkey, approached them; he was never far from the ponies, of whom he seemed to take care. But his leg was still a little wonky from an injury he'd sustained in a fire before the hotel opened. Thinking about that still filled Pippa with dread, of how close they'd come to losing some of the animals ... It made her shudder.

'Hey,' Pippa said, going over to her sister and trying not to grab Toby from her arms.

'Hello,' Harriet said. 'Right, which one of you wants first hold?'

She was definitely getting better at letting people near her child.

'Me!' they both said.

'Gemma, you have him first; after all, Pip, you've had more time with him lately.'

43

Gemma clutched him to her and kissed his head.

'You really are the most beautiful baby,' she cooed.

Harriet and Pippa exchanged a glance. Was she broody? Pippa wasn't sure if Freddie was ready for fatherhood. He was barely ready for adulthood, after all.

They watched as Gemma started walking Toby around the field.

'He's pretty relaxed about being handed around,' Pippa said, as Toby seemed happy with Gemma.

'Um ...' Harriet didn't look pleased. 'I expected more loyalty.'

'With a mother as neurotic as you, that's a miracle. He obviously takes after Connor,' she added with a laugh.

'Shut up! I'm not neurotic.' Harriet swiped at her. 'Well, only a bit. But there's something I need to tell you. Have the accountants arrived yet?'

'No, they're due at three for tea, it's all organised,' Pippa replied.

'Great. So, I just had an email through the booking system. A woman wants to book in for at least a couple of months.'

'Really? Who is she?'

'I don't have much info, to be honest. Her name's Brooke Walker. She's from California, is thinking of moving here to start a business and wants a quintessential English experience.'

'But two months will cost her a fortune. I know Hector's on mates rates, but he's still paying a lot and he can afford it.'

'She must be well off, too. I gave her a quote, with a small discount, and she agreed straight away. She also said she'd pay two months upfront and then see if she wanted to extend. The good news is that we can fit her in, even with the other bookings, and the brilliant thing is that this'll be a healthy amount of money through the winter. In fact, if she stays two months that'll take us to spring and if she stays longer ...'

'Gosh, with her and Hector we'll have two long-term residents. What else do you know about this woman?'

'I'm waiting for her to answer the questionnaire. She did say that she had a British heritage she knew very little about, which is one of the reasons she was coming, along with the idea she might settle here and run a business, but I've no idea about anything else. Hopefully, we'll hear more soon; I'm quite intrigued. I have no idea how old she is, even. She's arriving in a week's time and I said that we'd organise the airport transfer.'

'Brooke, that's a very American name,' Pippa mused.

'Who's Brooke?' Gemma asked, rejoining them.

'Some woman from California who wants to stay here for a couple of months,' Harriet explained.

'God, she's bound to be blonde and beautiful,' Gemma lamented. 'And thin. I'll bet she's thin.'

'Gemma, I hate to point it out, but you're beautiful and slim – not thin but slim,' Pippa said. 'And if she is, the only man who might be remotely interested in her is Hector.'

'But he's only got eyes for you,' Harriet pointed out. 'But then Freddie only has eyes for you, Gem, so there's no problem.'

Gemma looked unconvinced. That was the only thing with her, Pippa worried. Gemma still wasn't the most confident of women and her brother probably wasn't the best at picking up on this. Pippa was going to have to watch that, because if Gemma needed reassurance, she'd have to point that out to Freddie.

'By the way, I've got a re-homing-cum-adoption day to organise for the dogs. Gemma, have you got time to help me in the next couple of weeks?' Harriet asked.

'Sure, I'm on top of my college work.'

Gemma was studying for a business degree; the hotel had given her a taste for starting up something of her own, but she worked so ridiculously hard she was always ahead. And top of her class. For someone who lacked confidence, she was very good at what she did and Pippa never failed to remind her of this.

'Great, why don't we meet later and brainstorm? I'll call you when I know what Toby's schedule is. Speaking of which, he's due a feed.' Harriet took him gently from Gemma.

Pippa looked out over Meadowbrook. It really was the most magnificent place in the world, she thought. There was nowhere quite like it. And with that, she headed back to the house to greet her latest guests.

Chapter Six

'Bloody hell! Who knew accountants could drink so much?' Freddie's eyes were wide as he sat in the bar with Pippa, Hector and Gemma, the evening after their six latest guests had departed.

'I told you they all said they liked tequila. That should have been a warning sign,' Pippa laughed.

'Yes, well, that woman, Patricia, she was very frisky. She kept trying to touch my bum,' Hector complained.

'You know, you should stay here for free. No, you should actually be paid to stay here, the way you were the star attraction,' Gemma stated.

It was true. Everyone wanted to talk to Hector. When the accountants discovered he was staying there – thankfully not until their last night – the group had insisted he join them for dinner and then drinks. Hector had obliged with good grace, although he did go to bed earlier than them, citing work. Pippa thought it was to get away from the groping woman, Patricia. She was so mild-mannered when Pippa met her – as well as throughout the painting workshop and the cooking – so when she drank and became a bit of a cougar, they were all taken aback. It had been fun, though. They'd loved their stay and the bar bill had been great for

Meadowbrook's profits. They left with a flurry of compliments and assurances they'd return. She wasn't going to tell Hector that, though. Not yet. He really might demand to be put on the payroll.

'So, tell us about your new book,' she said instead, trying to change the subject as they sipped much-needed glasses of wine.

She had her feet up on the table. It was nice at times being at Meadowbrook without guests and it felt like home again. As much as she loved the hotel, she did miss having the house as a family home at times. But that was only natural. And as she was the only one who actually lived in Meadowbrook, it wouldn't ever be the same family home again.

'It's sort of a sequel, although I've introduced some new characters. Did I tell you that the first one might be being made into a film?'

'No way, mate, you never said. Congratulations!' Freddie sounded delighted.

'You know I was in LA before New York, going to all these meetings where everyone says they love you, they love the book? Well, on and on they went and often it comes to nothing. But I just got confirmation that there's been an offer and they want to get started straight away. So although it might not see the screen, my agent's confident it will.'

'That's amazing!' Pippa leant over and kissed Hector's cheek. 'I can't tell you how proud we are of you,' she said.

He blushed. Hector always looked young for his age; he wasn't quite thirty, but he looked even more like a schoolboy when he blushed.

'So, you have to write book two now. What about the film script?' Gemma asked.

'They'll be getting a scriptwriter in. I didn't think I knew how to write a book and I've never written a script, so I don't want to push it. But I get to consult on it and when I've finished this book, I'm probably going to go to LA for a bit.'

'To live?' Freddie couldn't keep the horror out of his voice.

'No, but maybe for a while. After all, why not? I'm pretty flexible, I've got no ties here.' He glanced at Pippa, who pretended not to notice. 'But the problem is that this new book has to be good. It's great that *The Coron Files* was such a success and the family intrigue seems to be the main hook – you guys were my inspiration, by the way.'

'Great, because in the book the family are all corrupt money launderers and possibly murderers,' Pippa pointed out.

'I did use poetic licence. I just said you were inspiration, especially you, Pippa. Where was I? Oh yes, there's a lot of pressure on book two, which is why I wanted to write it here, with you guys. I kind of feel the first book was largely created at Meadowbrook and so I want the same for this one. I like to think of myself as your writer in residence.'

'I, for one, think this calls for champagne,' Freddie declared.

'Fred, you know what Harry said about us drinking the profits,' Pippa cautioned.

'Oh, put it on my bill,' Hector laughed. 'I don't care about the cost. Having drinks with good friends to celebrate my film deal, it doesn't get much better than this.'

'I'm sure they'll give you a big discount,' Gemma teased.

'Oh, for goodness' sake, get the champagne, Fred, and pour. I'll deal with Harry if I have to. Hector's not paying for his own celebration.'

'Now that's the sister I like best.' Freddie jumped up and was back with a bottle of champagne in seconds.

Pippa thought this was the least they could do for Hector. Not only did he pay them, and not only did he entertain the guests, but he also put the hotel firmly in the limelight via social media. And he'd do anything to help them, after all. He deserved this – more than this.

'In fact, I think we owe you a few crates of the stuff. And seeing as you do all that social media for us, I'm going to put it down as a marketing expense,' Pippa said. 'You can have whatever you want at any time.'

'Including you?' Hector raised his eyebrows hopefully.

Pippa didn't know how to respond without being rude, so she just ignored him. She knew that Hector only wanted her because she was the only woman who resisted his charms. It was flattering, she guessed, but she needed a man and Hector was still a boy in too many ways. Besides, she'd explained to her entire family when they questioned why she wouldn't even consider him. The minute she succumbed to him, he'd go off her. That's what happened with men like Hector. She couldn't cope with the rejection that would inevitably come.

'Gus just texted. He said he and Amanda are going to grab a bite to eat at the pub. Shall we join?' Freddie said, saving Pippa.

'Let's go,' Pippa said. 'Then it'll feel like a proper celebration.' And it would hopefully stop Hector looking at her with his moony eyes.

'Harry and Connor aren't coming. She's probably got that baby stuck to her again,' Freddie moaned.

'Oh, Freddie, you're so mean about your darling nephew. Connor and Harry are new parents, they need time to get used to it, and I think it's wonderful the way they spend time together. As a family.'

Again, Gemma looked wistful, so Pippa quickly mobilised them. This wasn't a safe discussion. Having Hector declare his 'love' for her was almost preferable, in fact. Life had been good, if not great since the hotel opened, but Pippa could sense a shift. She didn't know what, but Gemma seemed almost as besotted with Toby as Harriet and as she didn't have any family, she was pretty sure that she was more ready than Fred to have a child of her own, or at least for him to make a commitment to her. But she brushed those fears aside. Instead, they were going to have a nice meal and toast Hector's success. Nothing would ruin that.

However, as it turned out, Gus managed to ruin it. As soon as they walked into The Parker's Arms, Amanda shot Pippa an anxious glance and as Gus's head was almost stuck in his pint glass, she could tell that he wasn't happy.

'You look terrible,' Freddie said as they all sat down at the table.

'Thanks, mate.'

Hector was dispatched to get drinks, with Gemma offering to help. Pippa grabbed menus and when they were all settled, she turned to Gus.

'What's wrong?'

'My little girl,' Gus said, and then he opened his mouth and closed it again.

Amanda patted his arm.

'Fleur has a boyfriend. Not a date but an actual boyfriend. He's seventeen,' Amanda explained.

'Far too old for her.'

'Um, she's sixteen,' Pippa pointed out.

'Nooo,' Gus said and took a huge slug of his drink.

If it had driven Gus to drink, it had to be bad.

'Alfie, that's his name. Lives just outside Parker's Hollow. They met in the village shop, which is so innocent,' Amanda explained.

'There's nothing innocent about teenage boys,' Gus said, waggling a finger at them. 'He was probably trying to buy booze and cigarettes with a fake ID that he's paid for by selling drugs.'

'That's true,' Freddie replied and Hector nodded.

There was certainly nothing innocent about Fred when he was a teenager, that was sure.

'He's at the local sixth form, doing A-levels. Wants to be an architect and from what I can tell, he's a nice boy.'

Amanda sounded slightly harsh. She had the patience of a saint when it came to Gus, but even she had a limit. And Gus was famous for being an overprotective father; although, of course, he adored Fleur.

'He didn't call me Mr Singer when he first met me,' Gus said.

'I'd have him shot,' Freddie joked.

'He's probably on drugs,' Gus added.

'We all were at that age,' Hector pointed out unhelpfully.

Pippa gave him a prod on his arm and hissed at him to shut up.

'Oh, God, I need a whisky,' Gus said.

'No, you need to eat. Now, let's order and stop talking nonsense. Gus, your daughter was going to have a boyfriend at some point and I really don't think Alfie's a delinquent. We might have to deal with the fact that at some point soon, Hayley will, too.'

'Oh God, no.' Gus put his head in his hands.

Hayley, his stepdaughter, was privy to the same kind of overprotectiveness as Fleur from him, but as she was more interested in sport than boys it hadn't really been a problem.

'Alfie's decent. His mum and dad are both teachers. He doesn't have any tattoos or a criminal record and as far as I can tell, it's just a bit of hand-holding and snogging at the moment,' Amanda said.

'Don't say that, please,' Gus begged.

'I give up!' Amanda threw her hands in the air. 'Right, I'm going to have the vegetarian pasta. Anyone else ready to order?'

'Sorry,' Gus said. 'I know I'm being unreasonable, but it's so hard to watch my little girl grow up.'

'Listen, mate,' Hector said. 'You're pretty lucky that Fleur's sensible, clever and a credit to you. I know you'll always worry; after all, we were teenage boys once. Actually, I acted like one until fairly recently. All you can do is trust her, support her and get either Amanda, Harry or Pip to do the girl talk with her.'

'Oh God, not me. I mean we get on pretty well, but I'm still the evil stepmother,' Amanda stated quickly.

'I'll do it,' Pippa offered. 'If you get Harriet to do it she might turn into a bit of a ball-breaker. You know, teach Fleur how to make boys cry.'

Not that Harriet was like that anymore, but then she still thought she was. She was quite soppy about Connor, but she'd never admit it.

'Maybe I should get Harry to do it, then.' Gus cheered up. 'OK, thanks, Hector, you do make sense. And yes, my darling wife, let's eat.'

'Nightcap?' Hector asked when they were back at Meadowbrook.

It was nearly eleven and as the hotel was empty bar Hector, there were no staff around. When it was like this, Pippa had struggled being alone, even for the odd night. The house was so big and although it was home, had always been home, she still felt jumpy at every little noise. She was glad that Hector was here. They had a few bookings at the weekend but until then, it was just the two of them.

'Sure, we'll drink the good brandy. It's not in the bar, I keep it in the office, just like Dad used to.' She led the way.

They settled into the sofa, nursing their drinks. Pippa had tucked her legs underneath her while Hector stretched his long legs out before him.

'This reminds me of Dad,' Pippa said after a while.

'I wish I'd met him,' Hector said. 'I kind of feel that all you Singers are part of my family now, so it would have been nice to have known him.'

'He's still here,' Pippa said, gesturing to the huge portrait of him they kept in the office. Their father was a little on the vain side. He'd had the portrait painted years ago and he kept it in his bedroom when he was alive. Now, it was far more suitable for the office. None of the guests needed a full-size Andrew Singer staring down at them.

'Yes, he looks as if he'd be as overprotective as Gus. I feel that he's warning me off with his eyes,' Hector laughed.

'Don't be silly. You're my friend and he'd have liked you. Actually, at first he wouldn't but now, with this serious writing side of yours and stuff, he'd probably have liked you.'

'I'll take probably. Right, let's have a toast. To my new book and to Meadowbrook, where it all began to make sense to me.'

As they clinked glasses, Pippa was lost for words. She never imagined that Hector felt that way, the way she did, about Meadowbrook. It was quite moving and she knew then that her father would have liked Hector. He would have admired the way he'd sorted himself out, grown up and was what her dad would have referred to as a 'decent man'. High praise, indeed, Pippa smiled to herself.

Chapter Seven

'I don't see why I have to be the bloody driver,' Freddie moaned. 'I'm not a chauffeur, I'm a serious bar manager and co-owner of the hotel.'

'You picked Hector up happily enough,' Pippa pointed out.

'That's different, he's a mate,' Freddie whined.

Pippa laughed. Her brother acted like a toddler at times; she was almost expecting him to stamp his foot.

'Fred, I can't go because I'm needed here. We've got guests leaving and I've got to get Brooke's room ready. I've got a skeleton staff as there's some kind of cold bug going round, so someone needs to pick her up from the airport.'

'But why me?' Freddie persisted.

He didn't like being 'staff', even though technically he was, but then he'd always been slightly work-shy. Since he'd started managing the hotel bar and running all the hotel's social media, Freddie had began to work harder than ever, largely owing to Gemma, Pippa thought, but he still didn't like to do anything that he didn't want to. Which was a lot of things.

When they first lost their father, the terms of their father's will stated that the four siblings had to live together in the house for a year and work in the sanctuary. Freddie had been appalled when he was first put on chicken duty, although he was very fond of them now and he spoilt them. But, that hadn't happened overnight. It had taken a boot up Freddie's backside to get him to actually do some work – and that boot had come from their father, from his grave.

'Harry would kill me if we paid a cab to pick her up and included in her price is airport transfer. Fred, she's an important guest. She's staying with us for at least two months and she's paid the full amount up front, so we need to make sure her stay, from the moment she steps out of the airport until she leaves here, is perfect. I trust you to give her the right kind of welcome.'

'Hummph. What's this woman's story, anyway?' He folded his arms but she could see he'd thawed a little.

'It's quite strange, actually. She's only twenty-five, which seems very young. She's from California. Apparently, she has some kind of English ancestry who she wants to find out more about and is even thinking of setting up a business here.'

'Doing what? And when you say here, I'm guessing you don't mean Parker's Hollow?' Freddie frowned.

He had a point. This was a lovely village but young people didn't exactly pour in to set up businesses here. It was definitely an older person's type of village; although there had been an influx of younger families lately what with the new housing developments on the outskirts – much to the horror of many of the long-standing residents. It had crossed Pippa's mind to question why she'd chosen Meadowbrook, but Harriet told her not to pry. After all, they'd find out soon enough when she was staying with them.

'Not sure, but we do know that she's vegetarian and she eats a lot of eggs – free-range, of course,' Pippa grinned.

Their chickens laid eggs and as the coop had almost doubled with ex-battery hens in the past year, they had plenty at the moment.

She continued, 'And she drinks a lot of green juice. She sent the recipe over and poor Vicky's getting to grips with the blender and wheatgrass as we speak.'

'OK, so I'll go and get her from Heathrow. Please tell me I don't have to wear a chauffeur's uniform.'

'No, that would look silly, especially as you need to introduce yourself as one of the owners of the hotel. No, just look smart. Your best jeans and blazer would work well, I think.'

'How will I know who she is?'

'Oh, we made a sign for you. Don't worry, Fred, we've thought of everything. Oh, and take the Range Rover, remember. No Porsche.' Pippa didn't want the poor woman arriving terrified.

'You ruin all my fun,' Freddie mumbled before heading out.

Pippa was intrigued about their new guest. She knew so little about her but she was looking forward to meeting her. She was also looking forward to having another woman about the place, although Harriet had warned her not to try to push friendship on this guest. While Pippa had taken umbrage at the time, she knew her sister had a point. Pippa did know how to be professional but she could try a bit too hard to be friends with people at times. Gemma had been a case in point. When Gemma came to Meadowbrook to work for them, Pippa had determined they'd be best friends. They'd become so over time, which only proved her right, but she also accepted that she could be a bit pushy and Brooke was a paying guest. Pippa knew she'd have to remember that. Friendly but professional. Of course, if she was going to see a lot of her, a bit like with Hector, then surely it wouldn't be like the other guests, would it? Pippa knew she'd have to try to find the right balance.

'Hey.' Gemma walked in and found Pippa in the office.

'Gosh, it's like a revolving door around here. Freddie's just left, you've just arrived.'

'Oh, I missed him?' Gemma sounded anxious. 'I'm going to college in a bit. I was hoping to catch him before I left.'

'You guys literally must have just passed each other.'

Pippa's brows knotted. She knew Gemma well. When Gemma had come to work at Meadowbrook as their hotel consultant, Pippa and she had become close. Even though Gemma had tried to keep her and the rest of the family at arm's-length, they soon broke down her barriers. It wasn't easy and her situation turned out to be complicated. Gemma was serious and hardworking but anxious and almost secretive. They later found out that was because she wasn't actually qualified to do the job they hired her for – although she was certainly capable – and she'd stolen her old boss's CV. It had sent Pippa into a rage; she couldn't believe her friend had lied to her. But then Gemma had explained that her boss was horrible, her nan was in an expensive nursing home and she had nowhere to live, so she'd taken the first risk that she'd ever taken in her life... And she hadn't expected to get close to the people she worked with.

In the end, Pippa understood. Gemma had had a terrible time, had hardly any family and then her only relative, her nan, had died just before the hotel opened. Pippa had recognised that Gemma wasn't a bad person and she'd done an amazing job with the hotel. Eventually, she'd thawed and they'd reaffirmed their friendship, and when Gemma and Freddie got together, it had made Gemma more part of the family. And their relationship had seemed wonderful for the past year. Gemma was definitely a positive influence in Freddie's life and he helped bring out her lighter side. Everyone agreed they were made for each other; they were certainly very good for each other.

'Freddie and I kind of had a fight,' Gemma blurted out. Then she burst into tears.

Pippa led her to the sofa, sat her down and passed her some tissues.

'About what, Gem?' she asked.

'Oh God, I'm such a fool. I knew it was too good to be true. This life. Meadowbrook, the hotel, us then Freddie and the beautiful house...' Her words were interrupted by her sobs.

'Hey, it's not too good to be true. You deserve it all.'

Pippa put an arm around Gemma. This was the old Gemma, riddled with insecurity, never feeling good enough. Pippa felt her heart breaking for her. It had taken Freddie a while to get Gemma to agree to move into the barn conversion with him. At first she'd lived at the hotel, sharing Pippa's apartment – the living room had been a bedroom for a while – then she'd tried to rent somewhere nearer her college. But Freddie had begged her to live with him and eventually she'd relented. They lived with Albert, the cat that Freddie had adopted for her from the sanctuary to persuade her to move in with him. Albert had been Gemma's favourite. Pippa never knew her brother could be so romantic, especially as Albert loved Gemma but didn't like Freddie. Although when he first lived with them he'd hiss at Freddie, now he largely ignored him. But Freddie loved Gemma and Pippa thought her being there, with her boyfriend and her cat, and the rest of the Singers not far away, had given Gemma a new family and made her feel secure. But now, it seems she might have been wrong about that.

'You know I've been struggling. When the anniversary of nan's death came up I felt as if I went right back to when she died. I miss her, you know, and I still feel so lost sometimes. But I'm also lucky. I've got you and I've got Freddie and the family. But you know how insecure I was and still am sometimes. I try to fight it but it never goes away. Not properly.'

'I know, but my annoying brother loves you, Gemma.'

Pippa was stern, although sometimes Gemma did need a bit of a talking to. Mind you, Pippa did, too. That was how their friendship worked. Gemma would tell Pippa she worked too hard and Pippa would tell Gemma she was too hard on herself.

'I do know that, deep down, but Freddie's so confident, as you know. I'm not and I think I'm trying to push him into something he might not be ready for.'

'What do you mean?' Pippa asked, feeling herself go cold.

Maybe her suspicions were right. Her brother had never been a fan of commitment but with Gemma that was changing. However, Pippa knew that he had to make the changes in his own time.

'I mentioned marriage and babies. Seeing Harriet with Connor and Toby, well, it kind of makes me want that. I want my own family.' She dissolved in tears again.

'Oh, Gem. Freddie loves you and perhaps he should be thinking along those lines at his age. In fact, he might well

61

be. But you know, he's not the kind of guy you push into doing things,' Pippa said gently.

'I know. He said he didn't like children and he really didn't want a baby. He said he preferred chickens.'

Pippa couldn't help but laugh.

'That's such a Freddie thing to say. And you know he doesn't mean it. But, Gemma, he does love you, I can see that. Anyone can see that. But you need to give him some time.'

'I know, and there's no rush.' Gemma was only thirty, after all. 'I just can't help myself. You know, everything's going so well, so why am I trying to sabotage it?'

'Million-pound question. Listen, we need to spend a bit of girly time together, give Fred some space. Let him stew with his chickens. Once he gets back from picking up our new guest, that is.'

Gemma laughed. 'I could certainly do with that.'

'Let me settle in the new arrival and then perhaps we can have a trip into Bath for some shopping and lunch.'

'Sounds lovely. Thanks, Pippa, I don't know what I'd do without you.'

'You don't have to know.' Pippa hugged her. 'That's what friends are for.'

She just prayed Freddie and Gemma would work this out, because she didn't want to lose her friend and she also knew how much Gemma didn't want to lose Freddie. Not only that, but Pippa knew how much Freddie needed Gemma. She just hoped that Freddie knew it, too. She thought he did but equally, she knew that he was probably panicking about Gemma's grown-up demands. Just as everything seemed to be going smoothly, problems were mounting once more.

What with Harriet and the baby, Gus and Fleur, and now

this, Pippa was worried. Was there yet another storm about to break? She sincerely hoped not.

Pippa had run out of things to straighten. She had even straightened up Hector, who was working in the bar. He'd chosen a table by the window and was typing away. Pippa had taken him coffee after coffee, trying to keep busy. She didn't know why she was nervous, but it was probably because the hotel was quiet, so their new guest, Brooke, would notice everything. She wanted her to arrive and think how perfect, how wonderfully British it was, that was important to Pippa.

She had a group of women arriving the following day, best friends, who were participating in a painting workshop with Gus for a long weekend. That would certainly add a bit of life to the place but for now, she hoped that Brooke would fall in love with Meadowbrook. She was the first American that the hotel would welcome and she hoped the Englishness of the place would go in their favour. But she was worried that a young Californian woman would find it a bit dull or lonely being here alone for two months. Yes, she said she was looking at setting up a business, but what would she actually do every day?

She shook herself; she was fretting for no reason. She was polishing some already polished glasses at the bar, just for something to do. The rhythmic typing of Hector's laptop was fairly soothing and it was almost as if she were polishing in tune. The bar was designed with a nod to art deco, and the tables and chairs scattered around had been inspired by Freddie's obsession with *Bright Young Things*. It was quite dark, the furniture, but the floor-to-ceiling glass doors that led out to the patio brightened up the room. The bar ran across the top of the room, commanding it, and mirrors above reflected the bright array of liqueur that they provided. It really was Freddie's domain and it was a huge hit with all the guests.

'Hi.' Freddie bounded in suddenly.

Pippa almost dropped the glass she was holding. Hector looked up.

'Haven't you forgotten someone?' Pippa's voice was filled with horror. 'Where's our guest?'

'She's asleep in the car, or at least I hope she's asleep.' He didn't look happy.

'What do you mean? Is everything all right?' Pippa asked, chewing her bottom lip anxiously.

'Whether everything is all right, Pip, depends on your point of view. So there I was at Heathrow, stood with the sign ... actually, the other drivers who were waiting thought I was one of them and they struck up conversations with me about traffic. They were very friendly but what do I know about traffic? I know nothing about traffic, so I had to nod and agree that the M25 was the worst motorway ever and I don't even know if that's true or not.'

'Freddie, the guest?' Pippa pushed.

'Oh, yes, so I was waiting and after what seemed like ages, a blonde woman, almost hidden behind her luggage trolley, appears. She made her way over to me and blinked at my sign, so I went to greet her, told her I was Freddie Singer and then she fainted on me!' Freddie explained.

'You should be used to girls falling at your feet,' Hector joked.

'Well, maybe, but not actual fainting, though. We had to get help, first aid, and it took ages for her to come round. I got her some water and when she did wake up, she was really embarrassed. Kept apologising. So eventually we got her into the car – I had to push the luggage and they put her in a wheelchair; although she said it wasn't necessary. Anyway, when we got to the car, she sat in the back and didn't speak to me. When I asked her a question with no response, it became clear she'd fallen asleep. So I panicked the whole way back that there's something wrong with her. What if she's unconscious? Perhaps I should have stopped and checked.' He scratched his head.

'Oh my goodness, she might have passed out in the back of your car!' Hector piped up as he stood up.

'Yes, she bloody well might. So hurry up and stop asking me stupid questions.'

They all bounded out to the car.

They found Harriet staring into the car as they reached it.

'There seems to be someone asleep in the car,' she said, eyeing them all suspiciously.

'Open the door and check she's all right,' Pippa said urgently, panic fluttering in her chest.

It wouldn't look good if the guest fell ill, or worse, before she even checked in.

'Why, what's happened?' Harriet's eyes widened.

'Long story. Please, open the car.'

Pippa almost pushed Harriet out of the way and yanked the door open. She put her head in to check that Brooke was breathing.

'Aaargggh!' Brooke screamed, moving with a start and head-butting Pippa.

'Ow,' Pippa replied, recoiling and rubbing her head.

'So she's all right, then,' Harriet said, rolling her eyes.

She leant in as Pippa rested against the car, still rubbing her head and trying to ignore the amused looks on Freddie's and Hector's faces.

'Hi, I'm Harriet Singer. Welcome to the Meadowbrook Hotel. Sorry that we scared you but...'

Harriet turned to Pippa, who was still rubbing her head. It really hurt.

'Sorry, yes, hi, I'm Pippa Singer. Freddie told us how you'd fainted at the airport, so I was just checking you weren't unconscious.'

Pippa felt herself go red. This wasn't how she'd envisioned the arrival of their new guest. Not in a million years.

They all waited expectantly as Brooke unclipped her seat-belt, got out of the car and ran her hands through her long blonde hair. Pippa wanted to say 'wow'. She was about the same height as her, very slim, highlighted blonde hair cascading below her shoulders, with blue eyes, the clearest skin that Pippa had ever seen and the cutest button nose. Pippa couldn't decide if she had the Californian look or not, but she was certainly stunning.

'No, I'm sorry, I was fast asleep. It's been a bit of a journey.' She smiled, displaying the whitest, straightest teeth Pippa had ever seen.

She was wearing skinny jeans, white trainers and an off-the-shoulder sweater. She was beautiful, Pippa decided, and as she glanced at Freddie and Hector, who were stood slightly open-mouthed, they'd clearly noticed, as well.

'Welcome to Meadowbrook,' Pippa gushed, hoping that she didn't have a lump on her head. 'We're so delighted to have you staying with us.'

'Why, thank you,' Brooke said, her voice warm. 'I'm so

happy to be here, I really am. I'm sorry I fainted on you.' She looked at Freddie, who shrugged it off.

'Right, shall we get you settled in?' Pippa asked, remembering her role.

'Oh, please, that would be just great. I'm still a bit tired and wobbly from the journey, so I'd appreciate a bit of a rest.'

'Absolutely. Freddie'll take your bags up. Come with me and I'll get you checked in.' Pippa turned to Harriet.

'I need to grab something from the office,' Harriet mouthed and walked towards the house.

'Come on,' Pippa said, 'we've got a lovely room ready for you.'

'As long as I have a comfortable bed, I'm happy,' Brooke gushed.

She was definitely American. Pippa picked up her tote bag and led Brooke to the house.

When Pippa walked into the kitchen a while later, Harriet was sat at the table with Hector. Freddie had gone home after taking Brooke's bags up, saying he'd earned the rest of the day off. In fairness, after the scare that he'd got with Brooke, he probably had.

'Is she happy?' Harriet asked.

'Yes, but tired. She says she didn't really eat on the flight, which is why she thinks she fainted. I offered her food but she said she had some snacks with her so that would do her until dinner. She asked me to call her at six so she doesn't sleep for too long.'

'Great. What a way to arrive. She's very attractive,' Harriet said. 'In that almost cute, American way.'

'Typical hot LA girl,' Hector said. 'I mean she's gorgeous, but there are a lot of similar-looking women over there.

Although her skin's very pale, most of them have a bit of colour, but then she had just fainted.'

'No wonder you want to move to LA, then,' Harriet said.

'What?' Pippa glanced sharply at Hector, who turned red.

'Harriet, I didn't say I was moving there. And anyway, not my type, so I'm definitely not going there for the women.' He cast a longing glance at Pippa, who pretended not to notice. 'Anyway, she seems nice. Sorry she hit you.' He seemed happy to change the subject.

'She didn't hit me; we just clashed heads. And I'll live.'

Pippa noticed Harriet look at her sharply. She'd obviously snapped at Hector without meaning to. Probably because her forehead still smarted – or was that just excuses?

'I thought perhaps you and she could have dinner together tonight,' Pippa said to Hector, sounding a little softer.

'But I don't know her!' Hector sounded alarmed.

'I know that, but I wanted to set up a proper dinner in the dining room to welcome her and she can't dine alone. Tomorrow there's four women staying, but tonight...'

'Fine, but only if you join us,' Hector said.

'I agree,' Harriet added. 'It'll make Brooke feel more comfortable if you have dinner with her as well as Hector. You can barely expect her to have dinner alone with a strange man when she's just arrived. It might feel like a date or something. No offence, Hector.'

'None taken,' Hector grinned.

'It'll be a nice welcome but without being too unprofessional. Anyway, I'd better go.' Harriet stood up.

'Where's your baby?' Pippa asked as if noticing for the first time.

'With Granny Gwen. She insisted on having time with him

this afternoon. She's getting more forceful. I said I was fine and she basically wrestled the baby out of my arms. I should be catching up on sleep but I wanted to get started on the budgets for next month.'

''Course you did,' Pippa grinned. 'Oh, and by the way, Hector, dinner is vegetarian tonight.'

'That'll be good practice for LA. I think everyone's turning vegan over there. I would, although I'm a little worried about cheese. I really love cheese.'

Pippa glanced at him again. Was he really planning to move to LA for longer than he was letting on? And if so, why wouldn't he tell her that?

'Oh boy! this room is something else,' Brooke exclaimed as she walked into the dining room.

She had napped, showered and changed. She was wearing tight black trousers and a leopard print top. She looked sexy rather than cute. Clearly, this woman could morph into different looks. A skill Pippa hadn't mastered. She'd never managed sexy.

Pippa had taken a large glass of white wine up to Brooke's room shortly after six and Brooke had certainly come alive since her rest. She had enthusiastically responded to Pippa's offer of a tour and so had seen the basement pool and gym – which she loved – the drawing room – which she adored – and finally the bar – which she couldn't believe. 'It's awesome,' she kept saying. She seemed to love the house, which made Pippa feel so much better than she had when poor Brooke had first arrived.

'You met Hector earlier, but now you can be introduced properly,' Pippa said.

'Hector Barber at your service,' he half bowed. 'I'm a guest here, too – or, more accurately, the writer in residence.'

'You're Hector Barber, the writer?' Brooke's eyes widened.

'I am. Have you read my book?' His eyes lit up.

'No, but I've heard all about you from a friend who's a huge fan and she has the most ginormous crush on you. Wait until I tell her I've met you! Oh! and of course I could read your book while I'm staying here,' she said.

She was bubbly, effervescent even, and Pippa couldn't help but warm to her.

'I'll give you a signed copy,' Hector offered gallantly.

Pippa smiled to herself. He was being even more 'English public schoolboy' than normal and Brooke seemed to be lapping it up. Why wouldn't she, though? He was charm personified.

'You're really hot, in that typical English way. You know, a bit like a blond Hugh Grant when he was young. My mum's a huge Hugh Grant fan,' Brooke explained.

Pippa couldn't help but smile. She was definitely not afraid to say what she thought, which Pippa again slightly envied. She wished she had her confidence at her age. She definitely didn't have it when she was Brooke's age; although of course she was married to Mark then, who was very good at making sure she felt uncertain of herself.

'Why, thank you.' Hector's cheeks flushed and Pippa smiled.

'Great, now sit down and I'll tell them we're ready for dinner. I've selected a white wine to go with dinner, I hope that's all right?' Pippa asked.

She felt as if she sounded more English than she usually did – either because of Hector or perhaps because Brooke's perky American accent was such a contrast to hers.

'Sounds great,' Brooke said.

Hector insisted on pulling chairs out for both Brooke and Pippa, and after they were all seated, Pippa's lips curled with amusement. Thankfully on cue, their waiter for the evening arrived.

While they ate, Pippa was pleased that she'd insisted on them dining together. Hector was asking questions and Brooke seemed more than happy to answer them.

'Where do your parents live?' Hector asked after they'd established that they knew a couple of the same places in LA.

'Orange County. Or rather, my mom lives there. My dad died six months ago, so...'

'Oh, I'm sorry to hear that,' Pippa said quickly. 'We lost our father a few years ago now, so I understand.'

'Thank you.' She didn't meet Pippa's eyes. 'It was a shock, that's for sure. I mean, I'm only twenty-five and you don't expect to bury a parent at that age...' Her eyes filled with tears.

Pippa shot Hector a pleading look.

'So, what brought you here?' Hector asked.

'I guess I just started to think about my life a bit. I didn't have a job I loved, I'm single and I knew I had English ancestors ... I kind of thought I'm twenty-five, I should have some direction by now, so why not take a big chance, and that's how I ended up here.'

'Wow, that's incredibly brave.' Hector's voice was full of admiration. 'But why Parker's Hollow?'

'I know I have some kind of family tie to Somerset, so I googled hotels and as soon as I saw Meadowbrook, I fell in love with it.'

The smile on Brooke's face spoke volumes. It lit up the

room and Pippa couldn't help but want to beam back at her. She was infectious. And perhaps it would be nice to have another single woman around, Pippa couldn't help but think, although Harriet's voice in her head told her to slow down.

'Everyone does,' Pippa replied. 'And we're so glad you chose to stay here,' she added quickly. She didn't want to sound as if she was boasting or downplaying Brooke's comment.

'I'm sure my business will be more city-based, or at least in a town eventually, but there's always Bath, which everyone in America talks about, or Bristol, which I hear is a great city. I've done loads of research.'

She was full of enthusiasm which, again, Pippa found infectious.

'So, what kind of business are you setting up?'

Pippa hoped she wasn't coming across too intrusive. She tried to give Hector a 'please ask more questions look', but she was unsure if he saw it, as he seemed quite happy munching away on his dinner.

'Fitness. My background's in the fitness industry. I'm not full of details at this stage but you know, there's a lot of innovation in and around LA, so I thought it would be a great idea to bring some of it over here. I kind of thought that if I was going to have a new start, I'd like to bring something of LA with me,' she laughed.

Pippa marvelled at the ease she seemed to have developed already. Brooke seemed so relaxed and happy, not what she'd expect from such a young woman who'd left her home to start a new life potentially. Pippa would have liked some of her confidence, that was certain.

'That does sound good. So you exercise a lot?' Hector asked finally.

Pippa looked at Brooke's figure and guessed the answer was yes. Although Pippa had always been slender, she was allergic to exercise. Harriet was always running or swimming or something, the same went for Gemma, but Pippa was more of a couch potato. Harriet always said she'd get to a certain age and then she'd have to exercise because she'd start putting on weight, but Pippa's attitude was that she'd cross that bridge when she came to it. No need to panic yet. And running around keeping the hotel guests happy was probably a workout in itself most of the time.

'Sure, I love working out. I'll be using the gym, going for runs, you know. I'll also be checking out other gyms in the area at some stage.' She smiled, her perfect pearly white smile.

'Harriet used to run, but she hasn't so much since she had her baby. But Gemma – she's Freddie's girlfriend – runs most days. If you want company then I'm sure one of them'll join you. Actually, probably Gemma right now. Harriet's losing the baby weight by breastfeeding and worrying.'

They all laughed.

'That'd be great. Thanks, Pippa. What about you?' Brooke asked.

'Oh good God, no. Pippa doesn't ever exercise,' Hector said quickly. 'She thinks it was invented by the Devil.'

'What?' Brooke sounded horrified.

'Ignore him, Brooke, it's his British humour. Anyway, I did yoga for a bit,' Pippa replied defensively.

She didn't add that it had only been for a short time and that she'd fallen asleep when they were supposed to be meditating then woken with a start, dribbling, and had been too embarrassed to go back.

'But you're so slim,' Brooke said. 'Although being slim isn't the same as being fit,' she added.

'Good genes,' Pippa replied.

She and Freddie took after their mother, who was very small-framed, but Harry and Gus took after their father and had to watch their weight.

'I'm sure I'd love to run with Gemma at some point. And I teach yoga,' Brooke explained. 'I'll probably do yoga every day in the gym, and maybe swim, as well.'

Pippa thought her life sounded exhausting; although if fitness was her business then it made sense.

'Won't your mum miss you when you're away? I mean, are you two close?' Pippa asked.

'Oh my! this food is delicious. I hope it wasn't too difficult for me being vegetarian?'

'No, we also have experience in vegan food, actually. We serve lots of vegetarian dishes, but Gwen does a lot of vegan baking and we can adapt to whatever you want.'

Pippa decided to ignore the way she avoided her question. Brooke was a guest and she needed to remember that. Of course, she had hopes that as Brooke was here long-term, she'd become part of Meadowbrook. Perhaps not quite in the same way that Hector was, but at least a bit; although she'd keep reminding herself to stay professional. Otherwise, she'd have Harriet to answer to.

'That's why this place was so perfect for me. I'm going to love it here, I just know it.'

Brooke downed her glass of wine and let Hector refill it. Pippa raised her eyebrows. For someone so small she could certainly drink. As she giggled loudly at something Hector said, Pippa wondered if she was a bit tipsy. The long journey, the fainting, jetlag and coming to a new place, it was all probably a little overwhelming for her.

'Let's raise a toast,' Hector said. He was a bit tipsy too, his cheeks flushed, which was his tell. 'Here's to Meadowbrook and new friends.'

'Wow, that's so nice. To new friends and to Meadowbrook Manor.'

Brooke clinked glasses with them and Pippa had a feeling that this was going to be a fun few months at the hotel.

Chapter Eight

Pippa knocked on the door and waited.

'Come in,' Brooke said breathily from the other side.

Pippa turned the door handle and walked in.

'Hi, sorry to interrupt you,' Pippa started, standing awkwardly by the door.

Brooke had been here for a few days now and Pippa hoped her jetlag was easing. When the painting group, which comprised four middle-aged women who were all good friends, were staying, Brooke had kept herself to herself. She opted to dine in her room for all meals and although Pippa tried to persuade her to join the others, or at least Hector, she was resolute; she was still adjusting to the time difference and the weather. The women had been lovely, very quiet and well-behaved, but Brooke had barely been seen. She spent hours in the basement gym and Hector had taken her on a tour of the grounds but apart from that, Pippa had barely set eyes on her. It was fine – after all, she was allowed to do as she pleased – but still Pippa worried that she wasn't happy. One of Pippa's faults was her ability to fret about every little thing.

'Hey, no worries, come on in.'

Brooke was sitting cross-legged on the bed. She had a laptop in front of her and she was wearing her gym clothes. She looked gorgeous as always. On the rare times Pippa had seen her, she always looked amazing. In her gym clothes, she looked as if she'd just stepped off the catwalk rather than out of a gym. She almost made Pippa want to get fit. Almost, but not quite.

'I just wanted to check everything was all right. The other guests have just left, so it's you and Hector again until the weekend, and I wanted to ensure that you feel at home – you know, have everything you need,' Pippa smiled. 'And to check that you're happy here so far.'

'Everything's great. I've been keeping to my room a bit – you know, jetlag – and also I want to make the most of having all this time to rest while I can. But it's all good, Pippa. I'm very happy here,' she smiled, reminding Pippa of someone – probably a film star, the smile was so engaging.

'Will you join us for dinner tonight? We were going to eat in the bar. Freddie and his girlfriend, Gemma, should be joining us, as well as Hector.'

Brooke's eyes lit up. 'Sure, that'll be great. I want to apologise to Freddie for fainting on him and it'll be nice to meet Gemma. We can maybe arrange a run. I'd love to run outside but I'm terrified of getting lost,' she laughed.

'That's fabulous. If you need anything else, just ping me on the iPad.'

'Oh, I wanted to ask. I saw a group of old women arrive earlier from my window, but you said that there aren't any guests?'

'Sorry, I should have explained. They're our gardening club. They come and tend the gardens a couple of times a week. Really, they're part of the community. My other brother, Gus,

77

and his wife, Amanda, look after them. I hope that's not a problem?'

'No, I was going to say I'd like to go and see the gardens properly. Do you think they'd show me around?'

'Of course. Come down with me and I'll introduce you. They're all lovely, but a word of advice, don't let them hear you call them old,' Pippa laughed and touched Brooke lightly on the arm. 'They still think they're teenagers.'

Brooke sprang up. 'Got it. Thanks, Pippa. I really do love it here.'

There was an intensity to her voice that took Pippa by surprise.

'We're very happy to have you,' she replied as she told Brooke to wrap up warm and waited while she did so.

One thing she felt confident about was that the gardening club ladies would definitely love Brooke.

'Edie, this is Brooke.'

Edie, long-time member of the Meadowbrook community, soon-to-be Toby's godmother (self-appointed), was also the rose expert and she was cutting them back. The rose garden was famous and attracted quite a lot of visitors in its own right. It was mainly down to Edie's skill and she was passing those skills on to Gus. The Meadowbrook roses were so beautiful when in bloom it was breathtaking and they'd even won some kind of awards.

Before Edie had a chance to speak, four other women had approached. The women loved their gardens but they loved meeting new people more.

'I'm Rose and that's Margaret, Pat and Mary,' Rose said.

'Hello, Brooke, are you staying at the hotel?' Edie managed to edge herself in front of the other women.

They all started gently elbowing each other for space near Brooke. Just another day in the gardens, Pippa thought. Thankfully, the rest of the gardening club were busy in the vegetable gardens a little further away, so Brooke wouldn't be mobbed just yet.

'Yes, I am.' Brooke instinctively took a step back. 'And I just love the gardens. I was hoping that you'd show me around,' she asked shyly.

Pippa stood back.

'Are you American?' Pat asked.

'I am.'

'Do you have gardens like this in America?' Margaret asked.

'Not really, or not that I've seen. Nothing as beautiful as this, for sure. But I'm from California, which is more like a desert.'

Brooke had obviously said the right thing, as they all beamed at her.

'Right, I'll leave you to it. See you in the kitchen for tea and cake later,' Pippa said and she made her way back to the house.

She paused by the back door and looked. They were still all crowded around Brooke, but she was pointing at a plant and asking questions. It was sweet. She spotted Gus waving to her from the top of the garden and she waved back before she went inside.

'Hi, Gwen,' Pippa said as she found her in the kitchen. She went to give her a hug.

'I thought I'd make a cake for the gardening club.' She returned the hug. 'Sit down and I'll make you a cuppa.'

'Gwen I should be doing that. But OK, if you insist.' She sat at the table. 'It's bitter outside. I thought Brooke would be

79

complaining, you know, coming from the sun, but she seems to take the weather in her stride.'

'You said she had some kind of British heritage,' Gwen laughed. 'Maybe she's got an inbuilt way of coping with our weather.'

'True. I was hoping you'd be here. We've got a lot of baking lessons and workshops coming up and we may need to come up with some more help. You know, now you're managing to prise your grandson off Harriet a bit more.'

'I know, it's all in my calendar. And Hilary's helping out with some of them, now they're becoming more popular. I thought we needed more people, so I'm also training up a couple of the girls here. One of them's a very good little baker.'

'And will that be enough? I don't want you to wear yourself out.'

'Don't fuss. Although you're right, I am trying to spend a bit more time with Toby. They grow up so fast and I don't want to miss my first grandson's childhood. But Hilary's brilliant and she seems to enjoy having a "little job", as she calls it. I know she tends to stick to quiches, but she can actually bake anything. I think we should be fine.'

'Perfect. And how is our Toby?' Pippa asked.

Toby was doted on by his granny, as well as his auntie and just about everyone in the family. Even Freddie; although Freddie doted from a safe distance. Gwen was so excited when Harriet was pregnant and she was certainly desperate to get her hands on her grandson a bit more often. It seemed he changed every time she saw him and she didn't want to miss anything.

'Oh, he's so beautiful. I wish your sister would take it a bit easier, though.'

'Gwen, this is Harry we're talking about.'

Harriet didn't admit to struggling, she thought that was a weakness, so Pippa knew better than to say anything to her and if she said she was fine then she was fine.

'I know,' Gwen sighed. 'And I just have to make sure she knows I'm here to help whenever she needs it.'

Pippa nodded.

'Do you have any cake for us, Gwen?'

The chatter of the gardening club ladies interrupted them. The kitchen shrunk as soon as the ladies, who'd all taken their boots off, traipsed in and sat around the table. There wasn't quite enough room for them all, but Edie liked to stand by the Aga and a couple of the others joined her. Pippa saw Brooke put her head around the door.

'Is it OK for me to come in?' she asked nervously.

'Of course,' Edie replied, which made Pippa and Gwen grin at each other.

Edie liked to act as if this were her house and no one ever argued with Edie. But as a guest, and a long-term guest at that, then Brooke was welcome anywhere, Pippa felt. She didn't want to usher her out of the kitchen – that was no way to help make her feel at home.

'Please, come in and join us,' Pippa invited, showing Brooke in as Gwen fetched another chair from the utility room.

'This is the best bit of gardening club, apart from the gardening,' Rose announced.

'Yes, tea and home-made cake. Can't beat it,' Margaret agreed.

'Wow! it smells delicious. But is it vegetarian?'

The room went quiet.

'Of course it is, there's no animals in it,' Edie said as Gwen put the cake in the centre of the table. 'Whoever heard of an animal cake?' she cackled.

'It is vegetarian,' Gwen replied, her brows etched in confusion. 'It's got eggs and butter in it.'

'But they're not animals,' Margaret pushed.

'No, but they are animal products,' Brooke explained. 'But it's OK, I'm not vegan; although I'd be real interested in doing some vegan baking with you, Gwen.'

'And that's why I never understood Americans,' Edie said. 'You're a lovely girl, but how would you cope with no eggs or butter? What about crumpets, what do you put on your crumpets?'

'What are crumpets?' Brooke asked and was shot a number of horrified looks.

'Being vegan isn't an American thing,' Pippa explained, trying not to laugh.

Luckily, Brooke didn't seem offended; although her eyes flickered with confusion.

'Of course it is,' Pat said. 'They tried to bring it over in the war with those nylons they tried to woo the women with. But it didn't catch on.'

'What, because of rationing?' Gwen teased.

Pippa sneaked a grin at her.

'Not just that but because we're British and we don't hold with all that,' Mary argued.

Pippa shook her head but caught Brooke's eye and winked. There was nothing quite like the Meadowbrook gardening club. She just hoped Brooke wasn't going to get offended. Especially as she wasn't actually a vegan.

'Were you alive in the war?' Brooke asked innocently.

Pippa almost grabbed her to protect her. Most of the ladies turned white. Edie choked on her cake and Gwen had to whack her on the back quite hard to stop her from choking. Her face was puce.

'No, dear, we're all far too young,' Rose explained. 'But we know about the war from our parents.'

'Grandparents,' Edie quickly added.

'Actually, Brooke has British blood. She's here because her family is from around here originally.' Pippa changed the subject.

'Oh, you should have said.' Margaret beamed with pleasure. 'That makes you one of us.'

'Um...' Brooke started.

'Who is your family?' Edie asked, taking another slice of cake. 'I might know them.'

'I'm not real sure. It's my father's family. Walker's my surname, but I don't know a whole lot about them, yet.' Brooke was a little red-faced.

'The good news is that any British blood counteracts your American, so you can be English, after all,' Rose declared with a logic that defied logic.

'I can?' Brooke asked, seemingly still confused.

Pippa wanted to shake her head, but instead she concentrated on her cup of tea.

'Oh yes, I did a course in how to do a family tree and it turns out if you're a bit English you beat every kind of nationality.' Rose sipped her tea.

Pippa caught Gwen's eye then looked away as they both tried not to laugh.

'In fact, Brooke, I can help you trace your family. I have experience, you know. I did the course at the local library with a very renowned historian who once worked at a university somewhere in Wales, I believe, which is almost England,' Rose added.

'That's very kind,' Brooke replied carefully. 'I'll definitely take you up on that when I'm ready, Rose, thank you.'

'You might even find you're from right here and you could even be related to me,' Edie said delightedly.

Pippa was sure she saw all the colour drain from Brooke's face.

The sound of laughter from the bar rang into the hallway as Pippa left the office. She went in and found Hector, Brooke and Freddie all having a cocktail together.

'Hi,' she said as she sat herself on a bar-stool at the end.

For some reason, Pippa felt a bit like an outsider but quickly shook off the feeling. She was always the one Singer who worried about missing out. It stemmed from her being the baby of the family and often being told she was far too young to do things with her siblings. So, in fact, it was their fault she suffered from the fear of missing out, or FOMO, as Freddie labelled it.

'Brooke was telling us about her encounter with the gardening club,' Freddie explained.

'They certainly loved you,' Pippa said.

Brooke blushed. 'I adored them. They're so funny. I love that they think being English is better than being American,' Brooke giggled.

'We all know being British "trumps" being American, excuse the pun.'

Hector laughed so hard at his own joke he nearly fell off the bar-stool. How long had they been here?

'I love Americans.' Freddie clinked glasses with Brooke. 'And, Pip, Brooke's teaching me how to make skinny drinks – all the rage in America, apparently.'

'What are skinny drinks?' Pippa asked.

'Vodka or tequila with fresh lime and soda, sometimes all together as well. All with far less calories than other alcohol,' Brooke explained. 'Back home we know the calorific value of practically everything,' she explained.

'Another skinny margarita coming up. Will you join us, Pip?' Freddie asked as he grabbed a bottle.

Hector and Brooke went to sit at one of the more comfortable tables.

'I thought Gemma was coming up this evening, so we could all have dinner together?' Pippa asked, turning to Freddie.

'She's not well. She apologises, especially to Brooke – she so wanted to meet you. But she's been working so hard at college, I think she's just a bit run down and has a headache.'

'No, I'll skip drinks. Freddie, if you're staying here, I ought to go and check on Gemma.'

Pippa was torn. She wanted to stay and get to know Brooke better but she instinctively felt that Gemma might need her.

'Pip, that would be great. You know I don't do well around illness,' Freddie said, sealing her fate.

As they turned back to their drinks, Pippa realised she wasn't going to be missed. She felt irrationally upset at this.

'Freddie, I was telling Brooke that now she's met the gardening club ladies, she should see the animal sanctuary properly,' Hector suggested. 'I gave her a quick tour when we went for a walk the other day but I didn't get close to the animals.'

'Great idea,' Freddie replied. 'We can do that tomorrow. We'll take the buggy and I can show you the rest of Meadowbrook, as well. In case Hector missed anything.'

'That sounds great,' Brooke gushed.

'Count me in,' Hector added.

'Great,' Pippa smiled as she got up to leave. She was glad they were all making Brooke feel welcome.

'Fred said you're ill which is why you couldn't come up for dinner tonight?'

Pippa sat in one of the blue velvet armchairs that Freddie had commandeered from the house when his barn conversion was finished. Arthur, the cat, was purring on the sofa next to Gemma, who did look a little pale.

The living room in their barn had odd bits from the house in it, which weren't needed for the hotel, and somehow Gemma had made the eclectic mix of furniture work. The living space was huge and open-plan, with a dining table at one end and a living room the other. It was modern but with character, Pippa thought, and when Gemma moved in she added a few more feminine touches. It was a lovely space, actually, and it seemed to suit both Freddie and Gemma; a reflection of both of their personalities.

'No, I'm fine. I'm just upset because Freddie and I had another row. I said I felt insecure and he said that that was ridiculous. He asked how on earth he could make me feel more secure than he does already. I said I'd like a commitment and he replied that living with me was a commitment, that he wouldn't have asked me to move in with him, to a house on the family estate, if he wasn't serious. He said he loved me but that he didn't want to be nagged or pushed all the time.'

'He's got a point,' Pippa said gently, cupping her glass of wine.

The fact that she felt that Freddie had practically thrown her out of the hotel was now pushed further back in her mind as she defended her brother. She understood Gemma's insecurity – it was down to her upbringing, she'd been abandoned by both her parents and brought up by her nan – but she also knew her brother. He fell in love with Gemma slowly and there was no way he'd hurt her. Freddie might be the fun one of the family but he had the Singer heart. He also knew how vulnerable Gemma was. He'd thought long and hard before trying to get into a relationship with her. He'd even spoken at length to Pippa about it and he'd said he wouldn't try to do anything with Gemma until he knew he was serious.

'I know, but I'm always sabotaging things. Just when I might be happy I get scared and then things go wrong. Freddie even said that he'd speak to Harriet and arrange to get something drawn up with the solicitor to make sure that I have a share in the house if that'd make me feel better. I mean a solicitor's contract isn't exactly the romantic declaration I was hoping for.'

'Um, it's hardly a Tiffany solitaire, is it?' Pippa had to concede that one.

'Exactly, and I said that, and he said he didn't believe in marriage and no one he knew had a good marriage. I reminded him about Gus and Amanda and he pointed out it was a second marriage and that you're also divorced, so by his logic, only second marriages work. As neither of us have been married before, in his eyes we ought to steer clear. He's infuriating with his bloody logic.'

'I don't know what to say. I mean, Harry feels the same

about marriage, and I'm not the biggest fan after my divorce, but the problem is that although we all know that Freddie loves you, you need to feel secure.'

'Yes, and then I said about children and he said he saw them in his future, about five years at least.'

'That's not so bad. You're only thirty, Gem.'

'I know, and I'm doing my degree and I'd like to work for a bit, have a career, a bit like I did when I worked for you at the hotel, but I keep thinking he'll find someone better than me. You know, more suited. Like Brooke.'

'Is that what this is about?' Pippa was shocked. Where had that come from? That hadn't even occurred to her.

'I know I only met her briefly, but she's so confident and bubbly and gorgeous. I guess I'm jealous.'

'You do know that kind of irrational thinking can drive people away, don't you?' Pippa pointed out gently.

It hadn't crossed Pippa's mind that Freddie would be interested in Brooke; it just hadn't occurred to her. He seemed to enjoy her company, as did Hector, but he hardly knew her. Freddie loved Gemma, but he was a friendly, flirty guy, so Pippa could see why Gemma *might* worry. Although she was sure it was without foundation.

'Of course, which is why I'm so stupid. Do you think I should go to therapy?'

'Yes, and you can take me with you.'

'What's wrong with you?'

'I don't know. I think I might be a bit lonely.' Pippa's eyes filled with tears.

'Oh, Pip.' Gemma reached over and hugged her.

'It's been ages since the divorce and apart from the disastrous encounter with Edward last year there's been no one.'

Pippa found saying it, admitting that was what had been bothering her lately, was a slight relief. It didn't solve the problem but it was out there now and she couldn't take it back. Although she would only admit it to Gemma.

'Oh, Pippa, it's because you've spent the last year dedicated to the hotel. You never go out, you only meet guests and although most of the male guests who are single try to chat you up, you never reciprocate.'

'Because they're only here for a bit and they're guests,' Pippa replied. 'I need to keep it professional.'

It was true she'd been asked out a few times, but no one took her interest. In a couple of cases she was suspicious they were actually married.

'I know, and I agree, but maybe we should look at getting you dating again.'

'But how? I really don't know how to date.'

Her ex-husband, Mark, had wooed her when she was young and innocent. Then last year she'd met Edward at another hotel in the area when she and Gemma were doing research. He and she dated for a while but it turned out that not only was he trying to sabotage the opening of Meadowbrook as a hotel, but he was also married. There had been no one since then.

'We could look at the Internet. I mean, it can't hurt, can it? Especially as the hotel's quieter at the moment.'

'I don't know.'

Pippa chewed her lip unsurely. She felt a bit like Internet dating was akin to admitting failure. She knew plenty of people did it, but that didn't mean she should, did it?

'Either that or you start going out to meet men. Which means out of Parker's Hollow,' Gemma laughed.

Pippa thought about it and she wasn't sure that was her style, either. She didn't want to get dolled up and sit at bars in the hope of meeting someone. It wasn't her. Nor was the Internet, but at least she could do that from the comfort of her own home.

'OK, maybe the Internet.'

It seemed the lesser of two evils. At least she wouldn't have to leave the hotel.

'Great, and it'll be doing me a huge favour,' Gemma said.

'How?'

'Keeping my mind off my fear of losing Freddie.'

'We still need to deal with that, you know. Gemma, I don't want you to ruin your relationship. You two are so good together and Freddie needs you.'

'I know and you're right. I'll make more effort beating down my insecurity if you set up an Internet dating profile. How about it?'

'Deal!'

Pippa shook Gemma's hand.

'See, who needs therapy, after all?' Gemma laughed.

They clinked glasses before draining them to seal the deal. Arthur meowed loudly, which they both took as a sign of his approval.

Chapter Nine

'Can I get you anything else?' Pippa asked as she stood in the formal dining room with the seven guests who were enjoying a long weekend break.

They were a mixed group, two couples and three singles: a man and two women. Hector had said there was some late-night room swapping, so none of them quite knew the dynamic among them all. But of course it was none of their business and discretion was important in the hotel trade. Meadowbrook prided itself on being discreet; although Pippa had been shocked last year when it became clear that two couples who'd booked in engaged in partner swapping. She kept trying hard not to blush and Freddie said she was so naive, especially as housekeeping reported residue of drugs in the bathrooms when they left. Pippa didn't really know much about that kind of lifestyle, she was green, but running a hotel was certainly opening her eyes.

Anyway, these guests had spent their days lounging around the drawing room, mainly drinking and eating. They hadn't left the house. They were obviously quite wealthy, as they drank the most expensive wine and champagne, as well as Patron Silver tequila and the finest malt whisky. Pippa's eyes were already watering at the bar bill. Freddie had been working overtime. Which seemed to make him happy, as he and Gemma were still a little rocky. Pippa hadn't quite worked out how to fix that yet.

'Some more Bloody Marys, please,' James, the self-proclaimed leader of the group, asked.

'Sure, for everyone?'

'Yes, but less spice for me, please,' Carol, one of the single women, asked with a smile.

'I'll get them right away,' Pippa smiled and left the room.

Freddie hadn't arrived yet, as it was only breakfast and most of their guests didn't drink at breakfast. Pippa, who only had a rudimentary knowledge of how to mix drinks, googled it so she could follow the instructions.

'Hey, what's going on?'

Brooke walked in wearing her customary gym wear and looking incredibly cheerful. She'd been with them two weeks now. It was the beginning of February and although Pippa hadn't got to know her that well yet, Brooke was clearly trying to embrace Meadowbrook.

She'd hung out with the gardening club again and after Freddie took her on a tour of the sanctuary, she was now spending time there. It turned out she 'just loved animals', as well as gardens. She was enthusiastic about everything, in fact, and Harriet was even going to spend time with her later this week to talk her through how the sanctuary worked. She'd booked in a baking lesson with Gwen, saying it would be great to learn some traditional recipes as well as vegan baking before she went home.

Pippa was hoping that she could maybe spend more time with her, herself. She knew she had to be professional, but Brooke was young, here on her own and she was single like

Pippa. Pippa didn't want to push a friendship, of course, but she had to admit that it was nice, amid all the couples, to have another singleton around. They might, at some point, be able to bond over that. In the meantime, it wouldn't hurt to offer to take her out a bit, show her the area outside of Meadowbrook.

'The guests want Bloody Marys. I didn't like to tell them I didn't know how to mix them, it's Freddie's area, but we don't normally get asked for alcohol with breakfast!'

'I know, boy they can drink. I had a nightcap with them in the bar last night but I had to leave them to it. I was done and they seemed to be getting started. But hey, I know how to make the drinks, I used to work in a bar.' She joined Pippa round the side of the bar. 'Get me vodka, the tomato juice and Tabasco to start. Pull out the glasses and put some ice in.'

Pippa did as she was told, relieved that Brooke had arrived just in the nick of time.

'So, when did you bar-tend?'

'Oh, when I lived in LA during college. Everyone does it. We all hope to be discovered but I never was.'

'Did you want to be an actress?'

'No, but I thought I might get spotted for something, we all did. You even need headshots to get to work in the best bars. It's highly competitive, you know, because you never know who might walk in. After a while of bar-tending, which is a whole different world in LA, I went into fitness because it was something I enjoyed and was good at.'

'That sounds so interesting. I'd love to hear more about LA,' Pippa said warmly as Brooke started pouring out vodka.

'Sure,' Brooke said, 'but before they start screaming for their drinks can you fetch some celery?'

'Right away, boss,' Pippa smiled.

The guests were once again sprawled in the drawing room. Hector had gone to London for the day, to see his agent, and Pippa had enough staff at the hotel, so she decided to take some time out. She was just wondering where to go, when Brooke appeared. She was wearing jeans, a cute jumper and boots. She had a scarf around her neck.

'I'm thinking of going to explore, not sure where,' Brooke said.

'Would you like to take a walk with me? Or we could go for a drive? Whichever you'd prefer?' Pippa asked impetuously.

She was going out anyway and actually, it would be nice to have some company.

'Really? That'd be great. Can we go somewhere, like to another British village or something? I'd really just like to see the area, if you don't mind taking me?'

Brooke sounded enthusiastic and Pippa was happy to be a tour guide for a bit.

'I'd love to. Come on, we'll take the car.'

Pippa didn't often leave the hotel and she never went out with guests, but as she and Brooke sat side by side in her Mini, she enjoyed driving through the Mendip villages, showing off the countryside. She decided that they'd go to Wells for lunch, it was such a lovely town; although as it had a famous cathedral, it was technically a city.

'This is the smallest city in England, I believe,' Pippa said.

If she got to do tour guiding, then she might have to learn some facts. Not that Brooke noticed. She was so enthusiastic about everything that it was infectious. Pippa felt as if she was seeing the area afresh, through new eyes, and she could appreciate the beauty she often took for granted.

'It's awesome. The countryside's so pretty, not like where I'm from at all. But then I'm nearer the ocean than the countryside, I guess. And LA is a city, but not a city like this tiny one. Wells, you say?'

'Yes, it's historically important, I believe.' Pippa tried to sound authoritative for her American companion, although she really wasn't. 'But it's also very pretty. Would you like to get something to eat?'

They headed to a small café, where Brooke ordered a healthy salad and Pippa guiltily had a sumptuous-looking quiche with chips on the side.

'How are you enjoying your stay so far?' Pippa asked.

Pippa felt that she was getting to know Brooke a little. Although according to Freddie she was 'just adorable', and to Hector she was bubbly and made him feel enthusiastic about writing, Pippa didn't quite have the measure of her yet. She was definitely full of enthusiasm for Meadowbrook and she seemed to be keeping herself busy with plans for her business, but Pippa hadn't spent one-on-one time with her before today, really.

'Well, I really do love this area. Exploring has been great and you guys have been so welcoming. I think Harriet's amazing, the sort of woman you can't help but admire. So together, despite having a baby recently, and he's so cute, I just adore him already. And I love the animals. I told Harriet that I miss my dogs. My mom has three at her house and I used to spend so much time with them, so I'm going to help out with the dog walking. And I offered to help out with Toby, too. I used to be an au pair for a while and I really love babies.'

'Gosh, Brooke, what with helping out with the gardening club, the dogs and the bar the other day, you should be getting paid rather than paying us,' Pippa joked.

She had to admit, she was a little surprised. It seemed when she was busy with the guests, Brooke had been busier at Meadowbrook than she thought; although Pippa was sure Harriet would fill her in when they talked, something they hadn't done lately. Harriet was tied up and hadn't been to the hotel. Nor had Pippa had much chance to go down to the sanctuary. She made a note to go and see her sister later. Brooke was reminding her of life outside the hotel, something Pippa needed to remember a bit more.

'I think, Pippa, if I'm honest, it's because I could use the distraction.'

'From what?' Pippa leant in closer.

'My father's death was hard – you understand that, you all do – and then my mom and I ... well, we had a big fight not long ago. I kind of took a long hard look at my life and I didn't like what I saw. I felt as if I were failing.'

'But you're young, too young to be feeling like that, surely?' Pippa automatically reached out and squeezed her hand as tears filled Brooke's eyes.

'I guess, but you know by twenty-five, I should have some idea. You know, back home a lot of my friends are settled now, some married, some even with kids. So I realised that whatever I was doing wasn't working for me and then I made a crazy decision to come here. I figured that if I started afresh then everything might make sense.'

'You know, it's incredibly brave to come to a new country on your own, where you don't know anyone and you don't even have a job. I could never do anything so bold.' Pippa was being honest.

'Really? But you seem so together, like you could do anything you wanted to do,' Brooke said, sounding almost wistful.

'That's very kind of you to say that, I mean even think that, but my life's not as great as you might think. It may look like I have it all, but...'

Pippa wanted to open up and tell her about how she'd been feeling the way she did with Gemma the other day, to admit to loneliness, her failed relationships, her struggles, but she remembered that Brooke was a paying guest and she lost her nerve.

'Well, maybe, but you seem it to me.'

'Thank you, Brooke, that does make me feel better and honestly, I hope you're not too homesick. And I know you are a guest, but if you want to talk about anything, you know where I am.' Despite everything, offering a hand of friendship wasn't going to hurt. 'Especially if you want to talk about your father—'

'Sure thing,' Brooke cut in. 'So, can we go see this famous cathedral?'

'Of course we can, follow me,' Pippa said.

She didn't want to push Brooke because clearly she was going through enough at the moment and it certainly wasn't her place to pry.

Chapter Ten

Pippa briefed the staff first thing in the morning. It was Saturday, and including Brooke and Hector, the hotel was full. Four women, who were sharing two rooms, were here for a bridesmaids' hen do, thankfully a civilised one. Pippa had booked massage therapists and beauty therapists to come to the hotel and they'd turned an area by the pool into a mini spa for the day. Two couples who were keen ramblers had arrived on Friday and were going to be out most of the day taking long walks in the countryside, armed with packed lunches that Vicky was making up before breakfast. Occupying the final four rooms were four men, who all owned the same type of classic car and were going to a car show. They were beautiful old Jags and although Pippa knew nothing about them, Freddie and Hector had been salivating over them. Even Gus, who wasn't a car person, had sketched them excitedly. They were quite rare and worth a fortune, apparently.

But today was also Harriet's first big event post-Toby at the sanctuary – the dog adoption day – and Pippa needed to support that. Since the hotel opened Pippa had spent less time than before at the sanctuary, which made her sad, as she did love the animals, but there were only so many hours in the day. She'd been trying to make up for it in her quiet time, but it wasn't easy.

Although the hotel had enough staff who all knew what they were doing, Pippa still worried about leaving it. She was almost as bad as Harriet was about leaving Toby, even though the place was in good hands. When they opened they'd encountered a few staffing issues, which Harriet had guided Pippa through. Pippa was too trusting and, mistakenly, she tried to make everyone her friend, but when stock went missing from the bar, Pippa had learnt to toughen up and now she didn't let anyone work at the hotel who she doubted, trusting her instincts. And she operated a strict policy for staff, which was working well; although she knew full well if anything really bad happened, she'd get Harriet to help deal with it. She sometimes thought Harriet almost enjoyed firing people. She was the Alan Sugar of Meadowbrook.

She made her way down to the sanctuary and tried to put the hotel out of her mind for once. After all, she was literally only five minutes away if they needed her. She really did fuss too much sometimes. The hotel was thriving and she had to learn to step back when she could. If she didn't, she'd never have a personal life.

'Hi, Pip,' Connor said, running his hands through his hair before giving her a hug.

He was in the dogs' living quarters, which had recently been expanded so they had a bigger outside area, as well as luxury sleeping accommodation. It still upset her to see the domestic animals there, waiting for homes, but at least they had room to move around, the best food and a lot of love while they waited for their forever homes. It was almost like a five-star hotel for dogs, in fact.

'How's it going?' Pippa asked.

'H is frantic,' he said, referring to Harriet. 'Toby didn't sleep much last night and I begged her to let Mum have him this morning so she could get a few hours' sleep, but she insisted on bringing him here with her. I swear she's going to fall asleep standing up. Or on one of the dogs. It's not a good look.'

'My sister doesn't do things by half, does she?'

Pippa knew how important today was for Harriet, so she hoped that her lack of sleep wasn't going to ruin it for her.

'No, look at today. She's had no sleep, she's arranged this amazing dog parade, she's got the local paper coming – and by the way, they've been promised a picture of Hector with some of the dogs – and we're expecting over a hundred people. I know it's important to get the dogs re-homed and this drive will really help, but I don't want her to run herself into the ground over it.'

He ran his hands through his hair again. He and Harriet were made for each other, but they were very different people. Connor was passionate but so much more laid-back and he wasn't good at trying to get her sister to relax more. Goodness knows he tried, but she was a control freak.

'You and I both know how much Harriet has to be super-woman. Don't worry, Connor, she'll be fine.'

'Are my ears burning?'

Harriet approached with Toby in his pram.

'I was asking where you were.' Pippa leant into the pram, where Toby rewarded her with a gummy smile before shoving his fist into his mouth. She planted a kiss on his head. 'What do you want me to do?' she asked.

'I want to go through the order of the day with everyone involved. And you need to wear this.'

Harriet shoved a T-shirt that read 'Give a dog a home' at her. Pippa pulled it over her jumper. It was too cold to wear it on its own.

Gwen and Gerry approached.

'Connor, Harriet, it's far too cold out here for Toby, so we're going to take him back to your house and sit with him there,' Gwen said in her firm voice.

Gwen was a softy; growing up, she'd taken a maternal role with them but without overstepping any boundaries. However, when she wanted to be strict, no one argued with her. It was Gwen's way or the highway. Not even Harriet would question her.

'But—' Harriet started.

Pippa noted that she looked tired. And although she was wearing make-up, she couldn't help but see the bags under her eyes.

'You've got milk you expressed in the fridge and he'll be happier at home than out here. Not only that, but you need to spend some time concentrating on your event. These dogs need you.' Gwen sounded firm.

'But—' Harriet started to object.

'And as I'm shortly to be his godfather, it's my godfatherly duty to help out.' Gerry gave a mock salute.

'H, you must know when you're beaten,' Connor said, giving her a hug.

She shook her head but reluctantly relinquished the pram to Gwen. Actually, Pippa watched Gwen take hold of the pram and almost have a tug-of-war with Harriet before she finally let go.

'We'll come out later and see how you're getting on,' Gwen promised.

Harriet leant down and kissed Toby goodbye.

'You know, when I'm not with him I feel like a terrible mother,' Harriet said, her voice full of emotion.

'Nonsense,' Gwen said. 'You're a brilliant mum, a natural, and no mum needs to be with their child twenty-four seven – and no child needs to be with their mum all the time, either. Now come on, my beautiful grandson, it's time for Granny cuddles.'

'I don't know what's wrong with me,' Harriet said, wiping tears off her face when Gwen walked away and Connor was being cornered by Mike.

Pippa hugged her. It wasn't often that she saw Harriet cry.

'Oh, Harry,' Pippa said softly.

'I don't like having to ask for help. I thought I'd got better, you know, after Dad dying and Connor ... But it's still so hard. And that boy, he's so beautiful and I love him in a way I never felt possible, but all I ever do now is worry I don't deserve him, or that I'm going to fail him, or that I'm a crap mum.'

'Of course you deserve him, and all this...' Pippa waved her arms around. 'This for him, too. Our legacy, our father's legacy, you're building this and the hotel for him. Give yourself a break.'

'I know, I know, you're right. These dogs deserve loving homes.'

'Talking of dogs, where's Hilda?' Pippa asked of Harriet's rescued Old English sheepdog.

'We had to leave her at home. You know, otherwise she'd probably end up adopted by another family, she's such a flirt.'

The sides of Harriet's lips curled and Pippa could see glimpses of the old Harriet again.

'Good thinking. Right, let's go and get this brilliant re-homing day started.'

'Oh, look, isn't that Hector and Brooke coming?' Harriet asked.

Pippa looked and saw two figures in the distance; it certainly looked like them.

'I didn't know Brooke was coming.'

Pippa hadn't had much time to speak to Brooke since their visit to Wells, but she seemed happy and was spending a bit more time with Hector, she noticed. The two of them could often be found in the bar together, which was nice, Pippa thought, company for them both. Pippa was hoping to spend more time with Hector, but she'd been so busy trying to organise the hotel for the next few months that so far she hadn't seen as much of him as she'd have liked.

'They look good together. And she's not that much younger than him,' Harriet pointed out with a smile. 'Of course he's desperately in love with you, so that probably won't work out.'

'What, you mean Hector and Brooke?' Pippa asked. She hadn't thought about that. 'And he's not in love with me. He just thinks he is.'

'Would you mind if they got together?' Harriet asked, her worry forgotten as a teasing tone entered her voice.

'Of course not. If Hector and Brooke want to date then great. Anyway, Gemma's making me do Internet dating. I mean I'm not confident, but I'm willing to give it a go.'

'You, Internet dating? Bloody hell! I never thought I'd see the day,' Harriet laughed.

'Why not?' Pippa stormed.

Her sister could be so annoying. She had a habit of making her feel like a teenager again.

'You're just so fussy when it comes to men ... Oh! hi, Hector, Brooke, nice to see you. Thanks for coming to support us.'

'You know I just love dogs, so I'm really happy to help,' Brooke said breathlessly.

'Great, come with me and I'll get you some T-shirts.'

Harriet led them away.

Pippa was still irrationally annoyed with Harriet as she walked off with Brooke and Hector. But she didn't have time to stew, as a dog ran into her, practically knocking her off her feet.

'Sorry, Pippa. That's Paddy; he's a bit boisterous,' Connor said, scooping him up.

'No worries. Right, let's get this show on the road.'

Pippa shook herself, brushed dog hair off her jeans and bumped straight into Freddie, who was holding Gemma's hand.

'Hello, you two,' she said, happy to see them looking so together.

'Gem said I have to flirt with the women to get the dogs homed. Can you believe it? My own girlfriend, the love of my life, encouraging me to flirt with other women.'

'But only for a good cause,' Gemma laughed and kissed Freddie on the lips.

They definitely looked very together, and happy, which made Pippa warm with happiness for them. And she was also relieved.

'Bloody hell, do you two have to smooch all the time?' Fleur asked as she approached.

'She's only annoyed because her boyfriend, Alfie, couldn't join her today,' Amanda explained.

'I'm not impressed that he couldn't spare the time to help the dogs,' Gus puffed, secretly sounding pleased.

'Dad, he's got a university open day. In Cambridge.' Fleur rolled her eyes. 'You know, that university where only clever people go ...'

'So he says. He's probably buying drugs on a disused council estate.'

Amanda shook her head. 'Hayley's got a big hockey game and she's with her father this weekend, so she sent her apologies. Right, let's go and see where we're needed.'

'Ask Harry to separate Gus and Fleur – they seem to be bickering more than usual,' Pippa whispered to Amanda.

'You have no idea,' Amanda replied, rolling her eyes. 'This poor Alfie could be up for the Nobel Peace Prize and he still wouldn't be good enough.'

People seemed to be milling around everywhere, Pippa thought as she grabbed some leaflets from the office and headed back. They'd definitely managed to get more people there than even Harriet thought. There were quite a few families, some older couples, and a few who seemed a little awkward and were probably alone. But they all certainly seemed serious about re-homing.

Pippa watched as Harriet charmed a group of people who surrounded her, her earlier tiredness brushed aside. Connor was giving tours and introducing people to the dogs where he could. Freddie and Gemma were proving quite the double act, as they seemed to be extolling the virtues of dog ownership – when they didn't have a dog themselves, of course.

Hector was trying to keep quite a few women at bay. He was in danger of being mobbed and as Pippa went to rescue him, Brooke just pipped her to the post.

'Oh, Hector, can you come and help me, please?' she asked as Pippa stopped near them.

'Yes, of course. Excuse me, ladies, duty calls.'

Brooke linked her arm through Hector's proprietorially and led him to where Pippa was stood.

'Thanks, Brooke,' Hector said. 'They were trying to re-home me.'

'Nice job,' Pippa added, patting Hector on the arm.

'But I don't want a dog, I want a pony,' a little girl was saying.

Pippa and Brooke both turned at the same time.

'Darling, we live in a semi, we don't have room for a pony,' the father was saying, running his fingers through his hair.

'And you said you wanted a dog,' the mother added, seemingly a little pale.

'Hey.' Brooke went over to them.

Again, Pippa marvelled at how someone so young was so innately confident.

'Let me tell you about ponies. They're cute and all that, but you know, they don't like cuddles like dogs do, and half the time they just ignore you. How about we go and feed some of our ponies and you can see for yourself. I mean, I'm not a gambler but I'll bet you'll want to go and choose a dog after that.'

Brooke had crouched down so she was at eye level with the girl and the girl immediately seemed besotted by Brooke.

'Can I go and feed them?' she asked her parents.

'Yes, of course, thank you,' they said.

'Come with me; we'll see if we can find a carrot or two. Pippa, can you help?' Brooke asked.

Pippa nodded. How come she knew what to do all the time? Pippa wished she could be a little more like that.

'I can't believe how cute the tiny ponies are,' Brooke gushed when, having pacified the girl by letting her give them carrots, her parents had reclaimed her and she'd happily gone to look at the dogs again.

'They are,' Pippa said. 'And Gerald, the donkey, seems to look after them quite well,' she added.

He was like the father figure in the paddock. Then in the adjoining field were the goats – three adult goats and Kanye, a kid. As with all the animals at Meadowbrook, they had a story. There were Piper and Flo, who were sisters and who'd been rescued together, and Romeo, who lost his Juliet. They all thought it was a *ménage à trois* of goats and it may well have been, but when one of them gave birth to Kanye, it seemed Romeo had found his love and Flo was now the third wheel. It was all a bit crazy but Brooke seemed to take it in her stride.

They also had more pigs now. Geoffrey was the alpha pig and also Gus's favourite. They were mainly micropigs, who turned out not to be micro, and because they'd been so fashionable, unfortunately quite a few of them had to be re-homed when their owners became disappointed. The latest arrival was Kizzy, who'd been left at the sanctuary in the dead of night. She was a tiny piglet and Connor thought that she'd been rescued – or stolen, depending on how you looked at it – by vigilantes and taken to Meadowbrook. She was so sweet and Geoffrey had adopted her as if he were his daughter, and she was thriving.

'I think it's so sad that people hurt or abandon animals,'

Brooke said as if reading her mind. 'I mean I don't even eat them, but even if people do eat animals there's no need to abuse them, is there?'

Pippa couldn't help but like Brooke. She was open and warm. Although Pippa knew there was grief there, and Brooke still couldn't bear to talk about her father, she understood how that felt.

'I know, we have such a positive sanctuary here, but there's a lot of sadness behind it,' Pippa said.

'But I love the alpacas, their faces are so funny,' Brooke giggled.

'They really don't like anyone. Freddie tries his best with them and I think they're the only thing he's ever encountered that can resist his charm.'

'He is very charming, isn't he?'

Pippa looked at Brooke sharply. Did she have a crush on her younger brother? She hoped not; Gemma and he didn't need anyone to rock the boat.

'Yes, he is, and he and Gemma have the perfect relationship,' Pippa replied pointedly.

'Of course.'

Brooke sounded confused and Pippa's suspicion that she had a crush on Freddie wouldn't quite go away. No, that simply couldn't happen. Freddie loved Gemma, but they were going through a bit of a tough time, so he certainly didn't need some younger woman – who was hot, incredibly hot, actually – hitting on him.

'But now Hector, he's single, he's young, good-looking, successful and intelligent,' Pippa said.

God, he did sound good on paper. He was also the only single man she knew at the moment.

'Oh, I bet my mom would love him,' Brooke said. 'You know, he's so English, she'd probably try to hit on him herself.'

Not quite the answer Pippa was hoping for, but she could work on it. Pippa grinned as she petted Brian, the pony. She should really try to date, herself. Even if the Internet dating thing was as horrific as she suspected, it would be good practice. Gemma and Freddie would work out their problems, and maybe even Hector and Brooke would get together. It all sounded like quite a good plan. Although part of her didn't want Brooke and Hector to get together when she was single. Going back to being the only singleton at Meadowbrook didn't really appeal.

'I was thinking of introducing you to the cows but they don't like people. And unlike the alpacas, who just give you dirty looks, they can be quite aggressive.'

'Yes, Freddie told me about the time they chased him – and how they were gay but the one died and you got a woman cow and they had a baby, so not gay, after all! Freddie's so funny,' Brooke gushed.

'Hector's funny, too,' Pippa pushed. 'And he's single,' she added pointedly.

'Right.' Brooke's face contorted with confusion again. 'Shall we go and see if we can sign up some more adoptees?' Brooke asked, seeming to want to get away from the subject.

'Sure,' Pippa replied.

The crowd was thinning slightly, but there were still plenty of people milling around.

'Hey, that man looks a bit lost,' Brooke said, pointing to an older man standing on his own.

'What are we waiting for?' Pippa giggled, feeling some of Brooke's confidence rubbing off on her.

'Hey, I'm Brooke Walker and this is Pippa Singer,' Brooke said.

'William.'

They both looked at him but he wasn't offering anything else.

'Silly question, but are you in the market for a dog?' Pippa asked.

'Well, yes. I'm on my own, you see, so I could do with a bit of company. I saw this day advertised and thought maybe a dog and me, we could do each other a favour.'

'You know, having a dog is like having family,' Brooke said. 'I mean, you can't beat it. They're such great companions.'

'Right, well that's what I want.' William started to look animated.

'Let me take you to Connor and we can see what kind of dog would suit you. I'd say a Labrador myself, but you know, I'm not the expert.'

Pippa watched them walk off, marvelling yet again. She certainly sounded like an expert and Pippa would put money on the fact that William would re-home a dog, she thought, smiling to herself.

'Penny for them.' Hector reappeared.

'Just thinking how Brooke should work here; she's amazingly at home.'

'You know, part of that is that Brooke is quite the woman. She's definitely got balls, that's for sure, and part of it's Meadowbrook – you know, how it draws us all in,' Hector replied, draping an arm around Pippa's shoulders.

Pippa felt an involuntary shiver. He was right, that was what Meadowbrook did.

* * *

110

'I can't believe how well we've done,' Connor said later as they said goodbye to the last of the visitors and it was just the family, Hector and Brooke left, along with the sanctuary staff.

'Right, I have some champagne chilling, to thank you all for your hard work,' Harriet said, and she and Freddie started serving drinks. 'We couldn't have done it without any of you.'

'I reckon we might re-home about ten dogs after today,' Ginny, Connor's right hand woman at the sanctuary, said, beaming.

Ginny always cried when animals arrived, but she also cried tears of happiness when they were re-homed.

'At least,' Mike added.

There was a round of applause, started by the volunteer group who looked after the dogs.

'I had a couple of enquiries about cats, as well,' Clive said, 'even though we weren't doing a cat day. I still showed them, of course.'

'I'm so proud of Harriet for pulling this off.' Connor grabbed her, hugged her and gave her a kiss.

They raised their glasses. 'To Harriet,' everyone said.

'Thank you, although I don't deserve the credit for this. However, I must dash as I need to see my baby and to be honest, if he goes to sleep soon I'll be joining him.' She drained her glass and kissed everyone goodbye.

'Well, I'd invite everyone to my house for drinks but I know the hotel's full,' Gus said.

'Yes, which means I ought to get up there and make sure everything's all right,' Pippa smiled.

She was planning on checking everyone before leaving Freddie in charge and then spending the rest of the evening with Gemma.

'We'll have our normal family meal at The Parker's tomorrow, though?' Amanda said. The family went to the pub for supper every Sunday.

'It's a date,' Freddie said. 'And Hector and Brooke will join us, right?' he added.

'Will you?' Gus asked.

He was saying earlier how he'd hardly seen Hector since he'd been here and also how nice it would be to get to know Brooke, seeing as she was so interested in the gardens. The gardening club all raved about her.

'If that's all right?' Brooke asked.

'Of course, Brooke, great. We'd better go. Amanda, Fleur, stop trying to sneak drinks in, we're going now,' Gus barked.

'Great. I'll see you, Aunt Pip, Uncle Fred. Everyone else.' Fleur winked; she had half a bottle of champagne concealed under her jacket.

Pippa laughed at her niece, who'd undoubtedly get caught and have another tiff with her dad, as they set off back to the house. Gemma linked her arm as Freddie, Hector and Brooke strode ahead.

'Right, once you've sorted the guests out, we have a date with the Internet,' Gemma grinned.

'Oh goodness, we might need a few more glasses of wine before that.'

'What are you guys talking about?' Brooke asked as she hung back and fell into step with them.

'We're going to try to get Pippa a man via the Internet,' Gemma explained.

'Really? I thought you'd have men falling at your feet,' Brooke said sweetly.

'She does, but seeing as she only meets hotel guests, family, staff and the villagers there's not much for her to choose from, so we thought we might widen the search,' Gemma explained.

'Oh God, I'm regretting agreeing to this already and we haven't even started,' Pippa groaned.

'I know this might be rude, but can I join you? I'm missing my girlfriends and this sounds like fun,' Brooke asked shyly.

'Sure, the more the merrier,' Pippa said. 'It'll be like a girls' night.'

'Oh my goodness! that has to be a hairpiece,' Pippa exclaimed.

Gemma and Brooke laughed. The three of them were holed up in the snug, the one room in the hotel that wasn't available to hotel guests. It was the smallest room in the house, with an open fire, two large sofas and a TV but little else. It was what Pippa used to call the 'cosy room'. She often spent time in there in the evenings when her apartment felt too claustrophobic.

The rest of the guests were all in tonight. Some were in the bar, others in the drawing room, drinking, or playing games, chatting. Everyone was happy and Freddie and the staff had it all under control. So Pippa, Gemma and Brooke had come into the snug with a couple of bottles of wine and Pippa's laptop.

'What about this one? He says he's thirty but that photo was definitely taken a couple of decades ago.' Brooke pointed at a man in a black-and-white photo with curly dark hair and wearing an aviator jacket.

'Right, and no men with pictures of themselves topless need apply,' Pippa added as they scrolled through.

'OK, so forget that for now, we need to do your profile,' Gemma said. 'First, choose a picture.'

113

'Do I really have to do this?' Pippa groaned.

'Yes, you do. Brooke, what do you think of this picture?'

They looked at the screen. It was a picture of Pippa at Gus's and Amanda's wedding. She was laughing at something.

'Wow, you look so beautiful,' Brooke said genuinely. 'That was when you and Freddie got together, wasn't it?' she turned to Gemma.

'Yes, it was, and I was so happy.'

'When Freddie told me he said it in such a way there's no doubt the guy is crazy about you.'

'Really?'

Gemma flushed with happiness and Pippa relaxed. It seems she was wrong about Brooke liking Freddie – she'd misjudged her, or what she'd said, it seemed.

'You think that photo's really OK?'

Pippa never liked photos of herself. She'd been told she was pretty for most of her life, doll-like, blonde, delicate, but she didn't always see it. She was just her. It wasn't false modesty; she actually had a hard time accepting compliments. Maybe that was what drew her to Mark. He'd always preferred to criticise her rather than compliment. She bit back those thoughts. She probably needed counselling rather than Internet dating.

'My God, Pippa, I don't think you realise how good you look,' Brooke pushed.

Pippa was touched.

'Right, so I'm setting that as your profile. Now to your description.' Gemma had commandeered the laptop and wasn't letting Pippa anywhere near it.

'Divorced thirty-two-year-old. Runs a hotel with her family. Otherwise quite dull,' Pippa said.

'Do you have self-esteem issues?' Brooke asked, pointing her wine glass at her.

'Yes, she does, which is crazy as she's amazing,' Gemma replied.

'But I understand, I do, too. I went to therapy for it. I mean, everyone in the States does, right? So I found I had family issues and you know...'

'What family issues?' Gemma asked.

'I didn't always have the greatest relationship with my parents and now I barely have one with my mom. She's not happy about me being here ... I'm an only child, so I don't have brothers or sisters. I guess I always felt a bit like I didn't know who I was or where I belonged.'

'Oh God, I understand that,' Gemma said excitedly. 'I know it's not the same, but my dad left me when I was a baby. My mum followed a few years later and my nan brought me up. We were very close, my nan and I, but I always felt rejected by my parents and then my nan died just over a year ago.'

'That's so sad, but I understand the rejection thing more than you could ever know,' Brooke said.

'Why?' Pippa asked, feeling as if they were finally getting beneath Brooke's surface.

'Oh, it's probably textbook, although my parents didn't split up and they gave me a real nice life, but they didn't ever really seem to know what to do with me. It's hard to explain.' Brooke looked thoughtful.

'You should try,' Pippa pushed.

'Oh, Gemma, I forgot to say,' Brooke said, changing the subject. 'Do you fancy going for a run tomorrow morning? Show me some of the good routes around the place. I've been dying to run around the estate but I'm terrified of getting lost.'

'I'd love to, definitely. But now we need to go back to finding Pippa a date.'

'Great, I thought you'd forgotten,' Pippa said as she refilled all the wine glasses and prepared to finish her profile.

'Oh no, you're not getting away with it that easily. Pippa, you're the most amazing woman I know and you need to get yourself out there,' Gemma said.

'It's hard, I guess, being divorced so young,' Brooke said.

'Surely you're not?' Pippa was horrified at the idea.

'No, but I had this high school sweetheart and our families thought we should get married. When we broke up, it wasn't pretty. Even though he cheated on me, and we needed to go our separate ways, I mean the relationship had run its course. I think I was only with him to try to get my parents' approval.'

Brooke sounded sad and Pippa finally felt that she was getting to know her – very slowly and not that easily but a little bit, at least.

'And since then?' Pippa asked.

'Well, there have been a few men. I went out with this older guy and you know, he was so together and stuff, but after a few months I found out he was actually married,' Brooke said.

'No way! That happened to me, didn't it, Gemma?' Pippa said.

'Really?' Brooke asked.

'Yes, his name was Edward. Oh God, just thinking about him still makes me cringe.'

'Me, too! I felt so guilty, although I had no idea, and then angry.'

'Exactly,' Pippa grinned.

'Ughh, men! Sometimes I do wonder why we still even give them a chance but we do,' Brooke laughed.

'So are you looking for love?' Gemma asked.

'I'm looking for me first,' Brooke replied quietly.

Chapter Eleven

'Where are you off to?' Hector asked as Pippa stood by the back door, about to go out.

'I'm going to the sanctuary. I need to check on the ponies and the office. Harriet's finally taking a day off.'

'She is?' Hector sounded surprised. He knew Harriet well.

'Well, a day might be a stretch. She's got to take Toby to the health visitor for his weight check and then she's going to a class, baby massage or something, which is apparently now compulsory for parents. Now he's over four months old she said she needs to get him socialising with other babies. Probably part of her plan to ensure he's a genius without any social awkwardness.'

'The kid doesn't stand a chance! He'll be running the country one day.'

'Oh no!' Pippa laughed. 'They've got far loftier ambitions for him than just PM. Anyway, how's the book?'

Hector had been holed up the last couple of days. He needed to send part of his book to his publisher and to give him credit, he did work incredibly hard when he needed to. He'd barely left his room, all the staff vying to take him room service.

'I'm relieved that half of it's now with the publisher. I normally prefer to finish the whole thing before they see any

118

of it, but they need to start planning the marketing and now I feel that I'm on the home straight, in any case.'

'Does that mean you'll be leaving us early?'

Pippa had to admit she was getting used to having him around again; although it did sometimes make her forget that Meadowbrook was a hotel, especially when he and Brooke were the only guests.

'No, I have more writing, then editing. I'd like to stay for the whole three months. Do you fancy some company?'

'Sure.' They both wrapped themselves up in coats and scarfs then made their way out and down to the sanctuary.

'I'm so glad the dog adoption went well,' Hector said as they strode together. 'And dinner the other night in The Parker's Arms was fun.'

'It was, and you were a great help at adoption day, charming the women.'

'I think you rather charmed the men, actually, Pippa. They'd have re-homed the scary cows if you'd asked them to.'

'Ha, you flatter me too much.' Pippa felt her cheeks turning slightly pink. 'How are you getting on with Brooke?' she asked instead.

'She's great. So American, but I like her though; it feels as if she belongs here. But the other night at dinner she seemed to be a bit ... I don't know, almost sad at times.'

'Funny, isn't it? How people come to Meadowbrook and if they stay longer than a week, they automatically seem to become part of it. But Brooke's a strange one.'

Pippa stopped. It was true, Meadowbrook had a way of making everyone seem like they belonged there.

'How do you mean?' Hector steered her out of the way of a muddy patch and Pippa almost stumbled into him.

'She opens up – you know, the other night she was talking about her family and how she didn't have the best relationship with her parents – but at dinner last night she sort of clammed up. And I asked her yesterday how her run with Gemma was, and she just said fine and went up to her room. When I asked if I could get her anything she cut me off again. No explanation. It's like one minute she's friendly and the next she wants to be left alone.'

'I haven't seen that side of her. I know she was quiet at dinner, but all you Singers together can be a bit intimidating. There again, she's always open with me. I wonder what Harriet makes of her?' Hector said.

'Why, because Harriet's always so wise?' Pippa asked.

'No, because she's always so suspicious,' Hector laughed.

'I think it might be because she's grieving for her father. She doesn't like to talk about him, that's for sure.'

'But then Brooke, if her father's just died and if she had a complicated relationship with him, that makes sense, doesn't it?' Hector almost read her thoughts.

'Yes. We'll have to be extra sensitive with her. Maybe if you asked her out on a date she'd open up.'

'Pippa Singer, are you trying to pimp me out? Honestly, I thought you knew by now I only have eyes for one woman and that's you.' Hector stood and stared intensely at her.

Pippa felt her cheeks reddening again.

'For God's sake! Stop all that nonsense or I'll make you muck out the pigs.'

'Oh, and talk of the devil,' Hector said, ignoring her last comment as Brooke, holding onto two dog leads, waved at them from where she was walking with other dog-walking volunteers.

'Harry said she was helping with the dog walking. Goodness, she really is getting stuck in, isn't she?' Pippa said.

'Hey, guys.' Brooke bounded over. 'I've just been taken for a walk by these two.'

Pippa leant down and petted the dogs. 'It's so good of you to help out,' she said.

'No, I love it. I miss my doggies back home; it's the thing that makes me most homesick, so getting to walk them makes up for it a bit. I'm also going to groom them when we get back. Connor said I could help out with that if I wanted.'

'I'm sure Connor's over the moon to have your help,' Hector said.

'Sure. Whoops, I'd better go; they're not happy to stand still.'

After untangling herself from the dog leads that had wrapped around her legs, she headed off. Pippa couldn't help but think how at home she seemed and although that was nice, it sort of surprised her a bit. But she wasn't sure why.

Pippa enjoyed being at the sanctuary and Hector kept her entertained. He was quite nervous around some of the animals, for someone normally brimming with confidence, and although he didn't mind the tiny ponies or Gerald, he steered clear of the pigs. When they went to the office to check if anyone needed help, Ginny offered to make them coffee. In reality, she'd really offered Hector but had to make a cup for Pippa, too.

'Mike's with one of the men from the open day who's come to collect Lucky,' Ginny gushed, fluttering her eyelashes at Hector.

'Finally, he gets to live up to his name,' Hector replied with a wink.

Pippa rolled her eyes but no one was paying her any attention so no one noticed.

'Ah, so Brooke did work her magic, then?' Pippa said.

Lucky was a collie who'd been subjected to an ordeal with fireworks and hated noise. Another sad story.

'Yes, but William Masters who's adopting him lives alone. In his sixties, he's retired and just wants a companion, so they'll be perfect together, everyone thinks so.'

'No loud music or house parties, then?' Hector joked.

'Oh, Hector, you're so funny. No, we all think Lucky and William are the perfect match. It's been amazing since the adoption day. We've had so many applications to re-home. Which reminds me, Pippa, I've marked up the ones I think are right for home visits, but will you just double-check them, they're on the desk?'

'Of course.'

This was normally Harriet's role but Pippa knew what she was doing. When Harriet first found out she was pregnant they'd all had a quick crash course in the admin side of the sanctuary, in case Harriet was indisposed. Of course she never was, but they all knew how it ran in any case. Pippa went to the desk, where there was quite a stack of papers waiting for her.

'And the cats need feeding now, Hector. I don't suppose you fancy helping me?' Ginny asked hopefully.

'Sure thing, lead the way.'

Hector looked back and winked at Pippa and then she was finally left in peace. She'd just started going through the forms, when the computer on the desk pinged at her. She pressed the mouse and looked at the screen, then she wished she hadn't. Mike was the main user of the computer. He was one of the few paid, full-time members of staff, along with Ginny and Clive. There were a few paid part-timers, too, and as many volunteers as Harriet could press-gang into helping out. While Ginny had been given the lofty title of sanctuary manager, Mike was office manager. He worked closely with Harriet, while Ginny and Clive reported to Connor. Clive was more hands-on with the animals than the others.

'Oh God,' Pippa said out loud as she nearly spat out her coffee.

Staring at Pippa on the screen in front of her, Mike's screen, was a small picture of herself with the words 'we've found you a new match'. It was the Internet dating site she'd just signed up to and her profile was looking back at her.

Her body tingled with both horror and embarrassment. It felt so public. Who else in Parker's Hollow would know she was Internet dating? That she wanted to meet a man with a good sense of humour, and his own teeth? And as lovely as Mike was, he was nearly fifty. Twice divorced, the only thing they had in common was this place. She groaned. She'd put animal lover in her profile and obviously he would have done, too. This was beyond embarrassing. She willed the screen to go into sleep mode in front of her, but it seemed to taunt her for an awful long time before it finally did.

This was one of Gemma's worst ideas. OK, so she'd set the age limit to 35–50, but then she liked an older man. They'd tried to get her to lower it, even Brooke said that she'd be best off with someone more her own age, but Pippa had argued that she liked maturity. But Mike? Be careful what you asked for! Oh, poor Mike was lovely, there was nothing wrong with him, but he wasn't Pippa's type in the slightest.

But then she realised, as she remembered the others who'd

emailed her via the dating site, that she wasn't sure what her type was. At the moment, she was discovering only who she didn't want to date. All the men looked fine, or at least some of them did, but none of them held her attention. Yes, she knew you couldn't tell what a person was like from the computer screen, but it just didn't feel right. Gemma had said it was like Internet shopping but for a man. However, the thing was that Pippa hated Internet shopping. She wouldn't even buy so much as a pair of shoes from it. No, she was an old-fashioned woman who actually liked to buy things in a real-life shop. The problem was that since the hotel opened she'd rarely been anywhere to 'shop' or meet men.

When Mike returned to the office, whistling and happy about Lucky going to such a nice chap, she couldn't quite meet his eye. And she hoped when he did see his computer that he'd be far too embarrassed ever to mention it to her.

'I've been through all these, Mike, and I'm quite sure they're all suitable to go to the next stage of home visits,' she said, trying to keep her voice even and professional.

'Top job, Pippa. I'll go through them with Harriet when she's back. In the meantime, I was going to make a cuppa, can I tempt you?'

'Um, no, thank you. I need to go and find Hector and then I ought to get back to the hotel.'

She could feel her face almost catching fire. The first thing she'd do when she got back to the hotel was to delete her Internet dating profile. It clearly wasn't for her. She could only hope that all the single members of Parker's Hollow hadn't seen it before she got the chance to do so.

* * *

Pippa found Harriet outside near her house. Toby was asleep in the pram and she looked more relaxed than she had done lately.

'Are you all right?' Pippa asked, hugging her sister.

'Yes. You know, I really am. It turns out being with other mums isn't as horrific as I thought.' Harriet almost sounded gleeful.

'Harry, you shouldn't say things like that.'

'I know, but I thought they'd all be dull and talk about how much they love breastfeeding and sleep deprivation and poo, but it turns out we all feel the same. We're all sore from breastfeeding, ridiculously tired and not so keen on poo. I'm actually normal. One of the women even cried!' she announced cheerfully.

'Harriet!' Pippa swiped her sister but they both grinned. 'I did tell you that everyone struggled with being a new mum.'

'I know you did.' Harriet waved her hand dismissively. 'Everyone did but I didn't believe you. I thought everyone was really good at it apart from me, but it turns out no one seems to be. In fact, from today I learnt that quite a few people are struggling more than I am!'

She sounded far happier than she should when she said this but Pippa understood. Harriet, who was always a high-achiever in everything she did, always had been, didn't believe in struggling. Until now.

'Well I feel bad for them, those struggling, I mean,' Pippa pointed out.

'Of course – I do, too – but it means that I'm not as bad at this as I thought and maybe I'm not going to ruin Toby's life by being a terrible mum.'

'God, Harry, where do you get your ideas from? You're doing brilliantly.'

'I know that now. I can't wait to do more mum stuff! It really does make me realise that I'm not crap, and I like that.'

'But did you make friends? I mean, did you like the other women?' Pippa pushed.

'At the moment I love them all, but only time will tell. We didn't get the chance to talk about anything other than babies, not that I want to. There was one woman who worked in finance before she had her baby, so we'll probably get on, but now it's just nice to feel normal.'

'Talking of new friends, I wanted to invite Brooke to a girls' night, which means I need you and Gemma and hopefully Amanda to join us,' Pippa said.

She'd been worrying about Brooke feeling lonely and they had such fun that night in the snug that Pippa wanted to repeat it.

'Sure, but why? She's a hotel guest.' Harriet sounded perplexed.

'She's a young woman here on her own and she's here because she might want to settle down in the UK. I think she needs friends and at the very least we should show friendliness towards her.'

'Pippa, you don't need to make everyone your friend,' Harriet pointed out.

'No, and that's not what I'm doing, but she's vulnerable and she's also fun. You seem to like her and I know Gemma does. And the thing is that she can be open and warm, but then she clams up. She's a bit of a conundrum. I also want to find out some more about her plans for staying here and you know how good you are at asking questions.'

'Right, I hadn't really given that much thought,' Harriet said as if a light switch had been flicked on. 'I've been so wrapped up with Toby that I didn't think about it, but now … She's young, twenty-five and she's staying at a five-star hotel for two months, all paid for, so she can't be short of money. She isn't working but she says she's setting up a business, yet there's no sign of her doing much but dog walking, jogging with Gemma and hanging out at the hotel.'

'No. Apart from going out running, and me taking her to Wells, she's not been far at all.'

The way Harriet was talking was making Pippa more curious.

'That's weird,' Harriet concurred.

'I agree. And Hector said you'd be suspicious.'

'Hey, I'm not, I couldn't care less why she's here as long as her bill is paid, but I'm nosy. You're right, now I'm feeling a bit like myself again, I'm definitely curious.'

'So yes to a girls' night?'

'Sure, Connor'll love the chance to bond with Toby. He says it's like I don't trust him with his own son.'

'And do you?' Pippa asked dubiously.

'Of course, but as I said to you, I have this weird feeling of failure and when I'm not with him, I feel so guilty.'

'Thank goodness you met those other mums. I think it'll do you good to be with people going through the same thing.'

'Exactly. I thought I'd hate all these mum groups, that they'd be really boring, but I'm going to join more. Which means I need to take a bit more time off. But we should manage OK. It's not the busiest time for the hotel, after all, and I can do the accounts at home. But anyway, Brooke. Let's find out what her business actually is. You don't think she's some kind of secret hotel inspector?' Harriet's brows furrowed.

'No, she's too perky and no hotel reviewer would stay for two months. Anyway, if anyone can get it out of her, it's you.'

As Pippa kissed Harriet on the cheek and went to leave, she didn't notice that behind the hedge, Brooke, wearing her running clothes, stood, frozen, and had heard every word.

Chapter Twelve

'I can't remember the last time I had a girlie night,' Amanda said as she arrived at Meadowbrook's back door armed with wine and a broad smile.

She was wearing simple jeans and a sweater but her hair was loose around her shoulders and shining.

'Probably your hen night,' Pippa replied.

Amanda didn't go out much. She wasn't big on socialising, which suited Gus perfectly.

'You know, you didn't need to bring wine, we have a cellar full,' she added.

'I don't want Harry to accuse us of drinking all your hotel profits,' Amanda laughed as she handed the wine to Pippa.

'Good point.'

Pippa had organised tonight for them purposely on a Monday because the hotel was empty apart from Brooke and Hector that night, so it meant they could decamp to the bar. They had guests arriving the following day, so Pippa hoped it would mean they wouldn't drink too much. It was a theory, at least.

Amanda followed Pippa into the kitchen. Pippa grabbed some plates of snacks that Vicky had kindly prepared for them – it was a definite perk of the job – and then led the way to the bar.

'Where are the others?' Amanda asked. 'It's not like me to be early.'

'Gemma's on her way, she had to finish off some coursework, Harriet's coming when she's put Toby down, so she'll be a bit late, and Brooke should be here any minute. Come on, we might as well get started.'

Pippa poured drinks for them both and they went to sit at one of the bigger tables. Because they were there first, Pippa and Amanda sunk into the oversize purple sofa.

'Cheers. It's funny being here with no guests,' Amanda said, proffering her glass.

'I know. We were so busy over the spring and summer that I'd forgotten what it was like to be quiet. We're lucky we've got the corporate bookings, not to mention Hector and Brooke, but you're right, when we're here on our own I think of when we used to live here. And how Daddy lived here just with Gwen when I moved out.'

'It's a big house for just two people,' Amanda said.

'Hi.' Brooke appeared wearing an oversized jumper over skinny jeans. Her hair was loose and she wore her signature lip gloss.

'Nice to see you, Brooke,' Amanda said, standing up to welcome her with a hug.

'You, too!' Brooke replied effervescently.

'Sit down and I'll get you a drink. Is prosecco OK?' Pippa asked.

'Sure, that'll be great. Has Freddie got the night off?' Brooke asked.

'Yes, I had to get him to take Hector out so he didn't gate-crash our night.'

'Is he still mooning around after you?' Amanda asked.

Pippa blushed.

'Oh, I thought he liked you; he talks about you a real lot,' Brooke said. 'That's why I was so confused when you said that we should get together,' Brooke added as she sipped her drink.

'Hector's lovely but a bit young for me. I just thought you two might be well suited,' Pippa replied evenly. 'And I don't think he really likes me that much, he just thinks he does.'

'What? He's been crazy about you for years!' Amanda was incredulous, scuppering Pippa's plan for Brooke and Hector once and for all.

'Hi, sorry I'm late.' Gemma swept in and hugged everyone. She poured herself a glass of wine before settling into an armchair opposite Brooke. 'But I'm so glad to be here and away from my computer screen.'

'That makes me even later. But then try getting baby puke out of your hair,' Harriet said, breezing in, commanding the room as her presence often did.

Pippa was never exactly awkward but her sister oozed confidence, even when she didn't feel it. It was how she'd run her trading floor for years and made grown men cry.

Harriet blew kisses around the table, poured herself a glass of wine and sat down. She was looking good, Pippa thought. You wouldn't know she was sleep deprived – again, it was down to years of training on the trading floor, working all hours. It seemed it was a pretty good prelude to motherhood, in fact.

'Brooke, let's raise a toast, to you, to your stay at Meadowbrook and to getting to know you properly.' Harriet grinned as everyone clinked glasses.

'Thank you so much. You guys are so kind to welcome me this way,' Brooke replied.

Her voice was soft, Pippa thought; she couldn't imagine Brooke ever getting angry. She wondered if she ever did.

'Right, well, why don't we do an ice-breaker? Each of us'll go through a potted history and then we'll already know each other better,' Harriet suggested. She didn't have time to waste with small talk.

'A what?' Brooke looked confused.

Gemma exchanged glances with Amanda and Pippa, who were trying not to giggle. Harriet often approached everything as if it were a corporate exercise. Before she and Connor got together, on the odd date she went on she basically interviewed the guy, grilling him, practically demanding his CV before she'd agree to move from drinks to dinner. She said it was like that in New York – no one had time to waste so it was just efficient.

'I'll go first.' Harriet wasn't going to be dissuaded from her path. 'I'm the oldest Singer, recently forty. As you know, I live with Connor, whom I love, and Toby, my baby. I'm very lucky but life changed for me when my father died. I was a corporate hard-arse in New York in my previous life...'

'Which you'd never guess, right?' Pippa joked, thinking that perhaps the tone needed lightening.

As the others laughed, Harriet shot her a 'shut up' glance.

'So, anyway, I moved back here as per the terms of our father's will. We all lived here together for a year and we had to make money for the animal sanctuary. I found I loved it here. Not at first, mind, but then at some point it felt like coming home and I knew I was where I wanted to be.'

Everyone seemed surprised by the softness in Harriet's voice, but then she flicked her switch back as she so often did.

'Pip, you go.'

'Brooke already knows about me, don't you, Brooke?' Pippa said, unwilling to bore her by going through everything again.

'Sure,' Brooke agreed uncertainly. That night in the snug she'd told Brooke about Mark, about opening the hotel, about her friendship with Gemma. 'But, Harriet, you know you said about your dad's will, you know, about having to live here for a year? Well, can you tell me a bit more about that?' She leant towards Harriet.

'Right, well, the family was fractured at the time of Dad's death, which came as a shock. In his will he said we all had to live here, together, for a year, and it changed all of our lives. I fell out of love with investment banking and in love with Connor. Gus found his passion for painting, gardening and Amanda, Freddie got his act together and Pippa got divorced,' Harriet explained.

Pippa shook her head. It was a potted history of the year but fundamentally covered the main points, no emotion, no embellishment. Typical Harriet.

'So, Brooke, why don't you go next?' Harriet suggested, leaving her no option.

'Um, sure. Well, I grew up in Orange County and then I moved to LA for a while to go to college, but I didn't love it so I dropped out.'

'What did you study?' Harriet asked.

'Mainly LA nightlife,' Brooke replied honestly. 'I was supposed to do an arts degree but I didn't like it. I dropped out and found a fitness programme instead.'

'That makes sense,' Gemma said.

'I kinda didn't know what I wanted to do, but my dad said I had to go to college. He was so mad when I dropped out,

133

and Mom, too. It was like world war three in our house, so I moved in with a friend and tended a bar while I got into fitness. My parents really didn't approve of that, thought I should be doing something "proper".'

'Tell us about the fitness,' Harriet pushed. 'I'm guessing that your idea to move here, to set up a business, is based around that?'

'Well yes, I guess. I wasn't doing so well back home. Then my dad died and my mum and I had a big falling out. I needed to get away. I couldn't breathe.' Brooke looked sad.

Pippa reached across and gave her hand a squeeze.

'But why here?' Amanda asked. 'I mean, I love it here, but it's nothing like LA, or Orange Country, it's a tiny village.'

It was a good point.

'I don't know exactly,' Brooke started uncertainly. 'I found out that we had ancestors; my father's family were from Somerset. I started looking at the area and I knew about the cities ... I was going to go to Bath, actually, but then I came across Meadowbrook and thought, why not? It was impulsive, my mom's still mad at me for coming here, but now I'm here, I'm finding that I have very little reason to leave.' She had a wistful look on her face, as if she were elsewhere.

'And what about your mother?' Harriet pushed.

'That's complicated.' Brooke folded her arms across her chest as if to say that the conversation was definitely over.

'While it's great that you like it here, surely you can't stay at the hotel forever?' Gemma asked.

'I guess not...' Now she looked confused, as if this hadn't occurred to her.

As Pippa refilled glasses and pushed bowls of nibbles towards them, she thought that Brooke might retreat again.

'I can help you,' Harriet announced.

'What with?' Brooke sounded terrified.

If Harriet offered to help you that was often the reaction, Pippa thought. Brooke didn't stand a chance.

'Your business. I can help you with that, if you like. What is it you want to do?'

'I want to look at setting up a fitness business, using the latest trends from LA. There's a lot going on in the industry. I trained in a new class, a cross between yoga and HIT; it's really popular. I've made a list of local gyms that I need to visit and I've been researching popular classes in the UK. I think my way of training is different.'

'Sounds horrific,' Amanda shuddered. 'Sorry, it's just I only exercise by gardening,' she apologised.

'I need to do more research first,' Brooke stated, sounding more enthusiastic than she did at the beginning of the conversation.

'I think going to see some local gyms is a great idea,' Harriet said. 'And as I said, I'm happy to help with business plans and suchlike.'

'Thank you, Harriet. But enough about me. Amanda, so, how did you and Gus get together?'

'We met here, at Meadowbrook. I used to work for Andrew, their father, and I'd seen Gus a couple of times but not much. When Andrew died, Gus took over his role of overseeing the work in the gardens. He was so passionate, just like his dad in some ways.'

'What ways?' Brooke inched forwards.

'The way he loved nature and saw the beauty in the gardens. Andrew liked everything in order, but he also had a great respect for nature. Gus is like that, only a bit more creative.

135

A little bolder in his ideas, I guess. We both felt that what we did with Meadowbrook gardens, and of course that included the gardening club, had to respect Andrew's wishes.'

'Wow,' Brooke said, her eyes intense as she stared at Amanda as if drinking in every word.

Pippa saw how gripped Brooke seemed by everyone's story, how interested she was, and Pippa felt herself warming to her more. Pippa was a people-pleaser, which is why she was so good at her job running the hotel. If the guests weren't happy then Pippa wasn't happy and she felt as if now Brooke was practically her only guest, maybe she was focusing on her a bit much. Wanting her to be happy when she might not be after losing her father, wanting her to be settled before she was ready, perhaps. As Pippa relaxed into the evening, she told herself to chill out a bit. Brooke was fine, she was doing well, they were all getting on well so she needed to stop worrying.

At the end of the evening, when Brooke had said goodnight and gone to bed, Pippa called Harriet.

'I knew you'd call me,' Harriet laughed.

'I just wanted a debrief. It was fun in the end, wasn't it?'

Once Harriet's interrogation was over, they'd drunk more, ignored the food and laughed a lot. Brooke was actually very funny.

'Yes, and I like Brooke. I think she's just young and perhaps a bit lost. That's my professional opinion, so if we support and help her, I'm pretty sure she'll be OK. I'm not convinced she's not just having some kind of spoilt-kid tantrum with her mum, you know, and she'll go back to LA anyway.'

'Really? I still think there might be more to her than meets the eye,' Pippa reiterated.

She was thinking maybe Brooke came here for a man, maybe there was someone or something that drew her here and she wasn't ready to share it. That made more sense.

'No, Pip. You're way off the mark, and I'm normally the suspicious one. Her dad died, she finds she had ancestors from this area and she's lost, but she's probably taking her time because she's scared. You know, Pippa, she's the type that most women want to hate – you know, beautiful, confident, funny and intelligent – but you can't hate her because she's so nice.'

'She is nice, Harry, and I know what you mean, but I think there's something else going on. I just can't put my finger on it.'

'Bloody hell, Pip, you're beginning to sound like me. And I think you're wrong.'

'Maybe. I probably am overthinking it, but I guess time will tell, won't it?'

Pippa was still unsure if Brooke had told them the full story, but then as Harriet and everyone kept pointing out, she'd paid up front, so whatever she was doing here was her business and hers alone. Pippa really should be focusing on herself and not Brooke. Perhaps it was time for her to do just that ...

Chapter Thirteen

'Hector! What on earth are you doing?' Pippa gasped.
She'd just entered the drawing room and Hector seemed to have his head in the fireplace.

He turned around, still on his knees, soot in his hair and a smudge on his face, which Pippa resisted the urge to rub off. Even so, he looked impossibly handsome.

'I was trying to figure out how to light the fire.' He stood up slowly.

'Here, I'll light it. Honestly, Hector, you don't light it by putting your face right in.' She shook her head as she gathered logs and firelighters and started arranging them in the hearth.

'I do know that. Not that I'm good at lighting fires. Or I might be but I haven't really lit any so far. Then I started looking up the chimney and thinking about how they used to send kids up to clean them; I sort of got sidetracked.'

'Horrific thought.'

'Yes, it is rather, and then I wondered if it would make a good hiding place.'

'A hiding place for what?'

'A letter – you know, a love letter. But then how would it

ever be discovered? Or would it be discovered years and years later, long after the writer of the letter had died?'

Pippa wasn't sure she was exactly following this conversation but then many of her chats with Hector could be baffling.

'You mean perhaps it's windy outside, dislodging it, and then someone comes into the room and finds it lying on the fireplace? A miracle it's untouched, but perhaps it's wrapped in something charred and when they open it, the letter is perfectly intact?'

Pippa watched as the flames began to take hold as she sat on her knees, mesmerised by the way they danced. They'd grown up with open fires at Meadowbrook and she'd missed them when she lived with Mark, who insisted on those fake gas ones – only the most expensive. There was something about a real fire – the smell, the way the warmth crept around you like a blanket. It was so romantic, as well.

'Pippa, you're my saviour!' Hector interrupted her thoughts.

'I am?'

'Yes, you really are. I've been trying to find a hiding place for this letter in my next book. It's set in an old house, but it's Victorian not Georgian. I thought if it was in the fireplace, then surely it would never survive the twenty years I need it to, but with your way of explaining it, it might actually work, after all.' He was still sooty but at least animated, now.

'I'm so glad I was able to help you. Although, as you know, I have no idea really what you're talking about.' She patted his arm kindly.

'This book is becoming a bit of a struggle, if I'm honest. The first bit flowed, but now it feels a bit like wading through mud. I've been chained to my desk for too long, I guess.'

'You should take a day off,' Pippa suggested, putting the fireguard up.

'What a great idea. I need a change of scene. Where shall we go?'

'We?' Pippa asked.

'Yes, I can't possibly go on my own, not in the state I'm in, what with my suffering.'

'What suffering?'

'Writer's block. Call Freddie and tell him it's an emergency and you must take me out of this place immediately for both my own good and that of my book – my future depends on it.'

'Bloody hell, Hector, stop being so dramatic.'

As she thought about it, she decided a day off might actually do her some good. Getting out of the hotel would probably be just the tonic she needed.

They'd welcomed a family group of eight to Meadowbrook the previous day. Half of them were baking, the other half were painting with Gus. The hotel was fully staffed and, of course, there was always Freddie, who was probably going to be in the bar anyway, so he could keep an eye on it. She glanced over at Hector, who was watching her intently.

'You're on, but where are we going?'

'Let's go to Glastonbury and find some spiritual stuff.'

'Really?' She didn't have him down as the spiritual type.

'We can walk up Glastonbury Tor; it's quite inspiring. I don't really do all that hippie stuff, but it's a really beautiful walk. You never know, it might even inspire me and cure my writer's block.'

'Right, well let me change into something suitable for walking in and I'll drive us.'

'This is going to be the best day ever,' Hector said.

Pippa really didn't think it would be, but she found herself smiling at the idea.

She called Freddie and after he moaned a bit, he said he'd be right there. She had a look for Brooke, thinking maybe they could invite her along, but she was nowhere to be seen. She'd been a little vague at breakfast when Pippa asked her what her plans were. She'd seen her go off somewhere in her gym clothes, but Pippa wasn't her keeper, so she really had to stop her obsession with the poor girl and let her carry on doing her thing. Goodness, it wasn't as if she was hurting anyone and actually, she was proving a valuable addition to Meadowbrook in just the way Pippa hoped she would before she arrived.

'It's exhausting,' Hector declared as they neared the top. 'But so worth the view.'

Pippa felt a smile creeping across her face. The day was cold, crisp and bright, and Pippa felt as if she could see the world.

'I feel as if I'm tiny, you know,' Pippa said. 'Standing up here, being able to see for miles, and I'm a tiny dot. But I didn't have you down for a hiker,' she smiled.

'Shall we sit?'

He pulled his jacket off and lay it down. Pippa sat next to him, took two bottles of water out of her bag and handed one to him.

'You know, I don't exactly hike but in London, I often walk up Primrose Hill. There's something about being on top of a hill, looking down at the world. It makes me feel ... I don't know, powerful or something. Maybe it's the space around me – it's just so liberating.'

Pippa glanced over her right shoulder at Hector. He was

staring straight ahead, his cheeks pink, his hair slightly wavy in the breeze, but he had such intensity in his eyes – passion. She could see, at that moment, how he was such a good writer. She could physically see it in him.

'It's wonderful,' she replied, unable to find the words. 'I need to do this more often. I love Meadowbrook and the hotel, but I don't do anything for me anymore. Does that make sense?'

'Yes, it does. You need to live a bit. I know you love your work and your family, but you sometimes need to have that escape. All your siblings do. I mean, they don't live at Meadowbrook but you actually live there, you breathe it, and that's great, but you need to remember to take care of yourself as well.'

He sounded so sincere and concerned that for a moment Pippa felt emotional.

'You're right.' She pulled herself together. 'It's just that when opening the hotel I wanted to prove I could do it, that I was capable, and I think I've just forgotten to stop. Perhaps now I'll look at taking a whole day off every week and actually leaving the premises.'

'You've done a fantastic job with the hotel, Pippa, but you also need your own life.'

'That's what Harry says, and the others. Do you think I've got a bit of an obsession with it?'

'It's natural, it's your baby, the hotel, but it's up and running and doing well, so you can take a bit of a step back now.'

'I know, you're right. So, I'll try to remember to take some time off from now on. Deal?'

'That sounds like a great idea and I'll always be available to keep you company, you know.' He nudged her with his shoulder and they sat side by side, admiring the view in silence for a while.

Pippa felt alive for the first time in a long while and she knew Hector was right. He and her family had been nagging her for a while to take more time for herself. The hotel was doing well and they were building the business, but she had support, she had good staff, so there was no harm in taking time out. The others certainly did. She needed something to get her out of the rut that she was finally able to admit she'd been in. It was a lovely rut, a comfortable rut, but a rut nonetheless, and as she sat with Hector next to her she realised it was time to get out of said rut.

Brooke was sitting in the bar with a man who Pippa didn't recognise when she got back. Hector, who was newly inspired, rushed straight up to his room to get some writing done before dinner. Pippa had checked with Vicky in the kitchen, but everything was going well. You see, she chastised herself, leaving the hotel didn't make it fall apart. It was almost as if they hadn't even noticed she'd gone.

'Fred,' she said, approaching her brother, who was behind the bar moving things around and restocking the spirits

Pippa thought it must be his favourite thing to do, his baby, organising the already immaculate bar on a weekly basis. Freddie used to run a party company in London with friends of his, and he partied hard. After their father's death, they realised that he'd lost pretty much everything and he was on a slippery slope. But he'd turned his life around and although he drank a lot, by most people's standards – a hell of a lot – he'd calmed down. He'd done so before he got together with Gemma, but she'd been an additional good influence on him.

She saw that he was committed to Meadowbrook now and although he ran the bar and made up drinks, he also was in charge of their events, their social media and the marketing. Pippa knew he worked almost as hard as she did for the hotel, not that she'd tell him that. Freddie still had a big ego, something he hadn't managed to ditch and probably never would.

'Who's the man with Brooke?' Pippa whispered, glancing over at him but trying not to be obvious.

He looked tall, even though he was sitting down, and was wearing all black. Brooke was across from him, making notes.

'He's a local fitness guru, apparently,' Freddie hissed into her ear. 'They're having a "business meeting". I've served them soft drinks and snacks and they've been here for quite a while.'

The man, whose short dark hair seemed to glisten, had his head fairly close to Brooke. They seemed engrossed in whatever they were talking about and Pippa was intrigued.

'Well, hello,' Pippa said, interrupting them.

'Pippa.' Brooke looked up at her, her eyes betraying nothing.

'I just wanted to see if you needed anything?' she asked.

'No, thanks, we're fine,' Brooke replied, a slight blush to her cheeks.

Pippa raised an eyebrow as the man stood up. She was right – he was tall, and slim. His black uniform comprised tight jeans, a hoodie and black trainers. He was conventionally good-looking, but his jeans were exceptionally tight, she thought as she tried to keep her eyes on his face.

'Hi, I'm Chris PT,' he said, holding out a hand.

'Pippa Singer. So, how are you spelling PT?' It seemed an odd kind of surname.

Brooke seemed to have lost a little of her customary confidence, as she plastered a smile on her face.

'Oh no, it stands for personal trainer, ha,' he laughed. 'My actual name's Chris Reeves but everyone calls me Chris PT. I'm here to speak with Brooke about her business, or what could be our business, should I say?'

'Oh, that sounds exciting.'

'Yes.' Brooke found her voice. 'I hope you don't mind us working in here, though?'

'Of course not, Brooke, you're a guest here and you have the run of the place, which includes any guests of yours, who are just as welcome. Sorry, I shouldn't interrupt your business meeting, but if you do want anything, just shout.'

'Thank you so much, Pippa,' Brooke said before Pippa left them to it.

'Glass of wine?' Freddie asked as he poured himself a drink.

'I was going to wait until after dinner,' Pippa protested.

'It's your day off. The staff have dinner covered and anyway, it's rude to make your brother drink alone.'

'Where's Gemma?'

'She's out with her college friends, which'll probably do her good. I wanted to talk to you. You know, as you're her best friend, you must know she's feeling insecure at the moment and I don't know what to do. The other night after your girls' night she came home a bit worse for wear and accused me of fancying Brooke.'

'And do you?'

'No! God, no. Look,' his voice dropped, 'I know she's attractive, I'm not blind, but perhaps because I've matured and I'm in love, I don't look at Brooke in any way but as a friend. I adore Gem, you know that, but, Pip, I'm not ready for marriage or children. The idea fills me with dread, if I'm honest, and she's pushing a bit. I know that's the natural next progression, but I'm still getting my head around being a proper grown up.'

Freddie sounded so earnest that her heart went out to him.

'Fred, you've undergone a lot of changes in the last few years and although Gemma knows that, she didn't know you back then, so maybe she doesn't fully understand. You need to explain. Tell her that you've taken big steps but now, now you have a job, a girlfriend, your own home, it's already a lot and you both need to try to enjoy the relationship you've got.'

Pippa could see both sides but she desperately wanted to keep them together.

'You're right. I was thinking that if I took her away for the weekend, we haven't taken a break for so long, then I can explain to her how much I love her, love being with her, and ask her to be patient with me. I know she needs reassurance and sometimes I don't do that enough.'

'Look at you, Fred, you're an adult now!' Pippa hugged her brother.

'Are you two a couple?' Chris asked as he approached the bar.

'No, she's my sister,' Freddie replied with a horrified look.

Hector arrived, bounding up to them at the bar.

'Who are *you*?' he asked slightly rudely.

Brooke and Pippa both glanced at Hector in surprise.

'I'm Chris, although people call me Chris PT.'

'He's working with Brooke,' Pippa explained. 'He's a fitness expert and he's possibly going to be here more often.' She shot him a warning glare.

'Yes, we're discussing the idea of opening a new kind of fitness studio around here,' Brooke expanded.

'Now that sounds exciting. Where do you work now?' Freddie asked.

'At the Hopperly Spa, do you know it?' Chris replied. 'I'm the trainer there, look after the gym.'

'I know it,' Pippa replied.

It was quite fancy; she went there for a spa day with the others before Amanda's wedding. But she'd never seen Chris there. Not that she'd set foot in the gym, of course.

'They hired me to open the gym, but I'd rather expand my PT business and also run my own studio so I can be more innovative when it comes to fitness. That's the plan, anyway.'

'Sounds like you and Brooke are on the same page,' Freddie pointed out.

'Yes, well, we are and...' Brooke started.

They all turned their eyes on her.

'And we'd love to try to do a health retreat here at some point,' Chris finished.

'Here?' Pippa asked, confused.

'We were just toying with the idea of maybe trying something here, to try out some of our ideas. When you're quiet, of course.'

'If you want to book a week and run a retreat then that would be great, but unfortunately it would be your responsibility to fill it.' Pippa knew she sounded like Harriet, but she was a hotel manager, not a friend, after all.

'Great, maybe Brooke and I can work on that. It's just an idea initially. But we'd eventually like to find the best area for opening a new type of fitness place,' Chris said. 'We're going to look around.'

'Probably not here. This village is mainly full of old people and fitness isn't their thing,' Freddie pointed out.

'No, we were thinking a more residential, younger place, maybe a small town,' Brooke said.

'If you put a business plan together maybe you could talk to Harriet and get some advice,' Freddie said. 'More importantly, who wants a drink?'

'I'd love a vodka soda,' Brooke said.

'And I'll have the same, please,' Chris said. 'By the way, Pippa, are you single?' he asked, raising a hopeful eyebrow.

'No, she's not!' Hector snapped.

Freddie laughed while Brooke tried not to as Hector glared at Chris. Pippa's lips curled. She was going to answer him, truthfully, but then she looked at Chris and realised that she really didn't want to encourage him. Not least because his jeans were far too tight.

Chapter Fourteen

Pippa dashed into the office clutching her notebook. She'd been summoned by Harriet but was slightly surprised to find Freddie and Gus already there. Harriet had taken a seat behind the desk – usually Pippa's desk – and Gus and Freddie were side by side on one of the sofas.

'What's going on?' Pippa narrowed her eyes.

'An intervention,' Harriet said.

'About what?' Pippa asked.

'You, apparently,' Freddie replied. 'But I wanted it to be noted that I didn't know it was an intervention until I got here.'

'Gus?' Pippa pleadingly turned to her most compassionate sibling.

'Sorry, Pippa, but this is for your own good,' he replied.

'You see...' Harriet leant forwards on the desk.

She looked more like her old self. Maybe Toby was sleeping through the night now, because her hair was neat, she had no visible bags under her eyes and she looked immaculate. She was even wearing lipstick.

'Where's Toby?' she asked, instead of asking why they were here.

'With Gwen. Since I've been hanging out with other mums it seems I'm not as bad at this motherhood thing as I thought.

Letting Gwen spend time with her grandson is good for all three of us. But, Pippa, this is about you, stop trying to change the subject.'

'I still don't understand.' Pippa sank down onto the empty couch. She felt defeated already but she had no idea why.

'Pip, we love you. We've been so proud of you this past year or so. The job you've done with this hotel is spectacular,' Harriet said.

'It wasn't just me,' Pippa said.

'No, we were a team all along, but you have no life as a result of this. And before you protest, I know, because I was the same when I worked in New York at first.'

'That's ridiculous! I went out with Hector to Glastonbury the other day,' Pippa protested. She knew she was married to the hotel, and she'd acknowledged that, she'd even nearly Internet dated because of that fact. So what did they want her to do?

'That's our point.'

'Our point?' Freddie asked.

Harriet glared at him.

'Yes, our point.'

'What's your point?' Pippa asked haughtily. She didn't like this, not one bit.

'Hector,' Harriet said, folding her arms across her chest.

'What?' Now Pippa was even more confused.

'We've been thinking,' Gus cut in sensibly. 'You should give Hector a chance.'

'You want me to give Hector a chance?' Pippa asked.

'He adores you! You've been knocking him back for ages, almost since you first met him,' Harriet pointed out. 'And he's such a great guy. Well, now he is, anyway. He's handsome, smart, has a career and no longer does reality TV.'

'Or has sex on television,' Freddie added unhelpfully. 'Although you could have warned me that this was what the meeting was about, Harry.'

'In fact, he even turned down some shows, to be taken more seriously,' Gus said, ignoring Freddie. 'Pip, he and you would be so good together, if only you'd give him a chance.'

'No,' Pippa said. What the hell were they on? They all knew that as fond as she was of Hector, he was definitely not her type. They were all happy and just wanted her to be coupled off too, but because they all liked Hector, they'd decided on him. Jointly. Without even consulting her. What were they thinking of? It was ridiculous.

'What do you mean, no?' Harriet asked, looking offended.

'Look, I like Hector, but he's far too young. He's younger than me and we're friends – really good friends but nothing more.'

Pippa tried not to sound angry. She knew they were coming from a good place, even if they were coming from completely the wrong place.

'What we're trying to say,' Harriet softened, 'is that we worry that since Mark, and then Edward, you've been put off men because you can't trust them and therefore you're not giving anyone a chance.'

'I tried Internet dating,' Pippa argued.

'No, you didn't. You set up a profile and the Mike thing happened, so you gave that up, too,' Harriet replied.

'And the only reason Mike saw your profile was because you go for men who are too old for you,' Gus pointed out reasonably.

'OK, you might have a point about the older guys,' Pippa conceded. She felt the walls of the room closing in. She wasn't comfortable about the discussion they were having. 'But you have to let me meet men my own way, figure it out for myself. Just because all of you have found your bloody soulmates doesn't mean that I'm going to.'

'Not if you don't leave the hotel, you won't,' Gus said.

'Really?' Pippa felt angry. She was a soft person, a kind person, but she didn't like being confronted and she did know how to stand up for herself. 'You guys all met your partners at Meadowbrook, so I don't think that argument holds.'

'Oh, for God's sake, Pippa, the perfect man *is* at Meadowbrook!' Harriet sounded exasperated.

'I'm not going to go out with Hector just because he's here and available.' She could hear her anger bouncing off the walls.

'OK, I surrender, but think about what we've said. I don't want you to wake up one day and wish you'd been more open to finding love.' Harriet went over and hugged Pippa.

Pippa stiffened then surrendered to her sister's embrace. For some reason she was beginning to feel emotional.

'Changing the subject, you know we've got the committee meeting for the Easter event coming up, who's going to go?' Gus said.

Thankfully, he always knew when to change the subject.

'We should all go,' Harriet said. 'The hotel mechanics can be left with the staff and as the first event of the year, I think we should all be there.'

There were three annual events at Meadowbrook, held to raise money for the animal sanctuary: Easter, the summer fête and the Christmas fair. They'd all expanded year on year but were kept separate from the hotel; although, of course, guests could participate. They used to hold committee meetings – which involved quite a few of the Parker's Hollow residents – at the house but since they'd made it into a hotel, they'd moved the meetings to a private room at the pub. The residents, including a few members of the gardening club, the vicar and his wife, among others, missed spending time in the house, so they bribed them with an incredible spread of food and as much alcohol as they wanted in the pub to compensate. It had worked well for them. Pippa knew the house was important to the community and vice versa, but it was hard work finding ways to keep everyone happy.

'Great, well, if that's everything, I have work to do,' Pippa said, suddenly feeling the need to get out of the office, or away from her siblings, she wasn't sure which.

'Pippa, will you at least think about what we've said?' Gus asked, giving her a hug.

'Of course,' she lied.

As far as she was concerned, there was nothing to think about. If she was going to meet a man, a man who suited her, then it would happen, but she wasn't going to let her siblings' seeming desperation for her to be coupled off get to her. She was independent, she was happy – or she was happy-ish – and she'd figure the rest out for herself, of course she would.

She still felt slightly annoyed when she bumped into Brooke as she was checking the drawing room.

'Hi,' Brooke said, standing in front of her, seeming a bit awkward.

'Are you all right?'

'Sure. I mean, I wanted to talk to you. The other day, with Chris?'

'You mean Chris PT?' Pippa smiled.

'Yes, I met him when I realised I needed to get on with trying out business ideas and he's great. I mean, he's got similar ideas to me and he's ambitious. Not only that, but he's also passionate about fitness. He really wants to open a studio the way I want to, so that's good, right?'

'Sounds great. So, what's the problem?' Pippa sat on the arm of one of the chairs.

'I don't know, maybe cold feet or something.'

Brooke sat down opposite Pippa. She looked vulnerable and Pippa rarely saw this side to her.

'It's a lot, I get that, Brooke. You're in a new country, you're setting up a new business ... believe me, I could never have done that at your age. You've got balls, you know.' She borrowed Hector's terminology but it fitted.

'You think so?'

'God, I know so. You're incredibly brave and there's a lot going on. I think from the other day it seemed that Chris and you would be a good match – business-wise, I mean – and we'd love it if you could do a retreat or some kind of trial here to help get you started.' Pippa still felt protective towards Brooke, she realised – something that took her by surprise. 'Perhaps if we get any suitable bookings I could suggest that we offer a fitness option, if you want to try it out. I can't guarantee anything but it won't hurt to try.'

'Thanks, Pippa, that would be great.'

'Hey, anytime. And if you do feel overwhelmed and want to talk, you know where I am.'

Pippa walked away smiling. She felt as if she and Brooke had broken down another barrier and hopefully, she'd be able to help her, something that made Pippa feel good.

Chapter Fifteen

'Hey, little sis.' Gus enveloped Pippa in a hug as they met at The Parker's Arms for the first committee meeting of the year.

There were many ways they raised funds for the animal sanctuary, but the three annual events were not only important to the sanctuary, but also to the local community. The summer fête was the biggest, but the Easter event had grown since they started and it became harder to decide on a theme, especially as everyone had an opinion. With March beginning and Easter creeping towards them, they needed to get going with their plans.

Their committee was nothing if not colourful. John, the vicar, was the unofficial head, his wife, Hilary, was always at his side and members of the gardening club also came, as well as some of the older members of Parker's Hollow.

'Penny for them?' Gus asked as they put glasses, paper and pens around the table that had been set up for them.

'I was thinking of Samuel.'

Pippa bit back tears. Samuel was the oldest member of the committee and a big part of Meadowbrook, and had been for as long as they could remember. However, a stroke last year had meant he'd to go into a home.

'I know, I miss him, too,' Gus said and planted a kiss on top of his sister's head.

The room in The Parker's Arms was perfect for the committee meeting. An array of tables had been put together and it was great for the pub, because they made a decent amount of money from the meetings.

Harriet arrived pushing a sleeping Toby in his pram and Gemma was by her side. She was shortly followed by Freddie, who arrived with Gwen and Gerry. The committee members bustled in, full of excitement, and as usual it took ages to seat everyone and take drinks orders before finally, after about twenty minutes, they were ready to start the meeting.

'We need a theme, but I can't help but think we've already covered all the obvious ones,' Harriet started as she called the meeting to 'order' once everyone had tucked into the food and, more importantly, drinks. A few of the ladies had requested sherry and there were a couple of bottles of wine on the table.

'Can I pick up Toby?' Edie asked.

Active on the committee, as well as gardening club member, she often ran the bric-a-brac stall with Margaret. Because of their persuasive ways, it always made far more money than it ever should.

'He's sleeping.' Harriet rolled her eyes at Pippa.

They always brought an agenda to the meeting, but this was usually bypassed, meaning it generally took a further couple of meetings to get anything decided. Pippa knew it was because most committee members liked coming to meetings. It gave them somewhere to go and also a purpose, as most of them were retired. That was Meadowbrook and she was aware that deep down, they wouldn't have it any other way.

'It's fine, I'm his godmother almost.'

Before anyone could do anything, she lifted Toby out of the pram, which woke him up and provided him with an opportunity to show off how well his lungs worked.

'My goodness! Even deaf Samuel would have been able to hear that cry!' Rose, another gardening club and committee member, said.

'Do all babies sound like that?' Pete asked.

'Here, I've got a bottle for him.'

Harriet, trying not to sound angry, handed it to Edie and when she stuck it in Toby's mouth, he stopped crying immediately.

'Man after my own heart, likes his food,' Gerry announced proudly.

'Right, back to the Easter event,' Pippa said. 'We still need a theme.'

'I'd like to propose bringing back the real meaning of Easter,' John, the vicar, suggested.

'I second that,' his wife loyally piped up. 'Jesus and the Crucifixion.'

Pippa rolled her eyes and looked at Fred, who was trying not to laugh. Thank goodness Gus jumped in, because no one else seemed to know what to say.

'We've always said in the past – and I mean this with all due respect to both Easter and Jesus – that we can't have a half-naked man nailed to a cross, it wouldn't be suitable for children, and we do need to raise money, you know,' he pointed out gently.

'Fine,' John said, sounding disappointed, although why, as he'd tried to get this passed every year and was always vetoed, Pippa had no idea.

'But we'd love for your morris dance troop to be heavily involved, of course,' Harriet added as a means to pacify him.

'You know, you still haven't officially set the date for the christening,' Hilary pointed out, going off at a tangent.

'I know, I'm so sorry.' Harriet's face began to redden. 'We've been meaning to but we've just been so busy.'

'Next month's good for me. Pin Connor down. Where is he, by the way?' John asked.

Connor was normally at the meetings, but more often than not these days he seemed to be working.

'At the surgery; there was an emergency,' Harriet said. 'I'll get him to call you tonight.'

'Oh, goody, I do love a christening,' Doris, one of the raffle ticket sellers at these events, piped up.

'I do, too, although I prefer weddings,' Mary, her raffle-selling partner, added.

Pippa noticed Freddie looking intently at the table.

'Of course, I'll need a hat. Gemma, dear, will you take me shopping? Last time she took me to some wonderful charity shops in Bath and I picked up a few bargains, I can tell you,' Edie said.

'I'm not sure even I'll be wearing a hat,' Harriet replied.

'Yes, but I'm important, I'm going to be godmother,' she announced to the table.

'As am I,' Pippa cut in.

'Best if only the chief godmother wears a hat,' Edie decided, giving herself a promotion that didn't exist, but no one dreamt of correcting her.

'And as godfather I'm going to get a new suit,' Gerry announced.

'Why am I not godfather if she's godmother?' Freddie hissed at Harriet.

'Oh, Fred, I can't have both you and Gus, and I couldn't choose between you, but Pip's my only sister.'

'That's convenient,' Freddie huffed.

'I really don't mind,' Gus said reasonably.

'Anyway, you don't even like babies,' Gemma pointed out.

'No, but I've got a feeling I'll like Toby when he's older. A bit like how Fleur managed to grow on me eventually,' Freddie explained.

'Don't let her hear you say that,' Gus pointed out.

The meeting was definitely off track, so much so that Pippa knew that no matter what happened now, it wouldn't go back. They were all talking outfits for the christening that Harriet would now have no choice but to schedule. John was suggesting hymns and some of them were asking Gwen about the catering for the afterparty.

The door opened and Hector appeared with Brooke.

'I heard you were all here. Sorry I'm late, but is there anything I can do to help out with the Easter event?' he asked.

'What? Oh, I'd almost forgotten about that,' Edie said. 'We were talking about the christening.'

'What christening?' Brooke asked.

'Toby's. You'll still be here by the sounds of it, so we'd love you to come,' Edie said. Harriet opened her mouth as if to object, but then closed it again.

'Who are the godparents?' Hector asked.

'Gerry, Edie and Pippa so far,' Harriet explained.

'You need another man, to balance things out,' Freddie pointed out as if to put himself forward again.

'You're right, Fred. Hector, how do you fancy being Toby's second godfather?'

'Who? Me? Of course. I'd be absolutely thrilled. Honoured.' His smile stretched across his face, but as Harriet winked at Pippa, Pippa could only scowl back. Just because they were both going to be godparents didn't mean they'd get together. God, her siblings could be so annoying. They'd always ganged up against her in childhood, too.

'Great,' she smiled. 'I'm sure Connor won't mind that you've decided without him,' Pippa shot back.

'Actually, he already suggested Hector. He quite likes you now you don't have sex on TV and he even read your book,' Harriet replied testily.

Pippa was utterly defeated.

'I promise I'll be a good godfather,' Hector said. 'I'll take it very seriously.'

'And you'll make a very handsome and fine-looking godfather, too. Imagine the pictures of us together!' Edie said.

Pippa laughed, forgetting to be angry. It would be an interesting christening ...

'Right, this calls for a celebration. Can I get anyone another drink?' Pippa offered and they all excitedly accepted.

As drinks were fetched and toasts made, it seemed that the Easter event was all but forgotten.

'So, what's the theme for the Easter event going to be?' Brooke asked as she, Pippa and Hector walked back to the hotel together.

'No idea. They all got distracted by the christening. To be fair, they usually do. It takes us at least two or three meetings to get the event finalised.' Pippa was being warm, probably

160

because she'd been drinking earlier in the day and she wasn't good at it. Even John, the vicar, had succumbed to half a bitter. 'Thankfully, we have almost two months until it's actually Easter,' Pippa observed.

'I hope I'm still around. I know I booked two months, but I really think I need longer. I mean, I can't believe how quickly time is passing. And now I've met Chris ... things are really starting to happen.' Brooke's time with them was flying by.

'We'd love you to stay longer and I'm happy to block your room out, so at least it's reserved for you,' she offered. She had to admit she was used to having Brooke around now.

'Great, it's just that, well, now I'm thinking that the business side really might be a goer, we're going to start looking at venues closer to the city. Oh! it's going to be so exciting.' Brooke was brimming with enthusiasm.

'And you don't miss home at all?' Pippa asked tentatively.

'I do, but I love it here. I think I might be ready to start tracing my family soon, as well,' she confided. 'I'm scared, which is why I've been putting it off, but now I'm excited to find out where I actually come from.'

'We love having you here,' Hector said. 'And if you need any help with anything, let me know,' he said courteously.

'Thanks. I know I've been going through a lot of my own stuff, but you guys have been real kind to me. I think it's time I told you that I appreciate that.'

'You don't need to thank us and I for one am getting used to having you around,' Hector continued.

'Ah, thanks, Hector, I feel the same.'

Brooke linked her arm through his as they made their way to the front door. Pippa couldn't help but smile.

A figure was stood at the front door and as they approached, she saw it was Chris PT, wearing his familiar uniform of tight black jeans and a fitted hoody. His hair, the same colour as his jeans, almost shone.

'Hey, Chris,' Brooke said. 'I hope I'm not late?'

'Not at all. I'm a few minutes early.' He leant his long, lean frame against the door. 'And how are you doing?' he asked Pippa with what she guessed was supposed to be a sexy smile.

'Oh, dear Lord!' Hector replied, taking Pippa by the arm and pushing past Chris into the house.

Chapter Sixteen

Pippa rushed to get changed. She'd managed to persuade Harriet to go shopping with her earlier in the week and they'd hit Cabot Circus in Bristol to buy outfits for the christening. Harriet had settled on a lovely dove-grey dress and Pippa had decided on a suit. It was a little on the conservative side but it fitted. It was a deep green colour and Pippa, ever practical, knew she'd wear it again. Harriet complained that she looked fat in everything, but in reality she was practically back to her pre-pregnancy weight, apart from her boobs, which were bigger. Pippa, being fairly flat-chested, was envious. However, it was lovely to spend time with her sister, just the two of them, which was rare these days. They'd had a lovely lunch and she couldn't remember when she'd laughed so much. Connor had taken the day off, although Gwen was also going to be clucking around, so Harriet wasn't even worrying about Toby. After they'd got back to Meadowbrook, Pippa and Harriet had promised they'd spend more time together.

Pippa shook out her hair. She'd been to the hairdresser the previous day, thankfully, because this morning she had to check out all the guests, get the staff all organised for the christening reception later that day and also help housekeeping with some of the rooms that needed to be turned over for the following day. She barely had time to breathe, let alone worry about her appearance.

She applied minimal make-up and headed downstairs. Hector was pacing the entrance, looking incredibly smart in his fashionable blue suit; his hair was neat and his shoes were so shiny she could see herself reflected in them.

'Hey,' she said, giving him a hug.

'You look beautiful, Pippa,' he said awkwardly.

'Thanks, and you look really handsome,' she replied. 'But nervous...'

'I am a bit nervous. I've been reading up on the godfather business and I rather think it's a little more serious than I first realised. And I'm not sure how much I believe in God.' He sounded stricken.

'Don't tell John, the vicar. I'm guessing you're maybe over-thinking the whole thing. It is serious, Hector, but Harriet and Connor have chosen us to be a support for Toby, which we would be anyway, so look at it like that.'

'So, I don't have to ensure that his spiritual guidance is up to scratch, read the Bible to him or teach him about God?'

'No. If that was what Harry wanted, she wouldn't have chosen any of us. No, you get to be an important part of Toby's life and buy him expensive gifts, basically.'

'Ah, that I can do. But what about if anything happens to Harriet and Connor? Won't I have to bring him up?'

He looked so serious that Pippa had to resist laughing.

'I'm having him,' she replied quickly. 'But you, along with Gerry, who's his surrogate grandfather anyway, and Edie who, well, goodness knows what role she'll play, well, we'll all be there for him, that's what it means. And nothing's going to happen to Harry and Con.'

'You know, that's quite a good book idea. What if these parents made someone godparents and the godparents wanted the kid so badly they had the parents bumped off so they could get the kid? I should write that down.'

'Oh, goodness, Hector. Don't tell Harry that or you'll be un-godfathered before you even get through the church doors.'

Pippa shivered. She, Hector, Harriet and Connor walked down to the church together. Gemma and Freddie were bringing Brooke, and the others were meeting there. Gwen was already waiting, wearing a lovely woollen dress and big pashmina, and Gerry stood next to her, seeming slightly uncomfortable in his new suit. He looked so proud and Pippa felt a rush of love for him. Gerry, who still hadn't managed to get Gwen to put a label on their relationship, despite the fact they practically lived together, had slipped into their family without being pushy or demanding. He was so 'there' for them all that Pippa was glad he was going to be a godfather, even if he had invited himself to perform this role.

Freddie got out of the car and opened the door for Gemma then Brooke. Pippa waved. They all looked smart in their Sunday best. Brooke had asked Pippa's advice for what to wear, pleading that she had nothing suitable. Pippa, who was always willing to be helpful, had lent her a dark red dress and a coat, as it was still chilly for March. Gemma was wearing a trouser suit with heels, which explained why Freddie had driven.

'Hey, is the boy ready to get dunked?' Freddie asked.

'He'll probably cry. Where's Gus and Amanda and my darling nieces?' Pippa asked.

'Gus is bringing up the gardening club in the minibus, and Amanda will be here any minute with the girls and Alfie.'

'Alfie?' Hector asked.

'He's Fleur's boyfriend. Gus hates him but it's time he met the family; after all, he's her first proper boyfriend,' Harriet explained as she, Connor and Toby arrived.

'Gus won't be happy,' Freddie said.

'Which is why Amanda sent him to fetch the ladies. She's clever, my sister-in-law.'

Harriet smiled. She was looking gorgeous, every inch the proud mother. Even Connor, who never liked to wear a suit, still managed to look almost smart.

Amanda arrived on cue with Fleur, Hayley and a teenage boy who looked a little like Justin Bieber. Pippa smiled as introductions were made; her niece had done well.

After kisses were exchanged, John, the vicar, appeared with Hilary at his side.

'Are you ready for the big moment, young man?' John asked, bending down to the pram where Toby was asleep, his fists clenched.

'How does he sleep through all this noise?' Fleur asked.

'Takes after his father,' Harriet replied.

'Not when he was a baby,' Gwen started. 'When he was a baby he was a terror to get to sleep and he barely napped at all.'

'Oh, Mum, enough with the baby stuff.' Connor's face reddened and he sounded like a little boy.

'Oh! before I forget, I need to apologise,' Gemma said.

'What for?' Pippa asked.

'Edie's hat. It's sort of, really, really big. I mean, even for the mother of the bride it would be over the top,' she grimaced.

'I wouldn't expect anything less from Edie,' Harriet laughed. 'After all, this is her day, really, we all know that.'

The minibus pulled up and Gus hopped out, opening the door. Most of the villagers had arrived now, but last off the bus was Edie, wearing a hat that rendered Pippa speechless. It was not only enormous, but it was also covered in feathers and what looked like silver balls. It was extraordinary. And coupled with Edie's silver dress, she looked nothing like any godmother Pippa had ever seen.

'You can start now, the chief godmother's here,' Edie announced.

Pippa dreaded to think what the photos would be like. It took three of them – Freddie, Gus and Hector – to get Edie and her hat through the front door and then everyone fought to get the 'good' seats, which took even longer. But finally they were all ready.

'Are all church services this long?' Hector hissed as John rounded up the sermon. 'I thought this was just a special christening and would take five minutes.'

'Shush! John likes to do everything properly,' Pippa whispered back.

But he was right; it had been a long service. Fortunately, Toby had stayed asleep. Unfortunately, Freddie, who was on the other side of Pippa, kept nodding off, too.

'Can we have the parents and godparents at the font,' John finally announced.

Gus was taking the photos, being the most artistic one of the family, and Pippa laughed inside as Harriet and Connor stood holding Toby with Edie, her hat ensuring no one else could get near. Pippa, Gerry and Hector may as well have been outside the church door.

'I want to go first,' Edie said. 'As chief godmother.'

'Um,' John, the vicar, looked confused.

'Just let her,' Harriet hissed.

'The thing is that normally every godparent agrees at the same time,' John said.

'Oh no, I'll go first and then you can do the others at the same time.'

No one argued, not even the vicar. Toby woke up crying, but as Edie grabbed him out of Harriet's arms, he quickly settled, which seemed to support her argument further. When John had to take him to put the holy water on him, he almost had to wrestle him out of her arms. Then he cried when the water was poured on his head and Edie looked at John as if he were the Devil himself. Finally, Pippa got the chance to hold Toby.

'Can I get a photo with you, Hector and Toby?' Gus asked.

Hector moved as close as he could to Pippa and beamed.

'You know, you guys look so good together,' Harriet said as she stood by Gus. 'Like a proper family.'

'They really do,' Freddie agreed.

Pippa felt herself blushing, although Hector was still beaming.

'My turn.' Edie elbowed Pippa out of the way. She didn't want Toby this time but Hector, putting her arms around him. 'I think we make the perfect couple, actually,' she said forcefully and Pippa laughed.

'I couldn't agree more, Edie,' Pippa concurred as Hector turned a slightly odd shade of green.

Pippa grabbed Gemma and they drove back to the house, leaving the others to walk. She knew she'd probably get the wrath of Freddie later for 'stealing' the car, but she was prepared for that, because not only did she need five minutes away from the craziness, but she also needed to check that everything was ready for the party before everyone turned up at Meadowbrook. Harriet was going home first to change Toby and get all the stuff he'd need; she was probably going to use the time to get five minutes' peace, as well.

The service had finally ended after Edie, Rose and Margaret sang 'All Things Bright and Beautiful' rather enthusiastically, which made Toby cry the whole way through; although they could barely hear his cries above their singing. After that, the vicar had tried to herd everyone out of the church, which took a while. Even assurances of food and drink back at the house didn't hurry them up, as each of the ladies queued up to hold Toby. But at least that gave Pippa some time before they all descended on the hotel. It was a proper Meadowbrook christening.

The house was warm as they went in. The staff had all done a fabulous job and the bar was already set up to welcome the guests. Vicky had a wonderful spread of food waiting for them in the dining room, so Pippa really didn't have to do anything.

'How are things with you now? I haven't had the chance to catch up lately,' Pippa said to Gemma as they waited for the party to start in the bar.

'Good. I meant to thank you, Pippa. Freddie said you're going to get cover so we can go away next weekend. And I think we need it. You know, it's weird, but although we live together, what with the hotel and my course, we don't spend that much time alone. I'm not complaining, because I get to see you and the family a lot, but maybe this whole insecurity I've been feeling stems from us not having enough time alone.'

'Makes sense. I think you should make the most of the

weekend. My brother loves you, and you need to see that and not push him away.'

'Thanks, Pippa, and you're right, I need to relax and enjoy our relationship.'

The door burst open at that point and the noise level almost went through the roof.

'Oh, Gemma, that hat's going to kill someone,' Pippa said as Edie knocked someone flying when she walked in.

'I know, but she's very fond of it,' Gemma replied.

'It's your fault she bought it in the first place, so I charge you with getting it off her head,' Pippa challenged.

'I tried to talk her out of it,' Gemma protested, but she conceded defeat.

'Edie,' Gemma said gently.

Pippa was right behind her, pushing her forwards, as close as they could get to Edie without losing an eye.

'Yes, love.' Edie sprung round, knocking a glass out of Gerry's hand.

One of the waitresses rushed to clear it up.

'You'll need to take your hat off in here,' Gemma said gently.

'But why, it's such a lovely hat,' she replied as Gwen ducked to get past her.

'It really is but, Edie, it's so crowded in here, and hot. I don't want the feathers to wilt,' she added as a second thought.

Pippa beamed with pride – the woman was good with problem-solving.

'You think they might wilt?'

'Yes, in the heat and with all these people ... If you give it to me I'll put it somewhere safe,' Gemma finished.

'OK,' Edie replied uncertainly and Gemma quickly took the hat before she changed her mind.

It was put safely in the office and Pippa finally felt they could enjoy the party without fear of a guest being killed by a hat.

Pippa was helping Freddie to sort out the music, when Gus blustered up.

'I hope you know my daughter's being corrupted by that boy,' he said.

Pippa glanced over to where Fleur, Alfie and Hayley were sat around a table with Gerry; they appeared to be playing cards.

'What, Gerry?' Freddie asked.

'No, Fred, of course not. He's corrupting Gerry, too. They're gambling.'

'What *are* you talking about?' Pippa asked, amused.

She'd deduced that if anyone was a bad influence in their relationship, it was Fleur. She was up to her usual tricks of sneaking drinks and as far as Pippa could tell, Alfie was trying to get her to behave.

'They're playing cards,' Gus replied.

'Bloody hell, Gus, at least they're not having sex!' Freddie said.

'Don't say that word.' Gus put his hands over his ears.

'What are you lot talking about?' Harriet asked as she arrived clutching Toby's baby monitor.

'Fleur and Alfie,' Pippa said.

'He's sensible, she's not. If I were his parents, I'd be more worried than you are, Gus,' Harriet observed.

'But he's a boy!' Gus still wouldn't let go of his outrage.

'They're playing rummy with Gerry, Gus, it could hardly get more chaste than that. Pippa, you might want to go and see Brooke, I think she's a bit drunk.'

'Is she all right?'

'I'm not sure. Rose told me that she was talking to her about tracing her family but then she started crying.'

'Did you try to see if she was all right?' Pippa asked. 'You know, find out what's wrong?'

'No, 'course not, I came to get you. After all, you're much better at this sort of thing and anyway, I want a drink.' Harriet smiled and moved on.

Pippa shook her head and went to find Brooke. She glanced at the clock, which showed it wasn't quite 6 p.m. yet – she had a feeling it was going to be a long night.

Brooke was standing outside at the back of the house. They'd opened up one of the patio doors in the bar as it was getting very warm, despite it being fairly nippy outside.

'Aren't you cold?' Pippa asked.

'No, I'm fiiine.'

'Are you?' Pippa reached out and touched Brooke's arm.

'Yessssh.' Her voice was slurred. 'Look, I just had a feeew too many glasshes of champagne. I think my glassssh kept getting topped up without me noticing.'

'I know, I think I might have drunk more than I thought, too! I'm a little tipsy myself,' Pippa lied. She'd barely had time to drink, she was so busy trying to keep the guests in line.

'I guessh I was feeling a bit homesick; you know, it's hard sometimes.'

'I know, and you can go home anytime you want. If you want to go back early that's fine, I'm happy to give you a refund, although we'll miss you,' she added quickly, not wanting Brooke to feel that she was trying to get rid of her.

'No, I can't go home, you don't understand.' She looked at the floor.

'Then tell me.'

'I can't, I just can't.' Brooke's voice was full of pleading.

Pippa wondered if she was going to cry. She was going to try to find out more, when Hector rushed out.

'You're wanted inside. The morris dancers are about to do their special Toby dance,' he announced.

'What's morris dancing?' Brooke asked, seeming to pull herself together.

'Oh my, you mean you don't know?' Hector said. 'You're about to see one of England's finest traditions.'

'Not sure I'd go that far,' Pippa cut in. 'Brooke, the vicar's also the head of the local morris dancers and they perform at all the Meadowbrook events.'

'I'm so confused,' Brooke said.

'And in a minute you'll be even more so,' Hector said as he took both their arms and led them inside.

'Hector, shut up,' Pippa said.

'Am I even drunker than I first thought?' Brooke asked as she sat with Pippa and Gemma as the dance came to a close.

It was certainly one of their more enthusiastic performances, with bells, sticks and handkerchiefs galore. They hadn't dropped as many things as usual either, to be fair.

'No, that really just happened,' Gemma said.

'It's like nothing I've ever seen before,' Brooke said. 'But I kinda liked it.'

'You've now had the full Meadowbrook experience: the animals, this house, our family, the gardening club and now the morris dancers,' Pippa giggled.

'You never know what's happening next in this place,' Brooke said.

'You really don't. When I first came here I so wanted to be

173

a part of Meadowbrook.' A wistful look passed over Gemma's face. 'I didn't realise that I was a part of it all along,' she finished.

'Really, that's how you felt?' Pippa gave her a hug. 'And now you're family,' she said. 'And, Brooke, I know you might be a bit homesick, but while you're here, and we want you to stay as long as you want, I want you to feel that this is your home, too.'

Brooke looked tearful and just nodded.

'Oh, God, you girls aren't being soppy, are you?' Freddie asked as he and Hector appeared.

'Right, Hector, take Pippa and Gemma over for a dance and Brooke, Edie's insisting on having one of your skinny cocktails, so I need you to help me make it,' Freddie said.

'You see, totally at home! We've got you working here and you're paying for the privilege,' Pippa laughed.

'Ah, welcome to that particular club,' Hector finished as Brooke happily went with Freddie to make more cocktails, her earlier upset forgotten and replaced by a smile.

Chapter Seventeen

'What do you mean?' Pippa asked, her brow furrowed.
'I mean,' Gus said, 'that Brooke has booked a private art lesson with me and I wasn't sure about payment as normally we do this through the hotel. But we're having it now, the lesson, I mean, so I needed to check.'

'Why on earth has she decided to do this?'

'I don't know, do I? I mean, if she wants to do an art lesson then surely it's not for me to question why. She just asked me if I'd teach her, as she's always loved painting but has never really been sure where to start.'

Pippa felt a bit sorry for Gus. She was still feeling a little out of sorts towards Brooke, although she wasn't sure why. Well actually, if she was being honest with herself, she was. Since the christening Brooke had spent a couple of hours with Gwen baking vegan cakes. Then she'd spent ages with Harriet, not only helping with the dogs, but also learning more about the sanctuary, and she'd even babysat Toby! Pippa couldn't believe Harriet when she'd told her that and apparently, Toby loved her. Was there nothing this woman couldn't do? Then she'd spent time coming up with new cocktails with Freddie. So why did it bother her so much?

As much as she fought against it, Pippa couldn't help feeling a little bit jealous. She was always hearing how wonderful Brooke was these days and she wasn't part of it. She knew she was being silly, but as she was busy with the hotel it felt a bit like she was totally out of the Singer loop. Pippa liked to know everything going on at Meadowbrook and she felt left out.

Brooke ran a few times a week with Gemma, who'd become a huge fan, and even Hector took post-writing walks with her on a regular basis, gushing about how fun she was to be around. Was she jealous? Probably. Pippa was a sweet, friendly, welcoming person, but she was also quite sensitive and for some reason this hurt her. Even though she told herself she was being silly and totally irrational. After all, it was good that Brooke was getting involved while she was here.

'Right, well, are you happy to do a painting lesson? I mean, you have time?'

'Of course and I love doing them,' Gus beamed.

'Then why don't you do one for free this time? Brooke's spent a huge amount of money at the hotel.'

Pippa tried to sound magnanimous. After all, this was Pippa's issue, not Brooke's, who'd done nothing wrong. She knew she had to stop her ridiculous thoughts.

'I'm fine with that.'

'Perfect.' Pippa had an idea. 'Oh! and Gus?'

'Yes?'

'While you're alone with her, see if you can find out what's going on with her father's family. Her father came from this area, but she hasn't tried to track down any relatives yet. I'm just a bit mystified about it.'

Pippa knew suspicion wasn't a good look but, actually, after Brooke's tears at the christening, she was more concerned than

176

suspicious. Although it still didn't exactly add up, she was worried that Brooke was more distressed than she thought.

'God, you know, sometimes you sound so like Harriet.'

Gus's brows seemed to knot with confusion and Pippa wasn't sure that was exactly meant as a compliment.

'I'm teaching her painting, not interrogating her! Remember, Brooke lost her father and she's grieving, Pip, and we all remember how strange and alien that can be. I feel for her, she's obviously a bit lost, but I can understand her need to get away. And perhaps having some loose connection to the UK just gave her a place to run to.'

Gus looked earnest and Pippa knew he was right. She was probably the one overthinking everything, as usual.

'I know it makes sense. We all wanted to run away when Daddy died, didn't we? Only he stuck us here and wouldn't let us. But, Gus, I'm not trying to be like Harriet. I don't think there's anything untoward going on but I'm worried about her. She might be more fragile than we think.'

'OK, OK, I can check she's all right, if that really is what you mean?'

Gus looked stern and Pippa nodded.

'But remember, Brooke's an only child and having a difficult time, so I think she just wanted, or perhaps needed, to get away. Now she has, she doesn't quite seem to know what to do with herself, or her time. We need to be there for her if she needs us, that's what we do,' Gus continued.

'And that's what I've been trying to say,' Pippa shrugged. Or it's what she should have been trying to say, at least.

'Hi, Hector. Do you fancy coming down to the sanctuary?' Pippa asked once Gus and Brooke had gone to the summerhouse for her painting lesson. Feeling skittish, Pippa actually craved some stable company.

'Of course, whatever for?'

'I'm going to collect Toby for a couple of hours. Honestly, since these baby groups Harriet's like a different person. She lets me get my hands on her son far more,' Pippa giggled.

Harriet had stopped trying to be supermum and doing everything herself, finally letting people help her, much to the delight of Gwen, Connor and Pippa. Although she still texted every five minutes to check he was all right when she wasn't with him, it was progress.

'Can I help babysit my godson, then?'

'That's why I came to find you. I thought we'd go for a walk and then he can come up to the hotel. The handful of guests we have are all occupied and anyway, we can always take him into the snug. But don't you have to work?'

'I, Pippa Singer, am ahead of my word count, so I can give myself the rest of the day off. And getting to spend time with you is an added bonus.'

'Oh, stop it, Hector, you're such a dork.' She punched his arm. 'Come on, if we don't hurry, Harriet might change her mind.'

'Well, don't you both look the perfect family with my son,' Harriet teased as both Pippa and Hector pushed the pram together.

Pippa poked her tongue out at her. Childish yes, but sometimes with her older sister she felt that the annoying little sister role never quite left her. Hector blushed, Pippa noticed, and rolled her eyes.

'Right, in that case we're going to take him for a walk into the village and see how many comments we get about what a handsome family we make,' Hector joked.

'Although he definitely looks more like Connor than you, Hector, which is a good thing, by the way,' Harriet said.

'He looks like a baby to me,' Hector replied.

'Anyway, if I really am entrusting my son to you, then I need to get some work done. I've got to do the budgets for the sanctuary and the hotel; they seem to come around far too quickly.'

'And Brooke's having a painting lesson with Gus,' Pippa said casually as she started to turn away, unsure why she was telling Harriet this.

'Oh, good, it might take some of her nerves away – you know, now she's traced her father's family to Bristol. She's getting closer, but it must be a bit nerve-wracking for her.'

'Bristol?' Pippa scratched her head. Brooke hadn't actually told Pippa that she'd started looking into finding her family.

'Yes, and as Bristol's a big place, she's been feeling a little overwhelmed as to where to start searching. I suggested she start on the Internet, but apparently the Walker family name is fairly common in the area. I'm not sure what her next move is because, quite frankly, it's none of our business. Although I have offered to help her, not that I have much time, and she said she'd probably take me up on that offer soon,' said Harriet, filling her in.

Pippa hadn't heard any of this, but then perhaps Brooke felt she could confide in Harriet more easily. She shook her head. No, Pippa was the one people talked to. Harriet scared people. Pippa felt even more keenly that she was missing out.

'I guess,' Pippa said at length, 'that I'm not used to feeling left out.' Saying it out loud might help her make sense of it, she thought.

'I thought as much,' Hector said. 'And I don't think you can see it that way. From my point of view, Freddie and Brooke both like making cocktails; she was telling us how she worked in all these fancy LA bars a while back. And she and Gemma like running. She misses her family dogs at home, which bonds her to Harriet. Then there's Gus with the gardens and Gwen with her baking. Full credit to her, she's learning something to keep her busy while she doesn't have a job, or many friends around her,' Hector explained rationally.

'So, basically, I don't have anything in common with her,' Pippa said.

'Of course you do, or you probably do, but you run the hotel and as far as Brooke's concerned, that's where she's staying. She can't exactly get involved with running it with you, can she?' Hector continued, making perfect sense.

'No, but that brings me back to what I've been feeling lately. I have the hotel but nothing else.'

'You do, you have your family, friends, me, but the hotel's your thing, your focus, the way my book is mine. I think you might be projecting your feelings on to Brooke.'

'Bloody hell, I need to get a hobby,' Pippa said, her mind starting to tick over. 'I've got it. I'll ask Brooke to do some exercise stuff with me. They say it's good for mental health, after all.'

Hector's eyes couldn't hide the horror. 'You hate exercise.'

'Yoga, I might not hate yoga. I did it once and it was a bit boring but I could give it a go, and Brooke loves yoga. Perhaps I could find a decent yoga class for us to go to together. It'll stop me going potty about her if I spend a bit of time with her.' To Pippa, it made perfect sense.

'Right.' Hector shuffled awkwardly. 'You know, that wasn't what I meant.'

But Pippa had stopped listening to him. She couldn't bear to think she wasn't popular. She knew that probably said a lot about her ego, but she was fragile, she'd been hurt in the past and she'd lost a lot of friends when she'd married her now ex-husband, so it was understandable, wasn't it? She felt lonely; she was only human. A human with so much going for her that she felt guilty even to think that there was something missing in her life, but there was. She craved friendship, approval, people. Even as a small child, she'd never liked the feeling of being left out. It scared her how needy being left out made her feel and with Brooke she could sense that immature, childish emotion returning. She knew she needed to grow up, to be an adult, but in many ways Pippa knew she was still that scared child who missed the mum she never knew. The one who worried that her siblings would leave, which they eventually did, and then even her father, the one person she'd always relied on, left her.

'Come on, let's go back to the house,' Pippa suggested.

They found themselves passing the summerhouse and as Toby slept on, Pippa and Hector paused. Brooke, hair loosely tied back, was wearing one of the oversized shirts that Gus kept for lessons. As Gus stood near her, she was behind an easel, paintbrush in hand, her tongue clamped between her lips in concentration. On the canvas, a small splash of colour was taking shape. Actually, from where they stood, it looked good. Then Gus said something and Brooke laughed, her face lighting up as she did so. Hector looked at Pippa for a few minutes.

181

'She's happy,' he said finally.

'She looks happy and honestly, I'm pleased,' Pippa said, finding it hard to tear her eyes away from the scene.

But as Toby emitted a small cry, indicating he was about to let out a huge wail, they were forced to hurry off.

Chapter Eighteen

'You want us to do yoga?' Brooke asked, her brows raised. Pippa tried not to feel offended by the surprise in Brooke's voice.

'Yes, well, you see, I'd love to do yoga. I tried it once a long time ago and I've always regretted not pursuing it.'

It wasn't quite the truth. What she'd discovered during her ill-fated yoga classes was that she had the balance of a drunk. A really bad drunk.

'I could teach you, if you like?' Brooke offered.

Her voice was less horrified, although it still had a hint of uncertainty in it.

'That'd be great, but I was thinking we could find a class. It'd probably have to be Bath, because they'll have the best classes, and I thought you might like to ... you know, get out of the hotel a bit and have a change of scene.' Pippa wanted to find something they could do together, but she wasn't sure being in a teacher–pupil relationship was what she was after.

'That sounds good and I don't mean to be rude...' Brooke chewed her lip uncertainly. 'But, Pippa, I'm quite advanced at yoga, so we'd need different classes. I was thinking that if I taught you, not only could we start from the beginning, but it would also be good for me – you know, for my business. To get some practice in, as I haven't taught for a while.'

Pippa nodded slowly. Yes, that was possibly a very good idea. She'd be doing Brooke a favour.

'How's it going with the business idea?' she asked breezily. She didn't want to sound as if she was interrogating her.

'Yeah, good. It's taking a bit of time, but then we want to get it right if we're going ahead. I think Chris and I make a great team. He's a great fitness coach and he's found a potential studio in Keynsham. It's on a new development. It's not ready yet, but he said that Keynsham's a good area for us – pretty residential, apparently – so we're putting together a business plan. We visited the other day and it's going to be a great space.'

'Oh!' Pippa couldn't quite hide the surprise in her voice. 'That's brilliant, great news!'

'Yes. Chris has been working on it a lot so he hasn't been around much, but we're definitely trying to get this going. I think he'd be a really great partner. He's really committed to the industry and he's got lots of good ideas. I have to say, I'm excited now that we're moving forward.'

'Really, just a good partner?' Pippa couldn't help but giggle.

'Business partner!' Brooke raised her eyebrows. 'One thing I learnt from my dad was not to mix business with pleasure. And to be honest, I think Chris feels the same. We're not going to ruin anything by getting involved; although he is quite hot,' Brooke conceded.

'I suppose, although he's not my type,' Pippa said.

'So what is your type?'

'I guess a bit older, mature. I like a man who's got a strong presence. I guess more of a corporate man.'

'And how has that worked out for you?' Brooke asked.

'About that yoga...' Pippa said, avoiding the question, then she laughed. It was nice to have another singleton around to talk about men to, actually.

'No time like the present. Shall we go down to the gym to do it?' Brooke asked.

'What, now?' Pippa didn't exactly have anything else to do but she hadn't expected to start so soon.

'Yes, go and get changed and I'll meet you in the basement. Honest, Pippa, it'll be fun, and I promise I'll go gentle with you.'

'Now, try to stretch this a bit more.' Brooke manhandled Pippa, who wobbled but didn't fall, mainly because Brooke had hold of her.

'Ow!' Pippa squealed.

'Do you want to stop? I'm not sure you're enjoying this.'

'Nope,' Pippa said stubbornly as she moved into another impossible position.

If this was beginners' yoga then she was in trouble. And if this was Brooke's idea of going easy, she was as gentle as a boxer. Pippa was sweating in a way she never had. She thought the idea of yoga was that you didn't sweat. Or hurt. Or feel as if you were on the verge of collapse. But she wouldn't give in. This was the only way she'd bond with Brooke and she was going to do it even if it killed her. It probably would kill her, in fact.

'Drink plenty of water,' Brooke said afterwards as they both sat on the yoga mat having finished with a bit of meditation, which is the only part that Pippa enjoyed. Although she wasn't meditating, exactly – she was trying not to think about the million things she had to do.

'That was great,' Pippa lied. Although going forwards, she'd have to try to convince herself she enjoyed it, because she was going to do it again. She enjoyed spending time with Brooke, even if it was going to kill her.

'Did you think so?' Brooke looked delighted. 'I tried to do beginners, but I might have pushed you a bit. In LA I always did yoga from a more dynamic perspective and Chris said that in the UK there were lots of different types of yoga, some more gentle, so I need to get my head around that.'

'The class I went to years ago was very different but yes, I did enjoy it, thank you.'

'I need to do a bit more research, actually, but this is the kind of yoga I want to teach. I also do other classes, if you're interested in trying something different?'

'No, I think I'll stick to yoga for now. But I'd like to do it again, if you don't mind? Maybe give me a day to recover, though!'

'I'd love to, Pippa, and yes, let's do it the day after tomorrow; we don't want to push it. It's great practice for me, so you'll be doing me a favour, actually.'

'Anytime,' Pippa said, but she didn't mean it. 'So, we have a date. I was going to ask, if you don't think I'm prying, if you'd made any progress in tracing your dad's family.' Pippa wasn't sure if she overstepped the mark, but she decided to bite the bullet.

'No, sure, I don't mind. I found out that they're from Weston-super-Mare, which gives me a place to start. Chris says it's by the sea but not like LA.'

'It's nothing like LA. But I thought Harriet mentioned that your family was from Bristol?' Pippa asked.

Brooke flushed. 'Oh, yes, I traced them to Bristol but then

I found out they were from Weston originally. Chris said he'd take me there,' Brooke said, sounding enthusiastic. 'I'm really nervous so he said that if we visited the place first, before doing more research, it might be a good idea.'

'Right, I see. Well, Bristol's a big place, so starting in Weston might be easier.'

Pippa was about to ask more questions, when Hector appeared, wearing his swimming trunks with a towel slung over one shoulder. He looked tanned and although Pippa tried not to stare, she couldn't help but notice his six-pack as he put the towel down and dived, seamlessly, into the pool.

'Wow! he's so cute,' Brooke whispered.

'Fancy him?' Pippa asked, thinking back to the earlier fear she had that Brooke was after Freddie. Something she'd since dismissed.

As much as Brooke seemed to enjoy spending time with Freddie, Pippa could see it was purely platonic, especially as she and Gemma were friendly now.

'Not really my type, if I'm honest. I like more of a rock star type,' Brooke said. 'You know, tattoos and rougher-looking.'

'Really?' Pippa was surprised.

'Anyone can see how much he adores you, anyway,' she added.

'Oh, Hector only wants me because I'm the only girl who hasn't fallen at his feet,' Pippa argued. An argument she seemed to be bringing out a lot lately.

'No, I haven't fallen at his feet, either,' Brooke pointed out. 'And he shows only a friendly interest in me.' She raised her eyebrows and laughed.

Pippa couldn't help but laugh along with her. They stood up and Pippa found her limbs were already aching.

'What have you two been up to?' Hector asked, swimming closer to where they were by the side of the pool.

'Yoga,' Brooke explained.

'My God, Pippa, you look as if you might keel over,' he said.

'Thanks, Hector. Brooke is a great yoga teacher – she certainly put me through my paces,' Pippa said as she smiled and tried her best not to feel affronted. Did she really look that bad?

'I like yoga, can I join you two next time?' Hector asked.

'No,' Pippa shot.

'Yes,' Brooke said at the same time.

'Great, when are we doing it next?' Hector said, ignoring Pippa.

'The day after tomorrow; I'll let you know the time. This is brilliant! I'm almost teaching a class! Oh! Pippa, I have you to thank for this.' She hugged Pippa.

Pippa's plan had worked but at what price? She now had to endure more yoga *and* have the added humiliation of Hector witnessing.

Harriet was in the office after Pippa had showered and changed.

'I hear you did yoga?' Harriet's eyebrows arched.

'I did. Is nothing secret around here?'

'No, Hector told me. Is this part of a crazy plan to get to unravel Brooke's evil plan?'

Harriet raised an eyebrow once more, which Pippa noticed had been tidied for the first time since Toby's birth, almost.

Harriet was obviously more her old self now if she was visiting the beautician again.

'Don't be ridiculous!' Pippa tutted. 'I think we just had this misunderstanding. You know, I felt as if I didn't spend any time with her but you guys all did ... So instead of being suspicious of her – which, by the way I'm not – I thought I'd see if we could spend a bit of time together and bond.' It seemed logical in Pippa's head, anyway.

'I'm glad you're finally seeing sense where she's concerned. Although you must be a bit desperate if you were willing to exercise,' Harriet laughed. 'How was it?'

'Excruciating, but I do think that we bonded a bit,' Pippa said. 'And next time Hector's going to join us.'

'So, is Brooke good, then?' Harriet asked.

'I guess so. I don't know anything about yoga but it bloody hurt,' Pippa said. 'She said it was dynamic. I don't know about that, but it was definitely hard.'

'You know, if you do this morning class with her, when we have guests we could offer it to them. Say it's quite a workout but they might like it. Brooke gets to practise and if people take her up on it, we could pay her,' Harriet suggested.

'I like that idea. We've got this group of women coming in tomorrow for five days. They've got a book club and they're celebrating ten years together.'

'Do they know Hector's here?'

'No, and I haven't told him about them yet, either. My plan is to surprise them both!' Pippa laughed.

The book club would love Hector and hearing all about his new book, and he'd probably be delighted to chat with them. As long as Pippa asked him nicely, that is.

'Oh, you'll get him to charm them, I'm sure, and it'll be

great for the hotel. But try them. When they check in, offer them yoga. Clear it with Brooke first, though,' Harriet cautioned.

'She'd be delighted to have people to practise on, I'm sure. But can you check our insurance; otherwise they'll have to sign disclaimers.'

'Wow, Pip, good thinking. You're getting the hang of this businesswoman stuff. Right, I'm going to make a move and check that Connor hasn't lost Toby at the sanctuary. I always worry he might bring home Kizzy, the piglet, by mistake.'

'Harry, you are shocking. See you later.'

As she stepped outside, Pippa was amused to see Hector was helping Edie with the roses. Or, at the very least, he was carrying her tools. Pippa was surprised when she spotted Brooke, wearing an oversized coat she'd never seen before, out there digging up weeds with Margaret. Gwen was in the kitchen baking Brooke's favourite lemon cake. Brooke really was becoming part of the Meadowbrook furniture. It was easy to forget she was a paying guest. It'd be strange when she left, Pippa thought. And although she showed no signs of doing so, she knew she would at some point. She couldn't keep paying their prices forever, surely?

'Pippa,' Edie yelled, causing Hector to drop a trowel on his foot.

Pippa walked over to them, shivering. It was still cold and although spring was supposed to be here, it didn't feel like it.

'Hey, Edie.' Pippa gave her a hug as Hector hopped around from foot to foot.

Like a swarm of bees, the other women suddenly surrounded

them. Pippa kissed cold cheeks and enjoyed hugs from them all.

'Young Hector was telling us about you doing yoga with Brooke,' Edie said.

'Yes, I did it today; she's a very good teacher,' Pippa said as Brooke blushed. 'And Hector's going to join us next time.' She wasn't relishing the 'next time'.

'We want to do it,' Edie announced.

'Oh, we so do! I heard that it really helps with flexibility and we all need that, don't we?' Margaret said.

'I do. I can't remember the last time I touched my toes,' Rose added. 'Or seen them, for that matter,' she shrieked with laughter.

'And it's not all about sex, is it?' Mary added.

Pippa choked.

'Why would it be about sex?' Brooke replied, sounding confused.

'The thing is that Brooke's class is very fast-paced,' Pippa explained. If it nearly killed her, it might actually kill off the gardening club.

'I could do a gentle version for you guys,' Brooke offered. 'I think as you're so active in the gardens that maybe some stretching exercises might help. I think I could put something together to suit you all, actually.'

'There you go,' Edie said. 'Right, when shall we start?'

'The thing is, where are you going to do it?' Hector asked, seeing the horror on Pippa's face.

'There's not enough room for you all in the basement gym,' Pippa pointed out, realising it sounded worse than it should have done.

She didn't like to add that they couldn't possibly do it there up at the hotel because it was for guests only. The women didn't like to be reminded that the house was no longer always open to everyone.

'What about the village hall?' Rose suggested. 'Hilary might want to join us and there's plenty of room.'

'Great, then that's all organised, then,' Hector said.

'What do you think?' Brooke asked Pippa uncertainly as they stepped to one side.

'I think I might have to go on the Internet and order you some yoga mats,' Pippa replied. 'Because now they want to do yoga they'll do yoga,' she whispered. 'It has to happen.'

'OK, so I'll book the hall then, shall I?' Rose asked, coming up to them.

'Sure, it'll be great,' Brooke said with a smile.

'And after yoga maybe we can go to the library,' she added.

'Whatever for?' Pippa asked.

'Oh, Brooke found out her family are from Burton-on-Sea, so I said I'd help her trace them,' Rose announced proudly.

Pippa glanced over at Brooke, who was intent on looking at her shoes.

'Sorry, Rose, I get so confused with all these English towns and villages. I meant Weston-super-Mare,' Brooke corrected.

'Oh, I love it there. Maybe we can arrange a coach trip,' Edie suggested.

Pippa just shook her head as a look of horror crossed Brooke's face.

Chapter Nineteen

It was almost a shock to the system to be preparing for the busy season. It was the end of March and from Easter onwards, the hotel would be pretty non-stop. The first summer of the hotel had been manic. They'd been fully booked, mainly owing to discounts and special offers, but it had given Pippa a taste of how frantic running a hotel could be. And now she was being reminded of that again as she prepared for their first big booking of the year.

Poor Hector had to go and stay with Freddie and Gemma for a few days as they needed his room, although he said he didn't mind. Brooke was remaining where she was, she wasn't quite part of the furniture enough to move and she'd paid up front for her room. Thankfully, they'd managed to sort the booking without having to cause her any disruption. But Pippa had warned her that it might be a bit louder than usual, as they had a team of ten investment bankers checking in for a team-building exercise. Pippa prepared to greet four women and six men, and Harriet had told her it was important to get this right and that if this went well, then more bookings from the banking world could follow. But while they came with high demands, they also paid for those demands.

Owing to the fact there were only nine rooms available,

two of the women were sharing and they'd managed to make one of the rooms a twin rather than a double, just for the duration. It was a lot of work but they were paying a lot of money. Their boss's instructions to Pippa had been very specific. All done via his very efficient PA, she hadn't actually spoken to him. But his PA was ensuring that every little detail was covered.

The group, who worked closely together, had gone off track and needed to spend time bonding. Pippa and Harriet had put a five-day itinerary together for them. Day one, they'd spend settling in and a big dinner would be prepared for them in the evening. Day two, they were having a *Great British Bake Off* style challenge with Gwen. Day three, they'd roped Chris PT and Brooke in to put them through their paces with a boot camp, a long hike and then a fitness challenge in the afternoon. Brooke was thrilled; she said it made it feel as if she and Chris might have a proper business, after all. Day four, Gus was holding a painting workshop for them and they were going to paint Meadowbrook Manor, or a part of it.

Harriet had suggested bringing in the animals, but Harvey, the boss, via his PA, had said he wouldn't subject the animals to his animals. Pippa was trepidatious about what was in store. But then this was her job, so she'd be a total professional; although this felt slightly more serious than many of the bookings they'd had so far. She wasn't sure why, though. All their guests paid a lot of money to stay, but this was the most corporate they'd had. Also, Harriet had kept drumming into her how much money this could make in the future if they made a success of it, so no pressure...

She'd left no stone unturned; menus had been planned, with extra staff drafted in, and of course the bar was fully stocked. Freddie had ordered in the most expensive alcohol in the hope they'd be happy to pay for a lot of it. Harriet had also warned that if these bankers were anything like her and her team, they might not be delighted by the idea of baking, painting and doing those sorts of mundane activities, so they might be even more demanding when they were allowed downtime. Pippa could only hope they'd be nothing like her sister.

A luxury minibus with blacked-out windows started winding its way up the drive. Pippa and Freddie stood at the front door ready to welcome their guests.

'I feel a bit scared, to be honest,' Pippa admitted.

'I know, last year we were flat out but it seems that we've been a bit spoilt with the quiet season. This feels like the start all over again,' Freddie agreed.

'I know, it's not quite over yet – we've got a few more weeks of the quiet season, up until Easter, actually – but yes, we need to make the most of it, don't we?'

'We sure do. It's been good for Gemma, me being able to spend more time with her. I think next year I want to take her on a proper holiday; you know, when we're quiet again. Like a five-star holiday in the Caribbean, maybe.'

'Great idea.'

Pippa could imagine that Gemma wasn't exactly used to lots of five-star holidays and goodness knows she deserved to be spoilt.

'I want her to have an experience that she's never had. She used to go to Wales with her nan and she loved those holidays, but I don't think recreating those would do any good. No, I want to take her to a proper resort. Because she's not into fancy things, I thought we would book to do some snorkelling, maybe even diving and activities like that. She'd like that, wouldn't she?'

'Fred, she'll love it. What's brought this on?'

'I'll tell you later.' He gestured to the minibus, which had now stopped. 'I thought Harry might be here?'

'Oh, she would have been, but she's got a baby music group, which is now her top priority.' Pippa shook her head.

She'd have felt more confident having Harriet here, but then she knew, as manager, she needed to be able to deal with this herself.

'I can't believe our sister enjoys hanging out with a bunch of mums and babies, it's mad.' Freddie scratched his head.

'I think it makes her feel better knowing she's not the only one who finds it hard. She's coping much better with Toby since meeting those women and I can only fathom that it's because they're sharing the same experience.'

A cloud passed over Pippa's face. Yes, she was only in her early thirties, but she still wondered, being definitely single, if she'd ever have a child. At one time it was all she wanted and now ... For now, the hotel was her baby.

'Welcome to Meadowbrook,' Pippa said as the guests made their way towards them.

The man who headed them up was definitely Pippa's type, she thought, as she tried not to blush. He looked to be about mid-forties, with dark hair slightly peppered with grey. He wasn't overly tall but was well-built, wearing smart trousers, a shirt and jacket. Following him were the four women, who looked immaculate in jeans, jackets and boots, which were all designed to look casual but you could tell cost a fortune. Designer handbags dangled from their wrists. The men bringing up the rear were an array of ages, mostly wearing a uniform of chinos, warm jackets and boots or trainers.

'Harvey Carter,' the man said, holding out a hand.

As Pippa took it she felt a little faint at his touch, although his broad London accent surprised her; it didn't quite go with the image. He looked expensive. His brown eyes sparkled and when he smiled, lines played at his eyes, but his voice wasn't quite what she'd been expecting. He was definitely handsome, though.

'I'm Freddie Singer, this is my sister, Pippa, and we're very excited to have you staying with us.'

'Tell me that when we leave. I'm afraid my bunch of merry people – got to be politically correct, you see – might have you thinking otherwise in a day or two.'

'We'll see,' Pippa grinned. She couldn't help herself. Harvey's eyes were so brown they were almost black. 'Would you like to come inside and have a glass of champagne to start with?' She gestured to the door.

'Yes, we bloody would,' a voice boomed.

'What about our luggage?' one of the women said, flirtatiously batting her eyelashes at Freddie.

They looked to where the minibus driver was hauling designer holdalls and small cases off the bus.

'We'll take care of that. Freddie'll take you through to the drawing room and I'll get the luggage taken care of,' Pippa said, warming into her role. She did love it so much.

'Wow, a drawing room! It's very *Downton Abbey*,' another voice shouted and they all shrieked with laughter.

This would be a good stay, Pippa thought, and anyway, Harvey looked as if he could handle this lot easily. She tried not to think about how much she'd like him to handle her.

That definitely wasn't professional. But, unfortunately, as she watched him lead his group inside, none of her thoughts about him were professional, and she'd only met him for a second.

The noise from the bar suggested that everyone was happy. The rooms had been well-received and dinner was raved over. Harvey had been especially complimentary. Pippa just wished she didn't blush every time he spoke to her. She felt like a silly schoolgirl. Harriet had phoned to check everything was all right, Hector had decided to keep Gemma company at their house and so far all was going smoothly. Pippa was about to go into the bar to join the guests, when she practically walked into Brooke.

'Are you all right?' she asked.

'Yes, sorry, I just wasn't sure about going in. They seem quite...'

'Intimidating?' Pippa suggested.

'Yeah. I mean, some of the men are pretty hot,' Brooke giggled.

'Anyone in particular?' Pippa asked, hoping that she didn't mean Harvey.

'The cute guy with the red hair,' Brooke said, pointing at one of the younger guests.

He was tall with unruly red hair. Pippa raised her eyebrows.

'Cute,' she said. 'But he doesn't look like the tattoo type, Brooke.'

'No, but he's a bit like Prince Harry, so I can forgo the tattoos for that!' Brooke laughed.

'Right.' Pippa was lost for words; he looked nothing like Prince Harry apart from the hair colour.

'Shall we go and join them?' Brooke asked, chewing her lip uncertainly.

She seemed nervous and Pippa's heart went out to her.

'Yes and I'll be right by your side. I could use a drink, anyway,' Pippa winked.

She was never fully off the clock, but most of the work had been done for the day so she could enjoy herself a little. Also, socialising with the guests was part of her job.

They approached the bar and Pippa couldn't help but notice some of the men's eyes widen when they spotted Brooke. She was wearing jeans and a long jumper, her slender figure visible and her long blonde hair snaking down her back. She looked stunning.

'Hi,' Pippa said, honing in on the group of three women who were closest. 'Is everything OK for you?' she asked with a warm smile.

'It's super,' Trudy, one of the ladies, said.

Pippa thought that, on first glance, they might be difficult to please, they were so expensive-looking, so groomed and designer-clad, but they were actually all friendly and quite lovely so far.

'We love it here. We won't want to leave, ever,' Kathryn added. 'Although the way our male colleagues behave you might want us to! I was thinking, though, that I'd love to come back with my husband, for a romantic break; he'd love it here,' she gushed.

'You'd be most welcome and I'll give you a special rate,' Pippa offered, so pleased by the compliments.

Harvey approached.

'Ladies, can I get you a drink?' he asked, casually draping an arm around Pippa's shoulder. She nearly fainted.

'I'll get Freddie to do my favourite skinny margarita,' Brooke said, approaching the bar.

'What's that?' Heidi, the third woman asked.

As Brooke explained, they all decided they wanted one of those, too. They went to the bar to see how Freddie made them, leaving Pippa with Harvey.

'You don't want a skinny drink, then?' Harvey asked with a wink.

'No, I'll probably have a full-fat glass of wine in a moment,' she replied, unable to resist smiling at him.

'Let me get that for you, we've got bottles galore littering the tables.' He gestured to where the rest of his group were scattered, all drinking and talking animatedly.

A couple were outside smoking and two were sitting down studying the cocktail menu. It was all going swimmingly. The women were clustered around Freddie at the bar, who was entertaining them with his more elaborate cocktail tricks. The rest of the staff were all busy serving, and trying to keep the place clean. Pippa's eyes shone with pride – this was the hotel at its best.

'Just a small glass, I'm still working,' Pippa said.

'In that case, I'll make it a large. I don't want you to be too sober as my unruly bunch get more and more drunk. They can be a little uncontrollable,' he laughed. 'I've heard the boss is particularly hard to handle,' he said into her ear as he gently touched her arm.

'Oh, gosh,' Pippa replied, barely able to string a sentence together.

'And not only is this hotel beautiful, but it also has one of the most beautiful women I've ever seen in it,' he continued flirtatiously.

'You mean Brooke?' Pippa managed to get the words out.

'No, I mean you. You're so bloody gorgeous I don't know how I'm going to cope the next few days.' He reached out and pushed a lock of her hair behind her ears and she was lost.

Pippa could feel the blush from the tips of her toes to the tips of her ears.

'Are you all right, Fred?' she asked later as the bar had finally cleared out and she'd regained some composure.

The debris was mainly cleared away, but Pippa had sent the staff home and she was going to finish up herself. Or she might just close the bar off and get it sorted in the morning. After all, it was nearly 3 a.m. and she couldn't believe the stamina of the guests. A few had retired to bed, and Harvey had eventually cleared the rest out as they had a full day tomorrow and breakfast had been scheduled for nine. There'd be a few sore heads, Pippa thought. She wasn't sure how well they'd handle the baking, either. A vision of everyone burning themselves because they were still drunk entered her head but she quickly dismissed it.

She hadn't drunk too much but the combination of the wine and her flirtation with Harvey was taking its toll. She felt a bit light-headed.

'I'm not sure if I'm awake or if I'm asleep,' Freddie replied.

'You get home; I'll sort this out. I think I'll just stack everything on one table and then lock the bar, so we can deal with it in the morning when they're with Gwen.'

'Good plan. Are you sure you're all right if I leave you? Oh! and by the way, I saw Brooke disappear with the ginger bloke.'

'Really? I wonder where they went?'

'For a walk, I think, but that was ages ago. I'm sure she's fine; she is an adult, after all.'

'Of course,' Pippa agreed. 'Right, off you go then.' She ushered Freddie out.

She put the glasses together, made sure the outside doors were locked and then turned to leave, walking straight into Harvey.

'Oh, you startled me,' she said as he kept hold of her.

He snaked his arms around her and she felt warmth flooding through her. She hadn't experienced this instant chemistry in a very long time, if ever.

'Sorry, I went to bed but couldn't sleep, so I thought I'd see if I could get a brandy or something.'

He was wearing a pair of joggers and a T-shirt that showed the muscles in his chest. His hands on her arms were almost burning her. She knew what she should do – she needed to go to bed, so she should really just pour him a drink and send him back to his room. But then, after her siblings' intervention, trying to get her to have a personal life, saying that she was all work and no fun, which they kept reminding her about...

'I keep the good brandy in my office,' she said eventually. 'Let me lock up the bar and I'll share a nightcap with you.'

'My place or yours?' Harvey asked.

She thought of him in her father's old room. Although it was a hotel room now, she couldn't help but think of it as belonging to Andrew Singer.

'Come with me, through to the snug, it's cosier.' She felt her voice breaking up.

'Lead the way.'

Armed with a bottle of brandy and two glasses, she led

him into the snug. Before she'd had a chance to pour, he'd pulled her onto the sofa, almost on top of him.

'Harvey, I don't normally—'

She tried to protest but he silenced her with a kiss. It felt as if she were being awoken from a deep sleep. His lips felt like feathers brushing her at first but as she gave into him, the kisses became more insistent.

'Harvey, I can't. You know…' she said.

'Shush,' he replied. 'This is all I want from you. For now.'

She fell into his arms and lost herself in the depth of his kisses again.

Chapter Twenty

'Pippa, you are coming to yoga, aren't you?'
There was panic in Brooke's voice as she approached Pippa, who was straightening up the drawing room. Pippa took a breath. She was tired, she was confused, but today was Brooke's first 'mature' yoga class in the village hall. Word had got around that thirty people had signed up and Brooke was panicking. Somehow, Pippa felt that she was responsible, so she'd offered to go for support.

'Sure. Give me a few minutes to get changed,' Pippa said, needing to be alone before she headed down to the village with her car full of yoga mats.

Brooke still looked uncertain.

'Honestly, you'll be fine, and I'll be there,' Pippa said reassuringly.

The fund managers had only just checked out an hour ago and although Pippa hadn't got to speak to Harvey alone this morning, he'd slipped her a piece of paper with his number on before he left, which made her feel more excited than she had in a long while. After their first night in the snug, she was hooked. And although they'd finally gone back to their own beds that first night, she'd found she couldn't wait to see him the following morning.

Pippa had barely slept the last few days. Harvey was in her head and he'd got to her in a way no man had for ages. There was something about him that she was drawn to. He was handsome, yes, and he emanated success, but he was also funny and charming without being smarmy. He had a down-to-earth quality about him, as well. She shook her head – she was smitten. She'd managed to get through the following day, but she was now counting the hours until she saw him again.

Baking had been a success – they were all bonding the way they were supposed to – but it had been agonising waiting, as Pippa had had to stay up until the bar emptied – thankfully, a bit earlier, as everyone was exhausted – before she then waited for Harvey. He'd appeared, as she'd hoped he would, and invited himself for a nightcap in her apartment. Then she'd spent the night with him, against all her better judgement. She didn't sleep, sleep with him – that wasn't Pippa's style – but they'd kissed again for ages and she'd eventually fallen asleep in his arms. Thankfully, she'd set her phone alarm to wake her before everyone else, but she'd again been exhausted the next day. She'd even taken a nap when they were all out being put through their paces by Brooke and Chris.

The guests were all muddy but happy after their outdoor activities when they returned and they'd all retired to their rooms. But they'd also invited Chris PT to come to dinner that evening. Trudy had taken a bit of a shine to him and he'd charmed them all, which was good for business. Brooke and the man with the red hair were also getting very friendly. They were quite obvious about the fact they were getting together and Pippa heard her tell him to come to her room at one point. There was a lot going on those few days. She was pretty sure no one knew about Harvey and her, though. She certainly hoped not.

But now they were gone. She still hadn't slept with Harvey but he was hard to resist and they were definitely getting more passionate on each encounter. However, Pippa was a romantic and she didn't rush into anything.

She also felt that they'd got to know each other a bit. He was divorced, forty-five years old and had two teenage children, who he only saw when they wanted something. He'd dated regularly but hadn't met anyone since his ex-wife and according to him, the marriage broke down because he worked too much. He said he was trying to scale back now he was ready to meet someone again. Pippa opened up about Mark and the hotel, and how she was struggling to meet anyone she felt connected to, but she did feel connected to him. She couldn't explain it but there was something there.

They'd talked about her going to visit him in London, or going on weekends away, and she'd had a head full of promise when he left. She worried she'd been distracted from the hotel, but it was all running smoothly, so perhaps she could have a personal life and a work one, after all. Although, of course, the late nights had taken their toll on her and she was still exhausted, so she couldn't help but question her professionalism, or perhaps lack of it.

However, for now, yoga called.

'So, are you going to see that guy again?' Pippa asked as they set off in her car for the village hall.

'Rob? No,' Brooke replied.

'Really? You two seemed to get on well.'

'Sure, we did, but it was a holiday romance. You know, he

has this big life in London and I'm still finding my feet here, so I'm not looking for a relationship. By the way, thanks for letting Chris and I do the boot camp. It went really well and it showed me how well we can work together. We might try to do another one when the hotel's quiet, if you're happy for us to do so?'

'Absolutely. I have a feeling Chris was a bit of a hit with the ladies.' Pippa smiled.

Brooke was silent for a moment, then asked, 'Are you angry? You know, about Rob?' She chewed her lip worriedly.

'No, not at all, why would you think that?'

She tried not to think about the fact that she'd crossed the line with Harvey in the scheme of keeping him happy. She might not have had sex with him, but they'd hardly kept things professional, either.

'That's a relief, I just didn't want you to think we were unprofessional. But you know, that woman, Trudy, was after Chris all the time we were training. It was quite funny, really.'

'Apart from that, it all bodes well for you running a boot camp here. Honestly, I'm happy for you and Chris to put a package together and we'll brainstorm about how to sell it.'

'I'd like that so much. Thanks, Pippa. Although I have to survive this yoga class first.'

'That might be easier said than done,' Pippa teased, but gave Brooke a warm reassuring hug.

Pippa was surprised to see Hector and Freddie already in the hall.

'What are you doing here? Shouldn't you be at the hotel?' she asked.

'Nope,' Freddie replied. 'There's no guests, which you know. We were asked to come and move the chairs, which we've done, but I think I might just have to stay to watch. I mean, this is going to be priceless.'

Brooke's face drained of all colour.

'Fred,' Pippa hissed. 'She's nervous enough as it is.'

'By the way, sister dear, I saw how Harvey, our big, swinging fund manger, slipped you his phone number before he left, what was that about?'

'Who's Harvey?' Hector asked sharply.

He'd stayed away from the hotel for the last couple of days, so Pippa hadn't had to deal with him warning Harvey off.

'He was the boss of the corporate guests we just had and he gave me his number because he wants to talk about doing more corporate retreats here,' Pippa lied.

'That's what they're calling it now,' Freddie quipped.

'What's going on?' Hector demanded. He didn't seem happy.

'Nothing,' Pippa lied again before going to help Brooke lay out the mats and shooting Freddie a 'shut up' look. 'Get a move on, they'll be here in a minute.'

'I'm so glad I came,' Freddie said, standing at the back of the room with Pippa and Hector a short while later as the more mature members of Parker's Hollow attempted to do yoga.

Even John, the vicar, and his morris dancing squad joined in. Apparently, it might make it easier for them to swing their sticks and ring their bells ... John had had an extensive chat with Brooke to make sure that it wasn't anti-Christian. Pippa had to intervene and explain it was yoga, an ancient tradition, not devil-worshipping. She wasn't sure that John was exactly convinced, but he agreed to give it a go for his 'art'.

'This is better than telly,' Hector said, trying hard not to laugh.

'Edie!' Brooke's voice rang out. 'You need to put your left leg forwards, not your right.'

'That is my left leg,' Edie argued when it clearly wasn't.

Brooke looked at Pippa, who shook her head. It was easier not to argue. Brooke was amazing, Pippa conceded, as she kept her cool with them all. She was even unfazed when Gerry fell over during the tree pose and knocked into Hilary. They almost all went down like dominos. Then Rose and Margaret started talking about what they were going to have for dinner when Brooke was trying to get them to learn how to breathe.

'I know how to breathe,' Margaret said.

'Me too, I've been doing it for over seventy years,' Mary argued.

'Can I ask what the spiritual thinking behind the downward dog is? I'm not sure if this is actually anti-Christian, after all,' the vicar said worriedly.

'I'm not sure I can do the tree pose, aghhhh,' Rose said as she fell on Gerry.

The worst part was that when they lay on the mats at the end to meditate, half of them were definitely asleep and snoring. And when they managed to get everyone awake, they couldn't get up, so they had to be hauled up. Thank goodness Freddie and Hector had stayed.

'I think dynamic yoga is less tiring,' Brooke said after everyone eventually left. 'To teach, anyway.'

'But they all enjoyed themselves and that's the main thing. They love it when they get to do things as a community,' Pippa pointed out. Yes, it was chaos, but everything they did in Parker's Hollow was. 'Come on, let's go and get a drink at the pub. I'm buying,' she said, slinging an arm around Brooke.

'In that case, I'm in,' Hector agreed.

'Fred, why don't you call Gemma and get her to meet us there?' Pippa suggested.

'Sure thing.' He started writing a text.

'Shame Harriet couldn't come,' Brooke said.

'Oh, she'd have really enjoyed it,' Hector laughed.

'She really would! Come on, Brooke, you've earned a very large glass of wine.'

The pub was quiet when they walked in.

'There's Lucky!' Brooke squealed and she rushed over.

Lucky, the dog, had recently been adopted and was sitting by his new owner's feet. He looked contented and seeing this, Pippa felt they got to see the real importance of the animal sanctuary. Lucky was happy and had his new home, and William, who was alone before adopting Lucky, had a new companion.

'Hey, Lucky,' Brooke said, bending down to fuss him. She was such a dog lover.

'Hi, William,' Pippa said, 'can we get you a drink?'

'No, thank you, I'm good,' he mumbled in response.

'How's Lucky settling in?' Pippa asked as Lucky and Brooke were making a real fuss of each other.

'Fine,' he replied.

He was a man of few words and he looked at his pint so intently that Pippa got the impression he was finished with their chat, so she nodded and made her way to the bar.

'I'm so glad that Lucky's OK,' Brooke said.

'You're such a softy when it comes to those dogs,' Freddie said. 'You're right, though, normally when they're adopted we don't get to see them again, so it's nice to see him looking so happy.'

'William's always in here, apparently,' Hector said. 'Issy said he's a bit of a day-drinker.'

'As long as he takes care of Lucky, that's OK, isn't it?' Brooke sounded worried.

'Nothing wrong with day-drinking and the dog seems happy enough. Right, to the bar.' Freddie got the attention of the barmaid and ordered.

They sat down in a quiet spot and sipped their drinks.

'Seriously, this is one crazy town,' Brooke said.

'I know, although it's technically a village,' Freddie replied. 'But yes, it is eccentric. Those morris dancers doing yoga was something I never thought I'd see in my lifetime.'

'The vicar was surprisingly flexible,' Pippa giggled.

'Stop, stop this horror show right now,' Freddie said.

'Talking of horror, I was wondering if I could tag along to your Easter party committee meeting tomorrow?' Hector asked.

'God, I'd forgotten about that.'

'It's my turn to stay and man the hotel,' Freddie said gleefully.

Pippa scowled at him. There were only a few weeks to go and although they'd largely agreed on most things and even started the publicity, they still had a few things to finalise. Not that Pippa was in the mood, she realised. She felt too consumed about what would happen with Harvey and her. She hadn't thought through the next step, yet.

'Hey, can I come, too?' Brooke asked.

Pippa looked at her in shock.

'You really want to come along? It's normally a little unruly,' Pippa pointed out.

'That's an understatement,' Freddie said.

'I'd love to. We don't have big Easter events where I'm from so I'd be really interested.'

Brooke's face was flushed but she sounded sincere. Pippa had to remember that she was possibly lonely and at least she was now being much friendlier towards Pippa. This was what Pippa wanted, after all. Of course Brooke would be welcome.

'We'd love you both to come,' Pippa said. 'And although Hector has experience already, you'll truly have your eyes opened,' Pippa laughed and her phone pinged.

She glanced at the screen and saw a text from Harvey. She didn't want to read it, not with the others at the table, but she was dying to see what it said. She moved so no one could see and read the screen:

Can you get away this weekend? Hotel in the Cotswolds. You, me and a lot of champagne? x

'Who's that?' Freddie asked.

Pippa hoped she didn't look as flushed as she felt. She tried to think quickly. She didn't want anyone to know about Harvey, not yet.

'An old schoolfriend. She's over from France for the weekend and wants me to meet her in London.'

She was surprised how that tripped off her tongue. Pippa wasn't a good liar – after all, she never lied; she hated lying, in fact – but she couldn't tell them about Harvey. Not with Hector looking at her with his hangdog eyes. To be fair, she wasn't keen on anyone knowing. If her family got wind of it they'd interrogate her and make it a bigger deal than it should be.

'Which old schoolfriend?' Freddie asked, sounding suspicious, which just confirmed her initial thoughts about telling them.

'Maxine.' It was the first name that sounded vaguely French that came to mind. 'She lived nearby but her father's French so she moved to France a few years back. Anyway, you probably don't remember her.'

Pippa felt guilty but she hoped they'd believe her.

'No, although I did get flirted with by most of your friends so I should.'

Freddie looked as if he were wracking his brain for this person who didn't exist.

'Are you going to go?' Brooke asked.

'It depends. I'll have to see how the hotel's fixed.'

'A weekend away would do you good. You've worked so hard this year. I'm sure Gemma and I can step in,' volunteered Freddie.

'That's really kind, Fred. I'd love to go – you know, if it would be OK?'

'I'm happy to help out too, if it means you get to catch up with an old friend,' Hector said.

Pippa felt so guilty; he wouldn't be so keen to muck in if he knew the truth.

'Hey, I can help, too,' Brooke offered.

'But you're a guest. I mean Hector is as well, but you're a proper guest.'

'Oi, why am I not proper?' Hector asked.

'Because you practically live with us,' Freddie pointed out with a grin.

'Ah, yes.'

'But at the moment, so do I,' Brooke countered. 'And I'd like to help. I kind of like being busy now I've sort of started working again.'

Pippa let her mind drift to a weekend with no work and

the gorgeous Harvey, in a hotel that she didn't have to worry about, and she had to admit it sounded pretty damn appealing. She thought about how electrifying his touch had been. Even little gestures like giving her hand a stroke as he passed her made her feel as if she were on fire.

'OK, if you're sure, I'll go.' She texted back just one word:

Yes x

Chapter Twenty-one

Pippa found it hard to focus on the meeting. The Easter event committee were in fine voice this time. Harriet was chairing the meeting but she was already exasperated. Edie wanted the event to be more elaborate than ever but had no idea how and Hilary was trying to decide if she could add in a chocolate-making class, when she didn't know how to make chocolate. John, the vicar, was fretting about the slot for the morris dancers, Gerry was asking what else he could build, Rose and Margaret were arguing about the raffle prizes, and Mary was eating all the food that had been laid on for them and wasn't much help at all. Doris and Pete were sitting there observing everyone, seeming unsure what to say.

Gus was in a bad mood, after another row with Fleur, and was sulking. Hector was trying his best to be helpful, and Brooke sat there opening and closing her mouth like a goldfish. All Pippa could think about was her upcoming weekend and seeing Harvey again.

What should she pack? She didn't want to seem to be making too much effort – they were, after all, going to the countryside for a nice relaxing weekend – but she didn't want to look as if she hadn't made any effort, either. What about her underwear? It was clear that they'd be sleeping together, but she didn't want him to think she was slutty, not yet; after all, this would be their first time being together properly.

'Pippa?' Hector's voice interrupted her.

'Yes, sorry?' The whole table were staring at her.

'I said I'd dress up as Humpty Dumpty and Gerry will build me a wall. That way we can recreate the nursery rhyme and perhaps the children can throw foam eggs at me to try to get me to fall off the wall!'

'That's a brilliant idea!' Pippa, firmly back in the room and her thoughts away from her knickers, added, 'Wonderful. It's going to fit well with the other things we've decided.'

'Right, to recap,' Harriet said, obviously keen to get this meeting closed. 'Gerry's leading the Easter egg hunt; you're always a huge hit as the Easter bunny.' Gerry flushed with pleasure. 'Gus is running the egg-decorating station. I was also thinking we could do something with the chickens. I mean, I know we can't let the children in there to terrorise them, but maybe we could let the children feed them over the fence. Can Freddie be in charge of that?'

'Brilliant, I think we've cracked it. Excuse the pun,' Pippa said, fully back in the room.

Everyone laughed.

'And of course we'll have our raffle. I'll rope in people to help you sell tickets,' Pippa offered.

Rose nodded.

'I can do that,' Brooke said.

'Oh, and that nice man of yours can help, too,' Margaret suggested.

'Who?' They all asked.

'That Chris in the tight jeans,' Margaret said. 'He's got ever such nice legs.'

216

'You could both dress up as chickens,' Gerry suggested.

'I'm not sure...' Brooke sounded mortified.

'If you did it would be so good. The kids would love it,' Hector said just as Pippa was going to try to rescue her.

'Although, if she dressed as a sexy bunny girl, the men would buy more raffle tickets,' Edie suggested.

Brooke paled. 'Edie, that's sexist,' she said.

'No way, everyone knows I'm a rampant feminist,' Edie replied curtly.

'Great, it's all decided, then.' Harriet clapped her hands together, a smile curling at her lips.

'What about the morris dancing?' John asked, sounding a little put out.

'Well, you guys'll close the show, of course,' Pippa said. 'You're our grand finale.'

'Excellent!' The vicar flushed. 'And after that yoga lesson I think you'll be impressed with our new moves.'

After the meeting, Pippa was planning on retiring to her room, picking out all her outfits for the weekend and thinking some more about Harvey. But she'd barely pulled out her weekend case, when Freddie texted her summoning her to Meadowbrook's office. Sighing, Pippa made her way down.

The hotel was empty apart from Brooke and Hector in the drawing room. Hector was typing away on his laptop while Brooke was slumped on a sofa with a book. They looked as if they belonged in the room, Pippa thought with a pang. She never got to enjoy the house the way the guests did anymore. Not often enough, anyway.

Pippa was the first in the office. She tidied the desk from earlier and sat behind the largest one: her father's desk. It was her desk now, really, and although she shared the office, it was her desk in the main. She liked to sit there, look at the huge picture of her father that dominated the wall and think about what he'd do when she had a work issue.

Freddie burst in as if he were late, saw that it was just Pippa then went to the drinks trolley – again, her father's – and poured himself a brandy.

'Take it you don't want one?' he said.

'No, thanks, it's a bit early.'

'Yes, well, I need one.'

'Why?'

'I'll tell you later when the others are here.'

'What others?' Pippa asked.

'I've asked Harry and Gus too.'

Gus and Harriet walked in together, and seeing Pippa sat behind the desk, they both went to the sofa and sat down.

'What's this about?' Pippa asked.

'Brandy, anyone?' Freddie asked.

'God no, Fred, what are you doing?' Harriet said.

'The old Fred's back again,' Gus mused.

'OK, well, I might as well tell you. I think I'm going to ask Gemma to marry me.'

'Oh my God!' Harriet exclaimed.

'That's wonderful!' Pippa gushed. They'd officially be sisters.

'Congratulations, mate!' Gus went and shook his hand. 'My baby brother's all grown up.'

'Now, steady on. Here's the thing. You guys made me see that although I'm not for marriage, Gemma is. And she hasn't got anyone but us, which makes her insecure, and I love her. Therefore, I need to do what I can to ensure she does feel secure. And I know I want to spend the rest of my life with her. I'm just worried about the marriage curse.'

'Oh, not this curse thing again,' Pippa said.

'Look, Pip, you're divorced. Gus is divorced. Our mother died. Harry's never been married and is still with her first love. What if I marry Gemma and it goes wrong? What if it's the Singer curse or maybe even the Meadowbrook curse?'

'It won't,' Gus said. 'Pip and I both married too young to know what we were doing. You're older and I *would* say wiser but...'

'Although it doesn't always seem you know what you're doing, you actually do in this case,' Harriet pointed out. 'Gemma's the best thing that happened to you.'

'I agree and she's going to be so happy,' Pippa agreed.

'I need a ring, of course,' Freddie said. 'I want to do it properly but in a way that'll suit us, so I thought I'd arrange a dinner at the hotel when it's empty, just the two of us, in the dining room, because that's where I first met her, and after dinner I'll pop the question.' He fiddled nervously with his hands.

'That's perfect.' Pippa had tears in her eyes.

'We'll help you. Do you want to go ring shopping with him this weekend, Pip?' Harriet asked.

'I can't. I'm visiting my friend, Maxine.'

'Oh yes, the French girl no one remembers,' Harriet teased.

Pippa went red but thankfully this was Freddie's moment.

'OK, Fred, I'll come with you. Gemma needs something beautiful but simple,' Harriet said.

'Thanks, Harriet.'

'She's got something beautiful but simple,' Gus laughed. 'Our Freddie.'

'Oi!'

They all laughed and then Harriet insisted on them having a toast. Pippa was so happy and with her weekend to look forward to, everything was looking rosy.

Chapter Twenty-two

Before Pippa left for her weekend away, she called on Gemma. Freddie was at the hotel, so she knew she'd get her alone.

'I feel as if I haven't seen you in ages,' Pippa said, hugging her friend.

'My college work's been a bit crazy. I've got exams soon and I get so stressed. Poor Freddie's been so patient with me.'

'And so he should be. You're the same with him. Anyway, I need to tell you something and you have to promise not to tell a soul.'

'Not even Freddie?'

'Especially not Freddie.' Pippa knew it was a big ask, but it wasn't anything bad, so she hoped it would be OK.

'OK, he's not going to dump me, is he?' Fear flickered in Gemma's eyes.

'Don't be ridiculous!' Pippa said. 'He's head over heels in love with you.' She wished she could tell her about the imminent proposal, that would give her reassurance, but she wasn't going to ruin it for them. 'No, this is about me. You know I'm visiting my old schoolfriend this weekend?'

'Yes.'

'Well, I'm not. I lied, which I hate doing, but I met this guy; he was staying at the hotel.'

'The corporate retreat guy, Harvey?' Gemma smiled.

'How did you know?'

'I saw the way you two were looking at each other when I was helping Freddie with the bar. You thought no one noticed but ... And then Freddie said Harvey gave you his number.'

'Great, I thought I was being subtle. Anyway, we're going to a hotel in the Cotswolds. Gemma, I think I might really like him.'

'That's wonderful, Pip. Isn't it? I mean, is he...?'

'He's older than me, yes, but he's from a working-class background. He's very successful and before you say anything, he's not my usual type.'

'No, he struck me as down to earth and quite ... I suppose almost rough,' Gemma said carefully.

'I'm not sure he's rough, but he certainly wasn't born with a silver spoon and he's funny, as well.' Pippa knew that Mark was anything but funny and Edward wasn't exactly a laugh a minute, either. 'He's very different and anyway, we're spending the weekend together. I didn't want the family to know, because Harriet would start doing background checks, Gus would worry and Freddie would tease. But it's early days, so I just wanted to see how it went before I told them. However, you know where I am. I'll text you the name of the hotel so if there's a problem, you can find me, in case my phone doesn't work. But I'll contact you so you know I'm fine and Harvey isn't an axe-murderer.'

'He didn't seem the type and I trust you, Pip. You know you really do deserve this happiness, so try to enjoy yourself. But stay safe.'

'Love you, Gem.'

'Love you, too.'

Pippa followed the satnav instructions to the village in the Cotswolds that Harvey had picked. Part of her would have liked to go to London, to his place, because you can learn a lot about a person from where and how they live, but then there'd be plenty of time for that, she hoped. She smiled as she drove, thinking of the texts that Harvey had been sending, telling her how beautiful she was, how he couldn't wait to take her in his arms again ... it was all so romantic.

Pippa's relationship history had made meeting men very difficult for her. Mark had destroyed her confidence and her trust in her own judgment had been further beaten by Edward, the married rival hotel owner who'd tried to use her to stop Meadowbrook from becoming a hotel. Harvey was the first man she'd let even a little close to her since then, but there was something about the way he was so secure in himself that she hoped would rub off on her.

Pippa knew she'd come a long way this year, but she also had a way to go. She was getting to know herself for what felt like the first time and the problem was that there was much she didn't like. She believed that becoming self-aware was a good thing, but then discovering her negative characteristics was showing her that it might not be all it was cracked up to be. The need for everyone to like her, the fact she was such a people-pleaser, those traits were also a bit too prevalent at times.

She'd been drawn to Harvey's seeming straightforwardness. She didn't know that Harvey didn't have any skeletons but he was open with her and she did know that he was divorced. In fact, he was definitely single. One of the female guests on his retreat told her, after a few too many glasses of Malbec, that all the women in his team had tried to date him at some stage but he didn't mix work and pleasure. And although she couldn't let herself trust him one hundred percent, so far there were no warning bells. But, she conceded, it was early days, very early days.

He was the first man who'd made her feel interested in a while. Yes, he was over ten years older than her, but she'd always liked the older man. There was something about someone more mature that made her feel safe. That was the main problem with Hector. He was lovely, they were great friends and she found him attractive, but he was far too young.

So far, Harvey was perfect. He didn't need money, didn't need her hotel and wasn't married, so already he was streets ahead of the last two men in her life. She decided to relax and have fun; after all, she deserved it, didn't she? She felt a bit guilty about the fibs she'd told, but she had good reasons for doing so.

Another thing about Hector was although he was still clinging on to the crush he had on her, she was pretty sure that the minute she agreed to go on a date with him, he'd soon be over her. Hector was a classic case of a man who had women falling at his feet, so when someone didn't they had to pursue them until they did. Unfortunately for Hector, Pippa wouldn't play that game. She wasn't going to give in to him only to be discarded and ruin their friendship. See, she wasn't as silly in relationships as most people thought.

She shook her head as the satnav told her she'd arrived at the perfect country house that was to be her home for the next two nights – it was time to focus on Harvey, not Hector.

She texted Harvey from the car to say she'd arrived then sat and waited. They'd arranged to meet at six in the evening, as Harvey said he'd leave work early, but she didn't want to go into the hotel alone. Although she wasn't doing anything wrong, there felt something a bit seedy walking into a hotel on her own to meet a man. She shook her head – she was just being old-fashioned.

He texted ten minutes later to say he'd been delayed and that he'd be there in an hour and for her to go in by herself. She assumed it was traffic and as he was probably still driving, she didn't want to keep disturbing him, so she grabbed her bag out of the car and went to check in, trying not to feel silly about it.

The hotel was very pretty. Not like Meadowbrook but it was a farmhouse style, with lots of old stone and a big open fire in the reception area. She tried to ignore the feeling of being someone's 'bit on the side' that checking into a hotel alone made her feel. She wasn't doing anything wrong, so why did it feel like she was?

The receptionist was perfectly friendly as she explained her partner had been delayed – it felt good to say the word partner rather than man she hardly knew – and she was shown their room. It was gorgeously big, with views over the countryside, a four-poster bed and an old-fashioned clawed bathtub in the actual bedroom. There was a full en suite with a massive shower as well and as she fell onto the bed, sinking down into it, she beamed. This was utterly lovely. Harvey had done well and shown excellent taste already. There was a knock at the door and she opened it to a guy holding a bottle of champagne in an ice bucket.

'This was ordered for your arrival. Shall I open it for you?'

Pippa was about to say no, she'd wait for Harvey, but then

the bath looked so inviting and what was more decadent than a glass of champagne in the bath? So she nodded and let him into the room.

By the time she'd finished her glass of champagne the bath water was getting cold, so she dragged herself out reluctantly. After wrapping herself in a soft oversize towel, she sat on the bed and picked up her phone. It was gone seven. She poured another glass of champagne and dialled Harvey's number. His phone went straight to voicemail.

As she sipped her drink, she thought about the hotel she was in – after all, she might as well work if she was going to be on her own. The room was beautifully furnished but she knew the rates they charged here weren't that different to Meadowbrook. The staff were uniformed, which was some-thing they didn't do – they just ensured everyone wore the same colour to identify them as staff. Pippa thought she might change that in the summer; they could perhaps do something a little more. She'd think about that later.

She looked at the room service menu, which was standard but expensive, and she began to feel hungry reading about the 'home-made stacking vegetarian burger', but she couldn't eat before Harvey arrived. She was a little irritated – he was supposed to be here by now and he hadn't even had the decency to call her. She downed the champagne and refilled her glass. If the whole bottle of Veuve Cliquot was gone before he arrived, then it would serve him right.

At eight, she called again, but the phone still went straight to voicemail. Pippa was beginning to feel she'd been stood up, but even more humiliating than being left in a bar or restau-rant was being left in a hotel, miles from home. She was going to kill him when he turned up, or at least give him stern words. But then what if something had happened to him? What if he'd been hurt?

She logged onto the hotel Wi-Fi and searched the Internet for accidents. There were none reported. She got dressed in a black dress that she thought would be smart enough for dinner but not too much, although at this rate she'd only be eating in the room by herself. God, what did you do in cases like this? This was why she was better off single.

Just as she was about to succumb, call Harriet and tell her everything, begging her to tell her what to do, there was a knock at the door. She opened it to find Harvey on the other side. Her first emotion was relief, followed by anger.

'I know, I'm sorry,' he said, kissing her before she could even speak. 'I got delayed at work, then the traffic was horrific and my phone died. I couldn't find my car charger. It's been one of those terrible weeks and all I wanted was to be with you, so I feel like I've messed up before the weekend's even begun.'

'I drank all the champagne,' Pippa stammered. He was so good-looking – and standing there with his shirt slightly unbuttoned and his overnight bag slung over his shoulder, he seemed even more so. He also looked contrite, like a lost puppy, so she couldn't exactly be angry with him. 'I took a bath. Waiting for you seemed forever, after all, and then I had a drink and then another one. Before I knew it, it was all gone,' she said, her voice a little tipsy.

'I'll get more,' he said, walking into the room and picking up the phone. 'Or would you rather go straight for dinner?' he asked, raising an eyebrow.

'Well, I am really hungry – ravenous, in fact,' she said, trying and failing to be angry with him.

He walked over to her and wrapped his arms around her.

'But I think I need this more,' she said, feeling like a teenager again as she kissed him.

She was so cross that he was late but so happy he was here. As she let him lower her gently onto the bed, the happiness overtook her and the anger fled completely ...

In the end, they ordered room service and more champagne. They wore the soft, cosy robes that came with the room, and decadently ate and drank in bed. Pippa felt amazing. Harvey was amazing. She couldn't believe not only how passionate he was, but also how comfortable they were together. He wasn't posh, either, which was her usual type. He was rough around the edges and when he told her more about his upbringing, he was anything but middle class.

'I can't believe you used to shoplift,' she said as she snuggled into him.

'Only as a kid. I realised that if I didn't get myself on the straight and narrow, I'd end up like lots of the men in my neighbourhood, either in dead-end jobs or prison. So I got a job in a bank, worked my way up from total dogsbody to trader, worked harder than anyone else, and here I am. But the problem is that I'm married to my job. My ex-wife used to complain all the time. She liked the money, mind, but she didn't like the hours.'

'I work all hours at my job, as well,' Pippa said, trying to point out that she wasn't in the market to be a trophy wife. Been there, done that, never again.

'I know, I know, and that's one of the things that attracts me to you. You might be a posh bird, but you're a grafter, too.'

'I am, and I did come to being a career woman a little later in life than most but I love it now.'

She snuggled in further. It was so nice being close to Harvey. His arms felt as if they were more than capable of holding her and he smelt so nice...

His phone rang and he looked at it.

'New York,' he mouthed before answering. 'Yup?'

Pippa went to the bathroom to check her face. She was flushed but she didn't look too bad, despite the champagne she'd had. She could hear Harvey chatting away about things she had no clue about. Harriet would, she thought. Harriet would probably like Harvey and his city ways.

She splashed her face and went back to the bedroom. She got into bed as Harvey, phone still plugged on charge, was pacing around, talking loudly, swearing occasionally and gesturing animatedly. It didn't mean anything to her but she wished he'd get off the phone. It had been so romantic for a couple of hours, making up for his late arrival, but now that was gone.

He'd told her, in fairness, that he was married to his job, but until now she wasn't sure she believed just how much. However, when he did hang up and he came over to her, kissing her gently, she forgave him instantly.

'You are just too beautiful! Sometimes I don't know if you're real,' he said.

'Oh God, Harvey,' she replied.

Then she was lost in him.

They ate breakfast in the small dining room. She liked that there was no buffet. It was all on a menu, and coffee, orange juice, toast and anything else they wanted was brought to them. A little like Meadowbrook, but then in the dining room they did have some buffet items.

'Do you prefer this hotel to Meadowbrook?' she asked.

'Only because here I've got you to myself. And none of the rest of my staff are here.' He laughed and she joined in.

'I think it's very sweet here. I'm trying to see if there are ways to improve Meadowbrook.'

'They're very different. This hotel is lovely but it doesn't quite have the character you have. Or it does but in a different way. Anyway, food's good, but not quite up to your standard.'

'You really know how to win me around, don't you? What are we doing today?'

'Ah, well, the thing is, Pippa, I've got a report to write this weekend – don't say anything, I know, I know, but a deal came up last minute, which is why I was on the phone to New York so long last night. It's not going to ruin our weekend, but I need a couple of hours this morning to make a start.'

'I'll rephrase my question, shall I? What am I going to do?' She tried not to sound as annoyed as she felt.

'There's a lovely town not far. How about I drop you off there and we find somewhere to meet for lunch later? I'm sorry, but this happens. And in a couple of hours I'll be all yours again.' It seemed pointless to argue. 'I'll make it up to you, I promise,' he begged.

Pippa shopped in the quaint little high street. It was all very nice, cute shops and lovely buildings. But although she was enjoying herself, she wished she wasn't quite so on her own. She was so attracted to Harvey and she loved his company, but if their first weekend away together was inter-rupted by his work, then it didn't exactly bode well, did it? She thought that if she were trying to start a relationship with someone, she'd move heaven and earth to give them her undivided attention. Actually, she had a bit. After all, she'd arranged cover at the hotel so she could come here. She'd even lied to her family and he wasn't being very accommodating, was he? Harvey might not be married, but he had a mistress and it was work – or perhaps she was the mistress and work was the wife, that made more sense. Although at least he wasn't trying to hide it. Pippa had to weigh up whether or not Harvey was worth it. But with her cheeks flushed thinking of the previous night, she still felt he was.

She collected her shopping bags having bought a pair of earrings for Gemma, a necklace for Harriet, a cake cookbook for Gwen and some overpriced baby clothes for Toby. Then she wandered into a small secondhand bookshop and saw they had a shelfful of Dickens. Hector liked Dickens. He said he'd discovered him late in life but for some reason he enjoyed reading the classic books, which Pippa couldn't quite understand. She liked reading but was more into contemporary romance than classics. She picked up a leatherbound copy of *Great Expectations*. She had to get it for him, knowing how much he'd love it. Then she felt guilty and went and found presents for Gus and Freddie. At least that killed time.

She went to the small pub that they'd picked out for lunch when Harvey had dropped her off. She was ten minutes late but was relieved to see him waiting for her.

'I'm so sorry about this morning,' he said, taking her hand and stroking it.

'You say that a lot,' Pippa replied.

She'd always been a bit of a pushover in her relationships, she knew that, but she wasn't sure that was who she was anymore and it definitely wasn't who she wanted to be.

'I know, let me make it up to you. We'll have lunch and then there's a beautiful walk around here I thought I'd take you on. Get some fresh air and also give us time to get to know each other. I've booked dinner at the hotel so then we can have an early night.'

'I guess,' Pippa shrugged. He was difficult to remain angry at and what he was suggesting did sound perfect. 'But you have to promise me, no more work until after we leave tomorrow.'

'That I can promise,' he said and he went to get some menus.

'Do you date much?' Harvey asked as he held her hand on one of the local walks that he'd researched.

It was a lovely clear day and there were a few other people walking nearby, but for Pippa she felt as if they were the only two people in the world. He fixed her with such an intense look, as if he really wanted to get to know her, and she clutched his hand, feeling secure as well as happier and freer for the first time in ages.

'No, I'm hopeless. You know you say you're married to the job, but I am too, since opening the hotel. I don't trust easily, you know.'

'I know.' He fixed his eyes on her. 'I do know and I accept that it'll take time to trust me. I'm not the easiest person – not only the job, but I'm intense about life, too – and as you'll learn, I struggle to sit still. But I'd very much like the chance to show you that I might be worth it.'

Pippa melted. He sounded so earnest as they stood in the middle of a field, the countryside blossoming all around them, that everything melted away and for her it was the two of them.

* * *

Once again, they found themselves wrapped in each other's arms in bed. It had been the perfect day. They'd walked for miles, the countryside was beautiful and the day was spring-like. Conversation flowed and Pippa didn't think about Meadowbrook or her family once.

They'd returned to the hotel ravenous and ate a delicious home-cooked pie in the restaurant, paired with a lovely wine, before retiring to bed. Straight to bed. They were barely through the door than Harvey was taking her clothes off and Pippa had no objections. She wondered how easy it would be to fall in love with him and she worried that she was already on her way. Pippa didn't do casual. Never had and probably never would.

'Come down to Meadowbrook next weekend,' Pippa suggested. 'I can't leave the hotel two weekends in a row but we're fairly quiet and you can meet the others.'

She was jumping the gun, she knew, but with their situations, him in London, her in Parker's Hollow, not to mention their work, she knew she needed to see if this was going somewhere, and quickly.

'I'd love to,' he said and kissed her.

Yes, she decided, she probably was going to find it easy to fall in love with him, but then all signs pointed to him feeling the same.

Harvey was open with her. He'd told her about the pain of his divorce, his regret that he didn't have a closer relationship with his children and his desire to have a second chance. He wanted to settle down again but he refused to do so until he met the right woman. In Pippa's head, she was already the right woman. They'd talked late into the night and although she was tired, she wanted to know everything about him and tell him everything about her. She'd never found it so easy to talk to a man, or at least a man who wasn't family or Hector. She certainly hadn't had this ease with Mark, for she was always on her guard with him, and being with someone like Harvey only emphasised that. She'd never felt so desired, so wanted and so interesting as she did with Harvey.

At some point she must have fallen asleep, because she awoke when it was light, the sun streaming through the window. She rolled over but there was an empty space next to her. She sat up, startled, and saw that not only was Harvey not there, but nor was his stuff. He'd left. She blinked in confusion and then saw a note lying on the bedside table. She picked it up:

Had a wonderful time! You're some woman! I woke early fretting about this report and thought it would be better if I went back to London to the office to get it finished. I'm sorry if you feel I've skipped out on you, but I'll see you at Meadowbrook next weekend and know I'll be thinking about you all week. x

She wiped tears away. How could it be so magical and so bloody awful at the same time? She barely knew the man, but her emotions swung between anger and bliss like an out-of-control pendulum. She brushed off her tears and decided to see if Meadowbrook could sprinkle its magic on Harvey. If it did, then maybe it would work, after all. With more questions than answers, she decided to shower and dress then head home. There was nothing here for her now.

Chapter Twenty-three

Pippa drove angrily towards Meadowbrook. She'd sent Harvey a text saying it was wrong of him just to leave. He replied with an apology, saying he'd make it up to her at the weekend. Should she give him one more chance, despite the fact that much of the weekend had left her disappointed? But then, after all, when it was good, it was very good. She just didn't quite know how their first weekend together could be so confusing.

She decided she'd talk to Gemma about it, get her sensible take on the situation. Gemma wanted Pippa to find happiness, so any advice from her would definitely come from a good place. She felt marginally happier having made this decision. She also needed to check the hotel bookings for the weekend. She was fairly sure that they were full and although Harvey could stay with her in her apartment, she had to ensure the staff were all in place so she didn't spend the weekend working, which after this weekend with Harvey would serve him right but wouldn't exactly help her become any clearer about how their relationship would progress. Or even if it should progress.

The hotel was deserted when she walked in. Which was strange because it was still early and they had a group of four couples that weekend, all celebrating a birthday. She hoped

Freddie hadn't scared them off. They were due to stay for lunch, if she remembered rightly.

'Ah! Vicky, where is everyone?' she asked as she headed to the kitchen.

'Hi, Pippa, we didn't expect you back yet. Our guests are taking a walk before lunch. We gave them a map for the walk around the lake and back, so I'm just preparing lunch.'

'And where are my family?' she asked.

Typical Freddie, slacking off. He was supposed to be in charge. Obviously the staff could cope, but that wasn't the point.

'They're all down at the sanctuary.' Vicky looked at her feet. 'Look, I don't know what's going on, but there's a bit of a crisis, I think.'

'I just drove past and didn't see anything remiss,' Pippa said.

She'd glimpsed the cows lazing happily in the field as she drove past, as well as the alpacas and the ponies grazing with Gerald – in fact, all had seemed totally normal.

'I think maybe you should get down there. Hector and Brooke are there, too.'

Pippa headed off feeling slightly panicked. What was going on?

She found everyone in the sanctuary office. Harriet was at the desk, Connor was pacing, Gus, Amanda, Freddie, Gemma, Hector and Brooke were all stood around; Gwen and Gerry were even there. No one looked happy and the room seemed to shrink with all of them in there.

'You're back?' Freddie stated, ashen-faced.

'Oh God, what's happened?' she asked.

'Lucky,' Harriet said and burst into tears.

236

Connor went to hug her. Pippa spotted Lucky cowering by Gwen's legs; she was petting him and whispering in his ear.

'What happened?'

'That horrible man William brought him back and said he'd bitten him,' Brooke burst out, sounding both angry and on the verge of tears.

'Connor?' Pippa asked.

Connor shook his head.

'Pip,' Gus started calmly. 'William rushed in this morning with Lucky. He claimed that Lucky bit him for no apparent reason. Lucky seems distressed, but William explained that when he bit him, he shouted quite aggressively, which terrified Lucky. William showed us his wound, which he's making a fuss about, and he left Lucky here, saying he was going to the hospital to have it checked out.'

'It doesn't even need stitches!' Connor said. 'It was just a surface wound – nothing, really. Just a nip.'

'He said he's going to sue us for not warning him about the dog's aggression before he adopted him,' Freddie finished quietly.

'But Lucky's a softy,' Pippa said.

She carefully went over to Lucky and gave him a stroke. He whined but let Pippa stroke him.

'I told him when he adopted Lucky that the only thing that he should worry about was loud bangs, like guns or fireworks, which we know set him off, but there's been nothing like that,' Connor said. 'It was an unprovoked attack. I just can't quite believe it ... Did I get it wrong?'

'The thing is, that if he sues us we could be finished.' Harriet finally looked up.

Toby was sleeping peacefully strapped to her chest, blissfully unaware of the situation.

'I don't believe it,' Brooke stormed again. 'I don't believe that it was unprovoked,' she continued.

'We're insured, aren't we?' Gus asked.

'Yes, but that's not the point,' Harriet said. 'William's saying he's going to go to the papers, he wants us shut down. Oh God, imagine the bad publicity. None of our animals would ever get re-homed. They could even revoke our licence and we might have to close.'

'What are we going to do?' Pippa asked tearfully.

But no one seemed to know. Hector came and put his arm around her, which felt warm and comforting, so she nestled into his shoulder and cried.

After everyone, herself included, had calmed down, it was decided that Lucky would go and stay with Gwen and Gerry for the time being. No one believed the dog was aggressive; although if William carried out the worst of his threats, the poor dog could end up being put down. The idea of that further devastated them all. Lucky wasn't very lucky right now.

Harriet and Freddie were going to work on damage limitation, because they had to brace themselves for adverse publicity, and Gus and Amanda were going to go and see William, who lived near them in the village, to see if they could reason with him. No one seemed to feel very hopeful, but it was worth a try and sending the calmest members of the family to try to negotiate was sensible. It was clear that everyone in the office was both devastated and afraid.

'I'd better get up to the hotel,' Pippa said finally. 'One of us should be there.'

'Yes, thanks, Pip,' Freddie said.

'Brooke, do you fancy going out for lunch somewhere?' Hector said.

Pippa turned in surprise. 'You can have lunch at the hotel,' she suggested.

'I'd rather not,' Brooke said. 'I'm so upset, it might bring the other guests down and I don't want to ruin their stay. Thanks, Hector, that would be really great. It'd be good to get away for a bit and maybe we can think more clearly there.'

'Sure thing,' Hector said.

Gus and Amanda left to go and see William while Gwen and Gerry took Lucky. Connor took Toby from Harriet and followed his mum, and Hector left with Brooke.

'I'll come and help you,' Gemma said, putting her arm around Pippa.

Pippa nodded but didn't quite trust herself to speak. She linked arms with Gemma as they walked back up to Meadowbrook Manor.

'So, I know this is all a mess, but do you want to tell me about the weekend?' Gemma asked. 'We could do with something to distract us.'

'It was interesting. The village was beautiful, the hotel gorgeous – really romantic, in fact. The only problem was that Harvey wasn't always as romantic as the surroundings...'

Pippa took comfort in telling Gemma everything that had happened. By the time she reached the house, she'd exhausted the story.

'What can I say? After all, he did warn you he was a workaholic and he wasn't joking,' Gemma said.

'Yes, but our first weekend together, our first real date? Not only is he late, but then he skips off back to London without even having breakfast with me.'

'He's definitely not married?'

'No, divorced. He's a legit workaholic.' Pippa's head felt a bit clearer after voicing it all out loud.

'Do you think he's worth persevering with?' Gemma chewed her lip anxiously.

Pippa knew she, herself, could be quite difficult if people told her their opinions and she didn't want to hear them. Gemma had seen that first hand when Pippa had dated Edward, something Pippa still felt guilty about. Pippa was stubborn and it hadn't helped her in past relationships, but then she was headstrong and didn't like being wrong, even when she was.

'I don't know. My heart says yes, my head says no. And the problem is that I normally go with my heart, which is probably why I'm single.' Pippa tried to laugh but, unfortunately, it sounded more as if she were choked.

'Why don't you give it this weekend? I'll help out at the hotel so you can take a bit of time to get to know him and see how it is on your turf,' Gemma suggested.

'Yes, you're right. I've got nothing to lose at this stage by giving him another chance. I just wish all this with Lucky wasn't going on as well. It seems a lot.'

'Oh, Pip, it'll all work out; it always does one way or another.'

'I'm so glad we've got you, Gem,' Pippa said and she let her friend hug her while more pent-up tears decided to flow.

She was pleased that the hotel was pretty much running itself at the moment, but she knew that she needed to step it up a bit. After all, rooms needed refreshing before the busy season started, there was painting to be done, new bedding to buy, and they also had to decide on an advertising strategy for the next few months. But for now, for the next couple of weeks at the very least, she was going to try to focus on the animal sanctuary and what they could do to save it. Because when she'd gone back to her apartment on her own that evening and had had time to think, she realised how serious it was.

The fact was that Harriet wasn't really talking to her and when she messaged her, she only sent one-word answers to her texts. Freddie was proving equally elusive, saying as he'd worked all weekend, he wanted to take some time off. And Gus and Amanda had got nowhere with William, who was still threatening to sue and go to the papers. They had no idea what to do next. Harriet had warned them not to offer him money until she'd had a chance to consult their solicitor the following day, because if they offered him cash that might be seen as an admission of guilt. The sanctuary needed to survive – the animals depended on it. That was the number-one priority.

Hector and Brooke still hadn't come back to the hotel and Pippa had no idea where they'd got to. She almost called Hector to ask him but then decided against it. It really wasn't her place to track them down. But it all felt like one giant mess and she also felt alone in her thoughts. She had no idea what to do.

She decided an early night was in order after a shower, but as she tried to get to sleep she couldn't stop thinking about Lucky ... and the sanctuary ... and her family – her mind was whirring. It had all been going so well for them, this couldn't ruin it. Her father would be devastated if anything happened to his beloved sanctuary.

Pippa wracked her brains for a solution. Should she go and see William herself? Should she suggest hiring a PR company to help them? Should she quickly rally the village, the community? Or should they wait and see what this awful man was actually going to do? Maybe he'd calm down in a day or so and it would all blow over ... Pippa suddenly felt lonely. Yes, she had a big family and she had friends, but tonight, while sleep was eluding her, she felt ridiculously lonely and more than a bit scared.

Chapter Twenty-four

Pippa couldn't remember a worse week. Not for a long time, anyway, and definitely not since the hotel had opened. Thankfully, the hotel had been quiet all week; although at the weekend it was full and next week they had a number of bookings. Pippa had organised extra staff to carry the load while they dealt with the sanctuary situation. From when William had first threatened to sue, things had gone from bad to worse.

William had wasted no time in making as big a fuss as possible. Although he hadn't even needed stitches, he was making out that he was practically mauled to death. He'd immediately engaged a solicitor to represent him, a very aggressive one, possibly on a no-win, no-fee basis. Simon Hawker, the solicitor, called up the sanctuary to say how his 'client' was going to sue for injuries and also for distress caused by re-homing the pet that he'd grown attached to only to have to give him back after the 'vicious attack'. He didn't ask for an exact sum of money, but the implication from the hungry solicitor was that they wanted a big payout.

He'd also called up the local paper, who'd been clambering around the sanctuary, asking for quotes and taking photos. It was chaos. Especially as they had to rein Connor in to stop him from threatening the press with ... well, it was best not to repeat the threats. Mike from the sanctuary had tried to reason with them, but although it was a big local story, once they'd got photos and the Singers' 'no comment', they'd gone off to write it up. It had also been on the local radio and the threat was that if it carried on, the story might garner wider interest.

The Singers had closed ranks, along with the community, who thankfully were giving them their full support. John, the vicar, was going to pray for them, but as Harriet said, they needed more than prayers. Their family solicitor had put them on to someone who was better placed to deal with this kind of thing and Harriet had had many meetings trying to go over their options. Freddie was dealing with the press, saying that they refused to make comments until Meadowbrook Sanctuary had launched a full investigation. Basically, they were trying to buy time.

A couple of regular donors had immediately pulled out with funding and Pippa had been calling other large sanctuary supporters to ask them or, more accurately, beg them not to judge until the mess had been sorted out. She'd given assurances that it would be – with a confidence she certainly didn't feel but managed to muster up. Because she had to do something. She was relieved that most agreed, albeit a couple reluctantly, and the worst had been two large companies who said they'd have to put their sponsorship on hold until the outcome was decided. Pippa felt a little as if she'd done a bit to help, but each and every one of them were feeling frustrated. Poor Connor had never been so down and Harriet, who was usually a problem-solver, was unable to come up with a solution. Harry was trying to support Connor and remain upbeat, but Pippa knew she was feeling emotionally fragile, too.

Hector had used his social media and huge fan base to show his support for the sanctuary. He wasn't going overboard; however, he said he was confident that the sanctuary would be proved innocent. Goodness, it felt as if they'd done something criminal. But Hector proved a great support with some wonderful PR and Pippa was touched by how much he was willing to do. The problem was that none of them knew exactly how to make it go away.

It was unthinkable that the sanctuary might actually be in trouble. When their father had died, he'd entrusted – no, demanded – that they not only run the sanctuary, but also raise a certain amount of money to do so. One by one, each of them had fallen in love with the sanctuary and the work it did. It was part of Meadowbrook, a huge part, so nothing could be allowed to jeopardise it.

Brooke had surprised Pippa by stepping in to help with Toby. She was good with him, of course, having been an au pair for a short time – was there no job this twenty-five-year-old hadn't done? And although Pippa felt a little jealous, because Harriet was so grateful to Brooke, she knew she shouldn't, because they needed all the help they could get. Pippa was seeing sides to herself lately she wasn't keen on, but then as they were in the midst of a crisis, she didn't have time to dissect what to do about it.

It was threatening to be a disaster, but at the moment they were containing it. It was the best they could do. However, short of paying William off, no one knew how to make it go away. The sanctuary was in big trouble and no one could underestimate how much of a knife edge they were teetering on at the moment. Connor was devastated and blaming himself, and although Lucky had settled into his 'foster' home with Gwen and Gerry, no one knew what this meant for him, either.

Pippa got the staff to lay out the dining room. Before the guests were due that evening Harriet had called a meeting at the hotel so they could all sit down, review where they were and decide how to proceed going forward. Pippa had organised coffee and Gwen, who always baked in a crisis, had baked a lot of cakes. Although this was largely a family meeting, Harriet had invited Mike, Ginny and Clive from the sanctuary, John, the vicar, who was one of the most influential people in the village, as well as Hector and Brooke, who was involved whether Pippa liked it or not. Pippa was trying her best to stay calm. She'd also spoken to Harvey, telling him about the situation, but he still wanted to come this weekend. He was due to arrive later that evening and she was glad she'd have someone to distract her, someone to take the edge off the growing unease that she was feeling.

During the week they'd all rallied together, but in the evenings they'd all gone their separate ways, probably to recharge, and Pippa was feeling very much that she was on her own. But she wouldn't be this weekend – she'd have Harvey to hold her, reassure her and hopefully make her feel better. She wouldn't be alone. However, she had yet to tell everyone, apart from Gemma, about him coming and she was about to do just that.

They all sat around the table, including Edie. Edie had turned up because Gemma normally took her shopping on Friday mornings and when she heard about the meeting, she insisted on joining them. Toby was in his pram; thankfully, they'd arranged the meeting for his nap time, but Brooke said if he woke then she'd see to him. Of course she would.

'I'm not going to beat around the bush,' Harriet started, but then she never did. 'It's not looking good. We've got the papers running the story still and William's milking it, telling them that he's suing us for mental anguish as well now, because he loved that dog. There's a threat the story will go national.' She sounded grim.

'Bloody William,' Freddie spat unhelpfully.

'Quite.' Harriet rolled her eyes. 'We've spoken to a PR company, because although Pip's done a great job with our major donors, local families are also being put off. They specialise in crisis management and think they can help, but it's going to be difficult with the lawsuit going on. We're limited as to what we can do if they officially sue us, which is what they're threatening.'

'And although they're very good, they're expensive,' Freddie pointed out.

'Can we, you know, can our family trust pay?' Gus asked.

'Yes, if we all agree,' Harriet said. 'But the solicitors have suggested that in order to make this go away, it would be a better use of money if we pay William off.'

'Isn't that an admission of guilt?' Pippa asked.

'Not if he signs a non-disclosure. We offer him money on the basis that he drops the case and stops talking to the press, goodness knows he's done enough damage already. He can't talk about us or the situation again. And we're not admitting guilt but...'

'It feels like it,' Connor said angrily. 'And again, we're talking a lot of money. The sanctuary can't finance that.'

'No, it'll have to be taken from Meadowbrook,' Harriet said. 'I'll have to speak to the solicitors.'

'I feel so responsible,' Connor said. 'I'm sure ... I *was* sure

247

that Lucky was fine to be re-homed.' He had devastation written on his face.

'Connor, this isn't your fault. Everyone at the sanctuary felt Lucky would be a great dog to be re-homed and apart from his nerves around loud noises, he's a gentle, lovely dog,' Ginny said.

'Gerry and I haven't had a minute's trouble from him,' Gwen cut in. 'He's such a lovely, gentle fellow.'

'He's grand,' Gerry added.

'Do we know, for sure, that he wasn't subjected to a loud noise?' Brooke cut in. 'I know that there's a lot of shooting around here at times and although it's not firework season, it could have been something like that.'

'It's not shooting season anymore, though,' Freddie said, seeming to deflate. 'Although, of course, there's often shooting up at the farms.'

There seemed to be a glimmer of hope in the room.

'And we've only got William's word, so how do we prove otherwise?' Connor asked.

'I could go and flirt with him,' Edie suggested. 'See if I can get the truth out of him. You know, like one of the femme fatale types.'

The room was so silent you could almost hear everyone's brains trying to get around that offer as the glimmer faded.

Finally, Harriet spoke.

'Thanks so much for the offer, but we wouldn't want to put you in a dangerous situation,' she said carefully.

Freddie choked and Pippa could hear him mutter, 'More dangerous for William,' under his breath.

'But, Edie, we'll keep it in mind if all else fails.'

Edie was satisfied with this.

'And of course my morris dancers are happy to help,' John said.

'What, dance William into submission?' Freddie asked in a weak attempt at humour.

'No, Freddie.' John was keeping his cool as he always did. 'But remember, we've helped with security issues at Meadowbrook before. When that boy tried to let the animals out, and of course tracking down the person who bad-mouthed the hotel. We do have investigative and security experience, if you remember.'

'Of course, and you were so amazing in those cases,' Pippa shot quickly. They *were* helpful, in fact. It seemed Meadowbrook security was a bit of a morris dancer sideline. 'And we'll keep that in mind,' she added.

John seemed satisfied with this.

'So, what's the next step?' Amanda asked.

She'd rearranged work so she could be there for them; she'd been extremely practical and she was keeping Gus calm, which was no easy feat. Even Fleur had threatened to go and 'beat that bloody man up,' and no one thought she was joking. Fortunately she had exams at school, so she was at a safe distance while staying at her mum's.

'I'm going to meet with the solicitor again later today,' Harriet said. 'Gus, can you come with me?' she asked.

'Of course,' Gus replied.

Although Gus wasn't necessarily calm, he was sensible, so he was a good choice.

'Also,' Connor added, his voice devoid of any of its usual cheerfulness, 'perhaps someone could call William and tell him we're working something out with the solicitor but can he please not talk to anyone until we get back to him. It just might mean a bit more damage limitation. He seems to be trying to turn this into something like five minutes of fame. I heard the other day he'd told someone that he was in talks with breakfast TV!'

'Good thinking, Con.' Harriet reached over and squeezed his arm.

'I'll call him,' Amanda offered. 'After all, I spoke to him before and although I hate what he's doing, he was polite to me and I won't lose my cool.'

'Thanks, Amanda, that would be great. I'm not sure I could even bring myself to speak to him,' Harriet said.

'Is the hotel staffed this weekend?' Freddie asked.

Although he'd normally know this, Pippa and he had been a bit like ships passing in the night since the situation with Lucky, where one would manage the hotel while the other concentrated on the sanctuary and they kept swapping over to where they were most needed.

'I've got full staff and we've got a fair few guests. There's a family of four, a parent and two teenage girls, a couple celebrating their anniversary and a group of six women, one of whom has just got divorced and so they wanted a treat. A couple of the women have their own rooms and four are sharing.' Pippa paused. 'I haven't had the chance to tell you yet, but I've got a friend staying, too. In my apartment.' She concentrated very hard on the table.

'Not the mysterious French girl?' Hector asked.

Gemma chewed her lip anxiously. Pippa wished she didn't have to tell them now, what with Edie and John, the vicar, also being there, but she had to come clean.

'Not exactly. He's called Harvey and I met him ... we've been ... well, sort of talking a bit.' She felt her cheeks reddening as all eyes were on her.

250

'This really isn't a good time,' Harriet said, her eyes narrowed at her sister.

'I know, I know, but I explained that to him and he said he'll just muck in.' Pippa could feel her cheeks burning.

'Is this the guy from that investment bank who came here with Prince Harry?' Brooke asked a little loudly.

'No one told me Prince Harry had come here,' Edie said.

'He could have come to church,' John, the vicar, added.

'No, it was a guest who looked a bit like Prince Harry,' Pippa replied, her face still red.

'It's a date, then?' Hector asked.

Pippa couldn't help but hear the hurt in his voice.

'Um, well, um, it might be a bit,' she replied, going back to staring at the table.

'He seemed OK,' Freddie said, looking around the table. 'I mean he can hold his drink, which is always a good sign...' He tapered off.

'I have to go. Sorry, but I've just remembered I need to make some calls.'

Hector stood up so fast he sent his chair flying, but he didn't stop to pick it up as he rushed out of the room.

'What on earth?' Pippa asked.

'I'll go after him,' Brooke said, hurrying out after him.

'Poor Hector,' Harriet said. 'Pip, you had to know that would hurt him.'

'What am I supposed to do? Never date again?'

Pippa felt defensive. She hated upsetting anyone, especially Hector, who she was so fond of, but she'd tried to be subtle, not that she'd managed it, and perhaps this was what he needed to get over his silly crush on her. She was probably doing him a favour.

251

'No, but...' Freddie scratched his head.

'Pippa's tried to do this the right way and she deserves to be happy,' Gemma defended.

'Anyway, Hector only wants me because he can't have me. And he and Brooke have been spending a lot of time together lately.'

'Actually, they'd make a very good couple,' Edie observed. 'If he and I aren't meant to be then perhaps I should help him find happiness with Brooke.'

Brooke and Hector, Pippa thought. Why did that suddenly bother her so much?

She was just about to go into the dining room to check the table was ready. All the guests had checked in, they were happy and they were due to dine together. Minus Hector, who wasn't replying to her when she tried to find out if he wanted dinner, or Brooke, who was also giving her the silent treatment.

'Oh!' She jumped as Brooke appeared as if from nowhere. 'You scared me, I didn't see you,' she said.

'I just wanted to talk to you,' Brooke said, in a clipped tone.

Her eyes were narrowed, and Pippa had never seen this side to her.

'What about, Brooke?' Pippa asked. She felt as if Brooke was about to give her a ticking off and she wasn't happy about that.

'Poor Hector, he's so besotted with you and yet you let another man come here, where he's paying to stay so he can be close to you, to rub his nose in it.'

Pippa took a step back.

'Hang on. Hector and I have known each other for years. He first tried to chat me up when I was married, even. Of course I'm flattered, but I've told him a number of times that we're just friends. He's one of my closest friends, in fact. And anyway, if you knew Hector like I do, you'd realise that he only likes me because I'm the only woman ever to say no to him.' It sounded a little lame even to her ears.

'I don't believe you, Pippa. I do know Hector, having spent time with him recently, but you just see what you want. You think he's too young, too flirty, not good enough for you, but I see someone who knows more about love than you do, who adores you, who cares about your whole family, who'd do anything for you, and you treat him like dirt.'

Her words cut Pippa but her voice had softened. 'If anyone doesn't know the real Hector, it's you.'

Leaving Pippa speechless, she turned on her heels and made to walk away.

'By the way, I suggested to Hector that he go away this weekend so you don't get to rub his nose in it, but he said no, he needed to be here to support you all with the Lucky situation. You don't know how valuable, how honourable, how decent he really is.' She was angry again.

'Now hang on! Hector's one of my closest friends,' Pippa protested.

'Then I'd hate to see how you treat your enemies.'

Pippa was still reeling from the encounter when Harvey arrived. She'd called Gemma in tears, who was helping out in the bar tonight, so she'd rushed to calm Pippa down. She was so sweet but Pippa got the impression that she didn't totally disagree with Brooke. Gemma was just too nice to voice it. Pippa felt wretched. It was true that she didn't take Hector's

253

feelings seriously, but then if she did it would probably ruin their friendship and that would affect her whole family. Hector was a part of Meadowbrook and he'd never really said anything to her to imply that he was unhappy with them being friends. Most of the time, it was just harmless flirting, after all. Why was life getting so complicated? And was Brooke right? Because if she was then Pippa had to apologise and she didn't like apologising.

Although Pippa was known as the sweetest of the Singers, she was also known as the most stubborn. She hated being wrong and she had a real problem with saying sorry. She'd been like that since childhood. For now, though, she needed to concentrate on Harvey, who was perhaps her happiness, and she wasn't going to ruin that because of other people. She rarely put herself first but now she was going to.

Letting Harvey in, she ushered him straight through to her apartment. She had a cheeseboard waiting for him and a good wine. She didn't want to have to see anyone else tonight, not after the day she'd had, and although her family might want to meet him tomorrow, with the Lucky situation, they were too preoccupied to ask too many questions. In any other circumstances, she'd be grateful for that.

'You're a sight for sore, tired eyes,' Harvey said. 'Come here, beautiful.'

'I definitely have tired eyes too,' Pippa replied, kissing him. 'Wine?'

She poured two glasses and they settled on the sofa.

'So, is the dog thing resolved?' he asked, sipping his wine.

'No, and goodness knows what we'll do. We'll probably have to pay this guy off, get him to sign something to say he withdraws the allegations, without us admitting culpability.'

'It's the best solution. Give him money, he goes away and you can get back to normal.'

He made it sound so simple.

'But if we do that, without being exonerated, there's a chance we could still lose donors and the investigation could do so much damage that we'll never be able to re-home any pets.'

'Pay this bloody bloke off and get him to say that he was mistaken, that's what I'd do. Clearly, he just wants money.'

'It just seems so wrong,' Pippa protested.

Harvey made it sound like any other business deal.

'Life *is* wrong sometimes, Pippa. Now, can we talk about something else, please?'

His voice was sharp and Pippa was startled.

'Sorry if I'm boring you,' she snapped.

'Don't be like that, it's just I've come all this way to see you and I don't want to talk about a bloody dog. I want to talk about us and you and how gorgeous you are.'

His voice softened and so did she.

'Actually, it's all I've been talking about, so I don't want to talk about it anymore, either,' she conceded, feeling tired, suddenly, of everything. Including arguing with people. 'Let's take the wine to bed.'

The hotel was in good hands and now, as Harvey enveloped her in his arms, so was she.

She checked the hotel was all right as Harvey slept. She'd had a lovely night in the end and managed, with Harvey's help, to put all thoughts of anything but him to the back of her mind. The hotel was all set up for breakfast, it would seem. Gemma was on late duty and she shooed Pippa back to bed.

'This is your weekend off.'

'I took last weekend off, this seems greedy,' Pippa laughed.

'You deserve it; you've worked so hard. Go and have fun while you can.' Gemma hugged her.

'You don't think that Brooke's right and I'm a horrible person?' she asked yet again as the insecurity crept back.

'No. No, I don't. I think that it's a complicated situation, but we'll talk about it another time, when you don't have a handsome man waiting for you in your bed.'

'Which is most of the time, Gem.'

Pippa made coffee while trying to keep out of Vicky's way in the kitchen and she took them back to her apartment. She placed the cups on the bedside table and then kissed Harvey gently on the shoulder.

'Morning,' he said sleepily, slowly opening his eyes and stretching.

'Hey,' she replied. She felt happy this morning. It might be fleeting but she was going to revel in it. 'I made coffee and then I thought we could go into Bath for brunch. I know it's lovely here, but I need a day away from the hotel. Away from everything.'

'Sounds good to me. Maybe I can buy you something. Not only do you deserve it but it might just cheer you up.'

'Harvey, I don't need you to do that,' she said.

She couldn't remember the last time a man had bought her a gift. Actually, she could, it was Hector...

'I want to. You're going through a tough time and you're lovely. You make me happy. That's reason enough for me.' He kissed her insistently.

'In that case ... Oh, and just a heads-up, we're going to the pub tonight with some of my family.'

Harriet hadn't been distracted quite enough by the Lucky situation, after all. She'd demanded they meet Harvey at some point and the pub seemed like the safest bet. It would only be Harriet and Connor – Gwen would be babysitting – Gus and Amanda. Freddie and Gemma were on hotel duty. Fleur was with Alfie and didn't want to join the 'boring olds', and Hayley was with her dad. With it being the six of them, Pippa hoped it wouldn't be too uncomfortable; although she fully expected Harriet to ask far too many questions. But, of course, it could have been worse.

'I can't wait to meet your family. Your brother, Freddie, was a right laugh,' Harvey said.

'He's working here tonight but we'll have a drink with him before we go.'

'That's a shame. His girlfriend – Gemma, isn't it? She seemed very sweet, too, and the American, is she going to be there?'

'No, she's not,' Pippa said, thinking about how Brooke would probably be doing her best to keep Hector occupied that weekend.

And then she felt guilty. Brooke was just being nice – her harsh words to Pippa were out of concern – and she was taking care of Hector. Pippa would probably have to apologise to her, after all.

'She was fun. A couple of my boys took a shine to her; talked about her quite a bit when they got back to London, in fact.'

'Well, she did have a little fling with, what's his name? The red-haired guy, I think.'

'Rob. Good lad. Anyway, when I first met her I thought you and she were alike. I guess you're both blonde,' he laughed.

257

'No, she's nothing like me.' Pippa decided to end the conversation by kissing him.

So this was how it felt to be a normal couple, Pippa thought as she and Harvey strolled around Bath arm in arm. They'd been for an early lunch – it turned out that brunch was a little optimistic by the time they'd finally got out of bed – and now they were shopping. Harvey insisted on buying her a pair of beautiful gold earrings from her favourite Bath jeweller, and she was both touched and delighted.

As they looked in the shops, which was a good way to find out about his taste in things – conservative when it came to clothes and jewellery, it seemed – they chatted easily about their lives, their pasts, their likes and dislikes. There was nothing awkward about the time they spent together and conversation flowed easily. Although Harvey kept glancing at his phone, he hadn't done any work since they'd been together, which was a definite improvement on last weekend.

'I love this city,' Harvey said. 'You know, when I slow down, which I need to do one day, I could see myself living here.'

'You could? Really?' Pippa perked up.

She knew it was far too early to think long term, although as Pippa didn't do casual, she couldn't help herself. But the fact he lived in London and she in Somerset was something that bothered her slightly.

'Yes, I have no idea when I'm going to scale back on the old job, but I'm not going to be running at this pace forever. Unless I want to run into an early grave. Although I'm not quite over the hill yet.'

'And in the meantime, we could easily date like this, couldn't we? You know, weekends?' she said without thinking.

Pippa needed lessons in playing it cool, but it was a bit late for that.

'Don't see why not.' Harvey shrugged then, pulling her close to him, they carried on walking.

Pippa knew she shouldn't get carried away; it hadn't done her any favours in the past. With Edward she even saw them both running the two hotels together, after only a couple of dates, so she needed to take things slowly. But she couldn't help but picture them together, having many more days like this in Bath, spending their evenings at Meadowbrook with the family. It felt right. It definitely felt right, right now.

Pippa tried not to feel nervous as she got changed for the pub. She decided on a pair of jeans, a fitted black jumper and knee-length boots. It was beginning to get warmer. Spring was fully on them and she could almost feel summer approaching; although so far April had been quite chilly. Harvey was on his laptop in the living room, which she didn't mind as he'd been so attentive so far, and anyway, she needed space to do her hair and make-up. She'd handed Harvey a nice glass of wine while he worked and he'd suggested going to the bar for a pre-dinner drink, but Gemma had texted Pippa to warn her that both Hector and Brooke were there, so she'd dissuaded him. She wanted to avoid both of them. There was no way she was letting Brooke be rude to her in front of Harvey. She'd hatched a plan to sneak him out of the back door then walk down to Harriet's and Connor's cottage so they could all go to the pub together. She hoped her sister was on her best behaviour. Gus and Amanda would be lovely, but Harriet, well, she could be a pit bull. Although, of course, she and Harvey would have loads in common, so Pippa was hoping that they'd bond over the city.

The Parker's Arms was busy, but then it was every Saturday. Pippa had booked a table for the six of them, tucked away. She was thankful that William wasn't there, but then he normally went to the pub at lunchtime and in the early evening, so they were unlikely to have a confrontation. Pippa, Harvey, Harriet and Connor sat down and waited for Gus and Amanda, greeting various people they knew from the village while trying not to get engaged or drawn into conversation. For one night, no one wanted to talk about the Lucky situation.

'Shall I get drinks?' Connor asked.

He'd been perfectly friendly to Harvey so far, but it was clear that an animal-loving vet and a city boy didn't have much in common. Especially as Harvey had already – and embarrassingly – confessed he didn't like any animals. Connor didn't trust anyone who didn't like animals.

'I'll help you,' Harvey offered.

Connor paled.

'We'll have a bottle of Sauvignon,' Harriet said as she pushed Connor towards the bar, Harvey at his heels.

'Poor Con. Never did know how to deal with city boys,' Harriet observed.

'Not like you, then,' Pippa said. 'What do you think?'

'He's nice-looking, good bod, not your usual public schoolboy type. A bit old for you, Pip, as usual, but he seems OK so far.'

'Wow, OK, that's high praise coming from you,' Pippa teased.

'But, I know his type, married to the job, and I also know my sister. I'm not sure that you'd actually cope with it in the long term.'

260

'Harry, it's early days, so let's not worry about that yet.' Pippa tried to sound light, but it was as if Harriet were voicing her thoughts.

'Are we late?' Gus asked, bounding up.

'No, but if you go to the bar right now, you'll catch Connor with Harvey,' Harriet said.

Amanda sat down as he did so.

'You guys all right?' Pippa asked.

'Yes. Fleur's at Alfie's tonight, so one of us, probably Gus, has to stay sober so we can collect her later. God, wait until Toby's a teenager, Harriet, you end up as a glorified taxi service.'

'Thank goodness that's ages away. I want him to stay a baby forever – you know, so I can protect him.'

'I know. The hardest thing about being a parent is seeing how they get more independent. You're proud of them, of course, but you hate the idea at the same time,' Amanda laughed as the men returned with the drinks.

'What are you ladies talking about?' Gus asked.

'Children,' Pippa said.

'Do you have children, Harvey?' Gus asked.

'Yes, teenagers. One's at uni and the other's finishing sixth form. They only see me when they have to or want something. Bloody kids.' He glanced at the horrified faces around him. 'But I love them to bits, of course, and we're getting closer now they're growing up. At least I've done my bit with breeding; I don't need to worry about that anymore.'

Pippa nearly spat out her wine. Harriet glanced at her with concern. Thankfully, Harvey was oblivious, as he was talking about the 'real ale' he was drinking.

'Nice, and smooth. I like this one. I'll come here again,' he said. 'I do like a good local.'

'It's a pretty decent choice,' Connor conceded.

'We've got teenagers, so we know what you mean.' Amanda turned the subject back.

'They cost a bloody fortune. My ex, she wanted more kids, but I told her that I'd never get to retire if we did, so two was enough. There's school fees, then all the stuff they want to do for five minutes, like the violin and the flute, then it's all cars and houses. Neverending, the amount they want these days. Thank goodness they might actually be getting jobs in the next few years; otherwise I'd never get to retire,' he laughed.

Pippa could hardly breathe. Of course they hadn't had a conversation about kids, they weren't anywhere near that point, but Pippa wanted to be a mum. She was desperate to be a mother. Not necessarily in the next few weeks, but definitely in the next few years. Never wasn't an option. But then perhaps Harvey sounded set on this because he was single and if they fell in love, then he'd change his mind...

'Won't you miss work if you retired?' Harriet thankfully changed the subject.

'I'm not going for a few years yet. I'll probably trade my own account even then. It's in the blood, isn't it? Don't you miss it?' he asked.

'Sometimes I miss the buzz a little,' Harriet said carefully but at the same time grasped Connor's hand to reassure him. 'But with my life now, Connor, Toby, my family, the hotel, the sanctuary, there's always so much going on and I love it. It's a different buzz, but actually I think a bigger one.'

Connor leant across and kissed her.

'Yeah, not sure I'll be like that, but as I say, I can do private trading to keep my hand in.'

'Do you have any hobbies?' Gus asked.

God, Pippa thought, this sounded like a job interview.

'Nah, I don't have time. I played golf once but it was a waste of time. I have to go to the gym so I don't get too fat, but I don't have much spare time apart from that.'

Pippa smiled reassuringly at Harvey, but she didn't know why. He didn't seem phased by all the questions.

'Didn't you enjoy Gus's painting class when you came?' Amanda asked.

'It was OK, but I only did that, and the bloody baking, for the others. I can't be doing with all that arty stuff normally, but it was good for the staff. I wanted the team to bond and actually, it worked a treat. Really, you should thank me. I've told other department heads at the bank and they're all talking about booking. If you get a flood of them, I'll expect commission.'

'Tell you what, you can date our sister as your commission,' Harriet offered.

'Are you pimping me out?' Pippa asked. She laughed, hoping that it sounded light-hearted.

The problem was that here, in this situation, Harvey sounded a bit arrogant or something and Pippa wasn't loving it. He didn't even compliment Gus; in fact, he almost dismissed him.

'Anyway, Gus's painting workshops are wonderful, as are Gwen's baking classes. The guests love it.'

'Yeah, well, it worked a treat, as I said, for the bonding. I didn't need to get too involved as I'm the top dog anyway.'

'Oh, you really are,' Harriet said and Pippa tried to ignore the sarcasm that she could hear in her voice.

Steve, the owner of the pub, came over to take their order, which they normally went to the bar to do.

'I wanted to come over and offer our support again. I know

263

you wouldn't have re-homed that dog if there was anything wrong with it. And if you ask me, that William has a lot to answer for. I let him drink here still and, by the way, he's a big drinker, but I wouldn't trust him. I just wish there was something I could do.'

'Thanks, Steve.' Connor stood up to shake his hand. 'That means a lot.'

They all placed their orders and Steve left. It had left a bit of a sombre attitude over the table.

'Just pay the bloke off,' Harvey said. 'Get him to sign something saying he'll keep quiet and then it'll be over.'

'It's not that simple,' Connor snapped.

'No, it's not,' Gus said. 'Although he'll sign papers, some might see it as an admission of guilt on our part and it could do irreparable damage to the animal sanctuary.'

'Look, this guy's probably a bit of a chancer, but by the time you've finished paying the bloody solicitors you'd have been best paying him off in the first place. So, maybe a few people don't want to adopt from you for a while, but you know, people have short memories, they'll move on. Job done and maybe we can talk about something else.'

Pippa saw both Gus and Connor glance at each other. A look that said they weren't too keen on Harvey. Not again. Pippa's family never liked the men she dated. Of course, before they had good reason, but she really thought, hoped, that Harvey was different. Although tonight she was seeing him through her family's eyes and she wasn't too keen, either. Normally, when you introduced a new person they made an effort to be interested in other people, but not Harvey. It was like he was a different man when they were alone and Pippa was feeling confused.

'You're quite opinionated, aren't you?' Harriet said and Pippa wanted to put her head in her hands.

'I just tell it like it is, that's all. But I can see how important this animal thing is to you. I thought if you could get it to go away then you could put it behind you.'

He sounded mildly contrite and Harriet seemed to back down a little.

'So, you live in Central London?' Amanda asked, changing the subject.

'Yes, Notting Hill. A bit poncy but I like it.' He grinned. 'It's convenient and there's plenty of good places to eat. I'm a bit of a fan of city life, to be honest; couldn't live in the middle of nowhere like you.'

'I can't wait to visit your place,' Pippa said, trying to ignore the open-mouthed gapes of their dinner companions.

Thankfully, the food came and then they all concentrated on their plates as if they were the most interesting things in the world.

Chapter Twenty-five

'Right, so our solicitor's come back to us and said his solicitor – a man who's probably got a qualification online, by the sound of him – has asked for one hundred thousand pounds to make all this go away,' Harriet explained as they held an early morning meeting at Meadowbrook.

'Oh my God!' Freddie said as they all paled. 'That's ludicrous.'

'It is ridiculous. There's no medical report to support anything he's saying,' Connor stormed.

The problem was that no one was interested in the story of how William hadn't even needed as much as a plaster because as Hector said, who let truth stand in the way of a good story? The journalists were loving how the famous sanctuary, run by four 'spoilt' siblings, was under threat owing to negligence, possibly due to the wild parties thrown up at the house under the guise of the hotel ... or something like that.

'Our PR company's working overtime, but it's becoming increasingly clear that we're going to have to pay him off,' Harriet said.

They were in the kitchen at Meadowbrook, all of them, including Brooke and Hector, who were always around offering support. Pippa was trying to build bridges with

Brooke, but she was still unhappy with Pippa about Harvey. She hadn't said as much, but the atmosphere was still frosty between them.

'But surely not that much?' Hector asked.

'No, we're going to go in with a low counter offer. I want to offer him a few hundred pounds, but the solicitor says it'll be thousands, although nothing like they've asked. If we tell the press that they're asking for that much it might cast doubts on them about William, as well, or so I'm hoping.'

'I wish there was another way,' Connor said. 'I feel so responsible.'

'Stop that, Con,' Harriet said. 'I need you to stop this self-flagellation. After all, the animals need you, I need you and so does your son.' Her voice was soft.

'No one but William is to blame,' Brooke stormed.

'I quite agree, Brooke,' Pippa said.

Brooke gave her a short smile. Things were thawing a bit between them since Brooke's outburst the other day.

'So, our next move?' Gus asked.

'I'm going to leave it in the hands of the solicitors and also our PR company. If we pay him off, we'll make him sign a statement saying he overreacted. It's really all we can think of,' Harriet said. She sounded defeated and Harriet hated that. 'But if it saves the sanctuary from further trouble then it'll be worth it.'

'By the way, Pippa,' Connor said. 'Thank you for holding our sponsors off; at least they haven't deserted us. Yet.'

'They won't,' Pippa said. 'I'll speak to them personally to make sure of it, it's the least I can do.'

'They love you, Pippa,' Gus said. 'If anyone can charm them then it's you.'

As everyone murmured in agreement, Pippa flushed.

'I still think we should see if we can do something else about this,' Brooke said.

'Like what?' Freddie asked.

'Surely we're not just going to give into this man? And what about Lucky?' Brooke threw her arms up in despair.

Her voice was full of passion; Brooke did love the animals, that much was clear.

'Brooke, what choice do we have?' Gus said.

'I never give in, Brooke,' Harriet explained. 'But short of getting William to withdraw the allegation, we don't have a choice.'

'And he's made it clear he's not withdrawing,' Freddie said. 'Although we could send Edie in ... she'll think she's seducing him, but actually she might terrify him into agreeing to drop it.'

'We're not sending Edie in.' Harriet almost smiled. 'The thing is that we need to ensure Lucky keeps his life. He's happy with Gwen and Gerry, and I want to keep it that way.' She stood up to indicate that the discussion was over.

Pippa could see how much it was costing them and it was nothing to do with money. They hated being defeated and it seemed a loner called William who they thought would give a loving home to one of their dogs was actually managing to defeat them. Pippa dreaded to think what their father would make of it, but then no one, not even she, had any idea how to fix this.

'How's it going?' she asked as Hector sat in the bar with his laptop.

They hadn't really seen each other since Harvey had been and Pippa felt nervous around him.

'Pretty good. All on plan, so fingers crossed, it'll be all right,' he grinned.

'You know, you sound nervous when you talk about your new book.' She sat down next to him. 'But your first book was so brilliant that I really don't see that you have anything to worry about.'

'Thanks, Pippa,' he flushed with pleasure. 'You know, all the reviewers who said nice things about the book, most of them said it was surprisingly good, but your words meant the most. The fact you even read it meant the world to me.'

Pippa felt emotional. 'Really? Of course I read it! I was so proud you even wrote a book. It's a huge achievement. And then it got published, which is even better. You know, I don't find reading easy, but I was hooked, honestly, and I can't wait to read your new one, and I mean that.'

'I hope it lives up to expectations. You know, when you have one hit, it's such a worry that the next one will disappoint. I know I don't come across as insecure, but one of the reasons I wanted to write here was that I felt safe here, among friends, secure.'

'Oh, Hector, I had no idea.'

Pippa realised she took Hector and his bravado for granted. She liked having him around because he always had time for her, was always interested in her and made her feel as if she had a good friend, but did she do the same for him?

'When we're together, do you think I only care about myself?' she asked, feeling vulnerable.

What if she was a bad friend? What if that was what Brooke picked up on?

'Of course not. You even listen to me blather on for hours about the book and storylines. When I need to get out and clear my head, you always make time to come with me. You're one of the least selfish people I know.'

'Thank goodness for that. I was beginning to feel that I was self-absorbed.'

'What's brought this on?'

Hector's forehead wrinkled, which made him look even more attractive, for some reason. Pippa had to admit, writer, Hector, with his laptop, his hair askew from where he kept running his hands through it, was incredibly hot. She pushed those thoughts away.

'I don't know. Brooke said that I hadn't taken account of your feelings, you know, with the Harvey thing...' she shrugged.

'Pippa! My dear, sweet Pippa. I'm immensely jealous of Harvey, of course I am, and I think he's far too old for you and a bit of a twit from what I've heard, but you've made it clear you see me as a friend. I kind of keep a bit of hope alive ... Anyway, Brooke's a bit protective of me. We've become close. But if Harvey makes you happy then I'll just have to accept that and move on.'

Despite the fact he sounded sincere and mature, Pippa wondered why his words didn't make her feel happy. In fact, she felt a stab of something akin to disappointment.

'So, in the interest of that friendship, would you like to do something this afternoon? I think I could do with a change of scene.'

'I'd love to, Pippa, but...' He glanced at his phone. 'I've arranged to do something with Brooke, so we'll need to take a rain check.'

Pippa watched from a distance – behind a pillar – as Hector met Brooke by the front door. She was dressed up, jeans instead

270

of gym clothes, a smart jacket and her hair brushed. Hector kissed her cheek and as she hugged him, Pippa could see they were genuinely happy to see each other. She watched as they left the house and then, unable to resist, she made her way to the front door. She hung back as she saw them walk down the drive. They weren't touching but they were standing close and she could see warmth between them as they turned to each other to chat.

Pippa wasn't stalking them exactly, but she couldn't help but follow – at a safe distance, naturally. If they saw her, she'd tell them she was going to see Harriet. Actually,she might go and see Harriet. She hadn't had a debrief about Harvey yet and that would be a good excuse. She darted behind a bush as Brooke seemed to turn around but, heart pumping, she got away with it. She carried on, still at a fairly safe distance, as they disappeared out of the drive.

They both stopped to chat to Ginny, who was walking up from the village, and again Pippa found a wall to stand behind. She looked around the corner and ducked back as Ginny approached. By the time she felt safe to step out again, they'd disappeared into the village. They could have gone to the pub, or to the shops, or maybe they were just going to carry on walking. Pippa knew it was silly and she needed to put a stop to this nonsense. Besides, she wasn't a good stalker anyway and her nerves certainly weren't up to it, so she turned back.

Chapter Twenty-six

Pippa knocked on Harriet's door after her aborted attempt at following Brooke and Hector, hoping she'd be there and not at one of her ever-increasing mummy groups.

'What are you doing here?' Harriet said as she opened the door.

She was in the process of giving Toby a bottle, clutching him to her.

'I didn't get the chance to talk to you properly this morning, but I couldn't sleep last night. Or not properly. After Harvey left, I got to thinking and I needed to talk to you.'

'Pip, he's an arrogant knob.'

'Don't sugar-coat it.'

'He's not like Mark, or like Edward was, but he's so wrapped up in his own brilliance. Do you realise that at dinner he didn't ask any of us any questions, apart from whether I missed the city?'

'I hadn't noticed that.' She'd definitely noticed that, but she was embarrassed to admit it. 'But it was the first time he'd met you. Fred met him when he was staying here and he liked him.'

'Yes, but as Freddie said, he was with his team. He was

definitely the boss and in work mode. He hasn't met him socially and we have.'

'But when we're alone, he's nothing like that,' Pippa protested.

'Pip, if you like him we'll give him a chance. For once, I'm not suspicious of his motives. He clearly adores you by the way he looks at you. But, if I'm honest, I don't understand why you'd want to be with him. He's over ten years older than you and he doesn't want any more kids. So can you really see a future?'

'I wasn't thinking that far ahead,' she lied. 'You know, Harriet, I've been married to the bloody hotel for over a year now and I never complained, but I'm lonely. I'm sick of being the only member of our family who's alone and so if I want to have a bit of happiness, is that so bad?' Pippa felt like crying.

'No, Pip, it's not.' Harriet's eyes filled with sympathy. 'It's just that we love you and want the best for you.'

'What if Harvey's that?'

Pippa decided to ignore the baby thing for now; after all, they wouldn't be ready for that discussion for a long time. But for now she just wanted to feel the way he made her feel. That she was special, and wanted, and not alone.

'Then you'll have our support. If that's what you want. Now, can you hold your nephew while I go and make us coffee?'

Harriet thrust Toby into Pippa's arms and he smiled at her, with the most beautiful smile she'd ever seen. There was no way she didn't want a baby, she sighed, and it was as if Harriet was trying to remind her of that having given birth to the most beautiful one in the world.

They kept away from the topic of Harvey as they drank coffee and cooed over Toby. Pippa began to feel herself relax. She and Harvey had parted on good terms, he was oblivious to the effect he'd had on her family and they were going to sort out a time for her go to London; although she couldn't take yet another weekend off work. If she was honest, the dinner had damped her ardour for Harvey slightly. Harriet was right – he was opinionated and not interested in anyone else. And every time she tried to talk about the sanctuary or her family, he firmly changed the subject.

'Are you all right?' Harriet asked.

'I don't know, Harry. Honestly, I want a relationship, that's the truth, and maybe Harvey isn't right for me, but I'm beginning to hate being alone. At first the hotel was enough, but now it's up and running and everything's going well, I want more. I want a personal life. I don't want to be alone.'

'Come on; let's take Toby for a walk. He needs a sleep and we could do with some fresh air. And, Pip, you're amazing and everyone loves you. Including Hector. Especially Hector.'

'Hector doesn't love me. Why can't anyone get it? He just thinks he does,' she snapped.

Harriet threw her hands up in surrender.

'OK, I give up, I'll get my coat.'

On the walk they established some banned subjects – Harvey, Hector ... anything involving Pippa, in fact – but Harriet was right, the fresh air was good. It was a little breezy but bright and the sun was peeping from behind the clouds. Harriet pushed the pram and Pippa tried to relax a bit. With Harvey, she didn't need to throw herself into making any decisions – she just had to keep telling herself that.

'You know, I wouldn't hurt Hector,' Pippa said. 'That's why I kept Harvey away from him.'

'Oh, Pip, we know that, you're the loveliest.' Harriet gave Pippa's hand a squeeze. 'But we do feel that you don't take his feelings seriously. Not that it matters – he and Brooke were getting very close over the weekend, so you never know. Maybe if they got together then everyone would be happy.'

'He said they were just friends,' Pippa said defensively, without knowing why.

'OK, but would you have a problem if they did get together?' Harriet asked.

'Honestly, Harry, I've got no idea.'

Harriet stopped walking.

'What?' Pippa asked, banging into the pram.

'Sorry, my phone vibrated, I want to check it's not the solicitor.' Harriet pulled it out of her pocket, read the message and turned to Pippa. 'It's Brooke. She's asked us to meet her up at the house, urgently.'

'Why?' Pippa asked. Brooke, again ...

'No idea, but she said it's urgent, so come on.'

By the time they made the kitchen at Meadowbrook – which was empty of staff as they had the day off and there were no guests until the following day – Freddie, Hector and Brooke were all sat around the table.

'What's going on?' Harriet asked.

'No Connor?' Brooke asked.

Her cheeks were flushed a slight pink colour and she did look very beautiful.

'No, he's at the surgery, up to his ears in appointments this afternoon,' Harriet explained.

'What is going on?' Pippa asked.

275

'Can we wait for Gus and Amanda? They'll be here in a second; they're just finishing up in the garden,' Brooke said.

'No Gemma?' Harriet asked.

'She's at college. While we're waiting, you know tonight is the night I'm going to pop the question, don't you?' Freddie said.

'Of course! Your special dinner is under control,' Pippa smiled.

She was so proud of her brother. And delighted that Gemma would be her sister. So, it was in-law, but that was good enough. It made her family and although they already felt Gemma was part of their family, it would be lovely to have it official. She knew that it would give Gemma the security she needed, too.

'And I've got the vintage champagne chilling,' she added. 'It's all going to be perfect,' she smiled, her mood improved by the thought of her brother that evening.

'And Brooke and I are going out for the evening, so you'll have the place to yourselves,' Hector said.

Pippa felt surprised. No one had asked her to join them. Was Hector really annoyed with her about Harvey? He seemed fine with her earlier that day. Or was it that Brooke was still annoyed, which made more sense? Or was Harriet right and they were getting together?

'I'll go to Harry's, then,' Pippa suggested.

No one said anything. She was relieved when Gus and Amanda appeared at the kitchen door.

'God, it's a bit cold out there now. And the rain's starting so your timing's good,' Amanda said, sitting down next to Pippa and giving her a hug.

Pippa hugged her back. Amanda had a way of making her feel better.

'So, *now* can we find out what this is about?' Harriet asked. 'Toby'll be awake in a minute and screaming, no doubt.'

'OK, guys, I need you to listen to this,' said Brooke.

Brooke looked pleased with herself, Pippa thought as she put her phone in the middle of the table and turned the volume on speaker. A voice rang out:

'*Hey, William, how are you?*' Brooke's voice said.

'*Not grand with all this stuff going on, you know, with the dog,*' they heard William reply.

'*Let me buy you a drink, it must be awful,*' Brooke said.

She pressed the button.

Pippa narrowed her eyes. 'What's going on?' she asked.

'I bought him a drink and then I sat with him. You see, I spoke to John, the vicar, who reiterated how the morris dancers had helped out with security in the past, and I asked them to see if they could find out anything about the situation.'

'What, with William and Lucky?' Harriet narrowed her eyes, too.

'They asked around – discreetly, John assured me – but anyhow, they found out that not only is William a bit of a drinker, but he also walks Lucky over by Topps Farm just on the edge of the village.'

'Which means?' Pippa tried not to sound impatient.

'My investigators then informed me that Topps Farm were having a massive rabbit-shooting thing going on and so there was a lot of gunfire.' Brooke's voice was serious as she explained all this.

Gosh! she really had embraced Meadowbrook, Pippa

thought, if she was taking the morris dancers as investigators that seriously.

'What the hell?' Harriet said.

'Listen to this ...'

She pressed play and as William's and Brooke's conversation filled the room, no one dared breathe.

Pippa's mouth dropped open.

'Does he know you recorded this?' Harriet asked.

'No, not yet. You see, I knew from the vicar that William always went to the pub for an early lunchtime drink, so I've been going there and buying him the odd pint to get to know him. After the intel from the morris dancers, I knew I had to get him talking. It's taken a few goes but, finally, today I got the confession.'

'But how did you know that he'd confess?' Gus asked.

'I didn't, but I was pretty sure from the outset that this wasn't right. We all knew Lucky was a gentle dog but terrified of loud noises, so when John told me about the farm shoots, we thought it seemed likely that that could have happened. Especially as William drinks a fair bit, so he might have forgotten that Lucky was nervous. Anyway, John and I thought it was worth a try and if it hadn't worked, we'd have thought of something else.'

Brooke explained her plan and once again, Pippa felt guilty. She'd really put her heart and soul into trying to sort out the situation with Lucky. She'd got the morris dancers involved, for goodness' sake, and she'd given over her time to go and see William numerous times. That explained where she and Hector were going to when Pippa attempted to follow them. Now, it all made sense. It would teach Pippa not to be suspicious of her anymore.

It turned out William *had* walked Lucky near Topps Farm when they were shooting and it was the sound of the gun that caused the dog to nip him. The poor dog was innocent and William, who'd probably had a few pints, panicked. Then once he'd been bitten, he didn't want to admit it was his fault, so he blamed the sanctuary. Anyway, as he was already in the lie, it seemed to grow from there until he actually found he liked the attention, at which point he thought he might make some cash from it.

'How did you get him to confess?' Harriet asked, her eyes wide in wonder.

'Three pints and four whisky chasers. I might have planted the seed that I was glad he was doing something to bring the Singers down a peg or two, made out I didn't like you very much – sorry about that ... But then eventually he confessed, which is the bit you heard. I've got hours of recording and kept it all so they can't say we edited it, but to be honest, I think if you just tell him you know the truth, he'll back off. He's not a bad person, but he is a bit of a sad drunk, as far as I can tell,' Brooke said.

'Wow! You're a genius.' Harriet jumped up and hugged Brooke. 'How on earth will we ever thank you?' she asked.

'I don't need thanks,' Brooke blushed. 'I just wanted to make sure the sanctuary and the animals were going to be all right. And Lucky, of course. And all of you.'

'Well, Brooke, you're a superstar. None of us could think straight in all this, so thank goodness you were so clever,' Gus beamed. 'Harry, go and tell Connor right away!'

'I'll call him now, and then I'm going to call the solicitor and get him to confront William. We'll say that we won't make a fuss as long as he retracts the allegation and tells the truth to the press. Brooke, you're my hero!' Harriet was already in practical mode. 'But, Brooke, you're now going to stay at the hotel for as long as you want for free,' Harriet said. 'It's absolutely the least we can do to thank you for saving us not just a huge amount of money, but also the sanctuary.'

There was a round of applause at the table as everyone beamed.

'I agree. Brooke, you're now officially part of our family.' Freddie gave her a massive hug.

'I told her she was more than a pretty face,' Hector added.

'Well, I'm just so grateful, I know everyone will be. Brooke, none of us knew what to do and you did,' Amanda said.

'And of course the morris dancers will have to be rewarded,' Gus said.

'We'll buy them new bells!' Freddie quipped.

'I think it was just because I'm not so close to it that I could take a step back and be more practical. And by the way, Hector helped me with the plan, he needs some credit, too.'

'I wasn't the brains behind it, Brooke was. I was just there for moral support,' Hector said magnanimously.

'Well done both of you,' Pippa said, hoping that perhaps now Brooke and she could put the bad feeling behind them. After all, she'd done it for them – she really had proved herself. Pippa found she had tears in her eyes. 'I mean it, I don't know what we'd have done without you.'

'Thank you, Pippa,' Brooke said warmly with a big smile. 'I just wanted to make sure that Meadowbrook Sanctuary and all of you were all right,' she added.

'Hector, you're a marvel. You shall stay here for free, too,' Harriet said.

Pippa startled. Was Harriet drunk? They were overjoyed,

it was clear, and of course it was all thanks to Brooke, but Harriet, giving something away? Pippa felt her eyes sting with tears of relief. She really did feel grateful to Brooke and, of course, Hector.

'I wouldn't dream of it. I just gave Brooke a bit of support, it was really all her,' Hector replied gallantly.

The news was spread and everyone was overjoyed. The solicitor was charged with dealing with William, the PR company was going to start spreading the word in the press and Freddie said when he got the green light, he'd attack social media. He was happy to have something to do to take his mind of the imminent proposal.

'So, do you think you'll have the wedding here?' Brooke asked as they moved on from Lucky.

'It's up to Gemma, but probably. We met here, after all; we had our first kiss in the garden. I know the hotel's busy in the summer, but I'd like a spring or summer wedding so we can make the most of the garden,' Freddie said.

'You surprise me with how romantic you can be sometimes,' Pippa said, 'and we'd love to have the wedding here, regardless of the bookings, but it's up to Gem.'

'But you should help organise it. Our wedding was organised by Pippa, mostly, and she did such a brilliant job,' Amanda said.

'Thank you,' Pippa replied. 'Right, I think it's time for us all to celebrate,' she giggled.

'Hey! that's normally my line,' Freddie replied.

'Do you think he's done it yet?' Harriet asked as they sat in her living room drinking champagne.

Connor was practically dancing around. The weight he'd

been carrying on his shoulders had lifted and that was of course thanks to Brooke. They were virtually going to name a building after her at this rate. Or at least another animal. Connor's face looked back to normal and the worry lines he'd been wearing lately had disappeared. And although Pippa was still struggling with Brooke, she felt lighter, happier and relieved, too.

'No, Gemma or Fred would text as soon as he has,' Pippa said.

She was desperate to see Gemma, or to hear from her. She could only imagine how happy she'd be. Pippa was happy for them, but she was definitely ready for some of the happiness to come her way. With Harvey, maybe...

'God, I almost can't believe that Freddie'll be a married man soon,' Connor laughed.

'I know, but he's doing it for Gemma, really. That must be true love,' Harriet pointed out.

'Would you marry me?' Connor asked.

'As proposals go that's pretty weak, but no, because I know it's not important to you and nor is it to me. Toby's the only commitment we need.'

Harriet reached across and kissed Connor in a rare display of affection and Pippa burst into tears.

'I don't know what's wrong with me. Do you think all this is because I'm lonely?' She felt more tears welling up.

'Why don't you call Harvey and see if you can visit him this week? You can't go at the weekend as the hotel's busy and Freddie's off, but perhaps during the week for a night or two?' Harriet suggested, giving her sister a hug. 'It might do you some good and also stop you from feeling lonely.'

'But we don't like him—' Connor started.

'*We* aren't dating him. The break'll do you good.' Harriet sounded genuinely concerned for her.

'That's a good idea. I'll call him later. I want to celebrate with Gemma and Freddie first but then maybe I can go for a couple of nights later this week.'

The texts came through to their phones at the same time:

She said yes!

They refilled their champagne glasses and toasted the latest soon-to-be Singer.

Chapter Twenty-seven

She'd decided to take up Harriet's suggestion of a quick midweek break, as escaping to London seemed like her best bet right at this moment. She'd be back long before the weekend when the hotel was full once again, and Freddie and Gemma were going away for the weekend to celebrate their engagement, so she'd be busy, busy, busy. A couple of days' space would do her good. She needed to get her head together with everything going on, not that she was sure exactly what was going on.

'Isn't it great about Gemma and Freddie!' Pippa said to Brooke when Freddie, Pippa, Hector, Brooke and herself were all celebrating the engagement in the hotel bar late on the Monday night.

'Sure is,' Brooke replied, beaming. 'So, let me see the ring again, Gemma.'

Brooke was so excited for Gemma and Freddie. With the Lucky situation having been resolved, all was well between them again. Pippa had been slightly tentative with Brooke, in case she was still upset with her, but Brooke had been nothing but lovely to her so she'd relaxed around her. It was clear that Brooke had proved herself a worthy friend to them and Pippa had told her as much. She was surprised to see how emotional this made Brooke and they'd embraced. It seemed Brooke had forgiven her, after all.

'Can you believe it?' Gemma said. 'I thought, you know, earlier this year, that Freddie was so against marriage we'd never do it!'

'Well, he obviously saw sense, and I can't wait until you're officially my sister,' Pippa giggled.

'Of course, I want you to be my maid of honour. Oh my God, I can't believe it.' Gemma was radiating happiness.

'Are you going to have a long engagement? Oh, don't leave it too long. I can't wait for us to plan the wedding together,' Pippa said.

Gemma had engulfed Pippa in another huge hug while Brooke looked on.

'And as you're going to be sticking around to set up your business then you'll be here for the wedding, won't you?' Pippa asked Brooke.

'Hey, try keeping me away.'

All was well between them again.

'You know I'm going to be working most of the time?' Harvey said as he let her into his very smart, very minimal, modern house.

She wasn't sure what she expected, but it was clear that this was somewhere he'd simply bought, got a decorator to furnish and that was it. It was devoid of personal touches and also personality, she thought, although it was clear that the house was worth a fortune.

'I know, and that's fine,' Pippa replied, hugging Harvey. 'I just wanted to get away. I can go shopping, or maybe even to an art gallery, there's plenty to occupy myself with.'

'Great, but right now how about you occupy yourself with me?'

She did just that.

She'd been glad to get away. As soon as she'd sat on the train from Bath, she felt relieved to be leaving Meadowbrook and she didn't know why. It was perhaps the stress of the last few weeks, which, thanks to Brooke, was definitely over now. The press had printed the story, William was barred from The Parker's Arms, Lucky was officially now Gwen's and Gerry's dog, and all was well. Pippa had managed to speak to all the sponsors and they were fully behind the sanctuary once more. The publicity had even attracted more donations. And it was all thanks to Brooke. Pippa may have found her difficult to figure out at times, but now she'd seen her caring side, she was fully in the Brooke Walker fan club, along with everyone else.

Harvey didn't finish work until eight the following night, but she was meeting him at a restaurant in the city. Pippa had hit the shops to go and buy Gemma and Freddie an engagement gift, but she had no idea what on earth to get the couple who had everything, so she decided to speak to Gus and Harriet and perhaps they could club in together. She was so thrilled for Freddie and Gemma, she really was. She also vowed that it wouldn't force her to try to turn her and Harvey's fledging relationship into something it wasn't yet. Last night had been fun and passionate, but when she'd tried to talk to him about the Lucky situation and Brooke, he'd glazed over. He said he was pleased it was resolved but quickly changed the subject. It seemed Harvey was interested in talking about work, both hers and his, to be fair to him, but not personal stuff.

She couldn't help but think about conversations she'd had with Hector when they were alone. She'd talked about her fears, her hopes and everything, but she couldn't do that with Harvey. Actually, she could, but he made it clear he didn't want to listen. If he didn't like the sound of what she was saying, he'd cut her off, make a joke or just blatantly change the subject. She was learning that although she was having fun with him, was attracted to him – and she'd be lying if she said she didn't enjoy the passion – she was feeling more and more that they were never going to have the emotional connection, which she so craved. If only Hector could have Harvey's maturity, his age and his raw sexual attraction, or if Harvey could have Hector's mind, then she'd have the perfect man.

She pushed those thoughts away, because they were ridiculous, and she spotted Harvey making his way towards her. Her smile dropped when she noticed he had another man with him.

'Pippa, this is James. James, Pippa. Sorry, but we have a work situation we need to discuss, so I suggested he join us for dinner.'

As James shook Pippa's hand, she literally had no words.

She didn't know a bond from a future, she realised, as she tried to keep track of the conversation that didn't involve her at all. There'd been an issue with certain trades that day and James, who hadn't been part of the team-building exercise at Meadowbrook, and Harvey discussed it in a very animated way while Pippa ate her food and drank too much wine for something to do. She felt beyond awkward and was relieved when just as their main courses were cleared, James stood up.

'So sorry to have gatecrashed your dinner, but we're done now. See you in the office tomorrow, Harvey.'

'How was your dinner?' Harvey asked.

'Slightly dull,' Pippa replied.

'Don't start! I warned you when you wanted to come up here that I had work all week and you said you'd fit around it.'

'I know, I know. Shhorry. It's jus' been good to get away and I'm grateful, really, but to be fair, I've had too muuush to drink.' She could hear herself talking and her words were slurred. She giggled. Who cared if he talked about work? Who cared about anything?

'Right, well in that case, I'd better get you home. And I've got an early start tomorrow.'

''Course you have,' Pippa hiccupped as he paid the bill and then helped her up.

The two days had flown by, she realised as she took the train home. But as soon as she boarded the train, she also realised that she'd made a decision about Harvey. That morning, he'd left at five so he could go to the gym for an hour before work and Pippa knew, clearly now, if she hadn't before, that this wasn't going anywhere. She wasn't going to fall in love with him and he didn't really know her, didn't seem interested enough in getting to know her enough to fall in love with her. So, it was probably best to leave it where it was. They'd had a bit of fun, it'd been nice at times, but before she let herself get entangled with him, it was best to call it a day. All his gushing texts and fawning over her meant nothing in the scheme of things. Their relationship, or whatever it was, had ended before it had begun.

She had a feeling he wouldn't be exactly heartbroken. She grinned. She was growing up! She'd dated *and* she'd decided to break up with a man. This was the first time in her life that she'd done so. She was feeling a little proud of herself, in fact. Perhaps Freddie wasn't the only one who was behaving like an adult now.

She felt better coming back to the hotel. Renewed, in some ways. As soon as she put her bags in her apartment, she checked in with the staff then went to find Freddie. He was in the office, putting in the drinks order.

'How are you?' she asked, giving him a hug.

'Pretty good. Being engaged seems to suit me somewhat. How are you? You certainly seem to have a spring in your step!'

'That's because I'm the opposite of you. I've decided to call it a day with Harvey.'

'Really? Goodness, Pip, not like you to make such decisions.'

'I know, I know, I normally wait until it goes horribly wrong. The thing is that I liked Harvey, although no one else seems to, but he's so committed to his work and to be honest, I find him a bit dull. He doesn't seem interested in me, or my family, so I had an epiphany that there wasn't a future for us, so best not to waste anymore time with him.'

'That makes sense. Anyway, I'm going to finish this order then I'm off. I have to pack. We're going first thing tomorrow morning.'

'And are you going to tell me where you're going?'

'Actually, and please don't take the mickey, I'm taking Gemma to Paris.'

'Romantic.'

'I've booked an amazingly expensive hotel and we've got a whole weekend planned: Eiffel Tower, the river Seine, the Louvre...'

'Gosh, you're really doing the tourist thing.' Pippa was impressed; it wasn't like Freddie.

'Gemma's never been to Paris. And I didn't want it to be a cliché and propose there, so I thought I'd propose then take her for a really romantic weekend. I'll also give us the chance to do all the touristy things that she's never done.'

'Fred, she'll love it. You're the best fiancé in the world.'

'I am, aren't I?'

'Is there anything I should know?' Pippa asked.

'Yes, you need to do the final Easter event meeting on Sunday, but it's all organised pretty much. Can't believe it's nearly Easter already. Hector was asking after you, so maybe you'd have a word with him. I think he's a bit worried about being Humpty Dumpty.'

'Honestly, I think that's the least of his worries, but I wanted to see him. Is he in his room?'

'As far as I know.'

Pippa felt nervous as she knocked. They hadn't really talked since the Harvey thing and with Brooke being so angry with her, she wasn't sure if Hector was or not.

'Hello,' Hector's reassuringly familiar voice rang out.

She pushed the door open.

'Can I come in?' she asked.

Hector was at the desk, typing away.

'Sure, I need a break, anyway.' He turned to face her.

'Freddie said you're having second thoughts about being Humpty.'

'I'm not, really. The thing is that I know it'll make great publicity and I want to do that, but I don't want to seem silly.'

'Oh, Hector, there's nothing silly about Humpty Dumpty,' she laughed. 'I think the angle we'll go for is that you're so committed to our charity and so good with kids that you were willing to do this. And you're a star, we all think so.'

'Even you?' Hector smiled sadly.

'Especially me. I know we haven't chatted much, but every time I've seen you recently, Brooke's been with you.'

'Oh, she's great, isn't she? She's been giving me PT, which I need, because despite the fact I look in peak physical condition, it turns out I'm not.'

They both laughed. Pippa missed this, laughing with Hector. Harvey had made her laugh at first, but when they were in London, she only giggled when she was horribly drunk.

'You seem OK to me.'

Pippa treaded carefully. She knew that if she complimented him too much, she'd be in trouble for flirting, but she didn't want not to be his friend.

'Yes, well, Brooke's really helping and she's so much fun to be around. I'm enjoying her company immensely.'

Hector looked a little embarrassed. Pippa decided to change the subject.

'Right, well, I've got to get on, but how about we have supper tonight? In the bar. The dining room's only half-full, but I think I'd rather not eat with the guests – you know, me being staff and all,' Pippa suggested.

'I'll tell you what, let's do that, and Brooke can join us.'

'I'll go and invite her now,' Pippa suggested.

'This little piggy ... Oh! Hi, Pippa,' Brooke said as Pippa tracked her down in the drawing room, where she was looking after Toby.

Pippa had seen Brooke with Toby before but it still struck her how natural she was with him. But then she was with everyone. Once again, Pippa was hit by how composed she was for someone so young and she tried not to feel envious of that. Toby grinned and Pippa melted.

'You on babysitting duties?' she asked.

'Only for a bit. Harriet had to find something in the office and so I got to steal him away. He's gorgeous, isn't he?'

'Oh yes, he is.'

Toby rewarded them with another smile.

'How was your time away?' Brooke asked without hostility.

'You'll probably be pleased to know that I'm not seeing Harvey again,' Pippa said.

'Oh, Pippa, if you're unhappy, of course I'm not pleased. You know, it's just that Hector—'

'I know, my entire family wants us to be together and you seem to, too.'

'I think we care about you both and want you both to be happy,' Brooke explained.

'Well, the three of us can have supper tonight, if you promise not to do any matchmaking!' Pippa said.

'I'd love that,' Brooke replied.

It seemed that since Lucky and now her decision about Harvey, she and Brooke were really in a good place once again.

In the end, the three of them ate in the kitchen.

'You know, since the hotel's been quieter and I've taken a bit more time off, I've realised how nice that is to have more of a balance,' she said.

The three of them were quite comfortable together and dinner was turning out to be fun.

'Well, you know what they say – all work and no play,' Brooke teased.

'But she's got Harvey now,' Hector said, staring at his plate.

'Harvey and I are just friends,' Pippa said carefully. 'I mean, I probably won't really see him again, unless he has to do another team-building thing here,' she explained.

She tried not to notice how happy Hector looked.

'I'm glad you're OK about it,' Brooke said, breaking the silence.

'Oh yes, fine. By the way, how's Chris doing? Is he happy to be a chicken still?'

Pippa's lips curled. Brooke had proved to be a good sport yet again by deciding to be a chicken for the Easter event and Chris had apparently reluctantly agreed, as well.

'Chris is fine, great, so busy with plans for the new gym, but he's still coming to the Easter event. I mean, we won't let you down. But you know, the studio'll be ready soon, so I've decided I'm definitely going to stay in the UK.'

'That's great!' Hector said.

'At the hotel?' Pippa asked.

After all, Harriet said she could stay as long as she wanted for free to thank her for saving the sanctuary; although perhaps not forever.

'Are you sure you're happy with me staying now I'm not paying?' Brooke asked, looking worried.

'You know, we're delighted you're staying and want you to stay for as long as you want,' Pippa reassured. 'I just wondered if you were happy here, that's all.'

'I can't stay here forever. As lovely as Meadowbrook is, I know it's not my home. But if Chris and I do progress with the gym I'll probably move nearby, so I won't be too far.'

'And then I'm going to help Brooke find her father's family,' Hector announced.

'I know I should have done it by now, but I'm scared, you see,' Brooke said.

'Of what?' Pippa asked.

'Rejection. I've faced a lot of it in my life and if I track down my father's relatives ... what if they don't want me?'

She sounded genuinely scared, Pippa thought.

'Why wouldn't they want you?' Pippa said. 'You're fabulous! Look how much everyone here loves you.' It was true, they did. 'You've become such a part of Meadowbrook and any family you find would be lucky to have you.' Pippa surprised herself, with her words, but she saw the vulnerability in Brooke, something she hadn't seen in a while, and she was young, on her own. Pippa felt her heart go out to her and she wanted to reach out. 'In fact, if you want any more help, we'll all muck in,' she announced.

'Thank you. I might just take you up on that,' she said.

'I think we should start by looking after the Easter event,' Hector said. 'As long as I'm in one piece after being Humpty, of course.'

'That'd be great,' Brooke said. 'Guys, I really appreciate this. I've got names and places in my room, so when we're ready we can start with the Internet, I guess.'

'You haven't looked at all?'

'No. I'm too scared they won't want anything to do with me. And then what? I'll be rejected by yet another family.' Brooke suddenly burst into tears.

'Oh, Brooke, I'm sure they won't reject you,' Pippa offered, feeling a little heartbroken.

She might complain of loneliness, but she didn't know what it was to feel alone, not in the way Brooke clearly did, and she was so lucky for that.

Chapter Twenty-eight

As always, the Easter event was going to be a huge celebration. Not only had they saved the sanctuary, but also the positive press after William admitted that he was the cause of Lucky's distress had brought in new donors, and some very big ones at that. Harriet had started a new private sponsorship scheme and they'd acquired three baby donkeys, who Gerald loved, four more pigs and another alpaca, who thankfully Samantha and Sebastian had welcomed without any spite on their part. There were more dogs and cats coming in all the time, but the adoption drive meant that – post William – they were still finding homes for some of their animals. It was never enough, but at least that side seemed to be growing. After the unfortunate incident with William, though, they'd decided to add an extra home visit to their adoption process as part of a more vigilant check on each person or family.

Pippa had been frantically running around as the hotel was getting busier and she was interviewing more staff to carry them through the busy period. Corporate bookings were increasing and Harvey had, indeed, spread the word about Meadowbrook, as they now had other groups booked in from his bank. They were still talking on occasion, Harvey and herself, but they agreed to remain just friends. But then as they weren't really friends in the first place, that wasn't going to happen.

Pippa was surprised by the fact that she didn't mind. She'd almost gone through her first adult relationship decision, one that hadn't been forced on her by either a scamming husband or a cheating boyfriend. She felt as if she was finally growing up. But she also acknowledged that the short time she spent with Harvey had made her realise that she was ready for a relationship. Although she knew it wouldn't be easy, what with managing the hotel, she'd also learnt that things didn't fall apart when she wasn't there. Harriet said she was becoming more like her, so maybe it was time to concentrate on her personal life and not be such a workaholic. It was as if Pippa needed to find a life balance. She'd gone from not working at all to being all-consumed by work, so now she needed a middle ground. It was her Easter resolution. If there was such a thing.

She still felt nervous as she went down to the field at the crack of dawn to get ready for the day. They were blessed, fingers crossed, with a rain-free forecast. It was a relatively warm day and it felt as if spring was finally here after what seemed to be a very long winter.

The field was quiet but Pippa had expected to be the first there. Gerry had built the wall where Hector – Humpty – would sit, with crash mats placed either side. The Easter egg hunt was set to be held in one of the enclosed gardens, a little similar to the one they'd made last year when they had the Peter Rabbit theme. There were stalls set up for the raffle, bric-a-brac and also for the egg painting. And, of course, then there was the small marquee they'd used last year to serve refreshments.

It all looked ready to go as Pippa breathed in the early morning air and enjoyed the peace for a while, knowing how manic and exhausting the day would be, and that was as long as all went to plan. She was optimistic that this would be a great day for families. They'd pre-sold more tickets than last year and had more availability for others to attend on the day.

The hotel guests were made fully aware of the event when they'd booked. There was one family celebrating a seventieth birthday and both parents, two children and their partners, and two teenagers had said they'd love to join in. There was also a couple celebrating their anniversary who'd barely emerged from their room, so they didn't expect to see them. Vicky and the other staff were all there, holding the fort; although they were going to take turns to come down and help. The events at Meadowbrook brought out the best in everyone and it had become quite a draw from both Parker's Hollow and beyond. Pippa knew they could all be proud of that.

'Oh my God, I can't take it!' Pippa laughed, grabbing Gemma's arm for support as Hector appeared, trying to walk in his Humpty Dumpty outfit.

'He even makes being a walking egg kind of sexy,' Gemma grinned.

'Gemma, how could you?'

But Pippa had to admit that once he mastered walking, the egg, with Hector's face peeping out of it, was kind of cute.

'He's such a star for doing this,' Gemma said.

'I know, and then we've got Brooke and Chris PT dressed up as chickens, and Gerry as the Easter Bunny. It makes me feel as if I should be in some kind of costume.'

'I'm sure it could be arranged... At least we've got our

bunny ears on. Anyway, we might be needed to do some actual work today so it would hardly be practical,' Gemma laughed.

That was their excuse and they were sticking to it as the hordes of people began to arrive.

By the afternoon, Hector had fallen off his wall many times already and was a huge hit with the children. And their parents, of course. He'd been amazing, Pippa conceded. Even when the children missed hitting him with the foam eggs they'd made, he still pretended and fell off anyway to shrieks of laughter. Freddie was taking the money for the Humpty stall and he was almost crying with laughter as Hector struggled to get off the crash mats. He let him struggle for quite a while before going to help him each time.

Chris and Brooke had proved huge hits dressed as chickens. They'd been selling raffle tickets and doing silly dances, thoroughly entering into the spirit of the day. Pippa couldn't fault either of them – they were brilliant.

Gus's egg painting was also a huge hit and the refreshment tent was doing a roaring trade. The bric-a-brac and raffle were even making money, as no one got to walk past without parting with money. The Easter bonnet competition was being judged by Harriet, who in totally un-Harriet style gave prizes to each of them. She said it was becoming a mum that had made her do it, having made her soften towards children. Hopefully it was just hormones, Pippa thought, and next year she'd be back to her competitive self. Fleur and Hayley were looking after Toby most of the day, and Amanda and Gemma were floating around helping where it was needed.

Children lined up to feed the ponies and donkeys, supervised by Connor, and were largely on their best behaviour – the animals, that is, not the children. There had been one ropey moment when a ten-year-old boy climbed over into the chicken coop, but Elizabeth Bennet, Freddie's favourite chicken, had soon seen him off and, thankfully, he was in trouble with his parents rather than the sanctuary being blamed.

The children shrieked with happiness, the adults were talking and laughing, and, most importantly, they were parting with money. The animals were also all happy, which was the main thing. Gerald had eaten an Easter bonnet as per, which the children found hilarious, and the ponies lapped up the attention. By the time the morris dancers did their special Easter dance – which was pretty much like all their other dances – the day was hailed a great success and the sanctuary was back to where it should be, the awful Lucky situation firmly put behind them.

When things began to quieten down and she finally had five minutes, Pippa went to see Hector.

'You've been amazing,' she said genuinely.

'Thanks, Pippa. Do you want to join me on my wall?' He raised an eyebrow.

Pippa giggled and then climbed up.

'Nice wall you've got here,' she said.

'Isn't it just. Wow! I'm exhausted. Please tell me I don't have to fall off anymore.'

'You don't. Freddie's rounding up the stragglers to get them out of here and so you're free to go. You can even take your egg costume off, unless you've grown a little fond of it?' she teased.

'I think I will, I mean, I quite liked being an egg, though.'

'You're a good egg,' Pippa grinned.

'Too much egg-citement for one day. And before we get really carried away with egg jokes now we've finally "cracked it", I think I'll call it a day.'

They both laughed and before she knew it, Hector had grabbed her and flung her off the wall with him. As they landed, with her on top of him, they were helplessly laughing and Pippa had tears rolling down her face.

'Are you all right?' Brooke asked, still dressed as a chicken.

Pippa had told her that she and Chris were the cutest chickens she'd ever seen, which Brooke had found amusing. Chris was preening at all the compliments he received, as well. They were both good Meadowbrook sports.

'I've always wondered,' Hector said. 'What came first, the chicken or the egg?'

Leaving Brooke looking a little bemused, they collapsed laughing again.

'Well, Pip, you've pulled it off again,' Gemma said as they were about to go back to the hotel to get the evening's entertainment ready.

The Cooper family had the dining room to themselves, as the couple celebrating their anniversary had requested to dine in their room. Gwen had baked a birthday cake and they'd put plenty of champagne on ice. Normally after events, they had a big party at the house for all involved, but they couldn't do that tonight, so Pippa had organised it for the following Monday evening, when the hotel was briefly empty before the new guests arrived.

'We pulled it off! It was a team effort and everyone played such a huge part.' Pippa knew that she'd organised a lot of it – all the eggs for the children, the stall layout, the costumes

300

and so forth – but she felt as if her contribution was definitely mainly behind the scenes this year.

'I thought Chris was great – and Brooke, of course – but he made a fantastic chicken,' Gemma laughed.

'Amanda said that Fleur and Hayley were both trying to flirt with him. I mean, those teenagers flirting with an older guy dressed as a chicken ...! Luckily, Gus was too busy painting eggs to notice.'

'And with Fleur being in love and all!' Pippa laughed.

'Yes, well, apparently she said that flirting was all right and that she wouldn't act on it. Not that they stood a chance. Chris was a very professional chicken,' Gemma laughed.

'He was a good sport. And he'll be at the party on Monday night so we can thank him. You know, I think he and Brooke would make a good couple. I mean, they even looked good together as chickens.' Pippa wasn't sure where that had come from. 'Although as they work together I guess...'

'Yes, Brooke's told me that they both want to make some kind of business work here so they're keeping things purely professional,' Gemma replied.

'But that might change?'

'I don't think so. Also, Freddie seems to think that Brooke and Hector are having some kind of thing.'

'Really? Harriet implied the same but I haven't seen them as anything but friends,' Pippa said.

She knew that, very fleetingly, she'd wanted Hector and Brooke to get together in the past, but that was when she was worried Brooke might be interested in Freddie, which of course proved groundless. Now, she was more concerned that Brooke and Hector getting together would spell the end of her friendship with him.

'I'm not sure, but Freddie seems to think they're getting closer. Now we're engaged, he's trying to get everyone partnered off, so you'd better watch out,' said Gemma.

'Not sure there's anyone for him to try to fix me up with – and don't say Chris. He's not my type.'

'No, he's not, I agree. But you know, having dipped your toe in the water, so to speak, with Harvey...'

'I know, I was thinking the same. I certainly feel ready to date. But no more Tinder, please, or online dating. I might just have to start going out more. Oh God, I could even turn into a man-eater, you never know,' Pippa laughed.

'I can't think of anything less likely. Well, maybe I can – Freddie becoming one hundred percent sober.'

They both giggled like schoolgirls and Pippa felt happy. It had been a good day and she was still counting her blessings.

They reached the house and pulled themselves together.

That night, while the hotel bar was buzzing, Pippa noticed that Brooke and Hector were absent.

'Fred, do you know where Hector and Brooke are?' she asked.

It seemed that everyone talking about them potentially getting together had firmly put the idea in her head. And she had to admit, she didn't love it...

'Yes, he's taken her for dinner in Bath; I lent him my car. Said it wasn't an actual date, though. Apparently, she needed cheering up because she's worried about her family rejecting her or something.'

'Yes, she said as much last night. I'm just surprised Hector didn't mention it.'

'Look, Pip, I don't know anything for sure, but my suspicion is that he and Brooke might be getting closer. He's not said anything, but I think when he saw you with Harvey he finally accepted that nothing was going to happen with you and so maybe now he and Brooke have spent so much time together that...'

'You really think they might be, you know, romantically involved?'

'Harry does, too,' Freddie shrugged. 'And to be honest, as much as I love you, I want Hector to be happy. When you made it clear that you weren't interested, we all started rooting for them.'

'Of course, we all want them to be happy, especially Hector.'

Pippa didn't know why her cheeks were burning. Surely she wasn't jealous? How could she be jealous? She had no right to be. Even if them getting together changed her friendship with Hector, she should be happy for them.

'And they do have a lot in common,' Freddie added.

'What?' Pippa asked.

'They both love Meadowbrook,' he said and Pippa smarted a little.

Why wasn't she feeling as happy as she should at this? What was wrong with her? Perhaps her longing for a relationship now was stronger than she realised. Perhaps she was worried about losing Hector and even her fledgling friendship with Brooke. Or perhaps she was just being really bloody selfish.

Chapter Twenty-nine

Pippa hung up her mobile phone, cursed then panicked. It was changeover day at the hotel. They had guests coming in later that afternoon – a corporate booking, which was a real coup for the hotel, with top executives of a major retail chain – and all hands were supposed to be on deck. However, Pippa had spoken to Ross, who'd informed her that the house-keeping staff were all sick. One of them had the norovirus and it had spread like wildfire. The hotel was left with hardly any staff and no one to clean the rooms.

Pippa called Gwen first to rope her into cooking, which she was happy to do. Gwen didn't suit retirement and was always offering to do things. However, that still left the cleaning.

'Gem, are you at college today?' Pippa asked as she picked up the phone.

'No, I'm meant to be revising at home. What's up?'

'All the staff have gone off sick and we need to get the rooms ready. Fancy housekeeping with me?'

'Oh, great, my most hated job.'

'Gem, it's a total emergency and I don't know what else to do. I'm going to call Harry, too; she'll hate it, but at least she can make a bed.'

'What about Toby? If Gwen's up at the house cleaning then who can have him?'

'Hopefully Connor'll be at the sanctuary so he can keep Toby with him. Oh God, let me call her now. If she's not around, I might have to get hold of some of the gardening club ladies.'

'Please let Harriet be available in that case,' Gemma finished.

They'd roped in the gardening club ladies once before and it hadn't gone well. The rooms weren't cleaned thoroughly and instead they'd all had a whale of a time enjoying themselves and just pretending to work.

Pippa got straight on the phone to Harriet, who said that Connor was, in fact, at the sanctuary that day so could look after Toby for a few hours. Rather than complain about it, Harriet was all business and understood that this was a crisis, so was happy to muck in. This corporate booking had once again meant that Hector had been forced to vacate his room. Pippa had to admit that she was relieved when he'd told her he was going to London to see his agent for a few days and check on his flat there, so it wasn't going to be a problem. Also, part of her thought he might have moved into Brooke's room and she was still smarting. There was no evidence that they were together, but they were certainly very close, and having helped Brooke with the Lucky situation, Pippa wasn't sure what was going on with them.

Although at first she'd wanted them to get together, she wasn't sure now. Hector was important to Pippa – they were such good friends and she didn't want Brooke to take him away from her ... Gosh, she sounded like a jealous five-year-old. Maybe it was as simple as her being jealous of losing just a friendship, but she didn't like to think that she was. Or that there might be more to it. She wanted to be happy for them, but for some reason she couldn't make herself genuinely feel it.

Gemma, Harriet and Pippa all donned rubber gloves as they started with the rooms. Gwen, who was of course the best housekeeper ever when she worked for them, briefed them on how the rooms should be done and also warned them that she'd be inspecting them later.

'I don't even clean my own house,' Harriet moaned.

Vicky used to work for her a couple of times a week but since she was now working full time at the hotel, Harriet now had a lady from the village cleaning for her, who also helped out at the hotel from time to time. Of course she wasn't available today, typically.

'Look, it's time we stopped being so spoilt and did some actual manual labour,' Pippa said. 'It does us good to get our hands dirty sometimes.'

'And unlike you two princesses, I've cleaned plenty in my time and I even clean my house. Freddie doesn't really do much...' Gemma said.

'That I find hard to believe,' Pippa laughed.

'Should we have a tea break before we start?' Harriet suggested.

'No, we'll do an hour first and then we can have a tea break,' Pippa said.

'Oh God, stop talking and get going or we'll never get it done in time,' Gemma finished, brandishing a pair of rubber gloves.

* * *

'You know, that wasn't easy and I think it's good I experienced it, because our staff need to be more appreciated,' Pippa said as she sat at the kitchen table nursing a cup of coffee and some of Gwen's home-made biscuits.

'Pip, honestly, we do treat our staff well. We pay above most places round here, as you know, and the perks are pretty good,' Harriet said.

It was true. Their father, who'd run many successful businesses, valued his staff. He didn't think that trying to cut corners was appropriate and he said if you couldn't pay people well, then you shouldn't be in business. Meadowbrook was run on this ethos, meaning the staff were really happy, especially as training and promotion was encouraged. But they expected loyalty in return and largely got it. They'd had one bar person who'd stolen alcohol early on when the hotel first opened, but that had been dealt with and nothing major had happened since.

'Well, my loves, I'm impressed,' Gwen said when she'd finished her inspection. 'You can each have an extra biscuit.'

They beamed at Gwen as if they were children who'd been rewarded with sweets.

'But Brooke's room hasn't been done yet, before you all get too excited,' she added.

The three of them glanced at each other. Hector's was being used, so he'd moved his stuff into Pippa's apartment before leaving for London, they all knew that, but cleaning Brooke's room hadn't occurred to them.

'Does it need it? It's not like she's paying anymore,' Pippa said.

'Surely you should at least make her bed and check if she needs clean towels,' Gwen said. 'She might not be paying but she's still a guest.'

Pippa felt herself about to object, but then Gwen had that look on her face that said that she'd broker no argument.

'OK, OK, I'll do it. Just a quick tidy as Gwen suggested,' Pippa said reluctantly.

'Are you sure you don't want me to help?' Gemma asked kindly.

Harriet didn't offer.

'No, I'll do it. You guys have been amazing and, Gemma, I know it's not fair, but I need you to help out when the guests arrive. And, Harriet, I might need you, too.'

'That's fine. I've warned Connor he's on dad duty for the next couple of days and he's delighted to have Toby all to himself. Actually, I quite like playing hotel. I normally only get to look at the numbers.'

'Great, well let me go and do Brooke's room, and I'll see you guys later.'

'I guess we'd better go and check the drawing room,' Harriet remembered.

'I'll bring my feather duster,' Gemma quipped.

Pippa unlocked Brooke's room feeling like an intruder. When Brooke had first arrived, she'd told her that if she didn't want the room cleaned, or if she wanted to be left alone, to hang the 'do not disturb' sign that Gus had hand-painted. Unfortunately for Pippa, she hadn't hung it today. Brooke was out with Chris PT, working. They were increasingly gearing up for starting their new business and it seemed it was full steam ahead.

Even though it was actually her old bedroom, she still felt an impostor. Not that she could think of it like that, given they were friends, but it felt wrong. The bedding was piled up in a heap and there was a towel on the floor, along with clothes scattered around. Books littered the room – Brooke certainly wasn't the tidiest of people, it seemed. Pippa didn't want to do anything too personal, so she began by cleaning the bathroom, which was a total mess with loads of products lying around. But then Brooke was young, she reasoned, and living in a hotel room for months at a time probably didn't help, given it was such a small space for a long period of time.

As she tidied the products away, she was proud of herself for not prying too much into what Brooke used; although she was tempted to see if anything other than youth was responsible for her dewy skin. She cleaned the bath, the loo and the shower then put out fresh towels. There was something therapeutic about cleaning, Pippa decided as she hummed to herself. They'd been so spoilt by Gwen as children that they hadn't lifted a finger. Although when Pippa was married to Mark, she did the cleaning herself, as she couldn't justify not working and paying a cleaner. It wasn't as if Mark would have done it and he insisted on everything being immaculate. God, he was a tyrant, she thought. She folded Brooke's clothes, put fresh flowers in the room and made the bed, thinking how delighted Brooke would be to come back to a lovely neat and tidy room.

Just as she was about to leave, she couldn't help but notice something poking out from under the bed. There was a large holdall type bag with papers sticking out of the top. It made the otherwise now immaculate room look a bit messy and Pippa went across the room to move it, knowing how much it would have annoyed Mark. As she went to move the bag firmly under the bed so it was out of sight, somehow she dislodged some papers and they fell out. She felt bad, because she absolutely shouldn't look at them – after all, they were private and Pippa prided herself on how important privacy was for their guests – however, something caught her eye. She tried to turn her head away, knowing how wrong it would be, but her eyes were drawn back. She picked up the paper that she was trying not to look at and read:

Proposed legal action regarding Brooke Walker and the Singer family…

Unfortunately, once she'd read that sentence, she couldn't un-see it, and she needed to find out more.

As she read on, all the colour drained from her face and her heart started beating faster. She felt sick, she felt dizzy, and it was as if the words couldn't be real. She sat cross-legged, leaning against the bed, pushing her hair from her eyes and feeling sweat mount on her brow. She needed to stop reading, but with each paper a new piece of information was revealed and she found she couldn't tear her eyes away or make herself stop.

After she'd read all the papers, she carefully placed them back in the bag. Wiping tears from her face, she pushed the bag back under the bed and tried to decide what to do next. She needed to compose herself, and quickly, but how? She went to the bathroom and, seeing her reflection in the mirror, she felt as if someone had given her an electric shock as she wore the full horror of it all on her face. She splashed herself with cold water and after a while, she left the room and closed the door behind her.

She hadn't expected that. And now, she couldn't pretend she hadn't read what she'd read. But she had no idea what to do about it.

A glance at her watch told her that the new guests were due to arrive soon and she knew that what she'd discovered was far too big to deal with right now. God, for ages Pippa had thought there was more to Brooke than she seemed, but she'd grown to trust her, which she now realised she shouldn't have done. She should have gone with her first instincts. Brooke had managed to fool everyone, pretending to be their friends, or at least that was how it felt. In fact, lately, even Pippa felt as if they were friends. Despite all her early suspicions about Brooke and her initial distrust of the woman, it had never once crossed her mind that what she'd discovered would be the real reason she was at Meadowbrook.

'Is everything all right?' Harriet asked as Pippa joined Gemma and her, who were putting the finishing touches to the reception area.

Bright and vibrant, the fresh flowers smelt divine, Pippa thought, but she felt sick to her stomach.

'Yes, just a bit tired,' she lied. 'Right, what do we need to do before these guests descend?'

'Well, Pip, I thought maybe we should draw up a list of jobs for each of us for the next couple of days, so we know who's doing what, which might save us some time,' Harriet suggested.

'And I'm all yours, too,' Gemma offered. 'I've juggled college so I can help out.'

Pippa nodded. She didn't trust herself to speak. How she was going to get through the next few days, not just with the guests but with her family and also Brooke, she didn't know, but somehow she had to. It was far too dangerous to let anyone know what she'd discovered, not when they had guests

311

arriving. For now, she'd have to push it to the back of her mind and somehow get rid of the rising nausea, knowing that it was definitely not the norovirus, but Brooke causing it.

Chapter Thirty

If it hadn't been for the information that she held inside her, it would have been a great few days. But it was busy, exhausting, successful and horrible all at the same time. Pippa had barely eaten since her discovery and she felt sick all the time. She'd kept most of her chat with her family to the hotel and the minute she could clock off she'd hidden in her apartment, trying to make sense of everything when nothing made sense.

She wished that Hector was around, she had the urge to talk to him before she spoke to anyone else. She wasn't sure why, but possibly it was because he wasn't family. Not only was he a good listener, but he was also calm, and she definitely needed someone to calm her down. But, of course, that wasn't going to happen as he wasn't around. But her guests most definitely were – some very demanding but pleasant senior executives who liked everything to be just so. They'd got fully involved in Meadowbrook experience. They'd painted, had a *Great British Bake Off* style competition and they'd even been involved in the sanctuary for half a day, feeding animals and grooming the ponies, which they'd enjoyed. It was a real change from their corporate city life but they'd embraced it fully.

But when they were at the hotel, it was all expensive wine, whisky, vodka and tequila. Gerry had been sent out a number of times to collect things they didn't have, which was pretty unusual, as Meadowbrook usually stocked the best of everything; however, this group managed to challenge that supposition. It was lucky in a way that they were keeping Pippa, so busy that she could only think about Brooke when she was alone in her apartment, and because she was so tired, not even the worry was managing to stop her from sleeping. But when she woke, she felt an unfamiliar panic and anxiety that was alien to her as she remembered what she'd read in Brooke's room.

If only Hector were here, she thought once more. She really needed him, and now more than ever. A couple more days and he'd be back at Meadowbrook, the current hotel guests would have departed and she could finally tell someone what she knew.

Pippa felt sad. Her feelings about Brooke had been dismissed by everyone as just her being silly and although she thought there was something going on with Brooke at times, she didn't expect this. The enormity of the situation meant she didn't feel pleased about it, at all. In fact, she felt scared, wretched and alone with a terrible, horrible secret.

When she finally said goodbye to the guests, Gemma, Harriet and she collapsed in the drawing room. Although the staff were finally better, they still weren't allowed back until these particular guests had gone, just in case. They didn't want anyone to catch a sickness bug under their watch. Not at the prices they were paying. And they didn't need another threatened lawsuit when they'd only just got rid of William.

'I'm so looking forward to getting back to normal. Actually, working in a hotel is damn hard,' Harriet smiled. 'And I even think motherhood might be easier than this.'

'It has been hard work, but these guests were particularly demanding. God, it's lucky I had you guys to muck in. I don't know how to thank you.'

'And Brooke,' Harriet said. 'Her help with Freddie in the bar was amazing. You might want to be a bit warmer towards her. I thought you and she got on well now, but it didn't feel like it the last couple of days.'

'Yes, I did notice you were a bit frosty, Pip,' Gemma added.

Pippa scowled. It was on the tip of her tongue to tell her exactly what was going on with their precious Brooke, but she bit it back. Now wasn't the time. She still had a lot to process in her head. She knew that Hector was due back in a bit and she was going to text him, as soon as she was alone, asking him to meet her.

The hotel was empty tonight, thankfully, and the staff would be back to turn it around the following day, so Pippa could now focus on the matter at hand. She glared at Harriet and Gemma, but then decided they could enjoy a little extra time in their current ignorance.

'Sure, I'll make an effort,' she said, with no idea how she was going to get through between now and when she could speak to Hector and figure out what on earth she should do.

She almost jumped on Hector the minute he walked through the door with his weekend holdall. He looked tired, she noticed. He'd probably had several late nights and been out to London's hottest bars. Might even have made the gossip pages. She wondered how many women had been involved, then she pushed such silly thoughts aside.

'Had fun?' she asked, hugging him.

'Goodness, Pippa, that's some welcome. Anyone would think you're pleased to see me.' He flashed her a cheeky grin.

'You have no idea! I've made up your room, personally, and put your stuff back in. But, Hector, I need to ask you a favour. Once you're settled, can you come for a walk with me? It's sort of urgent.'

'A walk?' He sounded puzzled. 'Sure, let me just dump my bag.'

'Thank you.' Pippa felt relieved. Finally, she could unburden herself. 'Meet me by the back door.'

Hector was so easy to talk to as they walked around the Meadowbrook estate, and Pippa talked and talked. She went round and round in circles, cried and got angry, and Hector listened patiently to her, hugging her when she was upset, staying quiet while she railed. Finally, when she'd finished, she turned to him.

'What do you think?' she asked, although the question felt inadequate.

'Pippa, I can't believe it. I mean... She was part of all of this, and we were becoming such good friends. I even liked exercising with her, but I didn't have a clue. God, I can't believe she was keeping this secret all this time. I mean, Brooke...' Hector flitted nervously from thought to thought as he walked.

'I know, I mean, she was so good with everyone. I really liked her, I did. I know I worried at first, but that was because I'm insecure and I felt that we were the only ones with nothing in common. But after the Lucky business, I felt as if we were starting to bond.'

316

'That kind of makes sense a bit now.'

'Why?'

'You know, how angry she got about Lucky. How determined she was to get to the truth, for you guys.'

'I've kept it to myself until now. The running of the hotel was in such a mess and the guests were so demanding. It was bad enough keeping it together myself! I couldn't risk sending everyone else off kilter, but now I need to tell them.'

'Including Brooke?'

'No, I need to talk to my family without Brooke first. They need to know first and then we can decide together what to do. But believe me, it'll take a while to sink in. It still hasn't done with me. I still can't believe it.'

'No, I'm in shock, too. It's huge... I mean, I don't...' Hector seemed as lost as she was. 'She's such a great woman.'

'Hector, she lied.'

'Yes, she did. Sorry, but now so much makes sense – Pip, Lucky, William—'

'I don't want to hear it. Not now, Hector. I'll call a family meeting. Will you be there? I mean, you are family. And you keep me calm.' As she said this she realised it was true.

'Of course, if you want me there, I'll be there. But Gwen's the one who normally keeps you calm.'

'With you and Gwen we'll be safe, then.'

Pippa felt anything but safe, but as Hector put his arm around her, she felt that bit safer.

They were all squashed into the office. Toby was squirming on Gwen's lap and Harriet was next to her with Gus on the other side. Pippa was behind her father's desk, while Freddie and Gemma were on the other sofa with Hector. Gerry, who

317

Pippa had also included in the meeting, was perched on the other office chair. Connor was at the vet surgery and Amanda was working, so they couldn't make it.

'So, what's going on? No offence, Pip, but I've had enough of this place for a couple of days,' Harriet pointed out.

'I'm sorry. I know it's been a tough few days, but it's going to get worse and I didn't know what to do.'

Pippa bit back tears. She couldn't just cry – she had to get through this and be strong for her siblings.

'What is it, Pip, you sound really upset?' Freddie's brows were etched with concern.

'It's about Brooke.'

All hell let loose.

'Oh, for God's sake, I thought you and her were fine now?' Harriet said, sounding exasperated.

'She's been great,' Freddie added.

'She practically saved the sanctuary,' Gus said.

'Pippa, really, what is your problem with her?' Gemma asked.

They were all staring at her as if she were being unreasonable.

'You need to hear her out,' Hector said. 'You know I'm Brooke's biggest fan, but some information has come to light and, well, you need to listen to Pippa. I mean, you need to know about this.'

'Well, what is it, then?' Harriet sighed.

'I was cleaning her room the other day, as you know, when I came across some papers—'

'Oh God, you were prying, how could you?' Freddie said. 'I'd believe it of Harriet but not of you.'

'Oi, Freddie, shut up. Pippa, that's not good. I mean, we're a hotel, a five-star hotel at that! We don't snoop on our guests! You of all people should know that,' Harriet snapped.

'If she finds out, she'll be furious,' Gus added.

'I wasn't, I promise, I really wasn't,' Pippa shouted. 'I was tidying up and there were these papers poking out, so I just thought I'd put them back under the bed, but then there was something that caught my eye – our name – and of course once I saw that I had to look! I couldn't not, could I?'

'I suppose when you put it like that,' Gwen said. 'Carry on, love, let's hear Pippa out,' she finished.

'The papers I found ... I couldn't believe them, I still can't believe them! It's terrible! It's all so terrible, and I hope to God it isn't true.'

'What is it?' Harriet pushed. 'For God's sake, Pip, can you just tell us?'

'OK, fine, I *am* trying.' Pippa wiped the tears off her cheeks as Hector leant over to take her hand.

'Brooke's claiming that she's found her father's family, because her father is our father!' The words sounded like poison on her tongue. 'And not only is she claiming that she's our half-sister, but she's also taken legal advice on how to get her share of Daddy's estate!'

The silence was palpable.

'What the hell?!' All the colour drained from Harriet's face when she eventually broke the silence.

Freddie opened and closed his mouth. Gus kept blinking and Gwen sat very still, holding onto Toby, but shock was clear on her face. Gerry shuffled uncomfortably. Gemma grabbed Freddie's hand while Hector stood up and came over to put his arm around Pippa.

'Hold on,' Gerry said as Gwen's eyes darted between them

all. 'Are we sure that she's related to you?'

'No,' Pippa said. After all, she'd had the most time to think about this. 'Daddy wouldn't have cheated on Mum.'

'Pip, my maths might be bad, but Brooke's age ... so Mum would have passed away before she was born,' Freddie pointed out.

'Oh, right!' Pippa fumed.

That had been Pippa's only conclusion, that there was no way she was their sister. No way. She was an American con artist and she was playing the long game to get the most money. She'd been there, getting information, getting close to them all so she could con them out of money.

'I think she's involved in a very big con, it's the only possible explanation,' Pippa said.

'That does make sense,' Harriet concurred. 'There may be others involved – that Chris, I mean, do we know he's a personal trainer? He could be the brains behind it.'

'Doubtful ... have you seen how tight his jeans are?' Freddie said.

'He could just be playing dumb, though. I mean yes, he was happy to dress up as a chicken, but if he thought he and Brooke could con us out of this place then maybe that explains it,' Gus added.

'Hold on,' Gwen said. 'It could be possible. You might not want to hear this but although Andrew was loyal to your mum even after her death, I'm quite sure he was no monk. He travelled a bit on business ... I mean, he was only human. I'm not saying that Brooke *is* his daughter, but I'm just saying that it could be possible. You guys are jumping to conclusions, but we need to consider the option that she might be telling the truth.'

320

'What if Pippa was right all along? What if she's a really good con artist trying to get Meadowbrook? I mean, that's terrible,' Harriet said.

Harriet was again echoing Pippa's thoughts and sounding more like her old self, which Pippa found reassuring. Brooke may have pulled the wool over their eyes before, but no more.

'And it would explain why she was keen to get the Lucky situation sorted out – you know, to gain our trust,' Freddie added.

'What proof do you have?' Gemma asked quietly. 'I just can't believe she's a con artist. She's lovely, and lost, and she so wanted to be part of Meadowbrook, which if she was, you know, related to you also makes perfect sense.' Gemma's voice was gentle but Pippa didn't want to consider her words.

'I found letters going back and forth to a solicitor in America, stating that her mum told her that Andrew Singer was her real father after her own father's death. Then there were papers about how she was entitled to inherit posthumously, or something like that. There was a photo of our dad with who I presume is Brooke's mum, or someone else she was going to pretend was her mum. There was no hard evidence as far as I could see, but I could have missed something, I guess. It was such a shock,' Pippa sobbed.

Hector perched on the desk, grabbing her hand.

'I don't believe it!' Harriet stormed. 'I agree with Pippa, there's some kind of huge con going on. Maybe her mum met Dad once and now they need money, so they targeted us. She made us feel sorry for her by saying her mum and her were estranged. What if that was a story designed to get money out of us? What if her mum's behind this?'

They were all getting carried away with this theory now.

'That makes sense.' Pippa began to calm herself. 'It's got to be. Also, I found a load of credit card bills. It seems she's up to her ears in debt, which is how she's been staying here, putting it all on cards.'

'She was very good with the gardening club,' Gus pointed out.

'And the dogs,' Harriet added. 'She practically saved the sanctuary, whatever her motive. And Toby loves her.'

'And we had some lovely runs together,' Gemma pointed out.

'I so enjoyed baking with her,' Gwen said.

'And her cocktails were bloody good,' Freddie finished.

'But she's a fraud,' Pippa said, then stopped.

Staring at her through the open door was the very person they'd been talking about.

'You went through my things,' she said quietly.

Her face was ashen as she stood in her customary gym clothes.

'And thank goodness I did!'

Pippa felt angry on her behalf, on behalf of her family and her father. Pippa was normally the most gentle of the Singers, but not when she was riled. She had a temper, they all knew that.

'I'm not lying,' Brooke said. 'And I'm not a con artist, either. I'm your sister. I didn't know how to tell you, but that's why I came here in the first place.'

'What proof do you have?' Harriet asked, but she didn't sound angry anymore.

Brooke was shaking, Pippa noticed, and she felt guilty for shouting. Unless she was a con artist. After all, she was from

LA, she could just be a very good actress. She squeezed Hector's hand. It was all so confusing.

'My mum told me after Dad, the man I thought was my dad, died. It was awful! I had no idea that he wasn't my real father and when I found out, it was a huge shock. I contacted a lawyer but then I decided to come here and see for myself. I thought I'd know, and I did. And, by the way, I knew you wouldn't believe me, so I did a DNA test.'

'How did you do that? Dad's no longer alive,' Harriet asked.

Pippa was glad that Harry was back in control.

'I stole Pippa's hairbrush and a discarded piece of chewing gum of Freddie's. It came back positive! I've got the results.'

'Hold on, hold on! You think we'll take your word for this?' Pippa said. 'You come in here – and yes, Brooke, you did a very good job worming your way in with us all – then you have a dodgy DNA test and you're going to threaten us with legal action, try to take Meadowbrook? You think you can do that?'

'No,' Brooke replied quietly. 'But at first I was angry. Surely you can understand that? The man who I thought was my father wasn't and the family I did belong to were living in a manor house in England like something from TV. And I was angry with my mum for lying to me all those years. Of course, there's a lot more to it. But yes, I came here with the idea that I'd get what I thought I deserved. And I was angry and resentful, but I grew to know you, and I liked you, and that's why I didn't say anything.

'I thought I'd be so full of hate for you that I'd come, stay for a while and then reveal who I was, but I grew to like you all *and* Meadowbrook, and the community. I felt like I belonged somewhere for the first time in my life almost and no, of course

I don't want to sue you, but I do want to be part of your family. My family.' Brooke was crying. 'I didn't know what to do, I really didn't, but I was too scared to tell you, in case you reacted like this. You remember, Pippa and Hector, when I said I was scared to find my family in case they rejected me, well I was talking about you.' She started sobbing.

'We'll need proof,' Freddie said. 'Sorry, Brooke, I really like you and I actually don't think you seem like a typical con artist – although, of course, you can't be too careful – but this is all a shock and we can't just take your word for it.'

'Of course.' Brooke looked at the floor.

'I'm not buying it,' Pippa said. 'I don't believe a word you're saying, because if this were true, you'd have spoken to us before now, like any sane person would.'

Pippa was shouting now. Even Harriet flinched. Brooke turned on her heels and fled. Pippa burst into tears then.

'God, Pip, you didn't need to shout like that,' Harriet said, pulling her fingers through her hair.

Thankfully, Toby didn't seem fazed by the whole debacle, but Pippa felt guilty.

'That may have been a bit harsh,' Gwen said. 'Listen to me. You are Singers and you need to think about this. *If*, and I am saying if, she is your half-sister, you can't turn your back on her. After all, she might not be lying, she might not be a con artist, she might just be a very lost young woman who's just found out her father wasn't her father, after all. She might be telling the truth. Feeling betrayed by her mum and with no other family, she came to find where she might belong and this is how you react?'

'She's right,' Hector added. 'You guys are the most wonderful family I know. If she is—'

'She's not,' Pippa stormed.

There was no way she was accepting this. Brooke was a con artist, pure and simple.

'But if there is any possibility, love...' Gwen kissed Toby's head as he started to cry.

'He needs feeding,' said Harriet, who seemed to be in shock.

'You believe her, don't you?' Gus asked Harriet.

Harriet nodded.

'If you look at her, she looks a bit like a blonde version of me,' she said. 'I always thought there was something familiar about her, you know.'

'I agree,' Freddie said. 'There were characteristics that puzzled me, but now I realise they remind me of other members of the family. And she has the personality. I mean, with the Lucky thing, she was even behaving like a Singer.'

'No, just no!' Pippa cried.

'Pippa.' Gwen wrapped her in a hug. 'You've always been the baby of the family, so I know you might be feeling threatened, but you're also one of the most generous, loving people I know, so if Brooke is your sister, don't you think you ought to give her a chance?'

Pippa buried her face in Gwen's shoulder and wept.

'How do we find out for sure?' Gus asked. 'I mean, we do need to be one hundred percent.'

'Let's see this DNA test, for starters,' Harriet said. 'Although we might want to do another one, with a doctor rather than a weird Internet company who accepts used chewing gum.' She stroked Toby's hair. 'And we'll speak to her, calmly, about her mum. We'll ask her to explain, also calmly, and we'll promise to listen now, that's what we'll do.'

'OK, let's go and find her,' Freddie said.

'You go, we'll stay here,' Gwen said, taking Toby back. 'I'll give him his bottle.'

They argued for a few more minutes about whether they should go together or just one of them, and in the end Gwen, having had enough, sent them all out together.

'Good luck,' Hector said quietly as they left.

Gemma stood up to kiss Freddie. It felt as if they were leaving for something bad and perhaps they were. Whatever it was, Pippa knew that after this, life would never be the same for them again.

Pippa felt her stomach flutter as they made their way upstairs. What if Brooke really was their half-sister? It didn't make sense. There is no way that their father would have been happy knowing that he had a child out there that he didn't know about, or get to meet. Their father would have been devastated, in fact, to think that he had a child he didn't know about.

'Daddy wouldn't have let this happen,' she said suddenly, fiercely.

'Oh, Pip, it's clear that if it's true then he didn't know,' Harriet said, putting her arm around her.

'He wouldn't have let this happen if he did,' Gus pointed out.

'What a bloody mess,' Freddie said.

Pippa knocked at Brooke's door and waited. There was no answer.

'Come on, let's just go in,' Harriet said, moving Pippa aside and opening the door.

There was no sign of Brooke. It looked as if she'd taken some of her things, as well. She must have moved fast. They'd only been arguing over what to do for a few minutes, or was it longer?

'The holdall's gone,' Pippa said, realising that it was missing.

They checked the wardrobe and some of her clothes were also gone. There was no sign of her handbag and she'd taken her washbag from the bathroom. She'd left a bit of her stuff and on the bed, scattered, were some of the papers.

'Oh God,' Harriet said, picking up one of the pieces of paper. 'Here's the DNA test.'

They crowded round and although Pippa didn't understand it, she could clearly see that Brooke was a match to both Freddie and her.

'It looks real,' Gus said.

'It does,' Harriet added.

'Who knows how easy it would be to fake a DNA test!' Pippa still protested. 'I mean, it could be a forgery.'

'Look at this,' Freddie said, picking up a photo.

It was the photo of their father and a woman who was clearly Brooke's mum. They checked through the rest of the papers, some of which Pippa had already seen.

'I think she's genuine,' Harriet said finally as she read the printout of an email that Brooke's mum had written, giving details of their father that only someone who'd met him would have known.

'But...' Pippa chewed her lip. Surely not?

'We need to find her,' Gus said. 'Because Gwen's right, if she is our sister and she's pretty alone right now, we need to take care of her.'

'We cared about her anyway,' Freddie pointed out.

'We did, we said that she was part of Meadowbrook, and maybe she really is. We can't turn our backs on her,' Harriet added.

'But we don't know where she's gone,' Pippa pointed out.

Part of her felt terrible for Brooke while part of her was struggling with her own feelings. Did she really have a new sister? Was she no longer the baby of the family? Was that her problem – she liked being the youngest – or was it more than that? After all, her father had a daughter who he'd never met and never would. But then that meant that Brooke would never get the chance to meet her real father now, which would be devastating for her. Like she'd lost two fathers. Oh God, she had to think of how wretched Brooke must be feeling now. It was time for her to be her true, caring self.

'Call Chris PT,' Pippa said, remembering herself. 'He's her only friend apart from us.'

'Have we got his number?' Harriet asked.

'Oh, sorry, I have.' Pippa shook her head. She was feeling both stressed and anxious. 'But can you call?'

She pulled out her mobile, brought up his contact details and passed the phone to Harriet. The phone went straight to voicemail.

'Chris, it's Harriet Singer,' she said. 'Please call me back. It's urgent! We're really worried about Brooke. Oh! but maybe don't tell her that you're calling us. If you're with her. I hope you are. I mean, well, just call me back.'

Freddie shook his head.

'What do we do now?' Gus asked.

'No choice but to wait for Chris to call us. Right, let's go and see my baby.'

They found the others in the kitchen. Toby was asleep in his pram and Gwen was busying herself making tea.

'Any news?' Hector asked.

'She's gone but we don't know where.'

'I'm going to drive down to the village,' Freddie said. 'She can't have got far, she's not even got a car, so I might see her, or something. Call me if Chris rings.'

'I'll come with you,' Gus said.

'Why do I feel that it's my fault?' Pippa said.

'Oh, Pip, it's not. It's a mess but it's not your fault,' Gemma said.

'God, Pip, you said to me at the beginning you were unsure, but I brushed your concerns off, not that you could have predicted this, of course,' Harriet said.

'Oh God, Harry, if she is our sister then she'll never forgive me.'

'She will,' Hector said. 'And if she's your sister then I'm guessing all she wants is to be part of the family, and that includes you.'

'No, I'll bet she won't want to be part of my family,' Pippa said before starting to cry again.

It felt like hours before Chris phoned them back. Freddie and Gus had scoured the village but there was no sign. Gemma and Hector had gone to search her room again, but it was fruitless, because they had no idea what they were actually looking for.

'Chris!' Harriet snatched up Pippa's phone. 'It's Harriet.'

She put him on speaker and the family crowded round to listen.

'Hi, um, I guess you're calling about Brooke.'

'Yes.'

'She said she's your sister and none of you believe her.'

'We do believe her,' Harriet said. 'Sort of. Is she with you?'

'She's devastated. She said you guys accused her of being a con artist. I can see why – after all, she took ages to tell you

329

'– but then again, Brooke's a lovely person and certainly not a liar. She's one of the nicest people I've ever met, in fact.'

'Thanks for that analysis, Chris!' Harriet snapped. 'But, actually, we do know.'

'What Harry means is that we're worried about Brooke,' Gus interjected. 'Yes, we may have been a little sceptical, but then we were in shock. She's been here for months and not a word – you must see how that felt to us?'

'Yes, and I said as much to her, but she's scared. And she's young. I'm not that old, only thirty, but she's still in her early twenties and her life's been turned upside down a number of times recently. It's been difficult for her.'

'Chris, we get that, but we need to speak to her, can you get her for us?'

'Sorry, no.'

'What do you mean no?'

'She managed to get here and I tried to talk her out of it but I couldn't. I'm at the gym. I had a client I couldn't change and normally I'd drop everything for her, but then I need this job until I open my own gym, which of course I thought I'd be doing with Brooke—'

'Chris, calm down, where is Brooke?'

'In a taxi. I begged her not to and said I'd be free in a bit. In fact, if only she'd waited, I'm free now. But my client's one of the gym's most important members, so I was stuck.'

'Where's she gone to?' Freddie asked, sounding exasperated.

'Oh, to Heathrow. She said that you'd made it clear that you don't want her so she's going back to America. I tried to talk her out of it, but with my client and everything, there was nothing I could do. I mean, I was hoping she'd work with me, which is what we wanted to do, but of course we still had to figure out her work permit. There again, I'm guessing if she's actually your sister then she's half English, so she might be all right.'

'Chris,' Pippa finally managed to interject. 'So she's gone to the airport. How long ago did she leave?'

'About twenty minutes.'

'Right.' Pippa knew what they needed to do. 'Chris, we're going to go and find her. Keep your phone on you so we can let you know.'

'Do you want me to come with you?' Chris asked, sounding hopeful.

They all exchanged glances.

'No, Chris, I think it's probably best if it's just family right now.'

'Oh, OK. Good luck. Oh, and please get Brooke back!' Chris sounded upset.

'We will,' Pippa finished, sounding more confident than she felt.

Chapter Thirty-one

'I don't see why you have to drive,' Gus whined as Freddie grabbed the car keys to the Range Rover.

'Because you drive like an old woman,' Freddie bit back.

'I'm calling front seat,' Harriet said as she kissed a still-sleeping Toby then barked instructions at Gwen and Gemma as to what he needed.

'Why do you get to sit in the front?' Pippa complained. 'You always get the front seat.'

'I'm the oldest,' Harriet shot.

'I'm the second oldest, so I should drive,' Gus persisted.

'For goodness' sake, if you don't leave now she'll be back in LA before you even get in the car,' Gwen chastised.

'OK, fine, we'll sit in the back,' Gus said sulkily. 'And I'll call Amanda on the way, to explain.'

'Oh God, don't make me listen to you telling her how much you love her again,' Freddie complained.

'Right, out, now!' Gwen shouted.

They all did as they were told.

Pippa glanced anxiously across to Gus in the back seat as Freddie drove off. Gus was talking on the phone to Amanda, filling her in on the day's events. Listening to it, it sounded so surreal. They'd been living, sort of, with Brooke for four months now and all along she was their half-sister. Or alleged half-sister. Pippa still harboured some doubts, although they were shrinking. If Brooke wasn't a con woman, then why would she flee now? Or was she banking on the fact that they'd follow her? But then in the films if they have cons like that they reveal themselves straight away, don't they? Her head hurt with all the confusion.

'Amanda seems to think that she can see the family resemblance,' Gus said as he hung up.

'Really? Isn't it funny how now she's said she's related to us we all think we can see it,' Freddie said.

'Is that because she says she's our sister, or is there really a familiar likeness?' Harriet asked.

'Amanda says that she sees it more in her characteristics. She said, and I hadn't noticed, but she says that she has certain mannerisms that Dad had.'

'You know, I forget that Amanda worked with Dad before you two got together,' Pippa said.

Amanda had taken over the gardens at Meadowbrook before their father's death. She and Andrew Singer were quite close.

'I always thought she reminded me of someone – maybe there is something in that,' Harriet mused.

'I don't know,' Pippa started. 'Although her character is a bit like a mixture of all of us,' she conceded.

She had the strength of Harriet, the creative side of Gus, the fun side of Freddie and Pippa ... well, they probably shared more than she cared to admit.

'What the hell are we going to do when we get to the airport?' Freddie said as he accelerated.

'If we get there in one piece,' Gus murmured.

'We have to talk to her,' Harriet said. 'We need to make sure that she really is our sister. I know we've seen the photo, and the email her mum wrote, and also the DNA, but we need to be sure. My instinct is that Brooke isn't lying and sorry, Pip, but I don't think she's pulling off a con. We need to tell her that going forward, for legal reasons, we need our own DNA test.'

'And if it's positive?' Pippa asked.

She felt sick still. How could they have a secret sister? So their father didn't cheat on their mum, but how would he feel if he were here now? He'd be devastated at the idea that a child of his wasn't part of his life, she knew that. He was honourable. How could Brooke's mum have walked out of his life, had his child and passed it, her, off as another man's? It was all a huge mess.

'Then she's part of our family, Pip, like it or not.'

Pippa didn't know if she did like it or not. But, of course, she wouldn't turn her back on her. Pippa wasn't a bad person, just a little confused at times. Poor Brooke was alone and distressed, and if she was a Singer then she'd be treated as such. Pippa resolved to be a better person starting now and that meant welcoming Brooke into the family. After all, like Harriet, her instinct was telling her that Brooke *was* their sister. It was as if she knew it in her heart; although her head was definitely not as accommodating.

'Harry, have you found the terminal yet?' Freddie asked as they neared Heathrow.

Pippa had spoken to Chris, who'd managed to speak to Brooke, and found out she was heading to the American Airlines desk.

'Terminal three,' Harriet replied.

They'd been largely silent, all of them nervous and lost in thought. This was huge, Pippa knew, and the reality of possibly having another sibling hadn't fully sunk in. How could it? They'd checked in at home: Toby was fine, and Gemma, Hector and Gwen were sitting together, waiting for news. Connor was going to join them at the house straight from work, and Amanda was going to get the girls and go over. They had all their support system waiting at home. Who did Brooke have? Pippa wiped a tear away. Why had she treated her so badly, or if not treated her badly, thought badly of her? The poor girl had no one.

'She must be feeling desperately lonely right now,' Pippa said.

'Oh, Pip, she will be, but we'll be there soon.' Harriet turned round to reassure her.

'What if it's too late?' Gus said quietly.

'It won't be, not with my brilliant driving,' Freddie stated just as he pulled into a short-stay parking space.

They scrambled to get out of the car and ran to the terminal building in formation. Harriet spotted the American Airlines desk and rushed up.

'Did a woman buy a ticket?' she asked. 'She's about my height, blonde, very pretty, mid-twenties, name of Brooke Walker?' Her words gushed forth.

Before the bemused-looking lady behind the desk could answer, a small voice piped up.

'What are you guys doing here?'

They turned around and found themselves facing a tearful Brooke. She had her handbag slung over her shoulder and her holdall at her feet.

'Oh! Brooke.' Pippa felt her emotions overcoming her.

Remembering who she was, she grabbed Brooke and hugged her.

'My credit card was declined. I'm stranded,' Brooke said, sobbing into Pippa's shoulder.

'You didn't have a return ticket?' Gus asked.

'No, I only bought a one-way coming here. It was my ticket – you know, the ticket to happiness – but now I'm stuck here, alone.'

'No, you're not, we're here,' Pippa said, bursting into tears.

'Everyone's staring at us,' Freddie hissed.

Harriet steered them over to a quiet space. Brooke collapsed on the floor, still crying. Harriet raised her eyebrows.

'I'm too old for this,' she hissed as she sat down on the floor next to her.

The rest of them followed suit.

'I'm sorry,' Brooke said. 'I got scared and ran, but I didn't really know what I was doing. I was about to call Chris and ask him to come and get me.'

'Hold on.' Harriet took charge. 'You don't need to be sorry, but we do have questions. First, why did you come to us under false pretences?' Harriet wasn't one for small talk.

'When Dad – or the man I thought of as my dad – died, I felt so guilty because I didn't feel sad. We'd never been close and I always felt as if he didn't like me. My mum was diffi-cult, too. I know now it was because she'd had affairs – and not just with your father, either – and she was selfish. Having had too much drink, she told me after his funeral that he wasn't actually my father. He knew this, which explains why he didn't bond with me, but he loved my mother and put up with her behaviour – therefore, he had to put up with me.'

Her eyes glistened with tears and Pippa put her arm around her.

'When she told you, did you question it at all?'

'Yes, obviously it wasn't on my birth certificate. Your dad never knew. At first I was angry about that, why he'd abandoned me, but she assured me that he didn't know. Before I was born, she went to London for work. She worked for a big retail chain and she met your dad at the hotel they were both staying in. He was there on business, too.'

'How could she be sure that you were Dad's and not her husband's?' Gus asked.

'It turns out my dad couldn't have children. So when she found out she was pregnant, she couldn't lie to him about it. But she wanted a baby, so they decided to bring me up together. I don't think my dad had much choice. No one ever knew so he could save face, but whenever he looked at me he saw his humiliation. I'm pretty sure that's why we never got on.'

'It must have been a huge shock,' Freddie said.

The five of them sat cross-legged on the floor and as people passed them, almost stepping over them, they remained oblivious to the fact they were sitting on the ground in terminal three.

'I don't even know what my emotions were,' Brooke admitted. 'I was so upset, and confused, and then I started to get a bit obsessed. I got Mum to give me all the details; although she was reluctant at first.

'Anyway, I found out that my real dad was Andrew Singer, that he was dead – which was another shock – and that I had four half-siblings. I admit, my first thought was that I'd storm in and demand that you give me what I was due, which explains the solicitors' letters you found, Pippa. I mean, I was so full of resentment that I wanted to hurt you all. But then I thought I'd pretend to be a hotel guest and find out as much as I could before taking you to court.'

'So you were going to take legal proceedings against us?' Harriet bristled. 'It's not that I blame you, but it's unpleasant, and if you'd just talked to us...' she said in what could only be described as an understatement.

'Of course it's horrible. But you have to understand – I was so full of anger then. My whole life was a lie, where I'd grown up feeling as if I didn't fit in. I'd felt so alone, with no brothers or sisters. Then finding out there was a family out there who seemed to love each other, who worked together, who had everything when I had nothing ... well, it made me so resentful.'

'That makes sense,' Gus said.

'But then I met you. And you were so nice to me. And although I was a hotel guest, as far as you knew, you included me, you let me be part of Meadowbrook, which I found even more confusing. I didn't know what to do, but I did know that I didn't want to go down the legal route, I soon realised that.'

'But you seemed to enjoy being part of it, part of Meadowbrook,' Freddie said. 'I mean, you got involved.'

'I loved it,' Brooke said simply. 'Almost as soon as I arrived, after I recovered from fainting.'

'That makes sense now,' Freddie said. 'I mean, you fell at my feet, which lots of women do, but now I understand that seeing me, knowing I was your brother, well, it must have been a shock.'

'I saw my dad ... our dad in you when I first saw you and the stress got the better of me. But when I was in Meadowbrook it felt like home. Probably because I wished it so much. When I was little I used to wish I had brothers and sisters, and suddenly I did. You lot just didn't know it. You are all such amazing people, I just wanted to be part of your life.

'And then I didn't know what to do. I was so trapped in everything and it was awful. I was beginning to settle, like with Chris and the gym, and in the end I had no idea how I was going to tell you. I was so scared of losing you that I kept going. But I didn't have any money and my mum and I aren't talking, so I couldn't go to her for help, and then, well, then you discovered who I was.'

'God, it's a lot, it's so much to take in,' Gus said.

'What I don't understand...' Pippa started, needing to tread carefully given Brooke had unburdened – and she did understand, a bit more at least. 'Is why you didn't seem to like me as much as the others.'

'Way to go to make it about you, Pip,' Freddie teased.

'It wasn't like that. I just managed to spend time with the others more. You know, Gus in the gardens or painting, Harriet at the sanctuary or with Toby, and Freddie behind the bar. But you were always so busy running the hotel. I just didn't get to spend the same amount of time with you, which was why I was so pleased when we went to Wells and also when you wanted to do yoga.'

'I didn't realise. I guess it was a bit of a misunderstanding.' Pippa realised that they just hadn't had the chance to bond like the others, but maybe they would get the chance now.

'Oh goodness, this is so much to figure out,' Harriet said. 'I feel so bad for you, Brooke, but in a way, I'm glad it's all out in the open.'

'As long as you really aren't going to sue us,' Freddie added.

'I wasn't going to sue you, exactly,' Brooke pointed out.

'Ignore him,' Harriet said. 'I know, but you do have a point. If you are part of the family, then you're part of the family as far as we're concerned.'

'What do we do now?' Brooke asked.

They all looked at each other and it seemed even clearer that Brooke was related to them. With the five of them sat around together, they looked like a family, Pippa realised, and she knew in her heart that Brooke really was a member of her family.

Pippa stood up and held out her hand to Brooke.

'We go home.'

'I can't believe I've got another auntie,' Fleur said, launching herself at Brooke. 'I knew you were one of us. I mean, it's obvious. Not only are you incredibly hot, but you're also very good with animals, so it makes sense that we're related.'

'Thank you,' Brooke said uncertainly.

'Welcome home, love,' Gwen said, hugging her.

'Oh, Brooke, I'm so pleased you didn't go back to LA,' Gemma added.

'We'd definitely have missed you,' Connor said.

Even Toby smiled at her.

'And that's one happy ending! Even I couldn't have written that one,' Hector finished.

Chapter Thirty-two

'Welcome to your first family meeting,' Harriet said as they all sat around the kitchen table.

'Thank you,' Brooke blushed.

It had only been a week since they'd fetched Brooke back from Heathrow but it felt like a year. Not only was the hotel busy, but the Singers had also been spending as much time together as they could, catching up with Brooke's life and trying to get to know her now the truth was out.

'And you're officially family now. Not that we doubted you, but the solicitors needed us to do the DNA test, so we could apply for you to stay here in the UK.'

Pippa's head had been reeling. She'd relied more heavily on her staff to run the hotel while she came to terms with Brooke being her sister, a member of their family. And there was a lot for them to sort out.

Harriet had stepped in and was sorting out the legalities. Brooke wanted to stay in the UK, so they had to get her paternity officially recognised. The family solicitors were helping to find out what they needed to do regarding immigration. It turned out they had to get an official DNA test. But, Pippa thought, it was just a formality, as in their hearts they all knew already that she was one of them. And it turned out to be.

The solicitors also had to figure out how to get Brooke's inheritance sorted. The family were more than happy to share, but certain measures – for instance, not being able to sell the house– made things quite complicated. It would take a while to iron it out. Brooke insisted she didn't want money, but Harriet pointed out that she needed it. She had credit card debt that needed paying off and she had to live, so Harriet was taking care of that. Once again, Harriet was in her big-sister role, sorting everything out the way she always did.

'I can't thank you enough for all you've done,' Brooke said, her voice choked with emotion.

'If Dad were here, he'd have made sure you were welcomed with open arms,' Gus said.

Amanda grabbed his hand. The family were all finding this more emotional than they first thought.

'He'd have loved you,' Freddie added.

Gemma put her arm around him.

'And he'd be over the moon with how involved you are at the sanctuary,' Connor added while Toby gurgled contentedly on his lap.

'Andrew would be proud of all of you,' Gwen said, wiping a tear.

'We need to sort out somewhere for you to live,' Harriet said. 'I mean, the hotel's filling up and also, you can't live in a hotel room forever.'

'I could, actually; it's so beautiful here,' Brooke laughed.

'We've got plenty of room,' Gus said. 'You should move in with us for a while, until you find your feet.'

'And I've told you to go ahead with Chris and get the studio,' Harriet said. 'I've looked over the business plan and it seems sensible. We can advance you the money until it's all formally sorted out.'

'I don't know what to say,' Brooke said. 'It's so much. Gus, Amanda, I'd love to move in with you and get to know Fleur more.'

'Oh, she's your number-one fan at the moment. Anyway, we'd love to have you,' Amanda said.

'I'll miss having you around the place,' Pippa said, meaning it.

They'd bonded over late-night chats, a bit like she used to have with Gemma before the hotel opened. Pippa and Brooke were growing a friendship as well as building a new sisterly relationship. She knew that the years apart meant it would never quite be the same as with Harriet, Freddie and Gus, but she was growing to love her and it felt as if it was mutual. Although the others were right, they both had a very similar stubborn streak and they both wanted to be the baby of the family. A role that Pippa had no choice but to give up.

'I was hoping to come and work here. I mean, the studio won't be open for a few months and I need to feel useful,' Brooke said.

'Hey, I'll never turn away any help,' Pippa grinned.

'One more thing,' Brooke said.

'What's that?' Harriet asked.

'Would you mind if I changed my name?'

'What's wrong with Brooke?' Freddie asked.

'Oh God, Fred, she doesn't mean her first name!' Harriet laughed.

'You mean?' Gus asked.

'Yes, I'd like to be a Singer, if that's all right with you guys?'

'Oh, Brooke, you're already a Singer, so of course you can!' Pippa hugged her.

'Right, well, all that remains is to open the champagne and formally celebrate,' Freddie said.

'Any excuse,' Gus quipped.

'Well, it's not every day that you get a new sister,' Freddie persisted. 'And you know, that means we're officially outnumbered now, Gus.'

'Hadn't thought of that.'

'Should I go and find Hector?' Pippa said.

They all nodded.

Hector was in his room when Pippa knocked.

'Can you come and join us? We're having a drink to toast Brooke. You know, now she's definitely, one hundred percent, without a doubt, a Singer.'

'I'd love to. Pippa, how are you really dealing with it?'

'You know, I was convinced she was a con woman, but now she's actually one of us, I guess it makes more sense that she's not. I thought I'd hate not being the baby of the family anymore, but it's not so bad,' she laughed. 'Although, it's weird getting used to thinking of Brooke as my sister.'

'You're amazing, Pippa, and she's lucky to have you as a sister. Right, let's go for this glass of champagne.'

They found everyone in the bar. Freddie and Gemma were dishing out glasses. They toasted Brooke and then Hector cleared his throat.

'We have something else to celebrate,' he said. 'I've finished my book.'

344

'Well done, mate!' Freddie slapped his back before refilling his glass, then everyone else's.

'That's amazing.' Pippa kissed his cheek.

'So I'll be out of your hair by the end of the week,' he added.

'So soon?' Pippa felt startled.

'Oh no, we'll miss you, Hector. Are you going back to London?' Harriet asked.

'For a week I am but, well, I thought I might try LA. You know, now Brooke's moved here, I feel I should move there, rebalance it!' he joked while looking at his feet.

'For how long?'

Freddie sounded stricken. He was getting used to having his friend around.

'I thought I'd see. I'll pop back at Christmas – can't have Christmas in the sun, after all – but you know, maybe even indefinitely.'

As they all chattered about how much they'd miss him, Pippa felt a chill crawl over her. She was so used to having Hector around that the idea of him not being there was bad enough, but the idea of him being in another country, well, it didn't feel right. But then if that was what he wanted, then she had to respect that. And maybe, if she ever took a holiday from the hotel, maybe she could visit him. She could see Hector in Hollywood, with his books and his film deal and surrounded by adoring women. *No!* she wanted to shout. No, don't go, but she didn't say anything.

'Let's toast Hector. We'll miss you but you deserve every success.' Pippa hoped her voice didn't crack.

It wouldn't be the same without him here, this stay she'd

really got used to having him around. Even when she felt he spent too much time with Brooke, even when she was briefly seeing Harvey. He'd leave a big hole in Meadowbrook. And in her, she suddenly thought.

'To Hector,' they all echoed.

Brooke had gone to bed. Freddie was still drinking but Gemma was giving him 'the look', so he decided to call it a night. The others had all left them hours ago and Pippa was, for the first time in ages, properly drunk. The bar was a mess but could wait until morning. She went and sat on the sofa, taking a full glass of wine with her, which she didn't need but somehow decided she wanted it. There was so much emotion at Meadowbrook at the moment – a new sister, Hector leaving, the hotel about to get incredibly busy – everything was changing and Pippa didn't always like change. Hector sat down next to her. She realised how she'd let Hector be her anchor without her realising, but she was drunk so maybe she was just being silly.

'Are you going to miss me?' he asked.

'I actually really will,' she said.

'Do you remember when we first met?' Hector asked. 'You were married to Mark and I tried to chat you up.'

'You did, and you called Mark old, which meant that he hated you. But also you'd just been thrown off a TV show for having sex with too many women.'

'I know, I'm not proud of that. I know I made money the easy way, or the lazy way, maybe, going on all those TV shows, but you know, when I started writing, things really changed for me.'

'I know, and no one is more surprised than me that you're

actually good.' Pippa shook her head. Was that the right thing to say? No, possibly not.

'Thanks, Pippa; although hopefully you didn't quite mean it like you just said it. Anyway, you know, I'm not just a pretty face. I am serious about how I feel about you, you know. I mean, like I am about my writing. I fell for you the moment I first set eyes on you.'

'Oh, Hector, don't be silly, you didn't even know me then.'

'But over the years I've got to know you and I fall for you more and more each day.'

He looked so earnest and her stomach fluttered, but Pippa had had too much to drink. She couldn't trust herself – this wasn't a conversation to have when drunk. This was a conversation she felt too scared to have full stop, in fact. Even if she wasn't sure why.

'Hector, I'm really drunk, so you know, not a good time for this chat.'

He sighed. 'I've been trying to have this chat for ages but there's always some excuse. Pippa, I really need you to know and I need you to take me seriously.'

If she wasn't so drunk, she'd have felt sorry for him. And if she didn't suddenly see three of him, she might have taken him seriously. But she couldn't do this. Even if there was part of her, the drunk part of her, that wanted to, she knew she couldn't.

'Hector, sorry, but I've had far too much to drink and I really need to go to bed.'

She felt as if everything was spinning. It must be the drink, she decided as her stomach did somersaults, and she fled before anything terrible could happen.

Chapter Thirty-three

The hangover woke her. Her head pounded, her tongue was stuck to the roof of her mouth and she was desperate for a drink. Thankfully, she had the day off today. She vaguely remembered Hector trying to talk to her and she knew she couldn't face him when she felt like this. He'd have to wait.

She had to admit that her feelings towards him were beginning to confuse her. He did make her flutter, but then he always had; although she'd refused to take him seriously, convinced that the minute she succumbed to his charms he'd go off her. She still believed that. And he was also young. Pippa had only ever dated men older than her and Hector was younger. Only a few years but still ... She wanted to settle down and she wanted a child, but she didn't think Hector was ready for anything more serious than a dinner date.

Of course, she could ask him that question, but actually she didn't want to. Although, of course, if she told him what she wanted from him he might run a mile. But then she didn't want to lose his friendship. They'd grown closer and when he said he was going to LA, she'd realised how important he was to her. Also, of course, she'd been jealous when he'd spent time with Brooke before; although initially she'd encouraged him and her dating. Why was she so confused? What was

348

happening to her? Surely she couldn't be falling for Hector? No, no, no ...

So, he was one of the nicest people she knew. He was handsome, kind and interested in both her and Meadowbrook. More than that, he was part of the community and like family to them. And he was so handsome. Had she already thought that? But he was young and yes, he was successful – actually, incredibly successful – and he was also serious about his work and clever and interesting. She'd always thought of him as lazy, but with his books he'd proved that was no longer the case. And he wasn't a ladies' man anymore, was he? She couldn't remember the last time she'd heard about him being with someone. Even in the hotel, when the guests threw themselves at him, he didn't succumb. Was he really serious about her? She just couldn't quite bring herself to believe it. After all, there was too much at stake. If she dated him and he lost interest, which she was pretty sure he would, then it would affect the whole family. Freddie was particularly close to him and also, now he was Toby's godfather. Of course, there was no way that Pippa could jeopardise that relationship.

She felt ill but more than that, she was in a tizzy, so she did the only thing she could do and fell back to sleep.

A persistent knocking woke her. She reluctantly dragged herself out of bed and opened the door. Brooke, looking immaculate, stood on the other side.

'Oh, boy, you look horrible,' she said.

'Thanks.'

Pippa stood aside. She could feel her hair matted and sticking out. She didn't even want to look in the mirror.

Although her head was better than it had been earlier, she still felt dreadful.

'I'm sorry. Look, Pippa, I needed to see you and this was by your door. I think Hector slipped it under there.'

She handed Pippa a piece of paper. Pippa had to blink a few times before she could focus.

Dedication for Hector Barber's book number two

To Pippa, my one true love

'I don't...'

Words failed her. He was dedicating the book to her? That was just so amazing! But claiming she was his one true love? Really? Did he really mean this?

'Look,' Brooke started. 'I know that I was harsh with you over Harvey, but only because any fool could see what a wonderful guy Hector is and how much he adores you. You just seem so immune to it.'

'I always thought that ... that it wasn't real. I mean, his feelings. I adore Hector, but he's young and he's got a past.'

'We've all got pasts, even me, and I'm younger than both of you. Pippa, you always go for older men and it always ends up in disaster for you, right?'

'Well yes, so far.'

'But you seem to have a thing about Hector's age and he's only a couple years younger than you. God, you're so infuriating!'

'Isn't it a bit early on in our sisterly relationship for you to shout at me?' Pippa raised an eyebrow and pain shot through her head.

'No, because I've been trying for ages to get you to see what's right under your nose. This poor guy is in love with you and you refuse to see it. And what's more, I've seen the way you look at him, the way you change slightly when he's around. Your eyes light up, so I think you're actually in love with him, too.'

'I am?'

Was she? This was crazy. Did she light up around him? Probably, but he was one of her favourite people. Did she fancy him? Well of course she did, she was human and he was hot. Was she in love with him? Oh God, what if she was?

'I think you are, the rest of the family think you are. We've been talking about it.'

'Isn't it also too early in our sisterly relationship for you to be ganging up on me with our other siblings?' Pippa smarted.

'No, it's not. We all want you to be happy and we want Hector to be happy, and we think you'd be happy together, but instead you're both miserable.'

'I'm not exactly miserable.'

'You're lonely, Pippa. Remember when I first came to the hotel? Well, I felt you were a bit lonely and that's why you wanted things to work out with Harvey, but he was so wrong for you.'

'How could you tell that?'

Pippa knew little sisters were supposed to be annoying, she'd heard that from her siblings enough over the years, but an instant annoying little sister wasn't quite what she had in mind.

'He cared about work, money, and you don't care about those things. You care about people and animals and what matters. Harvey didn't.'

'That's true, actually. He wasn't very interested in anything to do with my family. But anyway, he's history, so why are we talking about him again?'

'I was trying to give you an example as to why you should be with Hector. He cares about the same things you do.'

'That's true.'

'And, well, I'm not sure how much I can tell you as it's a surprise, but he's going to prove it to you.'

'What?'

'I think it's best if I don't say anymore. Take a shower, get dressed and I'll wait here.'

'Brooke, you are beyond annoying, you know that?'

'I know. But I have a feeling it's worth it. But if I were you, I'd put some make-up on; you look pretty terrible.'

The shower made Pippa feel marginally more human. She took a little time to dress, selecting her favourite black jeans, a T-shirt and a floral kimono-style jacket. It made her look better than she felt. She blow-dried her hair, ignoring Brooke telling her to get a move on, and applied her make-up. Whatever was happening – and she didn't have a clue as to what it was – she was pretty certain that it was going to be a game-changer. She didn't understand it. Hector was off to LA, right? She was guessing from what Brooke was saying that the idea was for her to tell him not to go, but how could she? She didn't want him to go, but she also wasn't sure how to tell him that. She was too confused.

'Oh, you look nice,' Brooke said when she finally emerged. 'Gorgeous, in fact. Not like earlier.'

'Don't sound so surprised!' Pippa snapped.

But Brooke flashed her a bright smile.

'Let's go.'

'Where are we going exactly?'

'Oh yes, I forgot to tell you, we're going to the field. You know, near the ponies, where you do the events?'

'Why on earth are we going there?'

'You'll find out.'

Pippa followed Brooke out of the house and down to the field.

At first, she spotted her whole family. Everyone was there. Gwen and Gerry had Lucky on the lead, Harriet and Connor were stood there with Toby in the pram and Hilda at their feet, then there was Gus and Amanda, Fleur and Hayley, and Freddie and Gemma. They were all staring at her.

'Just what *is* going on?' Pippa asked as she faced them.

She wasn't good at being the only one who had no clue as to what was happening. She didn't like it and she wasn't big on surprises, either.

'OK, we're ready,' Freddie shouted.

Pippa's mouth dropped open as the morris dancers came onto the field and with them, dressed up to the nines in lederhosen, a funny hat and even bells on his knees, was Hector. Following them onto the field were the gardening club and the Meadowbrook events committee, led by Hilary. Pippa wondered if she was either still asleep, dreaming, or if this was a hangover hallucination.

'What the hell?' Pippa asked Brooke, who smiled and shrugged.

Music started from the morris dancers' sound system and Pippa couldn't believe that it was Beyoncé. As 'All the Single Ladies' rang out of the speakers, handkerchiefs started flowing, sticks were crossed and bells rang out as the dancers tried and failed to emanate the famous dance. Or their interpretation of it.

Everyone was crying with laughter as they carried on, despite the fact that it was a disaster. And although Hector was enthusiastic, he kept going the wrong way. At one point, he banged straight into John, the vicar, and they ended up in a heap and had to be helped up by a couple of other dancers.

Fleur and Hayley were stood at the front doing the correct dance. Edie had joined them and everyone was singing along: 'If you like it, then you should have put a ring on it.' Pippa shook her head. This was the maddest, craziest thing she'd ever seen. And it was pure Meadowbrook.

After the song, which sounded as if it were on repeat at least three times, finished, the morris dancers sat down for a rest and everyone crowded around. Hector approached Pippa, took his handkerchief and offered it to her.

'Milady,' he bowed. 'I'm not proposing. I know Fleur thought I was, but that would be presumptuous, as we haven't even been on a date,' Hector said. 'But I wanted to show you I was serious about you.'

'By putting bells on your knees and dancing badly to Beyoncé?' Pippa asked.

'Yes, perhaps that might not seem the most obvious choice, but I know how much all this means to you: family, Meadowbrook, the sanctuary, the community. And I wanted to show you that it means so much to me, too, not least because you mean so much to me. The song, well, it was sort of my way of saying that I want to commit to you before it's too late. Perhaps I should have gone for Ed Sheeran, but this lot can't dance to ballads, apparently.'

'But morris dancing?' Pippa shook her head.

'I thought that it summed up Meadowbrook and if you knew I was willing to try to do that for you, then, well ... And yes, I also know that Fleur and Hayley filmed me, so I'm going to end up humiliated on social media – my career may even be over – but then you'll know I *am* serious about you, once and for all.'

'You dedicated your book to me,' Pippa whispered, unsure what was happening.

'How did you know that?'

'You slipped the page under my door. Brooke picked it up when she...'

They both turned to look at Brooke, who was staring intently at the sky.

'I wasn't going to tell you. I was going to go to LA and just leave, but...'

'But?'

'Your family had other ideas. You see, a while ago I told Brooke I was going to tell you how I felt by doing this and so I practised with the morris dancers, but then you fell for Harvey, so we gave up on the idea. But Brooke told the others and they helped me to arrange this. A sort of last-ditch attempt to win your heart. To get you to see that I'm not just after you because you keep rejecting me. I'm after you because I'm in love with you.'

'Did you enjoy the morris dancing?' Pippa asked, her lips curled in a smile.

As the warmth of the sun seemed to spread right into her heart, she realised that this was real. This was how her siblings had fallen in love one by one, although without morris dancing, and now it was her turn. They all tuned into their feelings and Pippa ... Well, now she was acknowledging that hers were speaking to her loud and clear.

'A little too much, I fear,' he replied with a grin.

'Actually, he's a natural,' John, the vicar, said, slapping him enthusiastically on the back.

Pippa shook her head.

'So, what now?'

'Well, I don't have another song, if that's what you mean, but we could try something...'

'No, that's not what I mean. Hector, I don't want you to go to LA.'

'You don't?'

'No, I don't, and perhaps we could go out for dinner tonight, the two of us. I know that this wasn't a proposal, but maybe it's your way of asking me on a date.'

'A date would be a very good start.' Hector blushed.

'Oh, for goodness' sake, give her a kiss,' Edie shouted and the entire field cheered.

'Bloody hell, this wasn't exactly what I had in mind for our first kiss,' Hector said.

'But we'd better not let the crowd down,' Pippa said, feeling giddy with happiness.

It was as if all the feelings she'd been holding back gushed forth and she couldn't control them even if she wanted to.

She moved towards him and he put his arms around her. Goodness, it felt so right! And as she let her lips lightly brush his, she knew this was right – it felt right. And as everyone in the field erupted in cheers and applause, she also knew that she wouldn't have it any other way.

She kissed Hector again and she was sure the bells she could hear weren't the ones on his knees.

Epilogue

Six months later

'So,' Chris PT said as he stood in his and Brooke's new studio. 'Are you still single?' he laughed while Pippa giggled and Hector huffed.

'You know full well she's not, she's with me.' Hector put a proprietorial arm around her.

'If you ever get fed up with him, you know where I am,' Chris said with a wink.

'I'm not sure about him,' Hector said as he walked off. 'I mean, what is the point of him?'

'He's Brooke's business partner and look at what a great job they've done. He's also a friend now and you have to get used to him.'

They'd acquired the studio in Keynsham and Brooke was moving into a large, modern flat above it. She wanted to be near work and although they'd miss seeing her every day, she wasn't far away. Although they'd grown close, it would do Brooke good to have her own independence.

The studio had a fitness room for classes, a gym full of equipment and a personal training room as well as a space for treatments, like massage. It was gorgeous and although the Singers had all helped and done their bit, Brooke had shown that she was more than capable herself – a true chip off the old block, as Gwen said. She and Chris had come up with a great business model, and with both of them being young and ambitious, they already wanted to open other studios.

Harriet was the voice telling them to rein it in until they'd got this one up, running and successful. She'd been their self-appointed mentor, but actually she'd been incredibly helpful, if not a bit bossy in true Harriet style.

Brooke had settled into the family in so many ways, Pippa reflected. It was as if she'd always been part of it. And she and Brooke had become closer, as she was with the others. It was funny, but Brooke and Gus seemed to have the strongest bond, probably because although she was all about fitness, she also shared his passion for art and was actually quite a good painter, too.

Pippa was no longer jealous. She was the protective older sister now – a role she'd never played before – and she quite liked it. She tried, tentatively, to get Brooke to speak to her mum again, but she still wasn't ready to forgive her quite yet. But Pippa wouldn't give up. She knew that Brooke missed her mum and would at the very least like to make peace with her at some stage.

Gemma and Freddie had set the date and were getting married at Meadowbrook the following spring. Pippa was helping Gemma to organise it and was going to be her maid of honour. Hector was best man, along with Gus, so that seemed fitting. Pippa was excited for the wedding and although she didn't want to rush anything with Hector, she harboured a secret hope they wouldn't be too far behind. They hadn't been together that long, just six months, but they'd known each other for so long the relationship had accelerated. She couldn't believe, looking back, that she hadn't come to her senses sooner; it had been the best six months of her life. She'd never been happier, in fact.

'Auntie Pip, did you know they were serving wheatgrass rather than wine?' Fleur asked.

She was still with Alfie, who'd become a bit of a fixture with the Singers, and even Gus liked him now. Actually, sometimes Gus seemed to like him more than Fleur did.

Hayley was shyly shuffling around behind them. Luckily for Gus and Amanda, she was more interested in sport than boys and had already become one of the studio's first clients.

'Well, it is a fitness studio, Fleur, but don't worry, we ordered champagne for later; although you're still a bit young.'

'I'm almost seventeen, for goodness' sake. Uncle Fred had been drinking for years by the time he was my age.'

'Not the best argument to use,' Pippa laughed.

'I'm going to be eighteen soon,' Alfie said. 'But I'm not keen on drinking, to be honest.'

'No wonder Gus loves you, then,' Hector laughed.

'Yes, I almost dumped him because Dad said he reminded him of him!' Fleur's voice was full of outrage.

'Thanks,' Alfie said.

Fleur hugged him. 'Nah, I like you, you can stay. After all, who else would put up with my crazy family.'

Edie approached. She'd insisted on coming as a newly converted fitness addict – according to herself. Edie had even taken to wearing leisurewear. Tonight, she was in her favourite bright pink shell suit. It was quite a sight.

'So, Edie, are you going to be joining?' Hector asked.

'It's a bit far for me to get to, even though I've got a bus pass – not that you'd know to look at me. But Brooke's going to keep doing our yoga classes; the village wouldn't manage without them.'

It was true. Even the morris dancers kept going to the weekly classes and for many of the villagers it was their big social event of the week. It meant that Brooke had an important role to play in Parker's Hollow as well as at Meadowbrook, which their father would also have approved of.

'OK, let's go and pour champagne now,' Pippa said. 'Go and get Fred. He'll help you, Hector.' She kissed his cheek.

Hector had changed so much about Pippa's life, and all for the better. She was more relaxed now and she felt she'd finally grown into herself. After divorcing Mark, she'd found career. But now, meeting Hector, she was feeling as if she could finally be her whole self. She was still a career woman, but the loneliness had gone. That feeling of being anxious that she'd felt at the beginning of the year, the moody teenager she so often was, no longer existed. Being with Hector had shown her what a relationship should be like: a partnership, a friendship, but also passionate and equal. It was so strange the way before she'd always been the underdog in relationships. Even with Harvey she felt as if she was the one making compromises. And for some reason she seemed to have a deep-rooted belief that that was the way it should be. She'd talked it through with Gemma and decided it stemmed from the fact she was so young when she first met Mark that she'd just thought that it was normal and even after that, it had taken her a while to realise that it didn't have to be this way. But she was happy now.

Hector was a little bit annoying at times, though, and he

got on her nerves. He was messy and with his writing career, he lived in a different world quite a lot of the time. But the way he made her feel was worth those annoyances and they were minor in the scheme of things. He treated her so well, like a princess, in fact, and she was getting used to being spoilt. In turn, she enjoyed taking care of him. He had a lot on with work, so she was happy to step in and make sure that his domestic life went smoothly.

He was away a lot for work and Pippa missed him like crazy, but it also meant she got to concentrate on the hotel when needed. They'd come up with a balance, where they didn't live in each other's pockets, and it suited them both. They'd also discussed their living arrangements. The apartment in the hotel was small and they needed more space. It also would do their relationship good to be away from the hotel. Pippa had spoken to Harriet about finding a general manager and getting them to live-in, so that was on the cards. Hector thought they should buy a house in the village. It was a big step but one that Pippa felt she was ready for. Or at the very least ready to think about.

'So, do you think this is going to work?' Brooke asked her, interrupting her thoughts.

Brooke looked so young and vulnerable at times, but everyone was right, she also reminded Pippa of her father more and more. The way she tilted her head, the looks she gave ... Pippa wished he could have met her.

'How can it not? It's great, Brooke. You've done so well, especially with everything you've gone through.'

And Pippa meant that. She was immensely proud of how well she'd done. She'd lost a father, who wasn't her father, and she'd grieved for a father she'd never got to meet. She'd fallen

361

out with her mum and she'd gained four siblings. And she'd opened a business. As Harriet said, she was more of a Singer than even she realised.

'Quiet, please,' Harriet shouted.

She was relishing being the head of the family even more now they had a new addition. And, of course, now she'd settled into motherhood, she'd gone back to bossing them all around. Life was back to normal, or as normal as it ever was with them.

'I'd like to raise a toast. To Brooke and Chris and The Studio! May it be the huge success they deserve – which, by the way, I'm sure it will be.'

'To The Studio,' they toasted.

'And we have one last surprise for Brooke,' Harriet added.

Pippa gave Hector's hand a squeeze and went to stand with Harriet and her other siblings. Harriet handed Brooke an envelope. There had been several legalities and they were lucky that their family solicitor was so good that they were able to get everything sorted out in a relatively painless way. Although, of course, it hadn't been plain sailing.

'What is it?' Brooke asked.

'It's official! You're a Singer. Your paternity is legally recognised and now, like it or not, you're officially one of us.'

They all went in for a group hug.

Tears streamed down Brooke's cheeks. 'I absolutely love being a Singer. I'd just like to say how I've never been happier. Who would have known when I boarded the plane with my one-way ticket that I'd have found this!'

'It really was your ticket to happiness,' Pippa stated. 'And ours, in so many ways.'

'And I think we'd all like to say how much our father would

have loved you and been proud of you,' Gus said, emotion choking his voice.

'He really would,' Harriet echoed.

Pippa felt emotion fill the room.

'I wish I'd met him, but I guess he's in each of you,' Brooke said.

'And we see him in you, too,' Pippa said, putting her arm around her and giving her a squeeze as emotion welled up. 'You're definitely our father's daughter.'

'To Brooke Singer!' Freddie held his glass up.

'To Brooke Singer!' the room echoed.

Acknowledgements

Yet again I have been lucky enough to write about the Singer family. I do adore the Meadowbrook Manor series and am delighted with this third book. There are, as always, a whole lot of people who are involved in the book. So, a mountain of thank yous go to the following people. To the team at Avon, and especially my lovely editor Katie Loughnane, it was a pleasure working with you. Thanks also to everyone who works so hard for the books, Sabah, Elke, Dom and the entire Avon Team, it's always such a huge privilege to be published by you. Also, to Diane Banks and everyone at Northbank Talent Management for being great agents who are always on hand to support.

Thank you also to the lovely book bloggers – you overwhelm me with your support and help. Honestly, we authors value you so highly and owe a lot of thanks to you. The same to fellow authors who are always on hand to give reassuring words or virtual hugs. It's such a wonderfully supportive industry to work in, and I feel blessed to be part of it.

On a personal level, thanks to my family and friends, who I adore, and couldn't do this without, and you all know who you are. I am so lucky to have great people around me, and I love you all.

To Chris Reeves for being a good sport about appearing as Chris PT in the book – it's only loosely based on you, apart from the tight jeans of course!

And of course, huge, huge thanks to my readers. Without you there is no Meadowbrook, and no other books, so thank you so much for reading and letting me continue writing!

If you enjoyed *The Ticket to Happiness*,
why not go back to where it all started...?

Available now in ebook and paperback!

Take another trip back to Meadowbrook this summer
for sunshine, secrets and plenty of romance...

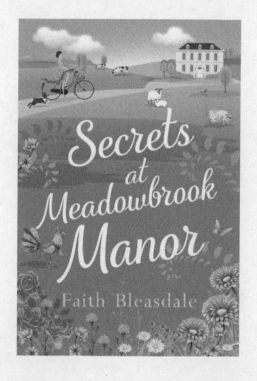

Available now in ebook and paperback!

Will a camping trip be the relaxing getaway
Daisy was hoping for? Or is her summer
destined to end in disaster...?

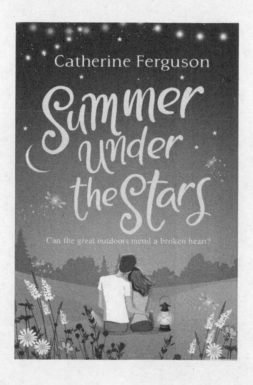

Available now in ebook and paperback!

Take a trip to the Highlands with Tracy Corbett's
new novel, perfect for fans of Heidi Swain
and Jenny Oliver...

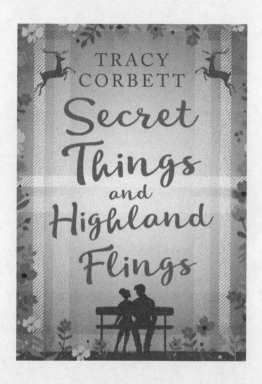

Available now in ebook and paperback!

Escape to Devon with *The Mini-Break* by Maddie Please. A funny, feel-good story that will take you on a trip you never knew you needed. Have you packed...?

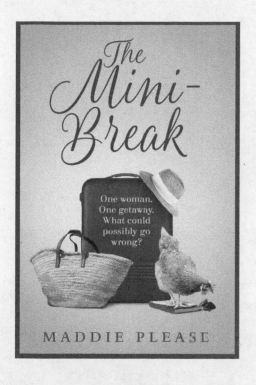

Available now in ebook and paperback!